LIGHT
ON A
PART
OF THE
FIELD

Kevin Holowack

light
on a
part
of the
field
a novel

NeWest Press
Edmonton, AB

Library and Archives Canada Cataloguing in Publication

Title: Light on the part of the field / Kevin Holowack.
Names: Holowack, Kevin, author.
Series: Nunatak first fiction series ; no. 54.
Description: Series statement: Nunatak first fiction series ; no. 54
Identifiers: Canadiana (print) 20200267523 | Canadiana (ebook) 2020026754X |
ISBN 9781774390146 (softcover) | ISBN 9781774390153 (EPUB) |
ISBN 9781774390160 (Kindle)
Classification: LCC PS8615.O473 L54 2021 | DDC C813/.6—dc23

NeWest Press wishes to acknowledge that the land on which we operate is Treaty 6 territory and a traditional meeting ground and home for many Indigenous Peoples, including Cree, Saulteaux, Niitsitapi (Blackfoot), Métis, and Nakota Sioux.

Board Editor: Thea Bowering
Cover design & typesetting: Kate Hargreaves
Cover art: "Driveway" © 2011 Paul Holowack
Author photograph: Josh Bookhalter
All Rights Reserved

NeWest Press acknowledges the Canada Council for the Arts, the Alberta Foundation for the Arts, and the Edmonton Arts Council for support of our publishing program. This project is funded in part by the Government of Canada.

201, 8540 – 109 Street
Edmonton, AB T6G 1E6
780.432.9427
NeWest Press www.newestpress.com

No bison were harmed in the making of this book.

PRINTED AND BOUND IN CANADA
1 2 3 4 5 23 22 21

part one

———◆———

a small
stroke

chapter one
- 1979 -

He lights a match.

The phosphorous glow throws shadows behind the irregular shapes of the barn and reveals three cows standing together for warmth. One turns to examine the dishevelled young man standing in the doorway.

A trough in the corner contains a thumb-deep reserve of water. The man forces the barn door shut and hobbles toward it, letting his rucksack fall to the hay. The match goes out when he leans over the edge of the basin, lowers his cupped hands and brings some of the liquid to his mouth. He gags. The cow-water mingles with his saliva. It tastes woody. Something that shouldn't be consumed.

Considering I stopped at the first shelter I saw, he tells himself, I should feel lucky for all this. He remembers the last time he vomited and collapsed. It was a month ago in Vancouver, a public library, an ordinary day in an ordinary place, now distant.

———◆———

In a nearby house, a radio mumbles. A young woman and a girl sit in the upstairs bedroom. The girl creaks a rocking chair. The woman watches the storm through the window. Branches like suspended puppets.

Last year, she remembers, there was a storm like this that threw a tree clear through the kitchen window.

"Do you think it'll happen again?"

"What are you talking about?" the girl asks.

A faint orange light slips between the cracks of the barn, flickers for a minute and disappears.

"There's someone in the barn."

The young woman puts on a jacket and walks out. When she opens the barn door, she brings with her a flood of lantern light.

The man in the hay is maybe eighteen, twenty, twenty-three? She bends over to get a closer look. A baby face but with stubble. A boy and a man at the same time, depending on the angle, like one of those novelty holograph pictures that changes when you flip it back and forth.

She leaves for a few minutes and returns with a plate of bread and cheese, a knife, and a glass bottle of water. She places the items by his elbow. He's still as dirt. Almost. Probably not dead.

———◦———

The rain continues overnight and into morning.

"I just brought him food and water, that's all."

"And the knife? I noticed it was missing."

"Yes."

Her mother sighs. "You're a silly girl, Gayle. A silly, stupid, silly girl."

"Why?"

"I know you're trying to help, but—why did you give a trespasser a weapon?"

Rain surrounds the house like static. Outside, grey light yawns through the clouds and falls on the yard, the fences, a truck pulling a trailer across the road, the trees, the barn—

"It's fine, Gayle. I'll call Davidson. He'll come with his sons and they'll drag him out." The mother grabs the phone, sticks her finger in the first digit, pulls, watches the dial churn back.

"Wait, Mum."

"What?"

"Those boys are morons. They'll throw him out like a vagrant."

"He is a vagrant."

"But he's my age, I think. Probably just some hippie. He's got a mum, too."

———◦———

The stranger is still unconscious when they return.

"He doesn't look so heavy," says the mother. "Looks like he puked on himself, too, so—where do we bring him?"

"To the sofa in the library. Put some old blankets down."

Gayle uses the edge of her coat to wipe matted straw from his face and then loops her arms around his shoulders. Her mother takes the legs.

———◦———

When he wakes, he's lying on a sofa in a large room filled with bookshelves, looked down upon by coloured spines.

There is no clock.

It's warm and he's sweating. A small fireplace crackles. He listens to creaks in the walls and the floor, the sound of the rain, for what he feels to be half an hour. Feeling more comfortable than he suspects he should, he sits up and takes a book.

Soon Gayle appears in the doorway. "Are you awake?"

"Yes."

"Are you hungry, thirsty?"

"I'm okay."

"You're not okay. We carried you in here. And we took your sweatshirt. It had puke on it."

The girl has a strange way of speaking, he thinks. Long pauses between her sentences, like she's talking with ellipses.

Gayle leaves to fetch a tray with a cup of tea, a small shepherd's pie, and a thimble glass of rum. She hands it to the stranger and stands looking down at him.

"I'm not a tramp"—he blows on the teacup rim—"if that's what you're thinking."

"What happened to you?"

"I'm sick, I guess. It comes and goes."

"Ah."

"And I drank from the trough. Couldn't have helped."

"You drank the cow's water?"

"Yeah."

"Why?"

"I hitched one long ride, but the guy let me off outside Salmon Arm. I just started walking. It was late so I went looking for a place to curl up and not be bothered. But then the storm came and I got lost. I was parched. Water seemed nice. Didn't think it would be so rancid."

"Cows don't care. Are you done with your tea?"

"Do you want anything? Money for the food, I mean. I don't have much on me, but—" He watches gravy break through the face of the shepherd's pie.

Gayle takes a few steps around the room, gazing vacantly at the books while the stranger forks bits of potato from the bowl. As she collects the dishes, she notices a book tucked under his knee.

"My name's Lewis, by the way."

"You have a book under your leg."

"I shouldn't be touching your things. Sorry."

"What is it?"

He isn't sure. He takes the book and reads. "1819 Odes."

"You wake up in a strange house in the middle of nowhere and start reading poetry? Why did choose that one?"

"I like poetry."

"You like Keats?"

"I think my aunt used to like him."

"Your aunt liked Keats?"

"Used to."

"Why, is she dead?"

"No, just realized he was sappy."

"And where is she now, your aunt?"

"Somewhere out there."

"Oh." Gayle isn't interested the stranger's aunt. "And you, where are you going?"

"Highway One."

"Highway One?"

"East, I mean. I'm going to Alberta." He smiles a straight-line smile. "How's that song go? 'Think I'll go to Alberta. Got some friends I could go workin' for. Weather's nice in the fall.' Something like that. You know it?"

"I'll leave you the rum. It's good for you. Kills bacteria."

After Gayle leaves, he opens the Keats book to a random page and takes a sip of rum. He's glad to be alive. And fed. He remembers reading the newspaper before he left Vancouver, a story about a man who pulled a woman out of a flipped car. The paper said he saved her life, a hero.

He wonders if something like this could make the newspaper: Hitchhiker's life saved by pretty girl near Salmon Arm.

Then he notices the smells of road grit and sweat.

He hobbles to his rucksack in the corner. There are a few spare shirts in there, and a razor, some soap, a notebook, an envelope with a few bills in it. Not much else.

Sunlight noses through the blinds, and he sets out in search of a bathroom to wash himself.

———•———

"I think he's lost, Mum," Gayle says across a table set with toast and tea. "Maybe homeless. Definitely harmless. Doesn't seem to know where he's going. And he mentioned some song about going to Alberta. Weird, hey?"

"I know what you're thinking, Gayle."

"Do you?"

"Okay. We'll let him stay. Who knows with someone like that? He might be gone by morning."

"Thanks, Mum."

"Did you tell your sister about our guest yet?"

"She walked in there while he was sleeping."

"She must be scared."

"Ami doesn't get scared. She just put her hands on her hips and said 'Is he a troll?'"

"A troll?"

"Must be something she read. She thought Lewis was sleeping like a troll, with his toes sticking out from under the blanket and all that. He's up already, you know, smoking on the patio. I can hear him."

"Ah, a smoker." The mother dips her toast in the tea and lets it drip out. "You know, Gayle, it might be nice to have another hand around here again."

"Mum?"

"We could get some of those odd projects done. Staining the fence, right? And the wood we got from that Mercer fellow needs to be cut. And we could always dig a few extra beds this year. It beats asking that unreliable Davidson kid. And I'll have more time for painting if I'm not doing chores, anyway. I'll go ask if he has any experience with cows."

"You're joking?"

The mother clears the table. "Have I ever joked before, Gayle? I only half-joke."

"Alright, Mum."

When the mother tells him he can stay, he nods and lets the last of the ash fall. Black, white, it scatters in the breeze.

"I've never worked on a farm, Miss—er, Ma'am—Miss?"

"City kid, huh? Don't worry. We're not real farmers. It's more of a hobby farm. And you can call me Ruth, by the way, not whatever you just said. I can give you an allowance."

"Thanks, Ruth."

———•———

The house has something called a "parlour" in it as well as the library and several spare bedrooms. He thinks it looks transplanted from another time and place but can't decide where. Maybe it's Victorian.

Gayle shows him the upstairs loft where he'll stay. The loft is spartan: a twin-sized bed, a sofa without cushions, a small desk, and two small lamps. Gayle flicks on both lamps.

"Ruth, your mother—"

"Yeah?"

"If I can ask, is she pretty rigorous?"

"Rigorous?"

"Yeah, I mean—*rigorous*. I just want to know how to act."

"I don't know. She's my mother."

"What does she do?"

"For a job you mean? She's an artist. Is that a job? I could never figure that out."

"And your dad?"

She scoffs and covers it with a false laugh. "He's not here—hasn't been here in a while."

The month of May arrives, and the days become longer. Every morning, Ruth sits by the parlour window with an easel. The sun floats up quickly in the mornings and perches in the sky, white-yellow, yellow-white.

She watches the yard, the accumulating wildflowers budding against the monotone grass. Violets, snowdrops, bull thistles, all looking like droplets on the fringe of a palette.

Dust rises in the sunbeam every time she adjusts her chair.

In the kitchen, the coffee percolator sputters and fills the pot slowly. It takes half an hour to fill. It needs to be cleaned out.

She watches Lewis drag a hose toward the barn where Gayle is milking the cows.

She dips her brush into a pot of Payne's grey.

———•———

"Would you like to learn how to do this?" Gayle moves aside so Lewis can see the entire underbelly of the cow. Her knees are on a stool and her hands are stretched forward to clutch the udder. She applies pressure from top to bottom, rhythmically. "They're gentle creatures, so you have to treat them gently. And they have amazing memories. If they don't like their keeper, they'll never give anything."

Milk sputters in the aluminum pot. It takes several minutes before it's full and ripples dance atop the cream. The cow blows a shaft of air from its nostrils and moves on.

Lewis takes the collar of the next animal and leads it to the stool. He sets a new pot on the floor beneath it. Saying nothing, he clutches one of the udders and carefully runs his hand toward the teat, applying pressure. But his hands slip. He can't find a rhythm.

Gayle grins. "It's coming slowly, but that'll change once they get used to you."

"How long have you been doing this?"

"Since we decided to get cows." Gayle lays her hand on his elbow. "It's hard not having many people to be with. Mum's pretty aloof and we're not close. So, I just wanted to say, thanks for staying."

She places her hand on Lewis's hand on the udder so that he can feel the warmth of her palm. This means *not so fast*.

"So many folk songs describe people like you," she says. "There's even an old tune that came on the radio last week, something about a young gypsy who rides a horse through the valleys. One day he meets this rich lady and woos her with his voice so he can snatch her away. But then she starts thinking about how happy *she* would be to abandon all her useless possessions, her ribbons and her feather bed. It's always a feather bed in songs like that."

"I can't tell if this is a compliment."

"It's not. Just an observation." She lets go of Lewis's hand and the udder, stands up quickly. "I guess I make up things about people when I don't know enough about them. You been cutting back? With the smoking, I mean. How many of those you got left?"

"I haven't counted. I had a couple packs on me when I got here. Gotta be prepared when you're on the road."

"And when you run out?"

"I'm not sure."

"You know, I sometimes imagine you're one of those runaways in a folk song, always on the move. You travel from town to town with a pack and as soon as you run out you hit the road again to find some more, never returning to the same place twice."

"I usually just head to the shop."

They each carry a pail of milk back to the house. "I remember the name of the song."

"About the gypsy?"

"It's called 'Black Jack Davy.' Goes something like, 'Black Jack Davy comes riding through the hills, riding so high and merrily. Something something, charm the heart of a lady.'" She half-sings, half-speaks.

"I don't know it." Lewis sets his pail by the door. "Do you want to know my true story? I'm not a folk song. My dad's name was John. He was a grocer. A businessman. A real hard-ass, you know. Nothing special. I spent my life working in the shop. They call me the bag bitch." He chuckles. "I shouldn't use words like that. I just wanna say I'm not so romantic."

"I never said you seemed romantic."

They leave the pails in the kitchen and Gayle leads him upstairs to his loft. He leans on the windowsill while she sits cross-legged on his bed.

"And what happened to your pop?" she asks.

"My pop?"

"Your dad."

"Sorry. I'd never call him Pop—it's too, don't know, *endearing*. What happened to him? He died, I guess. Had a heart attack. I was sixteen or something. So I went to live with my aunt. She's the one who made me interested in books and poetry and stuff. She's kind of a freethinker, you know. She wears bangles. She's poor as hell, but happy. Nothing like Pop."

"And when did you leave home?"

"Every year since I could walk."

"I'm sorry to hear this is as far as you got."

"That was a joke—"

"I know." She sees Lewis looking at the nearest mountain. "But it's fun to imagine being out in the open like that, living on your wits. Can I come with you, Lew?"

The word "Lew" sounds even stranger to him than the word "Pop." He imagines the two of them in a forest somewhere. A quiet place. Only two humans amongst the animals.

"Of course." He considers saying more, but Gayle is lost in thought and he doesn't want to disturb her.

———————◆———————

Gayle sits before the piano in the parlour and hangs her fingers above the keys. Lewis is out walking and Ruth is nowhere to be seen.

The house is eerily quiet for seven in the evening. No radio. No percolator. No mother. No father. Only the living shadow. The small, amorphous thing that lives on the shelf, in the corners, the periphery, and disappears when she tries to catch it with her eyes. It's been in the room with her for an hour. She's been ignoring it like an unpleasant smell or the unwanted gaze of a stranger, seeing how long it will last. It's harmless, she thinks. Neither kind nor malicious. When she can't take it anymore, she looks—

She shrugs it off and turns back to the piano. People always expect something of you when you sit in front of the piano. She puts her fingers over a chord—a D major—but doesn't press down.

Small footsteps come from the foyer, through the hall, into the parlour.

"How was swimming today, Ami?"

"The worst. I lost my towel and I had to put on dry clothes even though I was wet."

"You don't say." Gayle closes the piano, goes to the kitchen and begins preparing a boiled egg, slicing some hard cheese onto a piece of bread. Small bubbles gather in the pot and Ami comes back with dry clothes.

Gayle watches her little sister eat. "The new flower beds are almost good to go. I think we're going to put in some sweet peas. That way we get nice purple flowers *and* we can eat them later. Remember when we had those sunflowers out back, Ami?"

"Nope."

"It wasn't so long ago, but for you I guess it must seem like a long time. We have a picture upstairs of you pushing one of the flowers to your face—It must have been twice the size. And your fat little face. That was before you had hair."

A sound of someone shifting a piece of furniture upstairs—Ruth, above, moving something small: an end table or a chair. The boards always creaked. It's an old house, not good for fidgeters.

"Would you miss me if I disappeared, Ami?"

"Huh?"

"If I went away. Would it make you—sad?"

"Like Dad?"

"No, like Gayle. Your sister."

Ami scoops the yolk out of the egg and sets it aside.

———◆———

Past midnight, he can't sleep. He tires his eyes by reading a book from the library. He doesn't recognize the author and surrendering to someone else's words is difficult, especially when the book is old and contains complex, sprawling sentences.

With eyes full of darkness, he thinks about Gayle asleep two floors below, her thick eyebrows the colour of night. He tries to change his course of thoughts. Besides, he thinks, aren't all dark things the colour of night? Gayle's eyebrows, tar, the Model T, Keats's nightingale.

His cigarette turns to ashes and they fall red, white, then black. Only six left.

He remembers where he bought these cigarettes. It was at some truck stop near Chilliwack, just after he hitched a ride in a blue Buick driven by a large man in a suit named Tom. Just after Tom gave him a five-dollar bill, saying, "Take it, kid, you need it more than I do. Go get yourself some soup." The Buick sped away, flashing in the sunlight. He didn't buy soup. He bought these cigarettes. Now he closes the window. Something is expanding in him. An emotion that involves Gayle and the colour black.

In the morning, Gayle sits in an armchair reading a Virginia Woolf novel. Her eyes skate across the page, picking up one word here, another there. They don't want to connect, so instead she starts fanning the pages against her cheek.

Ruth is by the window with her easel. "Difficult reading, Gayle?"

"I liked the description on the jacket, but the book is awful. Seems like she says a lot, but nothing ever happens. Just people talking and thinking about stuff and really nothing."

"You have no patience, Gayle."

"There's no mystery, no big event, just people being sad and deep and none of the characters are really likeable—maybe one or two, but they're children. It's boring. I just want something to happen—a fight, an affair, a big fire. Whatever."

"Kinda like life, isn't it? Kids'll get sour."

Gayle shrugs. "I should phone someone about the washing machine. It's broken."

"Gayle."

"Mum?"

"Ami said you were talking about leaving?" Ruth's eyes remain fixed on the easel. The greens in the foreground are not quite right. She takes two tubes, squeezes parallel lines on her palette and uses a knife to mix them.

———◆———

Gayle goes to the basement and finds Lewis at the sink, working through a load of laundry by hand.

"Lewis—"

"Gayle?"

"You're doing a good job."

"It's not easy. Seems like it would be, you know. It's just soap and water."

"Try being a woman. Doesn't get any better than this."

He doesn't respond.

"That was a joke, you know."

"I know."

Gayle takes his arm and leads him upstairs, through the hall, to the library. They push open the heavy door and step inside. When there is no fire, the library is cooler than any other room of the house. Gayle scans the shelves and takes down a thick red book without a title.

"My father was a poet, you know. And a teacher, too. Did you ever wonder how a farmhouse ended up with a library?"

"I always thought it seemed strange."

She puts her hand on the cover. "Dad had the luxury spending his life collecting old crap and writing books. Imagine that. We used to live in Victoria, and then he got a new job in Edmonton. But before that, he bought this place for us. But he came and went."

"You should be proud of your father," Lewis says. As soon as these words leave his mouth, he feels annoyed with himself.

"Dad was kind of a—kook. Is it okay to call your own dad a kook? He was never really angry, though. Just different. He drank a bit, but so do most teachers. I read a story in the newspaper the other day about a teacher in Alabama who got caught snorting coke behind her desk before the class started."

"Is that his book there? The one you're holding. I mean, did he write it?"

"Sort of. It's nobody's now. It's a diary. I found it in his desk. Well, it's not really a diary. Just bits. Thoughts about this and that—something he wrote in Edmonton, I think. I don't understand it. And I can't read it, really. It's all about animals and nature and—time and eternity. Or something. Some stuff about death and sex. Funny combination, right?"

"I'm sorry," Lewis says.

"I heard Virginia Woolf filled her pockets with stones and walked into a river. Sometimes I try to imagine my dad doing that, but he doesn't have a story. He just vanished, you know—really—poof. Left us here to look after ourselves. He liked horses, too. We used to have a horse in a stable closer to town. She's dead now."

———•———

At midnight, upon snuffing out a butt, Lewis turns back to the darkness of the room and is not surprised to see Gayle's silhouette in the doorway.

"How many of those do you have left?"

"Three."

"Then what?" She steps toward him, puts her hand on his hip, leads him to the bed. "I assume you have a condom?"

After sex, she takes his head and rests in on her chest. A few minutes later, he sits up and lights a cigarette in bed. He uses the condom wrapper to collect the ashes.

"Does this make sense?" she asks.

"What do you mean?"

"Does what we're doing make sense?"

Lewis doesn't respond. Outside in the sky, a cloud wanders.

"About before," she says after a while, "I'm sorry. I don't wanna talk about my dad. Did I tell you I see a ghost sometimes in the house? It used to come around once a month or so. Sometimes I wake up in my sleep, paralyzed everywhere except my eyes, and I can watch it flittering around in my room. It's a shadow. It doesn't let anyone look at it directly. Kind of a shy, irritating ghost. A little rude, waking me up like that—I wouldn't say I'm scared, though."

"Ghost?"

She sits up and hugs her legs, presses her chin to her knees. "It's not *his* ghost. Don't think I'm nuts—I don't know if he's dead. Guess it doesn't make much of a difference. Sometimes when I was a girl and Ami was just a newborn baby, dad would take us out into the sunflowers to play hide-and-seek. It seems stupid now, but when you're small, sunflowers seem enormous, and if you have enough then you can get lost in them. Do you mind if I keep talking?"

"I don't mind."

She continues, "I don't think Ami understood anything, though. I still don't think she understands. We trampled so many innocent plants. Dad would weep sometimes, really weep, like he was one of those guys in the Bible who tore his clothes off and scratched the dirt with his nails. And that scared me. But his silence scared me, too. He was a little scary all around, I guess, and that's why we drifted."

A pause.

"What'll you do when we run away?" he asks.

"What do you mean?"

"I don't mean practical things, money and whatever. Things always work out. But your mom and your sister."

"How should I know that?"

"Maybe it doesn't matter. But me, I'm going to Edmonton for a while. It's a place to stop, work, make some money. You can come."

"Edmonton?"

"Yeah."

"Like my *pop*."

"Oh."

"I hope you believe in fate. I do. If it's too much, you—"

He waits for her to finish her sentence, but she doesn't. She pulls at a loose thread from the bedsheet but stops herself when the unravelling becomes too noticeable.

"It's a stopping point," he says. "In the long run I wanna go east. Far, far east. To the Atlantic."

"Why?"

"My aunt lived in Nova Scotia. She said it's the best place in the world. I don't know much more than that. Said it's an easy life, quiet and free. Bunch of hippies and draft dodgers and things. You can just find a job and stay there and not worry about shit. And there's always work on the docks. And from there you can get a boat to England."

"You're really a dreamer."

"I guess."

"Is that a hard life?"

"Not really."

———◆———

A cool rain comes in the morning.

In the parlour, Ruth makes a few dashes of blue across the sky of her painting. There are a few uncoloured blotches in the air where birds will be.

It'll be geese, probably, she thinks. They're becoming more common these days, returning for the summer to their home in Mabel Lake.

She looks out the window and sees Gayle walking across the lawn, toward the barn, with small droplets bouncing off the shoulders of her raincoat.

———◆———

In the barn, one of the cows lies down in the hay. Lewis is with it. It staggers when it tries to stand.

"What's wrong with her?" he asks when Gayle enters.

"If I had to guess, probably milk fever."

"Milk fever?"

"It means she's not eating properly, so it wears away at her bones."

"Is this normal?"

"I don't know. It happened before, a couple months ago."

"Is this my fault? I've been the one feeding them. Maybe they didn't trust me—didn't want to eat the food."

"They're animals, Lewis. They'll eat if they're hungry. Don't give them too much credit. It might be because the food's no good. We'll call the vet in." Gayle tugs the sick animal until it stands and ushers it to the side of the barn. She takes another cow and leads it to the milking stool.

———————

From the parlour, Ruth watches Lewis leave the barn, his eyes turned toward the damp grass. Gayle follows shortly after, her clothes covered in dirt.

No, she thinks, the painting will not have geese. The geese stopped migrating weeks ago. The white spaces require a different kind of bird.

Lewis enters. Ruth looks up from her work. "No work today, Lewis, with the rain and all. Take it easy."

"Thanks, Ruth."

He stands with his hands in his pockets. Ruth focuses on her picture, her brush poised and still above the sky. She lowers it and cocks her head, visualizing something.

"It's nice," he says.

"You're sweet."

"Straight out of your imagination?"

"Impressive, isn't it?"

Gayle comes in and hangs her coat by the door.

Ruth sets down the brush and turns to eye her daughter with the same critical squint with which she had been determining the contours of a distant blob. "Can you leave us, Lewis?" He leaves, and Ruth approaches her daughter.

"Don't tell boys what you're thinking, Gayle."

"What?"

"Otherwise you'll drain yourself out and there's nowhere to go from there. Remember when you were crazy about that big blond boy? What was his name? Mark Asshole?"

"Ansell."

"Sorry—bad joke. Half-joke. He was a mean kid though. Came from a mean family."

"I was sixteen, seventeen."

"How did it end for you?"

"What kind of lesson is this, Mum?"

"You're fragile like an egg, Gayle. You don't know anything about the world yet. I know you don't want to hear that, but that's the truth."

Gayle says nothing. Her mother's voice drones, as though she is distracted, looking through her.

"Let me start over. I'm not expressing myself very well." Ruth puts her arms around her daughter, who stands still, cold to the touch. She presses her dry lips to Gayle's hairline. "Don't forget your poor mother. You're my flesh and blood."

Gayle walks away and Ruth returns to her painting. From the adjoining room, Gayle turns back and sees her flesh and blood already absorbed in determining the perfect shape of a blob.

———— ◆ ————

Night. Lewis smokes by the window.

Gayle comes up behind him. "How many?"

"Two—soon one."

"Oh."

"We can stop in town on the way out, pick up some more. One thing the world never hides is its cigarettes."

"Hey Lewis—*whisper.*" She stands beside him and puts her hands on the sill. "Don't worry about the cows. They'll be fine. Mum'll sell them when she realizes she has no idea how to take care of anything. That'll be enough for her. It'll pull in some money—"

"Let's pack then."

"I did already. Did you?"

"Yeah, me too. I've been watching the road. Lots of cars around four, five, six. Coming back from work, probably. And BC loves hitchhikers. We only need to get as far as Highway One. If it gets tough, we'll spend a night in a motel and wake up early. No need to camp out. Edmonton isn't so far. We could do it in a day."

"Lewis."

"What?"

"You have mud on your face." She leans close and uses her thumb to wipe it away.

Like all faces, he thinks, it looks unfamiliar up close. Black eyes. Watery eyes. Blemishes.

She walks away and he notices something he's never noticed before: She walks with a limp, as though she has a stone in one of her shoes.

———— ◆ ————

Ruth asks Lewis to help her pick up seedlings from the greenhouse in Salmon Arm. She asks him to bring his bags.

"Already packed? That's convenient."

She drives a beige car with two doors.

"You've been doing a wonderful job, kid," she says as they drive. "With the fence stained and the beds all dug up, I'm starting to think you'll run out of things to do. But the fence looks beautiful. Just right. You've got good brush technique. You should consider being a painter."

They reach the sign welcoming them to Salmon Arm and pull into the parking lot of a strip mall with a greenhouse. Ruth turns off the car and sighs. "Gayle's a fragile girl. Like an egg. She was born with a deformed knee, you know. That's where it all started. I knew it right then and there: she couldn't possibly live in this world like the rest."

Lewis looks down, contracting and stretching his knuckles, drumming his fingers on his armrest. It occurs to Ruth that he's anticipating pain. It's something she's seen children do before getting vaccinated.

"And then her dad—I'm sure she told you about that. I don't know how she deals with it. It certainly isn't by releasing her emotions. That's what people do in movies, isn't it? They cry and punch walls and things. I think you know what I'm talking about. When's the last time you've seen a movie?"

"Maybe a couple months ago."

"A mother knows her daughter better than anyone. I have a sixth sense. You got it? I can't watch her forever. But she's fragile. That's what I wanted to tell you."

The rain patters on the parking lot. A man walks by carrying a potted tree.

Ruth stretches her neck against the headrest. "You're probably thinking, why is this old woman telling me all this, huh? But who knows? I'm slowly losing my intuition, letting a strange boy come stay in our house. I really thought you'd be a good kid with a good heart. Not an abductor."

He opens his mouth, says nothing.

"Where are you planning to go?" she asks.

"Edmonton."

Ruth reaches into her purse and shuffles through some bills, counts silently.

"For the bus." She holds the bills taut to smooth out the wrinkles and hands them over. "Go far. Don't ever contact my daughter again." She opens her door. "I still need your help to carry out the saplings, though."

———— ◆ ————

Gayle tries to get something out of Ami's hair. "Hold still."

"I hate holding still."

"Hay. You've been in the barn?"

The front door opens and Ruth enters carrying a plastic seedling tray. She places it on the floor and goes out again for more. She unloads the car by herself and then goes upstairs to her room.

Gayle examines the seedlings. Tomatoes. Broccoli. Sweet peas.

———— ◆ ————

The next morning, the sun is back. The only hint of the last day's rain is the softness of the earth. A single blackbird is perched in a tree beyond the window of the parlour. Ruth doesn't know if it's truly a blackbird or just a bird that is black.

Gayle enters.

"Gayle," Ruth says. "I was going to put geese in the sky, but what do you think of blackbirds instead?"

Gayle says nothing.

"Not for any real reason. Something has to fill that space. And at this distance, you can't really tell what kind of bird it is anyway. But I'll know."

"We need to call the vet. The milk fever's gotten worse. But they won't answer before ten o'clock anyway."

"Do you trust my judgement, Gayle?"

Gayle leaves.

Ruth turns back to her canvas and makes a small stroke in the sky—just a stroke and nothing more—to indicate a black bird at a great distance.

chapter two
- 1979 -

I n August, a letter arrives, addressed to Gayle. It's posted from Edmonton and bears the university stamp. She takes it, expecting news about her father.

Gayle, I'm waiting. The house is across from field from Queen Alexandra School. It's white and there's one big dying pine tree out front. I live in the basement. Ring the bell. If a man answers the door, tell him your name. He's a friend.

At the bottom, he wrote the address in blocky, childlike letters to ensure it won't be misread.

It's not her father. It's Lewis. He must have scavenged the envelope in order to send a clandestine letter and not alert her mother. She paces the library for a while. Her body is numb. She only knows she's cold because of the shivers.

She starts a fire in the woodstove and sits to write a letter to Edmonton, AB.

I'm coming. Wait for me. Don't move. Don't change. How long has it been? No more than a few months. But it feels like eternity. I've never felt this way before. I didn't think I was capable of it. I've been trapped here, but you are my ticket. I should have told you this before you left. I'm yours.

She stops. That sounds desperate, she thinks, and she doesn't want to come across that way. She starts again on a fresh sheet.

I'm coming. Gayle.

———◆———

She borrows her mother's car and offers to drive her sister to school, taking a few minutes to visit the local pawnshop. She starts with her own things—a guitar she never learned to play, a few eight-tracks, some clothes, jewellery. Then she moves on to things that aren't hers. It wasn't always their house, after all. The farmer who died in it before they came left behind a truck engine and, in the basement cupboards, boxes of a women's jewellery, bits of memorabilia, badges from the Second World War. She pawns it all.

She selects a random date to leave. Sometime at the beginning of September.

She knows from reading books that runaways have the best luck at midnight or slightly after. On her last visit to town, she finds a young man looking for quick cash who can pick her up at the top of the road and take her to the highway. She tells him to arrive at exactly 12:30 and idle behind the trees so the headlights aren't visible from her mother's window.

———◆———

When the night comes, she is a citizen of the world, a backpack over her shoulder, stepping through the hallway to Ami's room.

"It's just me."

"Gayle?"

"Remember when I said I'm going? Listen—I'm going."

"I don't understand."

"You don't need to understand."

Ami pulls her blanket to her face.

"And I'll call you," Gayle says. "Someday. But don't worry."

"Okay."

"Take care of mom. Just do what you're doing."

She kisses her sister on the forehead and descends to the parlour. Moonlight reveals all the familiar shapes. On the couch is her mother, sleeping. For all the time she spent complaining about her posture, about how important it is to sleep flat on the back, she's now curled into a ball, her knees hanging over the edge of the cushion.

Gayle had prepared a brief note and planned to leave it on her mother's painting stool. But it's no longer possible. The floor would creak. When she reaches the middle of the room, the snoring stops. "Ami?"

"Yes."

Her mother groans as Gayle dashes to the front door and undoes the latch. There is a glow beyond the trees—the pickup. Ruth emerges in the doorway behind her.

"You're following that boy?" She wraps her arms around Gayle's shoulders and strokes her hair. "Put your fucking arms around me—I'm your mother."

Gayle does.

"You'll find out," Ruth says.

"What?"

"You're wasting your time. I know all about running away. It doesn't work the way you think. Ruth turns on the porch light. "But who am I to judge *you*?"

"Mum—"

"But if you're going to that godforsaken city—keep an eye out for your dad, at least."

"Okay, Mum." Gayle takes a deep breath and presses the note into her mother's hand. She feels guilty about what it contains. She wrote it in anger, lethargy. It is nothing more than instructions for taking care of the cows. *I'll miss them the most,* she wrote at the end.

———•———

The driver says nothing until he drops her off at the motel on the highway.

"Good?" he asks.

"Sure." She looks out at the VACANCY sign with relief and fishes some bills from her envelope. One night in a motel, and then smooth sailing to Edmonton along the highways. Lewis said it would work.

———•———

Before morning, she stands in moonlight near the motel sign, hoping its pathetic floodlights will reveal her and her thumb, too.

———•———

Late in the afternoon, at a truck stop near Airdrie, she finds a ride north with an elderly woman from Calgary going to visit her son. Gayle tells her that she, too, is going to visit family but doesn't have enough money for a bus ticket.

———•———

The sun is setting by the time they arrive in Edmonton, and the woman veers far off course to bring Gayle to the address she provided, near Queen Alexandra School, in the heart of the city. Like Lewis said, it's a white house with a single pine out front. But it's far more ramshackle than Gayle imagined. The paint peels, shingles are missing from the roof, the grass is uncut and flatting over on itself.

No one answers when she rings the first time. She tries again, ringing the bell a dozen times in succession. She hears footsteps. Fingers crack the blinds of a window and soon the door opens on a man wearing pyjama bottoms and a sleeveless shirt. "Sorry. I was asleep."

"I'm—Gayle?" She says it like a question.

"Delightful. I'm Li Yong. Come in."

In the kitchen, the stranger asks how she is. He says it so nonchalantly that it shocks her: "How are you?"

"I don't know. Is Lewis here?"

"He's out right now. He gets home pretty late on weekends. I'm the home-owner. What's it, Sunday?"

"Are you his friend?"

"Yes."

"He told me he lives in the basement."

"That's true."

The kitchen, like the yard, is filthy. There are unwashed dishes piled in the sink, dust in all the corners and skirting around her shoes, which the man tells her not to remove, and newspapers—sports sections in particular—scattered around haphazardly. Ants march freely through a small triangular hole in the bottom of the window.

"Did he mention—anything? Me?"

"Many times."

She feels relieved. "Good. I guess. What's your name again?"

"Li Yong."

"Lee Yong."

"Sure, that's fine."

He shows her to the basement.

———◆———

She waits for an hour in Lewis's room before getting restless and taking a shower. Afterwards she realizes that her clothes are wet with rain and smelling of sweat, so she exchanges them for some of his—a too-large sweatshirt—and retreats under his sheets.

Eventually he returns. She hears rummaging in the stairwell and suddenly feels like a trespasser. Her instinct tells her to hide. But he doesn't come into the bedroom. He goes into another room, shuffling things, lighting a cigarette, sitting on a sofa with a creak. He turns on a radio and explores his options: news, a special about invasive species on the Canadian Shield, or a "Hard Rock Super Hour" featuring the music of Deep Purple.

A few minutes later, he goes to the kitchen. Soon the smell of hot meat wafts under the door.

It occurs to her she's made a mistake. The body in the other room, for all she knows, isn't Lewis at all. Many people smoke and eat meat, and the day of hitchhiking has installed in her a quivering fight or flight response. *Choose*, she tells herself.

She chooses flight and goes to hide in the closet. Irrational, but what other choice is there?

When he finally enters, she hears him search for something on the floor—his sweatshirt, most likely—give up, collapse on the bed and fall asleep.

She exits the closet. Moonlight fills the bed and she sees that it's indeed the man with a boyishly handsome face. Not one ounce of a stranger. She knows it well. She's kissed it. They've been intimate. Her fear vanishes. Slipping into the sheets beside him feels like the most natural thing to do.

She continues to observe the outline of her lover's face, freshly shaven, smelling of soap—not body soap, but dish soap—until he wakes from a dream and gasps. He finds her lying there beside him. Half-asleep, he lays his arm across her chest.

"Did you find the place okay?"

She stares into the dark holes that are all she can make out of his eyes. Her hands wander down to his hips. Warm and full of life, she thinks as she shuffles his pants down to his knees.

A current of pleasure runs through her. Sex takes no more than twelve minutes, after which he goes to the bathroom to clean himself off and returns looking sleepy but spry, like a wind-up soldier taking a few last steps before falling over into the sheets.

The room is an extension of us, Gayle thinks. By the grace of our bodies, it's become more humid, more fragrant, than it's probably ever been. Sex makes a room a home.

"It felt like a hole in me," she says, pulling him into the sheets. "I couldn't speak to anyone. Now it's here. It's true. We're free."

Dogs fight somewhere in the neighbourhood, beyond the cracked window.

"I've been working hard, Gayle."

"Has it been rough?"

"A little. But I don't want to bore you with all that."

"I came here to find you. *You're* what I want to hear about."

"Well, okay…. It's nothing. It took a while to find a job. They talk about Alberta like money shoots out of the ground, like there's a big boom and the businesses are just begging for more guys. It's not true, though. I was homeless for a while when I got here. Being homeless in the city is nothing like being homeless on the road. It's dangerous. I slept out under the bridge a few nights. It's fine for now. We won't be here long. This city's a—shithole."

"I'm glad you're okay."

"We have a lot ahead of us."

"Tell me."

"I'm going to save up, maybe for a few months more, just so we can have a fair go of it. I won't let you end up in a situation like I was in. I'm doing it so you don't have to. I'll take care of us. Lee's already helped me out. He's a good man, helped me find a job and let me stay on the cheap. I work in a shop, just like I used to do. A bag bitch." He laughs.

"Why's he doing it?"

"Didn't ask. Just because he's a good man. I met him in a diner when I was homeless and looking at the board in there for jobs and stuff. I guess he could tell I was down and out, so came up to me and asked me if I needed anything—I needed a lot."

He wiggles his arm free so he can reach down into the pocket of his jeans and find a cigarette.

For several weeks, he opens shop early and lets Gayle sleep in.

As caregiver to the cows, she hasn't slept in for years. For the first few weeks, she relishes in indolence and pays no attention to what day it is. She gives no thought to her mother, her father, or the future.

By noon each day, she's out walking. The streets of Edmonton are long and serene, aside from the occasional burst of exhaust of a passing Ford, Dodge, or Chevy. She walks as far as she can in any given direction until she encounters a place to rest—a strip mall, a McDonald's or an A&W, or a schoolyard with a bench—and then turns around.

After a decade of farm life, she finds the city's anonymity entrancing, the chain stores and consumer goods novel, the ever-present hum of traffic and voices dreamy. She disagrees with Lewis that the city is a shithole but doesn't care if he thinks it is.

———◦———

After a week, her opinion changes, and she finds the city boring, as though it were built from cardboard overnight and populated out of convenience. In Edmonton, people straight-facedly ignore her unless she interrupts them. No one says hello or gets in her way other than people asking for change. She doesn't remember Victoria being this way.

———◦———

The basement is plain and sparely furnished, ideal for someone who has no intention of staying. But there is still dust in the corners, soap scum in the shower, places where mice have torn insulation from the ceiling, laundry in piles on the floor. The kitchen contains only one plate, two cups, and two forks, and the fridge is empty aside from a package of bacon and a loaf of bread.

"It's okay for you?" he asks in the evening.

"I love it."

"With the mess and everything? I know you've never really been out before. I wanted to keep things perfect—perfect for you—but I didn't know when you were coming."

"It's perfect." She smiles. "Let's go get a beer."

"I got some wheat ale. We can drink it in the sofa room."

"The sofa room? You mean that other room?"

"Yeah—with the sofa in it."

They spend their evenings together with the radio on. There is no pressure to speak if they don't want to. As they wade through stations, she imagines his heart as an antenna. She learns a little more about how it works every time she lands on a program that makes him stop talking and turn his attention to it.

There are things they both enjoy—sometimes folk, rock, punk. They appreciate the straightforward rebellion of The Clash.

This is all she needs, she tells herself, for now and always.

"I heard that one on the radio while you were out," she says.

"Which?"

"That one folk song. We talked about it before—'Black Jack Davy' it's called. The one about the charming traveller who meets this pretty little farm girl and takes her away from her life of luxury and makes her take off her Spanish leather shoes and replace them with low-heeled shoes. It's always Spanish leather."

"Did Bob Dylan do it?"

"Maybe he wrote it. He wrote everything. But I just brought it up because there's this one line in the song, sung by the young man. He says, 'Come with me, pretty little miss. Come along with me, my darling.' But until today I always thought it was 'pretty little mess.' It doesn't make sense, but I liked it. I feel like a pretty little mess—your pretty little mess, in this house, our pretty little mess."

He sighs and brushes the hair from her forehead.

"But it's happened," she says. "You've stolen me away. I can be whatever I want, a pretty little mess, or miss, or whatever."

"And I've been thinking," he says. "I thought we'd stay here 'til spring. It's no good to travel in the winter."

"The winters here are supposed to be brutal. Minus forty every day, minus fifty at night, with wind like angry snakes. That's what dad used to say, anyway."

"You should get a new coat then."

"Are we good for that?"

"For what?"

"Money—for the coat."

"Yeah. We're good. I made sure."

"What about you? You're gonna go around in denim all year?"

"I'm okay."

By the end of September, the weather becomes cooler, the prairie wind more frequent. She grows to love the coldness of the house, the fact that she has to wear a sweater inside, the fact that they need each other's body heat to keep warm at nights, the fact that the shower runs out of hot water after less than ten minutes. It's an honest life, she thinks. It is as it is, and they desire nothing more than the small things that make them happy.

She buys a coat, a new scarf, and insulated shoes. Then things for the suite: spoons first, and then a bonsai tree she finds at the nearby farmer's market. It hardly makes a dent in her own stash let alone what Lewis gave her. And it's nothing she'll feel bad for abandoning, just something to give her eyes something to look at while she's sitting at home, waiting.

"I like trees," Lewis says when she shows him. "Why that one?"

"I've always wanted one of these little trees, since I was a girl. They make me think of faraway places."

"Anything you want, we'll get it."

"I don't want to bother you."

"I want you to be happy."

They turn to look at the bonsai on the shelf.

"We're pretty miraculous," she says.

"What do you mean?"

"This is what miraculous people do when they're waiting. They decorate their mess and drink beers. They just wait for the world to bring them someplace, right?"

"That's what I think, too."

———◆———

They go for a long walk down Whyte Avenue, along the rows of bricks and turn-of-the-century buildings now inhabited with shops. They stop in at the Princess Theatre to see a retro movie, deciding on Clark Gable in *Soldier of Fortune*, and then take dinner at a restaurant by the train tracks.

"I feel nostalgic watching old black and white movies," she says.

"When was it done?"

"I think the credits said the fifties." She scans the colours of her salad. "It's interesting how we can feel nostalgic for something we never saw in real life. It's really unusual. Maybe it's not nostalgia at all, but something else. Maybe people born today are going to feel this way about the seventies, you know, like they'll see it all through rose-coloured glasses."

"I get nostalgic watching movies at all," he says. "I haven't done it in I don't know how long. It still seems like a normal person thing to do. It's all kinda extravagant, too—like that theatre, all plush and red."

"That movie sure made the Chinese look like barbarians. Nothing like Lee, anyway. Maybe someday the Russians'll take us over and make a movie about Canadian barbarians. Or maybe not. I don't think Russians would be interested in us."

"It's funny, you know. Some people never like to talk about movies after they see them, but I think that's the whole point, otherwise—"

Their conversation is interrupted by a series of small explosions coming from the engine of a passing Ford.

"That noise," she says. "It gets me every time. This city can be so calm. But the noise—"

"Lots of young guys with too much cash. And old guys with too much cash." He picks at his food but doesn't eat.

"Hey Lew, are you sick?"

"Yes." He excuses himself from the building. Gayle doesn't eat without him, and both of their meals are cold when he returns ten minutes later.

"You look black and white," she says.

"It happens sometimes—"

"Yeah I know. You told me once that it comes and goes. Whatever it is. Like when we found you in the barn—remember?"

"Of course."

"You should see a doctor."

"It's not serious—and I can't afford it."

"We can afford it."

"No."

"And you smell like—weed."

"Yeah, sorry—it's good for the stomach. I feel better afterward."

"I haven't smelled that since high school," she says.

———◆———

"It's just weird," she says later in the sofa room.

"What?"

"There really are cowboys here. I thought that was a stereotype. They taught us in school that Albertans have a lot of cows and canola. I mean, I don't mind. It's kinda cute. And in the countryside I get it. But in the city, the get-up looks a bit out of place."

"I was thinking of getting some boots myself. Gotta do as the locals do while we're here."

They laugh at the thought of themselves in cowboy gear.

She goes to change the station to something local. Alberta cowboy music from Stony Plain. "Where do we go in spring, if we save up enough?"

"We could buy a car, maybe. Travel in comfort. We can take it far as we can, go east, all the way across Canada, to Nova Scotia. My aunt said it's the most beautiful place on Earth, the East Coast. We could even go down to the States, into Maine or New York. Hell, we could go all the way to Mexico. It doesn't really matter much, does it? We can sleep under the stars."

"We could go to England, right? You said we could once. They're supposed to love Canadians there. We won't have a hard life."

"My aunt told me you can drive your car onto a boat in New York and it'll take you to Southampton."

"How much will that cost?"

"We'll worry about it later."

"I'm amazed at us," she says.

"Me too."

"I'd like to help—make some money."

"You don't have to. That's my job."

"Like you're the hunter, I'm the nest-maker?"

"No—well, I don't know—what do you mean?"

"I want to help. Otherwise you'll burn out. You're already sick."

"But then we'd never see each other."

———— · ————

She soon finds a job as a waitress in a family restaurant specializing in omelettes. She buys the white and musky-yellow uniform but quits the next day, bothered by the repetitiveness of the job, of the sulphur-egg smell that clings to her, and the seemingly unfounded rage of the cooks.

Next she works in an elderly home, washing laundry, sweeping floors, handing out sandwiches and pudding at lunchtime. Here she lasts a little longer but quits when she grows tired of the incessant gossiping amongst staff, the way they make fun of the elderly behind their back, and the perpetual presence of ambulances, which are referred to by the residents as "chariots of death." Worst of all, she decides, are the stoic drivers who walk through the halls, chatting to the nurses about the weather while they pull the bodies from their stained sheets to "load 'em up."

———⁜———

"In the home, one of the nurses called this place Deadmonton."

"Why?"

"I don't know. Why do you think?"

"I don't know," he says. "Maybe it's because of the economy—I mean—because it's so fast-paced and unpredictable so everyone is tense. I heard something like that on the radio."

"But my dad loved it here. I think he did, anyway. He lived here for years. Came home only in the summer."

"Maybe he saw something in it. He was a poet, right? Maybe he liked the emotions. Death and stuff. I read Keats a little bit, you know, and one line always stuck with me: 'I've been half in love with death.' Is that right?"

Lewis shifts to his side and winces. Gayle lifts up his shirt and sees a series of bruises on his hip.

"What happened?"

"I tripped in the shop this morning."

"Oh darling," she says. These words make her feel older.

———⁜———

She finds a salon on Whyte Avenue and asks them to make her blond. Lots of girls in Edmonton seem to be dyeing their hair blond. There are more women with fake blond hair than there are men in cowboy gear.

"I mean blond like gold," she says to the stylist. "Like Farrah Fawcett or something, with highlights and layers and stuff."

The stylist says they can do it for under five dollars, which includes a shampooing.

"I love this feeling," Gayle says from under the current. "I've never done this before, you know."

"You've got lovely thick hair, but lots of knots."

"I used to live on a farm."

"Good for you, girl.... Come to the city to study?"

"No—I'm a runaway."

They both laugh as the stylist pushes deeper into her scalp and runs her fingers in small, circular patterns outward. Then she draws warm water to rinse out the shampoo.

"The hot water at my place doesn't work very well," Gayle says.

"Lots of hot water here, hun. Come now, let me dry it."

She is set before a mirror. Her hair is dried with a towel, brushed, and combed thirty times. Between small talk, she looks at her reflection and watches the line of her mouth curve upward.

"You've got a nice smile," the stylist says. "You could be in a magazine. Now, let's bleach—"

———◆———

"You're blond now?" Lewis asks.

"Yeah—I needed to change. It was a small investment—for the future."

"Change is good."

"Maybe I can get a good job now. Blond girls are more successful. I heard that on the radio once. Apparently there's some scientist in the States setting up wires to peoples' brains and making them look at pictures of blond women, just to see what happens."

He looks to the bonsai and shivers. "Good idea."

Gayle makes circles on his cuff. "You're not going to die, are you?"

"God, no."

"Why don't you take time off?"

"We need to save up, Gayle."

"But it's not even winter yet. What are you gonna do when the snow comes?"

"The snow's not supposed to get here 'til November."

"If you live 'til then."

"I'm not dying, for Christ's sake."

"Oh, Lew, I'm just—"

"Gayle, do you love me?"

"You know I do. Look what I've done for you. Look"—she gestures around the room, to the bonsai, to herself—"I'm here."

He turns the lamp off, lights a cigarette. The orange glow between his lips is the only remaining light in the room. In it, she thinks, he looks miserable.

part two

—◆—

the
soul's
things

chapter three
- 1960 -

A young woman throws her spoon—not her knife, she's sure of that—intending to miss and laugh it off. Her target is a chip in the paint above the shoulder of a broad man with elbows firm on the table, conquering the wall with his shadow. With a jerk of the arm, he deflects the projectile. Rosemary-dotted potatoes spatter behind him in the shape of an exploding star.

The spaniel curled up at his feet, which had been dozing even through the argument, flees the kitchen.

The man laughs and snuffs the candle.

"Let's go for a drive," he says.

"But it'll get cold—"

———•———

Forty-five minutes later, he clutches the wheel of a Chevrolet Delray, driving north on the highway, away from Victoria and toward the storm. The woman looks out the passenger window at pines thickening the roadside. Occasionally the headlights blast a sign: Wildlife Crossing, Provincial Park Turnout, Welcome to Mill Bay, SPEED LIMIT 50, 60, 50, 70, 50.

On this highway, which runs along the coast and bends to the commands of the cliffs, the speed limit can change with every turn. The driver pays no attention—he's white-knuckled, maintaining a steady seventy. Blood pulses through his pointer finger, below the slightly too-small wedding ring like sand through the neck of an hourglass.

"Slow down, Al," she says.

"Why?"

"Life. That's why. You're gonna end ours."

He slows.

"Better, no?" she says. "Nice, relaxing. A casual drive."

"You wish we stopped at one of those clubs on Douglas Street, huh?"

"I'm not a dancer."

"But we'll fix that. We'll start tomorrow."

When they do arrive anywhere ("anywhere" is what they'd agreed upon as a manageable destination), it's a tourist point indicated by a white gravel pull-off and a rectangular sign with a picture of a telescope, a single tree, and the sun, all roughly the same size.

The car parked, he slides his hand up her shirt.

"Better in the back seat," she says, "like teenagers."

"I've got a romantic side." He sings these words atonally, impersonating a crooner. A jig of the shoulders and he slicks back his hair, which promptly falls back into its original, conservative wave.

She spits a laugh, covers her mouth, and lies, "*Hey* Sinatra."

———◆———

Sex over, bodies tranquil, they exit the vehicle and descend the wet wooden steps to the point. The sign was misleading—there is no telescope, no sun. There are empty beer bottles and cigarette butts scattered around a wooden balcony with no safety rail, and the storm has knocked out the sky. They stand under a bough.

"A slow day up here," he says.

"I wonder why."

On a clear day, they'd be able to see a rough line across the strait, like paper torn carelessly: the mountains of the mainland. But today there's fog. Looking outward, she sees only an unfathomable number of ripples on the face of the water and the occasional scribble of lightning to the north.

"Count," he says. Hardly is the word out when they hear the crash. "Pretty close."

"I'm sorry, you know—"

"Hmm?" He smiles.

"For that whole thing." Hair streams down her brow. She pushes it back. "I don't even remember what we were going on about." She does remember—the accusations of infidelity, the spoon. She didn't know until being married that jealousy was in her nature.

"Who do you think I am, Ruth?"

"I don't even remember why I did it."

"We're on the same team. Come—"

She finds a place under his arm. The lightning and the sensation of being on a gangplank makes it all inconsequential. Anger, jealousy—"real life things," she thinks of them—don't matter.

"It's better we don't fight again," she says.

"You're so young. Naïve still. I say that as a compliment." He bends to pick up a rock.

"Yeah, I know." For a man of thirty-two, she thinks, he speaks wisely. Wisdom, whatever it is, is not something she ever valued until she met him.

He puts the rock in her hands. She rubs it between her palms, feeling its contours. It's a smooth rock, heavier than it looks. She throws it at a pine with half its roots exposed, living a precarious life on the edge of the cliff. She wants to see it fall. The rock flies past, but she doesn't hear it hit the bottom.

Soon a dark wind comes, sprinkling mud over their jackets. As he wipes his cheek, his smile disappears.

"What?" she says.

"It takes this kind of place to remind us how puny we are—in the grand scheme of things. *Drive my dead thoughts*—"

"Like those pictures of Kilimanjaro in that magazine last week? Or Sputnik? Right?"

"Water's the eternal symbol of purity, purification." Al takes a deep breath, steps away from her. "Have we been here before?"

"Nah."

"No—I suppose not."

"But lots of things look the same when the fog's in."

He stands at the ledge and looks down, examining the exposed roots reaching toward the beach below, which is narrow and stony and littered with bottles. It's a five-storey drop.

"Not so close," she says.

He doesn't respond—his eyes have glazed over. The familiar glaze. It's one thing in bed, in the kitchen, on the lawn, but it's another here. She takes his elbow.

"Move away, Ruth."

"You're gonna fall off—just a little slip, and there you go." She pulls him. He shakes her off. "S'not funny," she says. "You're scaring me."

"I'm getting thirsty." He holds his hand over the edge, palm up, catching rain. He brings it to his mouth to sip.

After he takes several gulps, she moves to his side and holds her own hands together as a bowl. She dips her lips into the storm water. Her hands shake against her will, but she smiles and sucks it in.

"It's beautiful," she says.

"*That's it.*"

Another line of lightning. It sounds before Ruth can count and she feels the tremors in the platform. The beer bottles vibrate and one falls over the edge. She drops the water and steps back. "Come back to me now."

He holds his arms out like a crucifix and laughs.

She hum-sings words: "Come to mama, come to mama. Your hand's a lightning ro-o-o-d."

Muddy hair is plastered to her cheeks, under her eye. She tears it away, pushes it behind her ears. The wind pushes it forward again and blocks her vision, knocks her off balance.

She lunges to grab him—"Fuck, Al—"

It doesn't strike them but the precarious pine. The current travels through the earth, the platform, their bones. As she watches the tree catch fire and tip over the edge, her jacket rises from her skin and quickly falls again, suctioning to her body. Her collar is a strangler around her neck. She is charged—and deaf.

She rips off her top button and turns toward her husband. He is floating, levitating across the threshold, over the rippling abyss. In her soundless world, she can focus. Time slows. She holds her breath. Al hovers there for what seems like an impossible amount of time—three minutes, five minutes—a metre over the edge, outlined by a dim blue halo.

Invisible hands place him gently on the platform, steady him on his feet, and release.

A rag doll, he collapses.

Overwhelming fatigue comes to her. She doesn't remember falling, and as she closes her eyes she wonders how she ended up on the ground, too.

———◆———

She wakes after an indeterminable amount of time with her sense of hearing returned, her body light, weightless even. She crawls to him but doesn't touch him. She doesn't know how the charge will respond.

Instead, she removes her jacket, places it over his torso and face, and kisses the small bump above his lips.

"Love you, Al. Get up."

He jerks. She pulls away the jacket and looks into his irises streaked with bright grey. His mouth bubbles open for a moment before the terror dulls into something like disgust, then nothing—just open. He kisses her on the mouth and holds his tongue between her lips, against her teeth.

"I can't stand up," he says.

With a heroic strength that she doesn't dare pause and question, she drags him up the wooden stairs to the car and helps him lift himself into the passenger's seat. She peels off his jacket and shirt, slides his belt from its loops, and tells him to kick off his pants while she pulls. Finally, she wraps him in a wool emergency blanket from the trunk.

Hypothermia—it's possible. She finds the keys in his discarded pants and lets the car idle with the heater on. It usually takes ten minutes to warm. She lifts his wrist onto the armrest so she can see his watch that, miraculously, still works.

Only then does she attend to herself. But afraid to look, she closes her eyes and mentally scans her body for wounds—

Her chest is open.

A jagged incision from her collar to her belly button.

Air moves in and out of her against her will. The car huffs rubbery air directly into her bloody rib cage and tickles. The car seat is sticky with blood, too. She holds her hand above her chest, counts to three, and makes contact.

It's an illusion. She's unscathed.

When she knows she's whole, she starts to cry in spasms and gasps. A joyful weeping from the stomach.

The shock seems to have heightened her sense of smell, which she uses to distract her from the moment at hand until she can gain her composure. Rubber air. Singed flesh. Rain. Rain!

She turns on the radio, takes Al's hand. His eyes are closed again, body unresponsive but breathing. "Listen, it's Sinatra."

The heat reaches maximum.

She's never driven before.

She jerks the Delray onto the highway.

No traffic because of the storm, she can maintain forty and not worry about switching gears.

When they arrive at the outskirts of the city, the streetlights appear to bring him back to consciousness. She looks over. His right eye is swollen shut, vomit is turning to paste on his cheek, but his lips are upturned.

"We're alive," he whispers.

"We're alive," she repeats, and then shouts, "Alive! I'm gonna make sure we're *per-fect*."

Swerving away from what she believes is a pedestrian, she hops the curb and accelerates into a brick wall, passing straight through it, the windshield shattering, husband ejected—

———————◆———————

A face, teeth—young, fluoride-white, perfectly perpendicular.

"It's a miracle he's alive," the face says. It's a nurse. She gestures to Al, who's in a bed—not the next one over, but the one after that. "How are you feeling now?"

Ruth commands her left eye to open. It's more stubborn than the right. "How did I get—"

"Again, ma'am, you have a slight concussion. Nothing to be worried about. If you feel dizzy, adjust your headrest with that lever or ring the bell if you need water."

"Okay—"

The nurse leans forward and continues in hushed tones, "I've been going around telling the other nurses, but of course you should know right away. Your companion's a real miracle case—considering what you've both been through." She explains that, despite not wearing his seat belt, Al has not a single broken bone. The nurse's words swirl through Ruth's consciousness as she explains that "acute spinal damage is pretty common but ... paralysis, internal bleeding and ... brain damage is a valid ... tests haven't ... some vicious bruises and swelling ... mysterious lacerations across his back but nothing that shouldn't ... a couple months, or a month if he's lucky."

"Okay."

"The reason it's a *miracle* though is that, according to first responders, when you hit the wall, you really *hit* it. The car burst right into the hotel lobby. Do you remember any of this?"

"No."

"Your companion was thrown, by the grace of God"—she folds her hands in front of her, swaying slightly forward and backward to punctuate her pauses—"through the windshield, directly onto a sofa. The receptionist had just stepped out for a dart. He's the one who called the ambulance. So no one was even present in the lobby. *What* are the chances?"

Ruth waits for the nurse's congratulatory smile to fade and says, "We were hit by lightning, too."

"Huh?"

"Just before—we were gone for a while—dead—but I came back first. That's why I was driving." The nurse leaves to relay the new information to the others and comes back with a team.

"Did you drag him, by any chance?" an elder nurse asks.

"Of course I dragged him—to the car. He was dead."

"It would explain the lacerations on his back. Perhaps there was something there, broken glass, rocks. How far did you drag him?"

"Far—up some stairs—"

"And you mentioned he was unconscious?"

"Dead. Levitating."

"Levitating?"

"For a few minutes. About this high." She sticks her arm straight out, parallel to the mattress. "Is this normal?"

The nurses look to each other and shrug. "Perhaps some hallucinations," says the eldest one. "Delusions from the impact to your head. I wouldn't worry about this now. Just rest. If it continues tomorrow, we'll scan for damage."

"I didn't hit my head 'til after. You've heard of it before? People in the air?"

"No, not exactly." The eldest nurse purses her lips. "Looks like it could be the second miracle of the day. You saved his life, ma'am." The nurses all smile and pretend to applaud. They maintain a gap between their hands in order not to wake anyone.

They leave, all except the young one, who Ruth whistles for as the others exit. She doesn't know why, but she trusts this nurse the most.

"I'm pregnant," Ruth whispers.

"*Oh—*"

"Do a test or something—to see if things're good."

"I'm not really allowed. I'm a student. I need to get it cleared." After some internal deliberations she adds, "My supervisor's off right away. We don't expect this kind of thing to come up so late."

"I really need to know."

"How far along are you?"

"I can't really remember. There's kind of a hole there. In my memory."

"When did you start getting symptoms?"

"The beginning of the month, I think."

"Okay." She sighs. "You'll have to check with another nurse during the day."

Ruth closes her eyes, expecting the nurse to leave. But she doesn't. She opens her eyes and the nurse is still there.

"I guess the miracles keep coming," the nurse says softly.

Ruth doesn't respond, so the nurse clears her throat and leaves. Ruth closes her eyes again and, when she grows dizzy, adjusts her headrest as she was told to do.

———————•———————

Ruth is released from the hospital the next morning. She takes a cab back to their bungalow in the suburbs and finds their spaniel dead inside an open cupboard beside the oven. She immediately slams it and vomits in the sink. It was her husband's dog. She never had time to get to know it. How long have I been away? she wonders.

She calls animal control and an officer arrives within an hour to take the body and apologize for the loss.

"Starvation," Ruth says, wiping her tears. "What day it is?"

"Monday, miss."

Not starvation, she thinks. It's only been a day.

"And it's most likely poisoning," the animal control officer explains. "It's common with household pets getting into cleaning supplies. The companies

are putting in all kind of scents and things these days. It's attractive to them."
He offers condolences once again and leaves.

She doesn't know what else to do so she screams at the top of her lungs, kicks a chair to the ground, and begins clearing the dinner plates they'd left behind, wiping up the potato splatter she left on the wall. The dog hadn't touched any of the human food. What a well-behaved dog, she thinks.

———•———

She visits her husband the next day, offering any help she can with washing, feeding and companionship. But he doesn't need Ruth's help. The nurses are there for that. They come whenever he rings the bell, and because he rings often, he's given his own room where he doesn't disturb anyone. Ruth visits for a few hours each day nonetheless and insists on being caregiver when she's present.

His only lasting mark, aside from the pale scars across his back from being dragged over broken glass, is a brown singe on his chest, roughly above his heart. She notices it during the first sponge bath.

"Looks like a star," she says.

This makes him smile. But it isn't true. The mark, she thinks, is a nebulous blob, a big dark amoeba. It remains looking fresh and singed long after the rest of his wounds heal over.

"It's warm," he says. "Here, feel—"

She puts her fingers on the blob and feels his heartbeat. It's true that it's warm. Unnaturally so.

The scars slowly seal and become part of him, but the burn always looks to her like an intruder.

———•———

She doesn't tell him about the dog. The nurses inform her that being in good spirits can facilitate an individual's healing process. It's a mysterious but verifiable principle of medicine, they explain.

As they expect, the miracle patient heals at an astounding rate.

"And would you believe someone from the paper came by to interview me?" he says.

"How's it feel to be famous?"

"Hardly famous. It's just a sensation story."

He stops talking so she goes for a walk around the hospital. The repetitive stained floors and the ever-present smell of decay and menthol-scented sanitation supplies make her nauseous. Her sense of smell remains unusually strong.

She goes to the cafeteria, orders a coffee, and sits in a corner table with the cup in front of her nose to neutralize the smell until she is approached by a nurse. It's the student, the young one, dressed in civilian clothes.

"Oh *hi*," the nurse says. "How are things?"

"My nose is acting funny." As a civilian, the nurse has shiny auburn hair and a loud, prancing voice. Ruth keeps the rim of the coffee cup against her upper lip.

She furrows her brow. "You have a cold? You should be careful not to spread it to the patients. It's an issue sometimes. You haven't been to the critical care ward, have you?"

"No—I just smell everything more than usual, since the accident."

"Oh, that's not abnormal after mild concussions. Are you here to visit your father?"

"My husband." Ruth lowers the cup.

The nurse blushes. "Lordy—I can't tell with the swelling. People can really change in the hospital lights too, you know. He had a beard when he came in—that usually does it."

"He's twelve years older, or thirteen I guess, depending on what time of the year—looks old for his age, and I look young but I'm not. I'm almost twenty."

"You know, come to think of it, I thought he was your father *because*"—she leans closer—"he's writing something—He's a poet, eh? "That's what he told me. I peeked at a bit of it. Said something like 'sweet child' or 'little child.' Told me not to tell you, so hush-hush?" She winks.

"It's how poets talk, I guess."

———◆———

"The nurse said you're writing again."

"Emily said that? Or—?"

"How many nurses do you have?"

He doesn't respond.

"Must be a good environment," Ruth says. "Nothing to distract you—"

"Better if I could use my right hand."

On the table beside his bed are scraps, words. They're embedded in napkins, torn pages, envelopes, bookmarks.

"What are you writing?" she asks.

"An article. On Keats. Something for work."

"Hogwash. I know when you work on something for school, you use notebooks. Don't think I don't know your quirks."

"It's a book then."

"Is it poetry this time?" she asks. "Or *about* poetry?"

The swelling around his cheeks and eyes has subsided, and the severe pupils are back—the dismal glaze.

"It's terrible luck to allow eyes on it before it's finished," he says.

They don't speak as she helps him to the bathroom. She stands outside and listens to him urinate. They don't speak for several minutes afterward.

"Bye, Al."

———◆———

One day the nurses bring him a newspaper with his photo in it, alongside an article about the "miracle" (the media also refers to it this way) of his flying through the windshield and landing on the sofa in the hotel lobby. He reads it out loud to Ruth with pride. It doesn't mention the lightning, the levitating. That's a private affair, no witnesses.

In the same newspaper, he begins scanning adverts for used cars.

"So soon," Ruth asks, "with the real-life things?"

"Real life?" he laughs. "Never—it's just to pass the time. We can probably get by without one, don't you think?"

He pulls a pathetic hospital pillow to his lap to rest the newspaper on. His right hand is still bandaged. He licks the fingers of his left to turn pages.

———◆———

She stops at a paint store on the way home and decides to make their bungalow a home. She chooses a new colour for the kitchen, dusty rose, and paints until two in the morning. The sales staff had suggested that neutral tones go well with anything, and she isn't equipped to replace the olive refrigerator or the lipstick-red window frame, or to steam out the white stains in the kitchen carpet left by the previous owner, which could just as likely be alfredo sauce as semen.

But the dusty rose dries quickly and, to her disappointment, becomes a straight pink.

She phones the store to complain, but there is no answer. She tries again. The line is dead, she thinks. But how do you call someone to repair your phone?

She catches the time on the clock above the kitchen table and laughs, seals the can of dusty rose, and begins to squeeze out the roller above a steel bucket. She squeezes faster and faster, beats the roller on the edge.

The phone rings. She lunges for it.

"What?" she says.

"Mrs. Windsor?"

"Yes.

"It's the Royal Jubilee calling. I'm Doctor Samuel Green. You're listed as Allen Windsor's contact."

"I know."

"Don't be alarmed. We're calling to let you know that he just underwent an episode involving seizures and loss of control over certain bodily functions."

"The hell's that mean?"

"Don't be alarmed. He'd complained of pain in his back and was administered a slight dose of aspirin—orally. A pill, I mean. Shortly after, he began undergoing contractions, shouting, crying, and he mentioned blurry vision. He called your name several times. Everything is under control. I'm just calling to let you know."

"I still don't know what's going on," she says firmly.

"I assure you your husband was administered nothing more than an Aspirin. Allergic reactions are possible, I suppose, though the pill is hypoallergenic."

"Should I be there?"

"Everything is under control. I'm just calling to inform you of what happened. It's protocol."

"Okay, Doc," she says, louder than she intended, and hangs up.

She sits on the kitchen floor, knees against her chest, balling herself with her arms.

---•---

At three a.m. she stands, stretches, and set to work on another coat of dusty rose.

---•---

"Not sure," he says when she brings up the episode. "Maybe they had me confused with someone else."

---•---

Exactly one month after the accident, he is home, entirely healed aside from the blob on his chest and the gaunt look to his face and figure.

In the evening, he sits at the kitchen table where, last time, he was hit with the spoon that set the series of deaths and miracles in motion. She prepares him a grilled a cheese sandwich with an egg in it.

"It's new to my repertoire," she explains.

He doesn't mention the missing dog. She doesn't mention the child in her belly. She sits beside him while he eats, arms crossed. He chews methodically. She can hear the clack of cheese in his jaws.

"We shouldn't fight anymore," she says. "That'd be best."

"It was worth it," he replies softly. "But no—never again."

He finishes half the sandwich in solemnity and leaves the rest, the underfried egg slipping out like spittle. "Excuse me," he says. "I need to walk."

She hands him his umbrella and coat and watches him tie his shoes at the landing. She stands at the top, looking down at him. "I'm really sorry I didn't tell you about the dog."

Mist swallows him. He returns an hour later to finish the sandwich.

---•---

She doesn't tell him she's pregnant until weeks later and expects him to be upset at her for hiding the information. But he isn't. He embraces her with one arm and cups her belly with the other.

"No one's gonna take a chance on a pregnant girl," she says.

"What's that, my glorious?"

"I'm definitely not gonna find work now. Everyone from design school went to Vancouver or Seattle. That's what we were supposed to do, for the good jobs. Everyone here's running small firms, so it's already tough."

"Don't even think about that now," he says. "Rest in your"—he beams—"*especially* enchanting glow." He lifts her and carries her to the bedroom, reminding her of their honeymoon (which took place, too, in their kitchen and bedroom). He rests her on the bed and she puts her hands behind her head, watching the old curtains sway.

"I never asked you," she says, "how do you like the new colour?"

"Your complexion is as milky as ever, my love. Statuesque. Italianesque. Like a nymph."

She laughs. "No, I mean the kitchen. I painted it with Pepto-Bismol."

"Anything you do I will love. That's a promise. I hereby pronounce you queen of the house."

They died—or nearly died—on the tourist point, she knows. But death doesn't change anything.

The only obvious change in his behaviour is his growing lust for food (he eats vociferously and constantly) and cigars. In her eyes, he *forces* himself to be a lover of cigars. The first two make him dizzy, full of coughs, but by the third he puffs with confidence like the man on the package.

The smoke smells like hickory sometimes, lavender at others. Sometimes a cocktail of both. He prefers to smoke on the lawn, in a coat, in the winter chill.

The lawn is a small, perfectly square patch of grass in front of the bungalow with no trees or flowers, surrounded by a short picket fence. He sits below an umbrella in a lawn chair with an armrest, writing on scraps, watching suburban traffic. The umbrella is for the rain.

She carries him a platter containing an ashtray and a glass of coke with ice, as requested.

"The smoke sharpens the pen," he explains to her. "It came up in conversation with a colleague—the cigar's uncanny ability to aid the poetic process."

"Good," she says.

"A man fresh recovered from an illness, as a man returning from a long trip, has a naturally heightened imagination. Everything is a foreign land. I must capture it before it's gone."

She returns to the house and watches him from the bedroom window. One stroke of the pen, then two. A procession of cars passing on the boulevard seems to push the poetry from him. He jots a whole sentence. The passengers in the cars eye him quizzically. He's an out-of-season sunbather, Ruth thinks. Every neighbourhood has an eccentric. After the man who burned all his garbage moved out, the eccentrics became us.

The last in the procession honks enthusiastically, and Al raises his hand to chin-height, rotates the wrist, waving like a royal.

———— ◆ ————

She notices something else. Returning from the dead deposited in their lives a love of darkness. They spend evening upon evening lying in bed, under covers, curtains closed, sometimes speaking, sometimes not. Often sobbing. Often laughing. Often naked.

They don't have features in the dark. These are the new personas they develop: the faceless ones, which, she thinks, her husband the poet may have a word for, but she doesn't.

"People are different in the dark," she suggests to the invisible man. "They're like different people." She can feel him smiling.

"It's true," he says.

"They're also different when naked. Do you think everyone does this?"

"Does what?"

"*This*. Being together and, just—this." He's the only man she's been with and she's never asked about his sexual history—it's far out of line. But she honestly wants to know.

"I know what you mean," he says. "I just love to hear you talk about it."

"I call us shadow people. Are we the only ones?"

"I guarantee you, Ruth—yes we are."

She feels a kick and moves his hand to her belly.

An overwhelming joy comes to them, a visceral thrill that causes their bodies to contract around each other and make as much skin contact as possible. They stay that way until the kicking stops.

———— ◆ ————

As queen of the house, she paints every room—four in total, five with the nook—and takes the bus into the city to buy cotton curtains and wooden curtain rods for the bedroom, handles for the kitchen drawers, placemats, rugs. She rearranges the furniture ceaselessly, shifts the bed so they sleep parallel to the window one day and perpendicular to it the next.

She tries to get all the supplies she needs for the week in one trip. She once enjoyed being on the bus, but when the pregnancy begins to show, she encounters only false smiles and paws that work their way onto her back, her stomach, run across her as though she's an apple that needs to be polished.

The touch of strangers makes her jerk away.

When her husband is with her, he explains it away, as though justifying a snarling dog.

"She's a little sensitive these days."

———◆———

She finds that shapes, colours, and how they interact comes naturally. Everything else does not. Each day Al comes home to a new house. He seems intrigued at first, but notices, or appears to care, a little less about the new look each time.

"How's my queen?"

"Bored. And when I'm not bored, I'm frustrated and sick. In the mornings."

"What do you mean? It's a strange word, 'frustrated.'"

"I can't cook. I can hardly clean. I'm not good at reading or doing intellectual stuff like you. And I'm forgetful as hell. I leave the paint open for days and it dries out. I can't even figure out the goddamn screwdriver and put up the curtain rod."

"Rave, sweet one."

He attempts to show her how to install the curtain rod, but also fails. He calls the hardware store and learns that there are various shapes of screwdrivers, various sizes of each shape.

"Now we know," he says.

———◆———

When November comes, he begins coming home later in the evening, leaving earlier in the morning, spending his weekends on the lawn with his jacket and poetry.

"I'm writing an article on Keats," he explains. "If I want to get anywhere, I need to publish. It's the truth."

"You're already a professor—eight years in school, right?"

"There's much more to it than that."

"I get it. You're a writer." She recalls some of the things he's told her about the writer's life. "It's an endless fight," she reiterates. "A life's pursuit or nothing at all. Right?"

"I haven't forgotten about *you*. I just need the alone time. Art is an act taken in isolation, just you and the winds."

"You're a hard-working man, Al."

"And your time'll come."

———◆———

As her belly grows, it becomes harder to climb on the stool to paint the ceiling and, she thinks, rather dangerous.

So she stops painting the house and takes up another kind of painting.

Her first attempt is a two-dimensional still life in an effort to imitate Matisse, who she learned about in the history component of her design diploma. She paints for two days, adding tone and complexity, using acrylics to speed up the process.

She calls the completed work "Three Eggs" and sits with it in the kitchen for an afternoon. But the acrylics, like the dusty rose, adopt new hues as they encounter the shifting light through the kitchen window. The intersections of colour—white and black, black and brown—are far shakier than she'd originally thought. The feeling of artistic elation subsides. She cries, embarrassed by her uncontrollable hand.

———◆———

At eleven p.m., Al emphatically kicks his shoes off at the landing, leaps the three steps with gusto and finds her in the kitchen, sitting on the floor.

"Guess what happened, Ruth? I was given an honour today. Truthfully, I wasn't supposed to know, but word got around that, apparently, the bright young minds at U Vic have selected me for an award. The category—what was it now?—Ah yes, *Most Inspired Temporary Professor* of English Literature. The M.I.T. prize—Mitt—"

She sets her painting against the wall, facing away. "Super-duper, Al."

"This may mean a substantial Christmas bonus."

"We can buy *anything.*"

"What's going on, my child?" He carefully lifts her to her feet. Then, palms against her cheeks, he holds her and gazes into her face as though it were a well.

"I'm bored—frustrated—sick—" she repeats.

He notices three real eggs staggered on the kitchen table.

"What are those for?" he asks. "Are we having omelettes?"

"I painted today."

He smiles, "Yes, you've made the kitchen wall the colour of your lips in summer."

"That was last week." She takes the canvas from the floor and hands it to him.

His eyes soften and he takes it gently, holds it at arm's length to avoid contaminating it with his breath. "It's outstanding."

"Really?"

"In the style of Matisse?"

"It's called 'Three Eggs.' I just spend so much time with the eggs that I wanted to do something for them."

He finds a leftover screw in a kitchen drawer and, with a proper Phillips head, screws it into the wall above the kitchen table and hangs the painting. He takes a step back, finger on his chin, and moves forward to straighten it.

"Perfect," he says.

Ruth begins to cry, and he leads her across the dividing wall into the nook, sits her in his desk chair.

"I was going to wait to show you this, but—" He runs out to the empty garage, returns soon carrying a heavy box with a hatch on top. "A record player," he says and sets it on the desk.

"SRP3.1."

"It's the model number. It's used but I tried it in the store and it works splendidly. The speaker is built in so it may not be very loud, but that's okay. Came with a record, too—"

"Which?"

"Sinatra."

"I knew it."

"Shall we then?"

One slow dance before they go to sleep. Two artists in love, she thinks, under the defective glow of "Three Eggs." She stumbles with the extra weight in her. With a firm grip on her lower back, he leads.

The baby is born in March, two weeks premature. She enters the world red with wispy black hair and a sideways kneecap. The doctors hand the baby to the surgeons and Ruth hears them say something to each other about "cutting it off" and putting it in its proper place. They tell Ruth the operation may cause chronic pain later in life, but most likely it will just result in a slight limp and hinder the child's ability to do high-intensity activities.

"I don't care," Ruth says. "She's fine?"

"Yes."

"Not—*singed*?"

"No."

They leave, and she falls back in exhaustion. Al rubs her feet and legs.

"Look what we've created," he says.

———◆———

Not long after, a nurse arrives requesting a name for the registry.

She looks wide-eyed at her husband. "*I can't believe we haven't decided on a name.*"

He leans close, whispers. She asks him to repeat. He does. She nods.

She turns to the nurse and says, "Gayle."

"With a y," he specifies.

———◆———

The child sleeps in a crib at the foot of their bed. Al takes a brief hiatus from work, during which the two of them, life-makers, curl up naked and warm and whisper to one another. If one falls asleep, the other stays up listening to their partner breathe until the baby wakes up crying.

"Who is Gayle?" she asks.

"What do you mean?"

"It's a beautiful name. I always thought it was spelled with an i."

"It's sometimes spelled with a y, but it's less common."

"She's unique then. Like us."

"She's exceptional."

"But what's it mean? *Gayle*? Doesn't it mean something—a storm, or a big wind?"

"I suppose it does," he replies, "but it's an ancient name. It means a parent's bliss."

New cotton curtains hang on the crooked though stable rod, blocking out most of the light.

chapter four
- 1979 -

Ruth leans back from the painting. A new colour will need to be mixed. Payne's grey with some kind of green to make the sorts of shadows that fall from moss-covered stones in summer. Her preferred method with landscapes is to work from back to front, alla prima. The world begins as a wash of sky. This uncanny, sky-exclusive universe is then populated with clouds, followed by the loose chins of mountains, then the nearer hills, the trees upon those hills, and at last the field, the flowers, the animals (black birds in this case), or the immediate meadows that draw and delight the eyes.

Painting alla prima means that shadows in the foreground are amongst the last things to be born.

And shadows are important. She remembers starting out with nature painting, not long after they moved to the countryside. She tried to sell some of her pieces at the Salmon Arm rummage sale, which took place in the church-yard and donated a percentage of its profits to projects undertaken by the Anglican missionaries abroad.

She didn't want to raise money for the church, though. In her late twenties, she viewed churches as mass brainwashing scams, so she set her paintings at a ridiculous price. She wanted to have her work merely looked at, not sold.

She sat behind her exorbitantly priced paintings—amateur works at that—and in her head she was fighting back against the Inquisition. It was a private half-joke. She laughed internally as she watched people observe her sunrises, nodding thoughtfully to the tune of beauty before seeing the price tag and raising their eyebrows in offence.

First, she learned that when something becomes unaffordable, it immediately becomes an object of criticism. In fact, it gives people pleasure to criticize things they can never own. She would listen closely to people who walked by, whispering things like "The perspective is a little wacky" or, less frequently but more memorably, "The shadows are distracting."

Next, she learned that when something attempts to resemble reality, it is much easier to see the flaws. Shadows *are* distracting. Ruth took this to heart and became attuned to them from then on.

At the next booth over was a man selling handmade clay pots. They were rough and had fingerprints in them, but he offered them at a two-for-one deal in the weeks leading up to Christmas or Easter and would engrave them with fluff like "Home is Where the Heart is" or "Jesus Loves."

Yet people loved those ugly pots in a way they would never love her landscapes. It's because they were useful. They could hold flowers, pencils, spatulas. Eventually, the people of Salmon Arm got used to her, the egotistical painter from Victoria, and they stopped nodding politely at her and her works. They stopped asking her about her inspirations. And she stopped attending the rummage sale.

Now she mixes a fresh green-grey and carries it to different rooms of the house to see it under various lights. No, she thinks, it's not quite right. It's already five p.m. so she hides the mixture under a wet paper towel, letting it wait until tomorrow.

———— ◆ ————

Gayle's leaving was it, the thing that cracked utopia. The pain and the memories are too much, so Ruth decides on a different method—to drown them out. She drives to Salmon Arm and visits the rummage sale for the first time in years, where she finds a man selling a used seventeen-inch colour television.

"Ruth?"

"How do you know my name?"

"I'm your neighbour—kinda. If you can call it that."

She doesn't know the neighbours. No other houses are visible from her property, and for the ten years she'd been there she's never made an effort to reach out to them.

"How do you know my name?"

"Sorry ma'am—I'd just read it in the papers when they ran that story about your husband a while back. It just stuck."

"He's in the paper again? What, is he famous?"

"He's well known in town, sure. I know you've been a private sort for all these years and I respect that. I don't mean to bother you with all this. But ever since he rode his horse through the province, he's been a kind of celebrity. That's the truth. He's a hero, I would say. So the town's been choked about what happened."

"I don't read the papers."

"I'm very sorry. You don't—know?" The man takes off his ball cap and holds it against his stomach. "Tell you what—what do you say I let you take home this machine here. It's the least I can do. She served me well for six years 'til I upgraded last winter. She's a bit finicky with the channel knob but she's got a good number of years in her yet. Name's Bill, by the way."

"Okay, Bill. But I don't know how to set it up."

———— • ————

He comes by on Saturday. She helps him unload the unit from the box of his pickup and carry it to the parlour. He takes off his cap, brushes the dust from his forehead, and looks around at the blank walls, the wooden furniture, and Ruth's unfinished painting by the window. "Nice place," he says.

"I cleaned."

He puts his hands on his spine and leans back until it cracks. "Thought I was gonna throw my back out carrying her in. They call these idiot boxes for a reason."

"A farmer like you, Bill? Working men are supposed to have strong backs."

"If the Tower of Pisa's allowed to bend, I can too. I'm not even a master-piece. My wife Liz says I'm gonna snap like a cracker if I don't retire soon—but that doesn't sound so good to me. Work keeps you young, eh?"

She offers him a coffee.

"And how are the girls?"

"How do you know I have girls?"

"Ah, sorry, ma'am—Ruth—I just knew. Must've been another something I heard around town. I'm very sorry."

"The girls are fine, as far as I can tell."

"Good."

"My eldest recently ran away to Alberta," she adds.

"Well—" Bill sits on the sofa and scratches his knee. Ruth sits across from him, saying nothing, listening to the sound of fingernails on denim. "So what are you producing here? I can hear some chickens from my place—those yours?"

"We don't have any chickens. A few cows, that's all. Three, to be exact. Soon to be two."

"What do you mean?"

"They're sick. My daughter Gayle—the one who ran away—she left me a note saying that the cows have some disease and that I have to take care of them or we'll lose them. Looks like anemia or something in the blood. Their eyes look runny."

"Well there's nothing goin' around as far as I know. My girls are just fine. Happy as pigs in mud."

"You have daughters?"

"No, I got a dozen cows. Look, Ruth, it's hard to see a woman on her own like this, worrying about her cows when you've got other things to worry about. Why don't I come by sometime this week and take a look at 'em. You can't really trust the vets around here. Seems to me that they're all after a quick penny."

———————— · ————————

The camera pans across a scene from the city of Kabul. A sea of faces, some looking at the camera in confusion or rage. An unseen commentator says something about a coup, a reaction to a coup. Then there's a statement by the Soviets. She didn't know Afghanistan was something she was supposed to be worried about, let alone something the Russians were worried about.

"We can watch cartoons tomorrow, right? It's Sunday."

"I guess so, Ami."

"That's what my friends do."

"Maybe. Off to bed now."

Ruth turns the volume to zero. She has to do it by hand because there's no remote. She wanders through channels until she finds a bearded man mouthing wordlessly before a panorama of the Grand Canyon. The way Bill talked about her husband, she expected to find him all over the news, some sort of curiosity case like when a lion and a tiger have a baby together in a zoo in Australia or little kids in Scotland get a surprise visit from Paul McCartney. But she doesn't find him, even after half an hour of wading through the swamp of important world events, so she resigns herself to watching the stranger standing before the Grand Canyon.

Thinking about nothing, absorbing nothing, merely basking.

One afternoon, she looks up the local Bills in the white pages and talks to five strangers before landing on the correct number. A woman answers the phone.

"Hello. Is this the—*Bill* residence?"

"Sorry?"

"Is this Elizabeth? Is your husband Bill?"

"Yes—"

"My name's Ruth. Your husband sold me a TV last week."

"Oh yes."

"Can I speak to him?"

The woman hesitates. "What's this about?"

"I'd like to thank him."

A few minutes later, Bill's voice comes on the line, sounding dusty and tired. "How can I help you, Ruth?"

"I just wanted to say thanks. For the TV and all."

"You're welcome, Ruth."

"And are you still willing to fix my cows?"

"Have you called a vet, Ruth?"

"You told me not to."

"Right, right. Yes, I said not to call the vet. They're no good around here."

"That's what you said."

"Well, I'll swing by tomorrow around eleven o'clock for a quick visit."

She spends the rest of the evening on a channel that plays soaps back-to-back from six p.m. to six a.m., wondering who's supposed to be watching soaps at those hours.

—————◆—————

Bill arrives at exactly eleven a.m. It's raining. He brings his wife this time and holds his jacket over her head as they approach the door. The furious knocking makes Ruth drop her paintbrush.

"What a mess," Elizabeth says when she steps in, a muddy pool forming around her feet.

"Ain't it just?" Ruth says.

"The forecast said it would be clear. Weathermen, garbagemen—two sides of the same coin if you ask me." She is a large woman. This is the first thing Ruth notices. She always notices peoples' bodies first. But she forgives herself for this, putting it down to all the time she spent examining herself in the mirror as a young woman and the fact that, as an artist, she needs to exercise her eye for shapes and angles.

"I'm just going to take a peek at the cows," Bill says and goes back outside.

Ruth invites the large woman into her home and offers a drink.

"I don't drink."

"Coffee or tea?"

"No, I don't drink."

"I also have cola for guests."

The woman accepts a cola, and they sit together in the parlour. The woman reminds Ruth of the smell of the church rummage sale.

"So my husband tells me you're living here all alone?" Elizabeth says.

"No, that's not true."

"Well, I'm sorry."

"My little girl's here with me." The house is silent. Rain runs down the windowpanes. "But she's at school right now."

"I see." The woman runs her eyes over the walls, the bare tables, the easel by the window, the television. "We don't have any children."

"It's not for everyone."

"It wasn't the Lord's will."

"Yes. Jesus wills in mysterious ways."

"God works in mysterious ways, indeed."

Ruth doesn't know how to talk to this woman. She doesn't know how to talk to people in general. She knows this and has long ago accepted it. But she feels a religious lesson coming on and wants to deflect it. She considers topics that might animate the woman. Parenthood won't work, so she considers politics, books, and painting, but settles on telling a joke.

"Knock knock."

"What?"

"It's a joke. Knock knock."

"Who's there?" the woman says, straight-mouthed.

"Jesus."

The woman sits up in her chair and takes a deep breath. "Jesus who?"

"Jesus Christ."

"I see." A few seconds later, the woman relents. "Jesus Christ who?"

"Jesus Christ, open the door. It's raining!"

Neither of them laugh. Ruth follows the woman's lead and begins scanning her own walls.

"You're an artist?

"I do landscapes."

"Where is that? Someplace around here?"

"It's from my head. A visual representation of my feelings."

"It's a very pretty picture."

They sit in silence until Bill enters the back door and wipes his boots on the rug.

"It's nothing to worry about there, Ruth."

Ruth jolts up, relieved. "Oh, good."

"It's milk fever, no doubt. You can see it in their eyes and 'cause they're trying to walk around and having a hard time of it, all a bit jittery. I seen it before. I got the instruments for it, though, and I can pick up some calcium borogluconate from a buddy in Enderby. Might take a couple goes." He looks to his wife. "We ought to get going then."

Elizabeth stands and wiggles her arms through her coat sleeves. "You know Ruth's a painter, Bill? She makes nice pictures."

Bill's eyes glimmer with an idea. "Why don't we ask her to do our portrait? You know I've always wanted to have our portraits done in front of the house— something to give my nieces to remember us by."

They turn to Ruth.

"Sure," she says. "Least I can do for your help with the cows."

Just before leaving, Elizabeth reaches into her purse and hands Ruth a King James Bible.

———◆———

Ruth uses a rag to wipe away the latest failure of a shadow, drops her brush into turpentine, begins tidying up for his arrival.

When he comes, he goes directly to the barn. She sees him pass by the window, not looking in. She follows shortly after and leans against the barn door, watching. He's gentle with the animals, puts his hand on the back of their neck and whispers to them while he uses his other hand to feel for arteries. They don't jump when the needle goes in and the contents are drained.

"Hey, Bill."

She startles him.

"Hi there, Ruth. Sorry, didn't want to bother you. Thought I'd just pop in here and get her done."

"Where's your wife?"

"I'm solo today. Nice animals you got here. You've been looking after them good."

"That's my daughter who does that—Gayle."

"Tell her she's doing fine."

"They don't like me nearly as much. I think I'll have to get rid of them soon. Do you know anyone looking for three old cows?"

"I can ask around, Ruth."

"Does your wife not like you coming here alone?"

Bill stands straight and adjusts his cap. He doesn't answer.

"It's nice to have company," she says.

Ruth goes back inside and makes a pot of coffee. By the time the percolator is done dripping, Bill's pickup is pulling out of the driveway.

———◆———

Seeing the word "wine" in print gives her a taste for it. *Let him kiss me with the kisses of his mouth; for thy love is better than wine.* She doesn't pause to question what an erotic letter is doing in the Old Testament. Maybe King James had mojo, she thinks.

She returns to the book with a glass of cheap Sauvignon blanc and fans through the pages like she's seen Gayle do many times, now understanding why—because a book like this has no starting point and no end. Reading it sequentially seems like a waste of time. She's too quickly buried in a sea of names and evocations, many of which she recognizes only from Christmas songs or art books. She'd prefer to treat the books of the Bible like a polite picnic, to get a flavour for each one but not indulge.

She picks Ecclesiastes and the Song of Solomon as her favourites because they appear to have the least to do with religion. Ecclesiastes appears downright nihilistic. There's also something intriguing about Revelation but she doesn't feel equipped to understand it. Maybe, she thinks, she could bring it up with Bill and Elizabeth. A conversation starter.

———◆———

At sunset, she lands on the Book of Ruth, which she always knew existed but has never read. Despite the story being rather boring compared to the Song of Solomon, she's amused to read about her nominal ancestor.

The Biblical Ruth lived in another universe. She was a simple, mundane, family-oriented woman devoted to her mother-in-law, even long after her husband died. And she worked in the fields, with her hands. She was poor, virtuous, and never took more than was given. It's hard to get a feeling for the Biblical Ruth, what she dreamed of or what she felt. The language of the King James Bible is too distant. Grammatically, it's rife with mistakes, and with its highfalutin, ever-condescending tone, it was surely written by a man who had no place describing the inner lives of women, anyway.

She wants to know what Ruth *looked* like, if she had good posture, if her face resembled her own at all. She goes to her husband's library and searches for a book of religious portraits.

Under ART & MISC. she finds a tall book called *Romanticism and Religion*, which is full of eighteenth and nineteenth-century oil paintings.

She fans through the glossy pages until she finds what she's looking for: the Biblical Ruth as imagined by some Italian painter named Francesco Hayez some hundred and forty years ago. She is standing in the centre of a vertical rectangular frame, before a soft brown and yellow countryside. For some reason her tunic has fallen from her shoulders, leaving her naked from the belly button up, even though her bottom half is wrapped in two separate robes. She wears a gold band around her right forearm and holds it out for examination. A bushel of wheat is tucked in her left elbow and her hair is wrapped. She gazes at something to the left of the viewer.

Ruth is drawn to the shadows, the hue of them. The loam-coloured shadows that encircle her eyes and dissolve as they approach the edge of her oval chin.

No, she thinks, her posture is not very good. She is hunched a little to her right and her head is nowhere near straight on her shoulders. In fact, she looks more like Gayle, with a bad knee and eyes always on the distance.

The image is intriguing because it's ripe with mysteries. Why is she topless? Was that the norm amongst Moabite women? It's common enough amongst the religious subjects of nineteenth-century artists. Topless Bathsheba, topless Mary Magdalene, topless Delilah, topless Eve, topless "Lot's wife." The whole gang.

On the next page is the same painting—almost identical, except that Ruth's tunic has climbed partway back up to her shoulders, covering her breasts, at least.

In the second version, the trees in the background are more distinct but the face is less defined, as though these two elements cannot fully co-exist.

———— ◆ ————

She drives to Bill and Elizabeth's farm. It's only five minutes down the road and is hidden behind a small wood. She takes a narrow lane through the trees and emerges between flat green fields where cows are grazing along with a single alpaca.

The house itself is small but immaculately kept, with a small, freshly stained porch surrounded by roses and hydrangeas just starting to bloom. Holding a collapsible easel and large sketching pad below her arm, she knocks. Bill opens it.

"Hey there Ruth. You're a little early, eh?"

"I run on a different clock."

"I see."

"You have a nice place here." She runs her hand along the railing and receives no splinters. "Puts me to shame."

A moment later, Elizabeth comes to the door wearing a pink dress. Bill is wearing orange plaid with his sleeves rolled up.

"I thought we'd dress up," Elizabeth says.

"I just thought we'd be like we are," Bill says.

"I dressed up already, Bill. Put on a nice shirt. Pink and orange just don't work together. It's true. Ask the artist."

"Sorry," Ruth interrupts, "but I'm just going to be doing some sketches of the farmhouse and the field. I need to study how the roses flutter. That's my trade. I can get your figures too, but just angles and curves and all that. I'll just plan out the portrait first and try out a couple perspectives. For now it's enough if you give me an *idea* of what you want to wear." She motions them to the bottom of the porch steps. "I'll come back another time for details."

"I see," Elizabeth says. "I thought we'd be standing still for a long time."

"Maybe an hour."

"Well Bill should put on a nice shirt anyway."

He goes inside.

Elizabeth stands with her hands together, dangling them over the pink frills that cover her stomach. It's not a good colour on her, Ruth thinks. It heightens the pinks of her face and makes her look over-heated.

"What do you think of neutral colours?" Ruth asks. She holds her thumb out and pretends to measure angles on the farmhouse façade.

"What do you mean by that?"

"Just that I work well in black, brown, white, yellow. But not bright yellow—more faded yellow, like sunflowers just before they die."

"Ah?"

"Those are my specialties. I'm not saying I'm married to those colours."

The woman's face grows pinker. "This is my favourite dress and I want to be remembered this way. But if *those* are the colours you can do, I'm sure we can accommodate you."

"Don't worry about it this time."

Bill returns wearing a black shirt and khakis and stands beside his wife at the bottom of the porch steps. "Better?"

No one answers. The couple stands an awkward distance apart, so Ruth takes Bill's hand and lays it on his Elizabeth's shoulder, then prods them until the gap between them is sealed.

She moves a dozen paces back, sets up her easel, and closes her eyes for a few seconds to focus herself and begins a charcoal sketch. As the minutes go by, Bill starts to fidget, opening and closing the hand on his wife's shoulder, and the gap between them widens again.

"What are you doing with your hand?" Elizabeth says.

"Sorry," says Bill.

"Is this not good for you?"

"I'm sweating, Liz. I got sweaty palms."

Ruth makes a few sketches to capture angles and a few to capture tones. She plays with different styles—loose, rapid strokes, or heavy deliberate lines and blocks. She works on multiple sketches at the same time and flips back and forth between them. When she's done working from that angle, she takes a few paces to the left and starts again. Then she returns to her original position and takes some paces back until she's out of speaking range.

"So," Elizabeth shouts after a while, "you've done many jobs like this?"

"Oh yes," Ruth shouts back. It's a lie. She's done landscapes and animals but never a portrait. "I have a passion for the human face!"

"Well I like the picture you had in your house. It reminded me of a postcard."

Ruth's eye is instinctively drawn to the non-human elements and she spends far more time detailing the shape and feel of the flowers, the grain of the wood, and making notes about the colours of the hydrangeas at half past four on a cloudy spring day, than she does studying Bill and Elizabeth.

She continues moving back until she is about fifteen metres away. She pauses for a few seconds, pretends to measure an angle, keeps going. She has all the sketches she needs but wants to play a private game, to see how far she can go before she makes them uncomfortable.

"Maybe it's better to—" Elizabeth says. Ruth can't make out the rest.

"It's for context," Ruth shouts back.

She sees Elizabeth's lips move, whispering something to Bill. She squints and thinks she can distinguish the words *mistake* and *God*.

Shortly after, Ruth closes her books and collapses the easel. The couple finally breaks apart, revealing a dark sweat stain on the shoulder of Elizabeth's dress where Bill's hand had been. Ruth saunters back from where she was, at least a hundred metres away.

"So," Elizabeth says when she finally arrives, "can we see them?"

"I'm afraid it's bad luck for me to show you."

"Bad luck?"

"I never show people unfinished works."

"The painting in your house?" Elizabeth furrows her brow.

"Yes. It's unfinished. It'll bring me some bad luck. Anyway—" Ruth digs in her pocket for her car keys.

"Would you like a drink of something before you go, Ruth?" Bill says.

"I'm in a rush."

"Well we have good faith in your work. And we'll pay well. I mean, we'll talk about payment next time. Don't worry about that."

———— • ————

"What are you watching, Mum?"

"I don't know, Ami. Some garbage."

"What, Mum?"

"A soap opera. You want something else?" She looks at the clock. "*Jesus, get to bed, child.*"

It doesn't take long for her to give up on soap operas. She's tried many—*One Life to Live*, *All My Children*, *The Young and the Restless*, reruns of *The Secret Storm*—but finds them worse than Revelation. Her soul is an enemy of the mundane. The lives of others, especially their bickering, doesn't interest her.

But the real issue isn't story so much as setting. The fact that some soaps can present an entire thirty to sixty-minute episode without ever leaving some rich family's domestic quarters makes her think of dirty water running down a clogged drain and, at the same time, of her own life. It's too far, it's too near.

She flips through channels as Ami patters up the stairs and puts herself to bed.

Eventually she lands on the CBC international news highlights. Better, she thinks. Destruction.

She learns that a bomb went off in Chicago. It was inside a package that was sent to a university professor but raised suspicions and was quickly handed over to campus security. It blew up when they tried to open it. No one was killed, but one victim almost lost a hand. CBC News predicts political motives and warns everyone—Americans and Canadians alike—to be aware of what they're receiving in the mail.

———— • ————

The landscape. Shadows are the only thing left to paint, and it will remain that way for now. Critical distance, she tells herself, will allow the shadows to form in my mind on their own—and later, all I need to do is pull them out.

She takes the painting upstairs, to the room above the kitchen that she uses for storage. Long ago, she and her husband had built a series of cabinets, measured and fitted with slots for holding canvas.

A storage space was something she'd wanted since she learned how to paint. It meant she could work to her heart's content and never have to worry where the paintings would end up. She wouldn't have to display them, she wouldn't have to hang them on the walls, she wouldn't have to sell them, she wouldn't have to throw them away, she wouldn't even have to think about them. She can simply keep them hidden and safe, tiny monuments to things her soul has seen.

She finds an empty slot and inserts her shadowless landscape between two other uncompleted landscapes from years gone by.

From another cabinet, she removes a blank twenty by thirty-four-inch canvas, which she had stretched and primed by hand a few months ago. She looks at the whiteness and smiles. This one has a destiny. Her first portrait. An heirloom for Bill's niece. Someone will treasure this someday. It will outlive her. What responsibility.

———— ◆ ————

At seven p.m., she drains a glass of wine and examines her sketches of Bill and Elizabeth from the other day. They're not terrible, she thinks. But what now?

She's never painted a portrait. Not only did she not want to, it's never come up. She's never been asked. Painting her husband or daughters never crossed her mind. He, for one, never expressed the slightest interest in having a portrait that their daughters could remember him by. Impressions are made in the heart, he would say—or something along those lines.

We are a non-sentimental family, she thinks to herself.

Thus, faces are a new country.

Ami comes from the kitchen and sees her mother hunched over the parlour table with her head in her hands.

"Are you having a bad dream, Mum?"

"I'm not asleep, Ami."

"Okay."

Ruth pushes her sketches aside. She immediately feels lonely without them, reaches back and inches them toward her with the tips of her fingers.

"What do you need, Ami?"

"We should watch TV, Mum. I have the medicine."

"What's that?"

"I have the medicine."

"I heard you. It's just—that's a pretty grown-up phrase."

"Miss Barker says it in class."

"Ah."

Ami turns on the TV and finds a channel playing cartoons—her medicine. Ruth joins her and they sit on opposite sides of the couch.

"What's this?" Ruth says. "I thought cartoons were only on Sunday morning."

"No, Mum. They're all the time."

"What are we watching now?"

"Coyote and Road Runner."

"What's it about?"

"The coyote wants to get the road runner."

"What happens when he does?"

"He doesn't."

"Fine with me."

———•———

"What loses me are the words—Ephesus, Smyrna—hmm—Philadelphia. I don't know a lick about any of those places. Who wrote that book anyway?"

"Revelation?" Bill asks. "That was Peter, who knew the Christ personally."

It's four in the afternoon, cloudy as before, and the couple poses at the bottom of the porch steps. This time Ruth is closer, studying the details of the faces, the highlights in the hair. Not needing to look at their posture this time, Ruth suggested that they all sit and pulled up a decorative garden stool for herself.

"Bill," Elizabeth says. "Peter did *not* write Revelation. It was John. Apostle John. The same John who wrote *John*, I mean, the Gospel according to *John*."

"You're right, Liz. Absolutely. I was thinking of something different. I get confused listening to the priest's little history lessons, to be frank. Lots of Johns in the Bible."

"The John who wrote Revelation was one of the disciples. With Mark and Matthew and Luke. Luke was a painter, too—the patron saint of the arts. Did you know that, Ruth?"

"Sure I did," Ruth says. "Saint Luke the painter. I knew another Luke. He taught me lines and typeface when I was in design school. I had a big crush on Doctor Luke, but he was married."

No one responds.

Chatting makes Ruth feel like a barber. It's an annoying habit of barbers, in her opinion, to pull banal information from the heads they are handling. She's never enjoyed small talk, and for this reason has grown her hair long. Not wanting to feel mundane, she does her best to steer the conversation away from the weather, current events, or the town of Salmon Arm where nothing ever happens.

"You hear about that new construction project they're gonna be doing on the 97?" Bill says. "It's supposed to take three years. They'll be ripping up the road in sections—supposed to be part of the new plan to get more tourists coming up from Kelowna and thereabouts."

"I haven't heard," Ruth says. "I never leave Salmon Arm, and my car can't break fifty."

"A waste of money, in my opinion. Tourists are coming up one way or another, and if it'll take all summer, I'd say the industry'll take a hit. Everyone'll be backed up for miles. It just means that in fall, when all the tourists go home, it's the locals who—"

"Sorry Bill, but I need you to close your mouth—"

Elizabeth laughs.

"I'm trying to get your chin," Ruth says. "That's all. I didn't mean anything by that." She leans forward. The chin juts out slightly and is covered in microscopic white hairs even though the hair on the head is grey and brown, like ash scattered in dirt. The jaw is square. Wrinkles stream outward from his eyes and seem ready to pour off the side of the face. It's the sign of a man who has spent his life squinting against the sun.

Looking closely at the human face produces an unusual feeling in her. As she shapes the jawbone or wrestles with the complexity of cracked lips, she feels those parts of her own face come alive. Intuitively, she frowns as the subject frowns, twitches as the subject twitches. She is, she thinks, drawing herself. She must focus on her own face and Bill's face simultaneously.

It's a method that works, so she doesn't question it. She ignores the rule of thirds, the rule of eights, the rules of sixteenths, the rule of ten thousandths, the fact that edges of the lips ought to line up with the edges of the eyes. Bill's face emerges naturally, like clouds have emerged naturally in her many skies.

When she achieves a likeness, she moves on to Elizabeth. This face is more difficult. It lacks the rugged, mountainous charm. It's a face, she thinks, that's spent its life rebelling against its own decay. The skin sags in places (unlike her own, which has only shrivelled), and the resulting crevices seemed held up by invisible tacks, an illusion caused by the muscles in the cheekbones flexing. The bottom lip is pursed. It's not a beautiful face, she thinks. She pushes away the impulse to disregard it for this reason but still, she finds it impossible to empathize with this face or feel its curves in her own.

She sketches furiously, exaggerates the sags, the double chin, the big eyes, the makeup applied more heavily to the left cheek than the right. She makes things up.

"Okay," she says. "I'm exhausted. It's hard on the brain, this stuff." She closes her book as she stands, places the decorative stool back on the edge of the garden.

"Thanks for your work, Ruth," Bill says. "We're excited to see your magic."

"I wouldn't say magic—maybe witchcraft."

"I would ask to see what you came up with," Elizabeth says. "But I know it brings you bad luck."

"We're excited," Bill repeats.

Elizabeth brushes dust and splinters off her dress—a pale yellow dress, like sunflowers just before they die.

———— ✦ ————

A CBC foreign correspondent to the United States announces that another bomb was sent by mail in Chicago. American officials are calling it an act of domestic terrorism. Someone they interview on campus (a student, probably) brings up Shirley Jackson's short story "The Lottery," in which a small American town randomly selects one resident to be stoned to death each summer to purge the community of bad behaviour and bring about a good harvest. The student shrugs, as though this odd reference says all there is to be said about the bombing.

The CBC foreign correspondent reassures the camera that this is *not* a random act of violence. "What we are witnessing is something planned and directed. Yet the motivation remains unclear."

The targets appear to be educational institutions, and judging by the sophistication of the explosive devices, the perpetrator is assumed to be a disgruntled student—"Probably a loner"—or a former university professor, presumably with a mechanical or engineering background. Universities across the country are amplifying security measures and asking anyone with information to contact police immediately.

"What's this, Mum?"

"Nothing, Ami. You're not going to understand."

"Can we—"

"Cartoons? Sure."

Ruth enjoys *Looney Tunes*. In *Looney Tunes*, no one dies. There are no foreign correspondents. There are no daughters. There are no faces. There are no opinions. There is no milk fever. There is no attempt to achieve reality, so there is no room for criticism or complaint. Everything exists in a universe where humans and animals are elastic. They can take a bullet directly to the forehead and the worst thing to happen is an elongated neck.

With a pen and a scrap of paper, using her lap as a surface, she doodles the Road Runner with his head stretched high, preparing for a run. She includes a speech bubble: *Meep-meep*. Why, she wonders, did I not study animation in school instead of graphic design and drawing? That's clearly the way the world is going. People don't want art. They want something else. Maybe then I'd be rich, she thinks. Self-reliant, carefree.

They watch cartoons until Ruth closes her eyes. When the comically long fuse on the Coyote's ACME dynamite runs out, Ruth is startled awake. Ami is gone.

———◆———

She struggles against the language of the King James Bible, but little by little she gets the idea.

The other Ruth is a widow from the country of Moab. Her husband was a foreigner from Bethlehem in Judea and, when he dies, all Ruth has left is her mother-in-law, another foreigner named Naomi. She is without friends or family of her own kin.

Naomi wants to return to Bethlehem and Ruth, having no livelihood or security in Moab, goes with her. When they arrive, Naomi sends Ruth to labour under another relative, a corn and barley farmer named Boaz. Boaz is wealthy and much older than Ruth.

Patriarchal Moabite custom dictates that, via her mother-in-law, Ruth also remains kin of Boaz for all time, although they are of different countries, and it seems that Ruth views herself as an alien, an outcast, and an outsider in Judea. Perhaps to distract herself from grief and loneliness, Ruth gleans corn night and day with hardly a moment's rest.

Boaz quickly takes notice of his productive, young, pretty, fertile labourer. He gives her preferential treatment and invites her to his home for dinner.

Naomi, sensing that her family line can be maintained by a marriage of Ruth and Boaz, tells Ruth to seduce him. After a gruelling day in the fields, he likes to sleep at the foot of a large mound of corn on the threshing floor and doze in the flakey sheaves until morning. Naomi tells Ruth to find him there, curl up at his feet and, when he rises, ask him to marry her.

Ruth lies at his feet and immediately wakes him up. The Bible isn't explicit, but they most likely have sex, and they rest together until morning, smelling of sweat and semen and corn.

———— • ————

She phones the Bill residence.

"What can I do for you, Ruth?"

"I don't really know—"

"Ruth—are you—I mean—I'm not really so good at dealing with these things."

"It's fine—"

"Are you crying?"

"No."

She can hear him walking, sitting, standing.

"Bill—you spend your whole life learning how the world works. You try and you try to learn because that's what life is all about. You try to make sense of something that makes no sense. You do everything you can to find a little island you can call your own, which is graceful and rich. Everything will be perfect, right? If we all had our own little island and there was nothing on it to fuck us up? But it's not like that, 'cause the world keeps breaking and taking everything away from you. There's no one there to look after you and nobody to lean on. Your husband goes away. Your kids go away. Everyone goes away and the world doesn't give a damn about you at all. Have you seen the news? Any day now there's going to be a bomb in the mail. That's what the world thinks of you."

"I'm coming over."

"Please don't."

There is more shifting, standing, sitting. She hears a door open and close.

"I'm lonely, Bill. I know this feeling. It's not good. But I'll be fine. I just need—I don't know—a confidant."

Bill takes a long time to respond.

"How's the painting coming along, Ruth?"

"The portrait?"

"Yes."

"Great. Listen—I gotta go. I gotta—go."

———◆———

Francesco Hayez put great care into Ruth's face.

It's roughly fifteen degrees off kilter from the Y-axis, yet stems flowingly from the neck, the body. The eyes are level, painted wide and looking even wider against the pinched Italianesque nose. The sun is orange and oppressive, but Ruth is protected by the shadow of her head-wrap. She doesn't squint, though the light in the fields must be fierce. Her bare chest, once virgin and white, is growing auburn like candlelight filtered through paper. A nineteenth-century lady in Judea, her chest will burn—but for now her face is flawless.

The eyes divulge the interior, an amalgam of emotions, perceptions, memories, and sensations, which swirl around with the physical world in an infinitely complex net of causation and succession. There is no gravitational centre.

The eyes of Hayez's Ruth, supernaturally calm, locked on an object behind the viewer, speak of a consciousness that is Singular. Her innumerable sensations—heat, stress, loneliness amid the alien corn—are all tied to that singularity, an anchor that allows the ancient Ruth to stay perfectly still despite it all, despite her countless years, her journeys through history, the accumulating chaos of her universe.

One thing. Being Singular, can it be characterized by a single word?

If time is an illusion, the thing could be anything from any time.

The game is to decide what that word is.

————◆————

Is that you, Boaz?

Who are you, Boaz?

What are you?

————◆————

She calls Bill and asks for the Salmon Arm newspapers that contain clips about her missing husband.

"Gee, Ruth—maybe they're around. We got a closet full of old papers. We keep 'em in there for fire starter in the wintertime."

"It's important for me to get that story."

Later that day, Bill drops off the paper but immediately makes up an excuse about being late for dinner.

"It's only half past three," she says. "You're not *that* old."

"Gee, Ruth."

"If it's about your wife getting jealous, you don't need to worry. We're all grown-ups. And your wife? Jealous of me? I'm a little old lady with a messy spine."

"It's not that, Ruth."

"Do you want to see my spine? It'll put your mind at ease. I'll show you—there's nothing to worry about." She clutches the bottom of her shirt and lifts it a few inches, exposing her hips.

"Oh boy, that's not necessary, Ruth. I believe you. I do." He blushes uncontrollably as he digs around in his pockets for his keys.

"Sorry—that was a bad joke. I'm lonely. Lonely people do inappropriate things. Don't tell your wife."

"I'm gonna let you get on with your day, Ruth."

"I've been thinking about your portrait night and day. You're a handsome couple, really. Bill—"

Bill nods, turns to leave.

"Thanks for looking out for me," she says.

chapter five
- 1962 -

Silver tinsel taped to the wall catches the chandelier light of the gala hall. Ruth has never liked Christmas—the pious kitsch and the kitschy piety—but it's too easy to complain about it. All through the party, she's been daydreaming about the creative ways she can ruin the event without being caught. Setting off a fire alarm, starting a painful rumour, tipping the tree into the buffet.

"Peace is just—a state of mind?" she asks the man she happens to be in conversation with.

"You could say so," the man replies. He speaks with a voice she thinks of as "brown." Low, some grit, an autumnal sway to it that complements his abundant beard. "Because in my view," he continues, "there are inner and outer phenomena, but the wall between them is an illusion. When you find inner peace, you can see outer peace, as they're really the same, even if we're raised to believe they're not."

"Phenomena?"

He scratches his beard. "It's a pretentious way of saying *things*—The Buddhists call them *dharmas* with a small d. So memories, dreams, emotions—they're things. Chairs, Christmas trees, human beings—also things. The illusion is that these two *kinds* of things are somehow different, as though they exist in different universes. That's the European thing to do, to insist everything has an opposite. But it's true that the inner world and the outer world interact with each other all the time. Like billiard balls." He holds up two fists, preparing to strike. "So imagine—"

Just then her husband returns from the bar, where he'd been discussing James Joyce with female graduate students. A glass of icewine occupies his left hand. He runs his right arm around Ruth's waist. "Merry Christmas, Phil," he says. "I see you've met my wife."

"Sorry," Phil says to Ruth with a grin. "I thought you were a student. Excuse me for the lecture there."

"What are we talking about?" Al says.

"The East," Phil replies. "As always."

They begin discussing Keats, the mind, other things only they understand. Phil congratulates him for landing the tenured professorship in Edmonton. Meanwhile Ruth turns aside, loses interest, looks around the room, the decorations, the all-professor band finishing their rendition of "Blue Christmas." Feedback from the microphone causes her to jump. Her husband notices and tightens his arm around her waist.

"Why don't you audit some of Doctor Parker's classes, Ruth, if you're interested in these things?"

"I'm not smart enough," she says. "I didn't understand a word of what you were just talking about."

"I could pull some strings," Al says, "and get you in there for cheap. You always say you're getting Stockholm Syndrome at home—"

"But Gayle?"

"We'll hire a sitter. We can cover it. We've earned it."

"It's an introductory class," Phil says. "Just for people who want to see the world anew. Nothing heavy."

———◆———

The university is easy to get to by bus. Since they destroyed the car, it's been the only way to get around. Ruth and her husband commute together Tuesdays and Thursdays, on which Phil teaches "Introduction to Eastern Thought and the Theory of Consciousness."

The shadow people they are in bed hide when they enter public. Al reads the newspaper on the bus, stories on recent Soviet advances in Central Asia and failed negotiations between East and West Germany, but he doesn't burden her with it. When she asks, he replies, this time and every time, "Russians being Russians."

He helps her find the building, hands her a bus schedule and says he'll be home late. He needs the evening for research.

"I thought you got the new job already. So why are you still—"

"It's a never-ending process. Bureaucracy. Fish eat fish. Don't wait up for me tonight, love." He kisses her lips, lingering moistly before marching away through columns of chattering students.

The classroom is in a basement, painted white and carpeted grey, fluorescent-lit and filled with a dozen long tables. She waits by the door in order to be the last one in. She sits alone at the back, a row between her and the nearest classmate.

Before class begins, Doctor Parker tells a joke. It involves a dying polygamist and his six wives of various ages, each one a little less beautiful than the last. The wives approach his deathbed one by one, and to each he asks the question, "If you truly love me, will you accompany me into death?" And each wife in turn replies, "I do love you, and I'll wait here until the last moment, but I refuse to accompany you into death." He throws them all out of the room, all except the last one, who replies, "Yes, I will accompany you into death" and crawls under the sheets with him. The wives represent money, fame, health, beauty itself. All except the last, the eldest and least beautiful, who represents karma.

Ruth watches the other students—looks of confusion, some of disgust at the mention of polygamy or the idea of crawling into bed with a dying man, and some of genuine interest.

"It's a joke told in Buddhist circles around here," the doctor explains to the class. "But like many things concerning death, it's not the kind of joke you laugh at. Though you can. It's a half-joke, if you will."

Face obscured behind his beard, eyes behind thick rims, always speaking as though nervous. She decides she likes Phil because he's shy, like her—and a comedic failure. No one ever laughs at my jokes either, she thinks.

———◆———

"And so, it's believed that meditation is essential to a good life like food is essential to a good body," Phil concludes a Tuesday lecture. "It's about the cultivation of a mind which, we recall, is hardly one iota under our control."

Ruth approaches him when the class vacates.

"How's it coming along, Ruth? How's Al?"

"He's busy a lot. Fish eat fish—I need your help."

"I have another class in"—he looks at his wrist—"half an hour. I can field a few eager inquiries."

"I want to know how to meditate," she says. "Because I always thought it was something people did on Salt Spring Island, or—India."

"I grew up on Salt Spring Island."

"I could tell. Because the beard."

He laughs. She smiles for having made him laugh. "The majority of students' interest only goes as far as the content of the exam," he says.

"I'm not really a student of anything. A lot of this stuff is beyond me. I could be a student, though, I guess, of this."

"Of course you're a student. Everyone is a student on their path. I too am a student."

"Doctor," she says. The word is uncooperative in her mouth. She isn't accustomed to doctors in anything but white. "Is this a religion? Are you religious? 'Cause I'm not. I was raised an atheist, and Al's religious but only in his own way, he says. But atheism's what I know and I'm happy with it."

"I will never speak a word on God's plan, on destiny, on heaven, or the end of time. *Nothing* is prescribed." He asks her to sit at the nearest available desk and pulls a chair across from her. Seeing him up close, she retracts her earlier impression that he is shy. He speaks fluidly, grammatically, as though reading from an invisible book. "Life is not about *concepts, theories.* The Buddha put it this way: Imagine I am pointing at the moon, which is truth. When I say 'Look,' I'm asking you to consider the moon, not the finger. The concept is the finger."

"I don't really get it."

"No one can say what the moon is but you. You just need to look at it."

"How?"

She walks beside him, through the hall, up the stairs. "On Salt Spring, we like the word 'cosmos.' It was a hit in the fifties. We talk about meditation as opening the spigot in our heads, letting it all flow into the cosmos—It's not pushing, it's letting. If that's meditation, then meditation can be anything. Just remember that, aside from the part of you that says 'open the spigot,' you don't have much control. We can learn to accept that."

———— • ————

A Thursday morning. Many dead moths are trapped in the plastic casing around the fluorescent tubes, filtering the dull classroom light like a canopy of leaves filters whitewashed skylight. Ruth fantasizes about this lecture taking place in a primeval forest. She's the first disciple of a new school of living.

Doctor Parker explains: "In Hinduism, as in Christianity, Judaism, Islam, there is a *kind* of soul—Atman. It means immutable stability. The Buddhists reply, 'There is no such thing.' This is a key difference. But is it really a difference? What we want to do is investigate how one lives their life in accordance to how they understand their soul, or lack thereof. So over the weekend, I'd like you to draft a provisional definition of 'soul'—make it as boring or as zany as you'd like, deny it all together if that suits your fancy. But keep this in mind: if you say 'There is no such thing,' then be prepared to explain how you could be the same person next class as you are now."

She walks with him after the lecture. They ascend the stairs and exit the building into the quad. Students hurry from class to class, but for once she is not alarmed by the motion, the brushing of shoulders. Doctor Parker emits a force field of calm.

"I'm not going to do the assignment," she says. "The soul and all."

"You don't have to. It's just an exercise."

"But I'd like to know the answer."

"The answer?"

"What is the definition of soul?"

"I can only tell you my answer, not yours."

He invites her to sit with him on a bench before a crowd of seagulls and removes a fist-sized ball of aluminum foil, peels it open to reveal a dozen pieces of bread rolled into perfect spheres. Ruth waits for six birds to be fed before he answers.

"A library of everything you've done for millions of years."

———— • ————

Instead of taking the bus home that day, she finds a pay phone, calls her house and asks the babysitter to work a few extra hours. Then she walks. The waterfront is not far from the university. She follows it south past mansions, hotels, yacht clubs. She opens the spigot. Delicious nothing.

At a major road—she doesn't know which—she turns right. She walks until well into the afternoon and arrives in downtown Victoria. As soon as she enters the grey, the inescapable traffic, it begins to rain. She finds herself halted at the intersection of Yates and Blanshard, side-by-side with strangers in overcoats.

A man offers her space under his umbrella. "Are you going far?"

She shakes her head no. The water reaches her skin, the blouse clings by the time pedestrians can safely cross Blanshard, but she stays in place. Soon another stranger asks her for a fire and looks her up and down. Ill intent. She shakes her head.

"A lighter?"

"Beat it."

The lights change again, but she doesn't cross.

She stays where she is, in the eye of the storm, for ten changes of the lights. It's the sound of thunder to the east, over the Strait of Georgia, that breaks the sensation of being immaterial.

Behind her is an office building with large windows. In the rain, the dimness, the reflection is clear. She sees her posture, a dramatic hang to her shoulders, crested spine. She approaches it. Horrid, she thinks. Behind the glass is the corner office where a suited man sits before a typewriter. The scene filters through her doppelganger, who has hair pasted in a thick line above her eyes giving the impression of a unibrow.

The office worker has a potted lily in the corner, wilting. On the desk, to his left, is a decorative sandbox with a miniature rake in it. He takes the rake and runs a few lines, leaving thin creases through the sunless, lightless, lifeless sand. As he rakes with his left hand, he continues typing with his right. The title of the document, she sees, has the word *Annum* in it.

Ruth feels anger at the pathetic and commonplace act the man is committing. She tries to seize this sudden emotion, understand what it is. Anger, she decides, is wet and cold. This conclusion comes as the man turns up from his task, throws up his hands, and mouths the word "*What?*"

Startled, she runs. She moves alongside the traffic until she recognizes a familiar number on a passing bus. She waves it down and rides it to the suburbs. Head dead on the window and hair stuck to the glass, she sees the world as a decorative sandbox, a graveyard.

———◆———

It's six p.m. when she arrives home. She lingers on the lawn, beneath the umbrella where her husband writes poetry. The lights are on and she sees, through a crack in the curtains, a figure pacing and holding her baby. She sits for a few minutes in a wet lawn chair, inhaling the rainy air.

The babysitter lets her in as she fumbles with her key.

"How come you locked the door?"

"It's late," the babysitter replies. Gayle sniffles in her arms.

Ruth hangs her wet coat by the door and excuses herself to change. When she returns, the babysitter is sitting at the kitchen table and Gayle is in her high chair.

"I'm sorry," Ruth says. "I walked home. I got lost in the rain."

"I been waiting for hours—I was gonna call the police." The babysitter's face is red. She's been crying.

Ruth removes some bills from her wallet—she doesn't count—and hands them over. "Maybe a bit more than the rate, but you deserve it."

"Are you okay? You were all wet."

"I like the rain."

"I was scared."

Ruth embraces the girl lightly, pats her on the back, lets go. "Do you want to stay for dinner?"

"I had some cereal."

"Oh, good—but I'm making eggs."

"I gotta go home. My mum's gonna pick me up."

Ruth gives the babysitter a glass of cola while they wait. She takes one long sip and sets it aside.

"Is your back okay?"

"What?" Ruth says.

"It looks like maybe it's hurting you—like this—" She cranes her back, emulating Ruth.

"My posture went to hell when I was pregnant. I'm trying to fix it."

"My mum has that. She goes to the doctor for it. A chiropractor."

"I'm only a few years older than you, you know."

They talk about school as they wait. When the girl leaves, Ruth hugs her again. "I promise that's the last time I leave you like that. The baby loves you. With me, she's always fussing."

As soon as the girl leaves, Gayle begins to cry. The crying continues well into the evening, despite how often Ruth says, "Shush up, Gayle" and bangs on the table.

———◆———

That night Al comes home at nine. He leaps up the stairs, lifts Gayle from her high chair and spins with her. "Hello! Hello! *Heeellloo*!" He turns. "And how are you, Ruth?"

"Dandy."

He puts Gayle back in her chair and sets a record on: Perry Como.

Ruth cracks eggs as Al chops green onions to the lazy rhythm of "Caterina."

"Ecstasy," he croons, "*sy-sy-sy-sy!*"

———◆———

She tells the chiropractor she strongly prefers not to be touched. He scoffs but relents and takes an x-ray under what he describes as "exceptional circum-stances." He diagnoses her with scoliosis.

"There are certain pills," he explains, "combined with certain stretches, that can release the tension in your body, especially your lower back."

"But the spine—"

"It is what it is. A curve, like an S—see." He poises his cigarette on the lip of an ashtray and picks up the x-ray. He sails his pinkie along the facsimile of her crooked spine and neck. "But it shouldn't cause any problems. It's just the muscle tension that's making it worse."

"How did it get there?" she asks.

"Not important. It is what it is, as I said. The solution is going to be the same and what matters is how to fix it. That's why you came in, no?"

She takes a prescription and a small pamphlet of instructional cartoons. The naked figures in the panels are faceless and accompanied by red arrows indicating which way they are to move.

"Do you have anything else?" he asks.

"Mhmm—"

"Go on?"

She pauses for a moment, gazes into the x-ray and murmurs, "Sometimes

I feel like I'm stuck in a well—or a washing machine—swirling around—everything muddled and trapped here with me. When I'm in loud places—I forget where I am. Is it a circulation problem? Are there pills for that? Or is it normal?"

"Hmm." He picks up his cigarette and resumes where he left off. He clears his throat and adopts a sudden change of tone, higher-pitch and patronizing. "Nothing I can do. You need to go to another doctor." He taps his cigarette hand on his temple, careful to keep the glow away from his hair. "Chiropractors deal with bones, you understand?"

———◆———

She returns the next day to file an anonymous complaint.

———◆———

She digs her thumb into the muscles around her hips and above her buttocks. The tension is obvious. Bunches of muscles, tangled ropes. It and the scoliosis, which she insists to herself is curable, distracts her from her meditation. She sits with her back to the wall to force it straight and can feel punching against her ribs. Caught between her heart and the wall, she surrenders, calls the babysitter, takes a trip to the store to buy mirrors.

Later she sets them up around the house. Four in the kitchen, two on either side of "Three Eggs," a body-length one in the bedroom. Another body-length and body-width one in the bathroom, opposite the mirror that was already there. If she stands directly between them, she can see herself ad infinitum.

She follows the instructional cartoon figures—pushing her shoulders back as far as they'll go and letting them fall, relax. It's the ideal form. She holds her arms straight ahead and, back straight, she bends at the knees until she feels heat in her calves and lower back. She repeats this for at least forty-five minutes each day, or until Gayle cries. Posture meditation.

———◆———

Al appears by the bathroom door one day, watching her watch herself. She sees him in the mirror first—shorts, shirt untucked, loose tie.

"You feeling—good?" he asks.

"What are you doing here?"

"It's Saturday."

"Yeah?"

"I like what you've done. It looks like a funhouse with all the mirrors in here."

"It's super *fun*." She resumes her squat, head turned, scrutinizing the projection of her neck.

He steps into the bathroom with her and begins mirroring her actions. The space is constricted. Just enough room for two adults to perform synchronized squats. Ten repetitions and he is out of breath.

"You shouldn't bend your back," she says, "and your knees gotta be here, straight down from your shoulders. Look—look." She adjusts his shoulder, removes his tie, and he tries again. "You're just a little stiff. It's common with men who sit all the time. That's what the cartoon says. Here, now this—"

She lies down on the floor and brings her knees to her chest, holds the stretch for ten seconds and eases flat.

He does the same. Three repetitions until there's a sharp tear.

"What was that?" she says.

"I tore my shorts."

She expects the mimic game to be over, but it isn't. They lie head to toe, the linoleum cold and lending static to their clothes. Black socks by her left ear. The baby silent in the adjoining room, asleep. The sound of light rain against the roof and the bathroom window. She loses track of how long they stay there.

"What are you doing?" she says.

"Just waiting."

"For what?"

"For you to stand up. I've got a hole in my shorts."

She squeezes his toes. "May as well make it last. How many days we got?"

"Oh, Ruth."

"A couple months?"

"And then I'll be home before you know it—Thanksgiving. When's that again?"

"I can never remember. September or October, maybe."

A Tuesday in June, her husband shelters her with a newspaper as they board a bus. The familiar sedated hum. The bald driver calls her "missy." Noble young men offer to vacate their seats for her until they see her husband. She appreciates the smell of drizzle through the single open window. The leaves on the boulevards. Her husband saying "Russians being Russians." Consciousness, a mirror, the surface of a pool, reflects all things but remains itself unchanging.

People in adjacent rows open vents to their personal lives, talk about their anxieties, relationships, whether Victorians ought to support the Canucks, opinions of the Viet Cong or whether Paul McCartney or George Harrison is the cuter Beatle. John Lennon is excluded, though redeemed as the "sassy one." She doesn't know The Beatles or the wars and doesn't want to. She thinks about "Three Eggs," her planned sequel ("Three Potatoes" or "Four Eggs"), about Phil, about empty houses and fear. She tries to think about nothing at all—but she can't. The mind is not within her control any more than the crossfire of idle chatter, louder and louder, creating a swirl, screaming rings around a planet, clothes in a laundromat.

"Ruth?"

"Hmm?"

"You were shaking. *Are you okay?*"

"Oh yes."

————◆————

She had lost interest in class as soon as Phil moved into specifics. She doesn't care to read the sutras, memorize words in Sanskrit or Pali, or listen to dates, the sequence of Dalai Lamas, or any numbers whatsoever. The term is nearly over. Attendance dwindles. The last day of class, there are only five.

Afterwards she offers to walk him to his office.

"We'll take the elevator," he says.

As they wait for it to descend, she asks, "Doctor, what do I do about *noise*?"

"Noise?"

"I can't get away from it. I went to the—real doctor. I told him I feel trapped in the world. Do you get it?"

"It means you're an exceptionally brave woman for coming here."

"I guess."

"And what did the good doctor say?"

"He wasn't good. He was rude, old. And a chiropractor. I filed a complaint."

He nods thoughtfully as though she'd said something insightful. "Have you been meditating?"

"Yes, on my posture."

"I see."

They enter the box. It ascends slowly. Inside, the ghostly smell of smoke, baby-blue ceiling, artificial wood panelling.

"Meditation is especially valuable to our society," Phil explains. "One might say it is more beneficial to us than to any societies hitherto because we have such noise. It's never quiet now, is it?"

"Our society is noisy."

"*Such* noise," he repeats.

"It's calm in here though," she says. "Maybe I should spend more time in elevators."

They stop between the first and second floors. Ruth touches the wood panelling, textureless and cool.

"I've never experienced this," Phil says. "The elevator appears to have stopped."

"Seems." She presses all the buttons. "I thought it was new."

"It's new—but technology is like the news itself. It doesn't survive the moment it was new."

He presses the buttons again, knocks on the metal door, stomps.

Ruth leans against the wall. They stay that way in silence, her leaning, him straight, feeble but with perfect posture, hands folded in front of him, holding his briefcase. Eventually he looks at his watch.

"I guess we wait," he says. "The building's empty. It's the last day of classes and everyone was eager to enjoy the nice weather."

After some time, they sit on the floor in opposite corners. In close quarters, she's uncomfortable looking him in the eye. But there's nothing else. The panelling, the ceiling, the numbers. He removes his glasses and his eyes shrink. A stranger now.

She closes her own eyes.

A pang inside her. She opens her eyes and finds him staring at his foot.

"How long did I have my eyes closed?" she asks.

"Perhaps thirty-five minutes. How do you feel?"

"Scared."

"What is that emotion, Ruth? *How* does that feel?"

"Lemons. Pressure."

"But let's look at the situation clearly. We are at a university. It's only a matter of time."

"You don't understand, doctor. I need to—" She crosses her legs, puts her hand on her crotch. "I'm so sorry."

"There's no reason to feel embarrassed."

"Been drinking a lot of water. For the muscles. Didn't think there'd be an emergency like this again. Thought one was enough." She rolls over, back to him. "Did Al ever tell you what happened to us? How we almost died, or did? I'm never sure 'cause no one can tell me."

"I read it in the paper," he says, tilting his head back. "They called it a miracle. A one in a billion."

"Do you think it was a miracle?"

"What do you think, Ruth?"

"I don't know. What's one in a billion mean? Everything that happens is one in a billion or more, isn't it? Sitting in this elevator is one in a billion. Just being born in one in a billion, so what's so miraculous about that?"

She closes her eyes again, smells his woodsy, masculine odour. She pretends she's speaking to a ghost. There are no bladders.

"There was a miracle that the papers didn't talk about," she says.

"What do you mean, Ruth?"

"Before the accident, we were hit by lightning. We'd just made love by a cliff, in the car—I mean, then there was a storm, we were outside. He got hit. I saw him flying. I saw him over the edge, and then—the miracle—he was put down again."

"We're not accustomed here, in the West, to miraculous events. In other parts of the world, or in past times, they happen without question. But we deny them."

"Al says we're exceptional, that we're like nothing else. Maybe the cosmos doesn't want us to die."

"I see."

"But it's happy to play with us."

She says nothing for some time, but her urgency grows. Phil pinches his shirt and airs it out, throwing the odour against the elevator walls, the ceiling. The smell plummets down on them again. She breathes only through her mouth in spurts.

"He's goin'—Al is—to Edmonton at the end of the month."

"And you're going with him?"

"No."

"What made you come to that decision?"

"I'm scared."

He says nothing.

"To leave the island," she adds. "I've never been away. And I don't know what's there. I don't even want to leave my house let alone go to some other city."

"Is it the same kind of fear as this, here in the elevator?"

She doesn't respond. She's a tight ball. She turns her mind to other things and forces her eyes shut. There is no time. She forces the current of her thoughts onto something, anything, and holds it there with deliberate violence until consciousness ejects.

———◆———

The hydraulic technician forces open the door with a crowbar. He takes Phil's hand and helps him over the gap.

Ruth is on the ground. The air is sour with urine.

"Lord," the technician says. "Is she—"

"She's okay," Phil says, trembling.

The technician bends over and puts a hand on her shoulder. She jolts up, touches her thighs and begins to cry. She too is helped over the gap, and the building custodian is called to bring spare clothes from the lost and found. She takes them without acknowledging anyone and changes in the bathroom. All men's clothes. She needs a belt to hold the trousers up.

Upon exiting, she avoids Phil and the technician and goes silently down the stairwell.

——————◦——————

It's six p.m. when she gets home. The babysitter lets her in once again as she fumbles with her key.

"I'm sorry."

"It's okay, Ruth. I wasn't worried like the first time. Baby's soft asleep in the crib."

Ruth starts down the hallway, toward the bedroom.

"Hey Ruth, are you cryin'?"

"Yeah—"

The girl runs to her and throws her arms around the shoulders of the borrowed sweater. "You don't haveta do that, Ruth. What's wrong?"

Ruth explains what happened—the elevator, the discomfort, fainting and wetting herself, the paralyzing embarrassment. Story finished, she asks if the girl can stay for dinner, blurting the question as an imperative: "You'll stay for dinner."

"Sure I can, 'cause school's done 'til the fall."

Ruth leaves to take a shower. She returns with her hair wrapped in a towel, shoulders back, smiling when she sees the girl hasn't left her. "I got Campbell's soup in the bottom right cupboard below the toaster. On a poster in the grocery, they said you can put two of 'em together and make a new flavour. The beef noodle and vegetable together make gumbo."

"I like everything," the girl says.

Ruth mixes the flavours and heats them on the fob. She serves the Campbell's gumbo with crackers and, while they eat, she asks the girl about school, her future, anything.

"You'd be a good sis," the girl says after a while. "You're a good listener."

"You don't need to cheer me up."

——————◦——————

Al enters as the girl leaves. He shakes her hand and produces a dazzling smile.

"You're here awfully late, Jean?"

"I was just keepin' your wife company, Mr. Windsor."

He walks her to her mother's car waiting in the street and comes back to the house, where he vaults up the stairs and thumps in the kitchen, rattling a spoon in the sink.

"Careful," Ruth says. "You'll wake the baby."

He sits at the table, eats what's left in Ruth's bowl. "Is there more?"

"No."

"That's fine. I had a big lunch, I'll have a big breakfast. How was the day, Ruth?"

"It's over. Been waiting for my saviour to come and pick me up."

He smiles and lifts her, twirls her like he does the baby. The towel falls from her hair to the kitchen floor and they leave it there.

"I heard there was an emergency on campus," he says, setting her down. "It was in your building—"

"I didn't hear anything."

He unpacks his briefcase in the nook, settles at the desk and scans his notes.

———•———

Hours later, he's still at work.

"Poetry or *about* poetry?" she asks from the kitchen.

"An article. Keats and the Eastern theory of consciousness. I just need a minute or two to get the ideas out. Maybe I'll call Phil about it, but frankly his viewpoint is a tad idiosyncratic for my taste. Hey, Ruth?"

"Mhmm?"

"You two are friends. What do you think, is he a real person?"

"*What?* Are you saying I have made-up friends?"

"Good lord, no. I just meant he's exceptionally stoic. It's a good virtue. Didn't think there was any more of that left in the world. Politeness is the hat of the ludicrous, as they say."

"I've never heard that one. But I guess it doesn't matter if he's real or not, does it? I'm not going to see him again."

"Why? Something happen?"

"Nah." She decides that if she ever tells him, she'll leave out the detail about wetting herself.

At midnight, he shifts from writing about poetry to writing poetry. She knows because he swaps his notebook for a receipt from his pocket.

Meanwhile, she gets a pencil and paper, begins pulling lines and shapes, texture and dimension from her imagination. The same objects she contemplated as a urine-soaked ball in the elevator. She draws a tree, then a stone, shades it in, makes it heavy, makes it stony, surprising herself that the object on the page materializes effortlessly, as though from nothing. It isn't present in the "real world."

Like billiard balls from the immaterial to the material—the stone comes from—

"Al," she says.

Twenty seconds pass as he tosses two words back and forth in his mind. He writes one. "Yes?"

"Why do you write poetry on scraps?"

"Because," he answers quickly, "it's about taking something infinite and making it small, a shard of infinity."

"And where do the words come from?"

"I don't know."

—from the library of the soul, she speculates. Millions of years' worth of material.

The day Al leaves for Edmonton, he takes a cab to the airport. It's early, dark. Ruth stands with him by the door, waiting for the cab.

"Call soon," she says.

"Of course, my cherished."

He looks out the window, to the lawn chair, the street. His squints at the chair as though contemplating whether he'll take it with him or not.

"You know," she says. "I didn't want to be a burden on you."

"Who put that idea in your head?"

"Nothing'll change, I guess, huh?"

"Nothing. You'll enjoy the calm and have all the time you need to paint."

He kisses her goodbye.

The same morning, she goes to the university to apologize to Phil. The bus is quiet, the summer's in, she hasn't seen him in over a month and doesn't know if he'll be there. Along the way, she contemplates how to name it: The accident? The event? Is forgiveness what I'm after, anyway?

She arrives at the building, takes the stairs to the third floor, knocks. No one. She wanders the halls until she finds an office with a light on.

"Professor Parker?" the stranger inside says. "Oh—you didn't hear?" He rummages through some papers in their office and returns with a newspaper. "Page ten."

Ruth takes the paper and reads it on the bench where Phil fed bread to the seagulls. She shuffles between articles, looking only at headlines, not wanting to sink into the flat, printed chaos that claims to be the world.

UNIVERSITY OF VICTORIA PROFESSOR SUCCUMBS TO FOOD POISONING

Phil Parker (58) passed this weekend. He spent his last moments in his second home in Rishikesh, India, where he planned to spend the summer teaching meditation workshops to tourists … contaminated food … possibly a reaction to insecticide … called a Spiritual Teacher … called a child of Buddha and Socrates … loved to feed the birds … no children….

She folds the paper on her lap and mourns to the tune of a hot police siren. A courageous gull attacks her shoelace and she lets it. Embarrassment, mourning—similar emotions, she thinks. Like an abscess cut with a razor, the slow gurgle of everything that was inside, the succeeding emptiness. Just as fast as the pain came, it leaves. Ironic, she thinks, how a man's life's work could be ensuring no one cares when he's gone. So unlike an artist.

chapter six
- 1979 -

Ruth sits down with the newspaper Bill brought over. She skims through used car ads, a feature about an upcoming junior school hockey tournament replete with photos of the Salmon Arm Rockets, and tips for clearing up leaves around your property before she lands on the story about her husband. It's at the back of the paper, before the trivia section and the crossword, tucked in the bottom right corner with no picture.

VANISHED PROFESSOR CONTINUES TO STUMP POLICE

Edmonton detectives have released new details about the disappearance of Allen Windsor (50), a professor at the University of Alberta undergoing a temporary suspension. Windsor was reported missing by a colleague last June after failing to appear at several scheduled mental health screenings. A month before his disappearance, Windsor had been evicted from his apartment and was living at the house of friend.

Windsor made local headlines thirteen years ago after completing a journey on horseback from Victoria to Salmon Arm. Windsor later purchased property near town and relocated his wife and their two daughters.

The disappearance is not believed to be criminal, but investigators are not releasing more information at this time. Anyone with information regarding Windsor's whereabouts is encouraged to contact the non-emergency line of the Edmonton police service.

She doesn't like the suggestion that she was "relocated" to Salmon Arm, as though she had no will, no say in the matter, when it was an entirely mutual decision, come to after many nights of them both sobbing in bed.

It saved them, being away from it all. Away from people, away from the news, the world. They had and needed only each other. They built cabinets, they fixed up the kitchen, they gardened. They were best friends. They were on the right path.

He was often away, but he always came back, and always wanted to come back, and the detectives should all be fired if they believe labelling him as an eccentric is enough to disqualify any serious consideration of the case.

She folds up the paper and uses it as fire starter.

chapter seven
- 1963 -

Al is coming home from Edmonton for Thanksgiving. Ruth feels obliged to make an event of it. She prepares the turkey in accordance with *Betty Crocker's 1962 Holiday Collection*. In the accompanying photo, the bronzed bird is served on a tasteful bed of half-moon onions and crimson crab apples and has a trove of breadcrumbs bursting from its rear. The succulent display rests on oval porcelain and is set on a red and white checkered tablecloth. The plate and tablecloth she found marked down at Woodward's.

Toward the end of the roasting time, she brushes her hair, ties her ribbon, dons a white and yellow polka dot sheath she bought recently to adhere to her office dress code. Gayle watches her change, banging sporadically on the edge of the crib, shouting, "Na!"

"No what?"

"Na."

It takes longer than she expects to get dressed. It takes longer than she expects for the turkey to roast, too. Luckily her husband is late. She pulls the crib into the nook and sits rapping her fingers on the kitchen table, inhaling rosemary, sage, mildew—

———◆———

He arrives by cab at six, shakes off his umbrella and hangs it on the door handle, untucks his shirt. He brought no luggage, only himself. He's put on weight, she noticed, but not a lot. It affects the way he walks, adds a hop—ironically, she thinks, giving the illusion that he is lighter, not heavier. He moves his new girth toward her, takes her fingers in his, allows her to rise on her own, and kisses her sloppily on the mouth with lips that taste like celery salt.

"You look nice, my love."

"*Thaynks* hun," she says, adopting for the moment a Southern drawl. "Been poppin' lotsa pills."

"From the chiropractor, for your muscles?"

She drops the accent and replies monotone, "Nah—laxatives. Something new I'm experimenting with."

"No, no. There's something else. The way you sounded on the phone, I'd have thought you'd become a wisp. You look healthy as spring."

"Things are more exciting since I started working."

"Tell me all about it—no, wait, that's a little vague. Let's start with what's immediate. How was your day?"

"Today I pitched a logo for a company that puts up chain-link fences."

"Oh?"

"They're called the Fence Fellows. The logo's blue and the O has a chain-link fence inside it."

"Okay, well, show me later, my love. Tell me about your colleagues, too. Are they good people?"

Gayle bangs her crib and he runs to her. He lifts her and spins, contorting his voice into high, wavering song, *"Hello-o-o-o-o-o!"*

Ruth leans hard against the back of her chair and cracks her spine. "She just cries to me and says 'Na.' That's her favourite word—when she's not crying."

"Na," Al says, kisses the baby's forehead.

"Na," says Gayle.

"I'm surprised she remembers you at all," Ruth says.

He puts Gayle her back in her crib, where she clutches the bars and stares longingly into the adults' kitchen universe.

"If you haven't noticed," Ruth says, "we're havin' a real American dinner."

"I can smell it. What's cooking?"

"Seagull. I'm skimping."

He squints.

"Turkey," she says.

He kneels before the oven to look, his descent sending the aromatic air particles of the kitchen into a frenzy.

"The oven light's dead," she says.

"It's quite dead—"

"Yeah."

"Pitch black."

Ruth kneels too, sniffs, opens the oven. Smoke billows into the kitchen and Gayle cries.

"Damn," she whispers. As though in a prearranged manoeuvre, she slips on mitts, carries the scorched bird outside and, in one swing, tosses it, the mitts, and the oven dish onto the lawn. "Dogs'll get it."

"It's okay, Ruth. I wasn't feeling hungry anyway. We can get by with the salad and potatoes, no?"

"There's none. There are onions and crab apples."

"I'll just have some beans."

"None. There's baby food on the bottom shelf. Mashed peas, I think."

He eats a can of mashed peas over the sink to prevent spilling on himself. "Maybe some pizza," he says.

———◆———

The pizza man arrives an hour later. Al answers the door.

"How's the lad?"

Ruth watches from the kitchen chair. The delivery man is easily in his late twenties if not early thirties. The word "lad" sounds unfitting, embarrassing even.

"Not bad," the delivery man says. "You know there's a whole turkey on your lawn, man?"

"Don't worry about it," Al replies. "Take it home to your dogs if you have any." He examines the man's suede jacket and gestures him inside, out of the rain. "Shirking the uniform today?"

"You mean shrinking? 'Cause of the rain?"

"You're not wearing the uniform today?"

"Yeah—it's not my thing."

"I like your spirit." Al nods. "To hell with bosses. You're exploring the world on four wheels. You must see plenty of things in your travels."

"Sure—I get to know the city pretty well."

"It's a noble profession, that of the courier. There's a long history to your line. What's your father do?"

"Lotta coke, man."

Al laughs and claps the delivery man on the shoulder. "How about you? You have any great ambitions?"

"Hoping for a promotion soon, to be a dispatcher."

"I mean, any dreams you seek to bring to fruition? Passionate dreams? Love, even?"

"I don't really get your question—but hell man, right now I'm dreamin' of the long weekend and a strong drink. You're my last delivery."

"You came to the right house, my friend." Al pays for the pizza, leaves it by Ruth's elbow on the kitchen table, fetches a bottle of whiskey and two shot glasses from a cabinet in the nook. "I've had this for a while—a congratulatory gift from my old faculty at the university."

The delivery man reads the label. "Top shelf, man."

Al pours two glasses. "To you, sir, and your dreams of"—he takes a breath, thinks—"being the best dispatcher there ever was or will be." They tip back.

"*Phoo*," the delivery man says, shaking his head. "Some bite."

Al leaves the man a generous tip and shakes his hand goodbye. He returns to the kitchen, retrieves two plates and a knife and begins slicing the pizza into large triangles.

"The hell was that about?" Ruth asks.

"I got a good impression from him. Clean, handsome. Kinda looked like James Dean, would you agree?"

"Everyone looks like James Dean these days."

———◆———

Over shallow plates of gasoline-coloured grease, they sit and stare at one another. He doesn't ask about her work again, or her colleagues.

"You've been painting, Ruth?"

"Trying. Can't."

"What's holding you back?"

"Nothing and everything. All this"—she swings her hand in a circle above her head—"But nothing really. I could. But with work, it's too much. I'm up to twenty hours a week."

"Art should not be simple." He stares at her, seeming to trace the curve of her chin with his pupils. He examines the ribbon in her hair but says nothing.

"My co-workers are good," she says. "They buy me gifts and stuff. I'm the only mother on staff."

He says nothing.

light on a part of the field   105

"Should I go on?" she says. "I could talk about serifs 'til your ears bleed."

"There's no need to speak, my love. I'm content in—your beauty, like a sailor is content to be lost when he's poised between the sea and the stars, the two immeasurables." He stacks the plates in the sink and leads her to the nook. "Have you been dancing?"

"I'm not a dancer."

"Tonight, we are dancers. In that dress"—he puts his hand on his heart, where the blob is—"I can't resist. I'm underdressed, but you—you look like an Italian sky, royal yellow, replete with seabirds and clouds sent asunder by the wind."

"You been there?"

"What?"

"Italy?"

"Yes—the Italy of my imagination."

He plays a jazz record. It's been a while since she moved this way, his palm on the small of her back, being led. In jazz—the kind of jazz playing now—there are no steps. "We are instruments," he says. "Improvise—"

She tries and struggles until a slow song comes and he pulls her closer, so close that her body adheres to his. She puts her feet on top of his, so she doesn't lose the steps.

"Sorry," she says. "I can't get the hang of it."

"Shall we try something else? Rock 'n' Roll?"

"I don't like guitars."

They continue with jazz until well into the evening until, eventually, she smiles.

"That's what I was waiting for," he says.

She deduces that an untouched body is like a spring. The longer it goes without touch, the tighter it becomes. She wonders if one day it can snap and no longer be a body at all. But little by little, the touch unwinds her.

"Can we make love, Al?"

"Ruth?"

"I was just thinking, I haven't been touched in a while. Does that bother you?"

He smiles. She sees a bit of mushroom in his canines and picks it out with her fingernail. He removes her polka dot sheath and carries her through the kitchen in her underwear.

The record plays out as they have sex in the bedroom.

"It ended right when we did," she says.

———◆———

She wakes up at two a.m. to the sound of a chair being moved in the nook. She's alone in bed.

———◆———

Morning. She looks beyond the checkered tablecloth, the empty pizza box, into the nook. He's dozing on the floor, atop a pile of wild blankets, without pants, and baby Gayle is asleep on his stomach with her head on his chest. A pen and an array of scraps on the floor beside him. Her dress folded over the back of his desk chair. She sees him slide the baby onto the blankets, rub his eyes, write a single word.

"You slept on the floor?" Ruth whispers.

"I didn't want to wake you."

"I slept good. It's been a while." The pizza box is too large to fit in the garbage below the sink, so she slices it in two with the knife. "You know, I picked up the paper for you. I know how you like it in the morning."

"You didn't have to, Ruth."

"Yeah, but I did." She takes it from its hiding place in the cupboard and leaves it on the kitchen table. "But it's three days old now."

He lifts Gayle back to his chest, holds her by the wrist, and makes her stand on him. "Hello, hello, hello."

"Na," the baby replies.

"She'll make a great receptionist when she grows up," Ruth says. "Hello to everybody."

Al turns his neck to the side, looks into the balls of Ruth's ankles, says nothing.

"I didn't mean anything by that, Al. A joke, a joke."

"What she responds to is simply tone." He looks back to the child. "Perhaps—perhaps she has a kind of sixth sense—something subtle, untarnished, still divine. Her soul is busy even if her mind is not. But language—not yet."

"You become Christian over in Alberta?"

"Hmm?"

"All the divine stuff. Someone at work told me Alberta was the Bible Belt of Canada."

"The soul exists outside of religion, surely. Probably in spite of it. You're twenty now. You'll understand someday, perhaps."

"Twenty-one." She boils water for his tea. "But let's knock it off. It's too deep for the morning."

He moves to the table and she sits across from him and watches him scan the paper. "Russians being Russians," he says. He reads with his finger on the page, tracking the sentence, and taps it at the end of each line of print. It's odd, she thinks, for a grown man with such a large vocabulary to read that way.

He makes it to the classifieds and dwells on them for a long time, appearing lost in thought. Eventually, a grin.

"Looking for another job?" she asks.

"No—"

"Obituaries? One of your enemies die?"

"No—"

"Well why are you smiling?"

"Ruth, sweet, we're doing well, money-wise. Better than ever before."

"Are we?"

"Listen—I'm going to run something by you. Do you like horses?"

She pauses, clicks her tongue. "Why the hell not?"

"Wonderful." He holds up his teacup as though making a toast. "A local farmer just outside of town is selling a brown filly. For a small fee, we can keep her housed and fed at a stable. A dear friend in Edmonton explained to me how it works. Abby. *Abby.*" He plays with the word, saying fast, saying it slow.

"You have a *dear friend* named Abby?"

"No," he bows his chin, looks at her punitively over the rims of her glasses. "It's a name I happen to enjoy. It draws my mind to the serenity of Wordsworthian reflections. Tintern Abbey. I thought of saving it if we ever had another daughter. Perhaps still—"

"You can't give a human the same name as a horse."

He waits for her to say more.

"But by all means," she says, "get an Abby if that's what you need."

———•———

In the afternoon, he calls, buys the horse, takes the bus to go see it. He arrives home in the evening.

"Where is it?" Ruth asks.

"She lives in a stable."

"No kidding? I assumed you'd ride back on it."

"I'm going tomorrow to get to know her a little better. She's well cared for out there, for a modest fee—"

"Sounds like a great way to spend your long weekend, Al."

———•———

The following day, the babysitter comes by when he's out with the horse.

"It's a holiday today, Jeannie."

"I thought you worked every day."

"I shoulda called. But if you're here anyway, you wanna come in for a cola?"

"I can do that, Ruth. I got nothing else today."

Ruth takes her coat and leads her to the kitchen table. The checkered tablecloth remains covered in crumbs and grease, the now five-day-old newspaper is still open to the classifieds.

"I love your tablecloth, Ruth."

"Got the idea from Betty Crocker. You know her?"

"My mum likes Betty Crocker."

"She's not bad." Ruth opens a bottle of Coke from the fridge.

The girl drinks from the bottle. "You have a good Thanksgiving?"

"The best of my life."

"Your husband come home to see ya?"

"Of *course* he's home."

The girl looks around at the mirrors, at "Three Eggs," at the pile of blankets still on the floor in the nook.

"He's out right now," Ruth says. "He bought a horse. It's kinda chaos in here, hey? We had a party last night."

"I love horses."

"So does he, I guess. Tell me about school for a bit, okay?"

Al returns early in the evening smelling like manure. He brushes bits of grass from his cuffs before vaulting into the kitchen.

"Oh, Jean," he says. "What are you doing here today?"

"Just keepin' your wife company, Mr. Windsor."

"Lovely. Company is what this house needs. It's bit a sad here, don't you think? Ruth doesn't like music anymore." He winks at Ruth. She glares back. "I was out riding today. The open air, the salty breeze. There's nothing like it. I'm famished."

"I heard you got a pony."

"It's been a dream of mine since I was a lad."

Ruth goes to the bathroom and closes the door, looks at herself between the two mirrors that cast her reflections back and forth infinitely. She looks deep into the chasm of Ruths, breathes, and returns. Ruth meditation. Al is sitting across from the girl, elbows on the table, focused on her face. The conversation has taken a turn.

"If you could live your life a second time," he asks, "would you skip over any of it, or live any of it twice?"

"I guess—I don't know—sir." She stutters and runs her fingers through her hair. "Probably until the age of twelve—those were good days."

"It's a big picture question. A way of gauging if you've lived a meaningful life. Do you have any dreams, ambitions?"

"I wanna go to college—and maybe have a pony someday, too."

"Al," Ruth says. "Jeannie's seventeen, finishing high school."

"Ah, well teenagers like pizza, don't they?" he asks the girl.

"I guess some of 'em do."

He calls to have one delivered. While he's on the phone, Ruth whispers to the girl, "He's acting unusual, Jeannie."

———◆———

The pizza delivery man is the same as before.

"What's your name, lad?"

"James. I was here couple nights back. You know that turkey's still sittin' on your lawn, man?"

"Well James, is this your last delivery of the evening?"

"Nah, I got one coming up in Upland, but I ain't into providing exceptional service to those candy-asses. Could use a stiff drink, actually."

"Candy-asses, eh?"

"Yeah—asses made of candy."

"Ruth!" Al calls to the kitchen. "Set the table for four."

She removes everything from the table, shakes the tablecloth outside, pulls the office chair from the nook. The pizza rests in the middle of the table, but the delivery man doesn't eat. Al pours three whiskeys and everyone but Jean clicks glasses.

"This is to you, James," Al says, "and the nourishment you've brought to this home." He stands to turn off the ceiling lamp and retrieve a thin candle. He lights it with a match from his breast pocket and takes his seat in his office chair.

"Life is a candle," Al begins his monologue, "short and bright. The slightest draft could make all the difference. There was once a wise young man who had seen too much, far too much, in the short time he was on this Earth, before the wind took into the air his quiet breath. An orphan, a doctor. You might say he saw the end at every moment of his life. For this we trust him. When he saw his own end was near, he taught one simple lesson that outlasted him and remains truer than the sun to this day. He told the succeeding generations not to waste their precious time. Be Beautiful, for Beauty must die. We must see Beauty in all things. Taste it and believe that some tastes are eternal."

No one responds.

"I choose friends wisely," Al goes on. "As friends of mine, you'll understand."

Gayle bangs the rattle on the crib and then she, too, sinks into silence. Jean begins eating her pizza with a fork, using the edge to hack off small triangles.

"Jean and James," Al says to Ruth. "What a nice ring. Don't you think?"

"Sure."

"They look like twins."

"Yeah," says James, leaning toward Jean. "I can see it."

Jean asks for a drink—Ruth brings her another cola from the bridge. She takes a sip, fidgets.

"Do *you* have dreams?" James asks her.

"I'm going to school soon."

"I been to school," James says. He pours another shot of whiskey and attempts to transfer the contents through the narrow lip of Jean's Coke bottle, spilling most of it on the tablecloth. "Me," he continues, "I studied mechanics for a few months. That was five, six years ago."

Al finishes his pizza quickly and takes Gayle from the high chair. Then he takes Ruth and asks her to join him in the other room, which means the bedroom. Alone, he kisses her, holding the baby aside.

"What's this whole show for?" she asks.

"If a man has a single goal in life that surpasses and survives all others, it's to leave behind imprints of love, moments to fossilize in history. They don't understand now. They're too young. But someday they will. Otherwise, I'm having fun."

"I get that," Ruth replies, not sure what he means by them being too young. Jean's only a few years younger than her and the pizza man is at least five years older. "I guess it's harmless."

"I love hearing your voice," he says. "I could swim in it."

"I don't believe that. We don't talk much, do we?"

"What do you mean, sweet?"

"When you were away, you phoned twice. You talked to Jean today more than you talked to me in—how many months?"

She counts months backwards in her head and he watches her, studies her face, her lips. She arrives at her answer but doesn't say it out loud. She looks around the room, the unmade bed, the mirrors, herself.

"A butterfly's life is more precious because it comes with its limitations," he says as he undoes the top button of her blouse.

"We can't," she says. "Not now."

They hear a door slam. She re-buttons her blouse and they go back to the kitchen to find it empty aside from the unfinished crusts and a half-empty bottle of Coke.

"Godspeed," he says, puts the baby in the chair, takes Ruth into the living room and puts on a jazz record.

———◆———

"I'm sorry, my love," he whispers when a slow song comes on.

"Why?"

"For not always being close to you. Tell me, what's in your heart right now?"

She rests her head on his chest. She aims for the shoulder, but it's too high. "You're worrying me."

After a moment he replies, "Make every moment like this. Until you wilt and fade, like beauty will do. You're cursed, you know that?"

"Huh?"

"A woman, young and beautiful—it's a curse. We're all cursed, but you a little more than the rest."

"Oh that? Yeah, I know that."

The song fades. They let it go and he tries again to unbutton her blouse. She responds by doing the same to him, freeing the top five buttons, revealing the broad chest, the faded pink nipples, and the blob.

He takes her fingers and leads them to the mark. Warmth flows like syrup into her bones, toward her wrist.

———◦———

"Ask me anything," says shadow Al.

"Are you gonna leave me?"

"Not in my wildest dreams."

"Then why do you keep—going away?"

"Because at this moment in my life I need—how do I say—my garret. Ruth, can I tell you something? I want you to know and remember this forever, for as long as we live, every time you worry."

"Mhmm—"

"Since the time on the cliff, I've been unable to shake the reality that life is precarious. Time is the most precious resource, and since then—since then, the work I do is this: I'm making a monument to you in my soul. I don't mean that figuratively. I've been working on something lately—something that eats at me night and day. It's a calling. A vocation—Do you know the word?—I'm composing now what I believe is my life's masterpiece."

"Oh—"

"Your lack of trust in me—I understand why—but it's not worth it. You know you're the only woman ever I've been with? But before I met you, I dreamed only of you."

"I didn't know."

"I've waited many lonely years for you, exactly you."

"When the monument's done—"

"Hmm?"

"We'll be like us again?"

They make blind love. The tension drains from her body and she clutches a pillow to her chest. Her sense of smell becomes sharper: the melange of bodily fluids, diluted whiskey evaporating from their mouths.

"Tell me," she says. "What is love to you?"

He doesn't respond right away. He shifts to his back, hands behind his head. "Unfathomable complexity. Just as the sky is, in fact, trillions upon trillions of particles catching light, though we see it as one and refer to it as one. Sky. We do this to love, too." He rolls to his side, facing the darkness that is her. "And you, Ruth?"

She responds immediately. "Love's when we look at all the beautiful things we've done for millions of years and add one more thing. It gets a little harder every time."

———•———

She wakes with a Third Eye. What did Doctor Phil Parker say? It was a tricky one. A Third Eye, he had explained, might be understood as the sense of sight doubled in the realm of the immaterial, into the infinite current coursing through all things. It can see through walls, through mountains, through skin. Matter exists, but it is not relevant now. Documented cases exist—Phil cited them in class—in which, in extreme circumstances such as a near-death experience or when a hero attempts to save a child from drowning in a river, a Third Eye appears. The child's soul will alight like a million candles, glowing colourless, say, forty metres to the south-east. Not white, but colourless. On the colourless glow before her, Ruth imagines black spots, nebulous blobs like the blob on his chest. Bits of the soul that have been burned. The Third Eye comes and goes within a fraction of a second. So pay attention, says Phil—

"You crying?" she asks.

"How did you know?"

She stretches a finger through the darkness, wipes a teardrop from his left jowl.

"You know, it was one of the best moments of my life."

"What?"

"When we thought we were going to lose it—funny?"

Gayle begins to howl, and he goes to calm her.

———— • ————

Early the next morning, he packs his luggage and calls a cab, retrieves the umbrella that had been hanging on the door handle for days.

———— • ————

Later that day, Jean calls to say she is quitting.

"What's going on?"

"Nothing Ruth—"

"It has to do with that pizza boy?" She pauses. "Pizza man—"

"He's a sweet guy, Ruth. Told me he's gonna bring me down the West Coast in his Spyder. We're goin' all the way to Las Vegas."

"That guy's got a Spyder? What about school or your mum?"

"Life's too short, Ruth."

"Can you cover just another week until I find another sitter?"

"I'm really sorry."

"Or come and say goodbye—to me?" Ruth hears noise in the background, cars, wind. "Where are you calling from, Jean?

She takes a moment to respond. "Somewhere in the USA—Washington, I think."

Ruth hangs up. She sits at the kitchen table with her face between her arms but doesn't cry. It's all a hollow throb, she thinks, this feeling of being abandoned. She vows to never hire another teenage babysitter. They're too young to understand other peoples' feelings.

———— • ————

She spends the last day of her weekend in lonely contemplation, avoiding all "real-life things" and taking stock of her arsenal.

In design school, she absorbed the terms *Object Hierarchy*, *Alignment*, *Focus*, *White Space*, *Vanishing Point*, *Complementary Colours*, and was able to see these things in her world. A line of doorknobs in a long hallway appears to angle toward a single theoretical vanishing point. This can also be observed in the bathroom, with the face-to-face mirrors.

Three objects aligned equidistant on a table: the closest is less likely to draw the eye than the middle one. Yellow and blue are long lost friends, purple and red are bedfellows. White Space and Object Hierarchy are evident in "Three Eggs," as one egg, the single brown one, is larger, and all three of them are off-centre, the right-hand side of the canvas being seventy percent taupe. Design is all a matter of matter.

Discussions with her husband produced terms like *Metonymy*, *Feminine Rhyme*, *Beat*, *Sublime*. Phil, at last, gives her *Formlessness*, *Reincarnation*, *Non-Self*, *Illusion*, *Non-Linear Time*—words that are entirely hollow, non-feeling. But, like light, they are paradoxically nothing and something. *Paradox* was another.

In between bouncing and feeding the baby, she sets to work on a new painting. Not the planned sequel to "Three Eggs," but something new. Something minute, spiritual, abstract, upsetting, sublime, a culmination of what she knows—

Colours: purples and blacks.

Shapes: stones and eggs and trees.

All carefully considered, all small strokes, nose close to the canvas. The *sensation* of a sweaty bed, the loneliness of spent fluids.

———◆———

I'm making a monument to you in my soul. She remembers the words as she paints. The sentence can be set on a fulcrum.

I'm making a monument—to you in my soul.

Seven syllables, five syllables. The first half of the sentence providing enough weight, especially with heavy-set noun "monument," to project the second half to the stars. The only part that bothers her is the swallowed hiccup, the unstressed dip, in the middle of it. Mon-*yuu*-ment. In her Canadian accent, it comes out as *nyooh*—an ugly sound not present in any other word she can think of.

chapter eight
- 1979 -

Ami is spending the night at a friend's. Ruth prepares supper for one.

As she microwaves Campbell's tomato soup, pushing a quiet simmer to the surface, these words sing in her head: *I'm building a monument to you in my soul.* Their musicality is why they stuck, and because they stuck she finds more intent in them than most things her husband said. The parts of him she doesn't understand become tied, in her imagination, to that simple phrase. It wasn't hollow language, like all his talk about the sea and the stars. It was a justification for everything.

She stirs the soup and places it back on the microwave dish for a second round. As she waits, she goes to the parlour, turns on the TV.

At times he seemed insane. He spoke in a voice that wasn't his, a voice extracted from another time. He attempted to sabotage his career with unwieldly, embarrassing poetry. But when these things happened, she reminded herself of his mission and knew he was not insane the way other people are insane. He wore his soul on the outside, a quiet simmer. If everyone did that, everyone would be insane.

What he made was not a work of madness. It was a monument to her. Why else would he have written six books of love poetry in the sixties and provided each one with the dedication *For my wife?*

She lands on *Looney Tunes* just as the microwave stops. She returns to find a third of the soup splattered over the interior of the appliance. It couldn't deal with the alien radiation. It had to burst. She wets a rag and wipes out the microwave in sloppy, unpainterly strokes.

But what good is a monument? What good are six books of love poetry? She never read them. He wouldn't let her.

And when he disappeared, she thinks, the monument came to a soft end, fallen to sand.

———◆———

But there is no end. Everything is caused by everything that came before it and causes everything that comes after it. Birth is a brief swelling of consciousness, death a dissolving into something else we don't yet understand and that is not simply human.

Looney Tunes is different though, she thinks as she drops a handful of crushed saltines into her meagre, now lukewarm soup. Unlike the news, it doesn't delude itself into believing all events mark the beginning or the end of anything.

The Coyote sticks his head into the barrel of a cannon to see if it's working properly. Maybe it's blocked. But it's dark in there. He has to stick his entire head into the chamber to see. And, as expected, it fires. The Coyote's face is blackened with gunpowder—

———◆———

—but after a moment, he's back. He's fresh and mischievous and has learned nothing from his first failure or his thousands before that. That's why he's content to fail, because time is not an issue, death is not a problem.

Now he ties rockets to his feet and slams on a helmet. Ruth smiles. He hits a boulder.

He is reborn again and again in non-linear time. So he needs no monument. He's already immortal. He can't get the Road Runner. If he did, his universe would end and the cycle of rebirth would be over.

———◆———

Artists can only go on if they do not learn from their mistakes, she thinks as she turns the TV off and sets her soup bowl on the windowsill to be rinsed by the rain. Turning off the TV always leaves her with a sadness that was never there when she had no TV.

It's like people. You don't want them until you have them.

She goes to her bedroom. Her husband's final letter is still in the top drawer of her night table, just under Gayle's departure note. She reads it again.

Some mush about love. Devotion. Beauty. Nothing she hasn't seen before. And then—*for I don't know how long. But for your good, I need to disappear. Until I return, believe I was never here to begin with. God bless you.*

———◆———

When he missed his annual visit, Abby the horse died from loneliness. Or neglect. Now she canters in the clouds, but the stable remains empty to this day. I don't want to be the one to break this to him if he comes back, she thinks as she closes her eyes.

chapter nine
- 1966 -

They are complete. He told her so in the dark last summer. Because he described them as "love poems" and dedicated them to her, she half expected them to come up on Valentine's Day. But she receives no call, no card, as usual. She isn't disappointed.

We're a non-sentimental family, she thinks.

The new babysitter brings Gayle home from preschool. She comes into the house with hearts drawn on her cheeks, carrying a card made by another student. Presumably, Ruth thinks, there was craft activity to indoctrinate children into kitsch-mania and make them soldiers of capitalism like everyone else.

Gayle hobbles to the nook without a glance at her mother. The nook is set off from the rest of the kitchen by a curtain and functions both as a storage space for her husband's hundreds of books and Gayle's bedroom.

"Any plans tonight, Ruth?" the new babysitter asks. It's an older woman with three children of her own. Since Jean abandoned her, Ruth is conscious of retaining a strictly professional relationship to everyone in her life: her colleagues and all five rotating babysitters who take her daughter to and from school and introduce her to laughing rascals her own age.

"I'm bogged at work," Ruth says. "I've got to go back to the firm if I can. I was hoping you could—"

"Take Gayle for the night?"

"If it's not too much to ask. She gets along with your kids so well. And it's Valentine's Day and all. Good for kids to socialize on Valentine's Day. I should've called you before you came all the way."

"Sure, Ruth. Sure I can."

"Cheque is still fine?"

"Not a problem, Ruth."

Ruth washes a glass in the sink and fills it with water. She gives it to the woman who drinks it all in a single, no-nonsense tip, straightens her jacket, recollects Gayle, and returns to her van.

Ruth doesn't go to work. It's too cold, too dark. She sets the kitchen table on its side to make room for her easel and decides that tonight she'll stick to quick-drying acrylics—thin, hesitant layers.

———◆———

It's a monochrome study of the concept of Fear, featuring a snowman she saw out the window of the bus last Monday. The snow melted the next afternoon, but the snowman will live in her soul for all eternity.

It's her fourth attempt at the theme, but it turns out even poorer than the rest. The kitchen lights are no good for painting outdoor scenes. The face of the snowman has to be redone three times and by then it doesn't meld with the rest. It hovers in front, as though the snowman is wearing a mask, a deformity of itself—a shoddy stab at an Erich Heckel—instead of looking at the viewer head-on like she wanted. Even for a snowman, she thinks, that's cowardly. The blurry coal and smudged visage say pity me rather than *feel* me.

———◆———

Late at night, she has the urge to phone her husband in Edmonton.

"Al?"

"Ruth, what's going on?"

"You're not in the middle of something, are you?"

"No—I can't talk long though. It's two in the morning. Did something happen?"

"No—I've just been painting. Working on snowmen. It's not going well. Tell me I'm doing things right, okay? I need a pep talk."

"Is Gayle asleep?"

She looks beyond the curtain to the empty bed, a mound where a pillow hides below the sheets. "Out like a light."

"Good, good. Well, I can't see them right now. But if you're doing it, then you're doing it right. Mistakes are just small steps toward what you want."

"You really believe that?"

"Why?"

"I've been thinking these days"—she pauses, weighing out her idea—"that it's ten percent of the artist's job to make art and ninety percent of her job to convince herself that it really *is* art and not just a hobby."

"All good artists doubt," he says. "I doubt everything except that."

"I'm getting frustrated at this one—"

"It happens," he says. "It's like writer's block. Sometimes you have to start over again and again and again like Sisyphus. Sometimes you have to kill, kill, kill your children. That's what writers say."

"I have to work tomorrow. I'm supposed to be typesetting some magazine about countertops. I'm behind schedule as always. I've already had a talking to from the boss." She laughs. "*Talking to*—Did I just say that? So trite. I have to get up in four hours."

"Hmm."

"I know you don't want to hear about that. Not your problem. Just forget it. That's not why I called. I'm hanging up soon—"

"I love you, Ruth."

"Thanks, Al."

———◆———

In the morning, she takes "Snowman #4" and puts it under her bed with the others. No more canvases are going to fit. She's going to need to kill it.

But not now, she thinks, and prepares to run for the bus.

Early spring, she hears of a free artist's workshop happening every Sunday morning in a gallery on Yates Street and works up the courage to go. She finds a non-Christian babysitter to cover the time.

It's a kind of meditation. A group stands in a circle, a line of easels between them and the day's subject, which ranges from flowers to human skulls to New Zealand pears. A taxpayer-funded instructor walks around, observing their progress, only offering advice if they ask for it.

Ruth begins by attempting to emulate the object, paying close attention to its contours and hues, ever aware of her own perspective, her height advantage over the thing at hand. But soon she realizes that she's the only one doing it this way. The rest of the painters, either because their eyes are poor or because they ignore their eyes, paint something that is only a vague echo of the subject. Instead they play—with colours, with shapes, with strokes. Endless playing, although no one appears happy.

In any case, the class spends more time drinking and smoking than they do painting, and they end sessions early to visit a nearby café and discuss their sorrows, the fact that society hates them, how capitalism has no room for them. Ruth joins them a few times, says nothing, only wanting to feel their pain in small doses and extract their philosophies.

"Art is revolutionary," says one. "It is inherently anti-capitalist because it has no use-value."

"Art aims to be pure spirit," says another, "and it's the only thing humans have that is not enslaved by so-called 'reality' or what we idiotically call 'nature.'"

"Art is pacifist," says yet another, "because it cannot in any circumstance be a force of oppression or violence. It exists in another 'realm,' which knows no war. So it is utopian—"

"Art alone can change how we view the world because it doesn't rely on logic, which has proven again and again to be futile when ninety percent of our actions are based on emotion, anyway, not reason."

"Technology has no place for art. Art on TV is not art. It's bullshit with no aura. Like Marshall McLuhan says…."

New ways, Ruth thinks, for an artist to convince herself that what she does is art and not a hobby.

But she becomes annoyed with the group after she learns her lessons, all those unrelated and sometimes incompatible packets of insight, and when the young men in the group become too friendly with her. She finds herself the object of too many utopia-seeking eyes, and leaves hurriedly one day, flustered after someone brushes her hand under the table.

———— ◆ ————

She keeps in touch with only one woman, a graduate student her age named Annabella Tavistock, who is thin as a baby poplar, preternaturally pale, and globe-eyed. She works with vast, aggressive splashes of colour, titling them, ironically, after ordinary objects, usually small ones: "Rabbit Foot," "Gumball," "Tooth."

She'd asked Ruth to meet her for wine several times and discuss art away from the others, away from the men. Ruth declined. But after leaving the workshop, she feels the gnawing of loneliness. Time around other people, she knows, like caffeine or prescription pills, means nothing in small doses, but doing it regularly produces an unhealthy dependence. The withdrawal is loneliness.

So she goes one more time, just to find Annabella and accept her offer.

"Someplace quiet," Ruth insists.

———— • ————

She learns that Annabella also left the group, and for the same reason as Ruth: too much attention.

"And not the *right kind* of attention," Annabella explains. "An artist should want the gaze of *wealth*. That's a necessary evil—a patron. That's someone who regrets their own life and wants to live free, vicariously, through art, using money, which has this stupid and desperate transformative power. Or, at the very least, we want *handsome* men, not those dime-store philosopher types." Annabella leans upon the table, reducing the gap between them. It's intimate, which Ruth appreciates. If all they look at is each other, then the rest of café ceases to matter.

"What do you mean?" Ruth asks.

"Writers, poets, musicians—whatever—people see them and they can move around, make noise, and all that. They love attention, any kind of attention, good or bad. It helps them sell. But painters have a harder go of it. We need to hammer people on the soul to get any attention, you get it? We're small, but we can make big, obnoxious things. We don't *get* a voice, so we hide and let the work scream for us. At least for now. Give it twenty years and all art will really be money in a different outfit."

"I got it," says Ruth, not at all interested in Annabella's predictions.

"You're lucky that you haven't been institutionalized." Annabella signals the waiter for more wine. "You're a renegade. The way you sat there all those times, leaning back, looking pretty, not giving a damn for anyone. You can rely on your *aura*. Most formal artists don't have that luxury. Picasso's not a great painter, you know? He's just more charming than his friends."

"I don't feel luxurious."

Annabella leans back, holds her palms up invitingly. "What do *you* do then, dear Ruth? Every artist has another life."

"Corporate design."

"What *moves* you, is what I mean to ask."

"I guess I'm a wife—and a mother."

Annabella laughs. She stops when she sees Ruth's offended look. "I'm not laughing at *you*. I'm laughing at the system. A woman with talent slaving away, forced into this domestic hole until she's too old to support herself. What a *dream*. You know, I'm celibate by choice."

"Why?"

"Because the second you show a man you have skills, you have potential and a brain of your own. I mean, if you ever do something impressive—he'll turn all that into part of your 'feminine charm.' Our culture sees women's talent as cute—or something edible. Five, ten years down the road and all your art's going into preparing brown bag lunches. Maybe we'd all better dress like men, and look like men, and then we'd be treated like humans."

Ruth doesn't respond. She doesn't want any more information regarding the system, only a moment of quiet in this café with this woman who seems to know a little and say a lot—yet say it with grace. Ruth sips her wine. She doesn't drink often, can't afford to. When her glass is empty, Annabella leans forward with a napkin to dry the edge of Ruth's lip.

"What do you plan to do now?" Annabella asks.

"What do you mean?"

"With yourself, your potential—what do you plan to make of it?"

"I don't know. I'm easily discouraged, I guess. I'm painting shit for no one but me. I have a stack of snowmen under my bed and I'm looking for a way to kill them."

"A stack of snowmen?" Annabella smiles, tilts her head flirtatiously. Ruth assumes by this point that the woman is drunk and looks around the café to see if they're attracting any attention. They are. A handful of men by the counter turn away when she spots them eavesdropping.

"Why don't you make something for me?" Annabella asks. "Art needs an audience, you know. Even if the audience never sees it, they're in the work while it's being made. They're *implied* in every stroke. You ever think of who you're painting for?"

"I guess I do."

"Make me something? We can trade, like a game."

"Okay," Ruth says. The men at the counter are looking over their shoulders again. "But I should go—I need to catch the last bus."

"Oh, take a cab, dear."

"I can't."

Annabella reaches into her purse, gives her a few bills.

"I don't want this."

"Oh c'mon, we'll split one." She winks. "My folks have money. It's kind of an allowance. And they wouldn't want a young woman riding buses around at night."

Ruth accepts, and they leave to hail a cab. Annabella concentrates on walking straight while Ruth turns around to make sure the men aren't following them. They aren't.

In the cab, Annabella writes her phone number on a napkin.

———— ◆ ————

What she makes for Annabella—instead of working, instead of mothering—is a series of absurd perspectives on ordinary objects. They are objects she doesn't have on hand and needs to extract from her soul: a vase carrying knives instead of flowers, the asshole of a cat, an egregiously large panini sandwich on a tiny table, a lampshade with teeth biting down on the bulb.

She stops meeting Annabella in person, nervous about giving her the wrong impression, but she calls the strange woman often. She doesn't know why. Annabella can't help with the paintings and can't even see them. She talks more about theories of art, the system, names of minor painters, and other things that become meaningless as soon as the conversation is over. On her part, Ruth talks about meditation, Phil Parker, paintings she wants to make someday, and her husband.

"He's not around much, huh?"

"He works in Edmonton, comes back every summer."

"Oh—"

"I've never really told anyone. I don't have many people to tell, I mean. I'm just like that. But it's a strange marriage. I don't have anything to compare it to, so I'll just say that. Just—I call him once in a while for advice—with projects, or when I'm stressed. But that's all. Nothing personal. It's like he's my shrink or something. Or my boss."

"It must get lonely."

"I don't know," Ruth says. "I guess it's like you said. Women ought to pretend we're men. Things'll change though. They always do."

The conversation always ends with Annabella asking Ruth to meet for another glass of wine or visit the gallery. Ruth always declines.

"If it's the noise," says Annabella, "I emphasize with you. I care. I can come to yours, or—"

"I can't," Ruth says, "with my daughter and all."

"Oh—"

"But I'll call you soon."

———◆———

Calling Annabella is a strange habit, she thinks. It doesn't help with the symptoms of withdrawal. It makes it worse.

It's as if there is a dear object someone has lost—a precious stone, a childhood pet, a home or a favourite tree—which miraculously materializes before them, and they reach to touch it only to have their hand pass straight through and send the object into ripples. Thinking of Annabella, she feels a thick, liquid sense of loss, but she doesn't know what was lost. Whatever it is, it refuses to be forgotten.

In her spare minutes before the babysitter brings Gayle home, Ruth lies on her bed and cries.

The project takes until the beginning of summer, when she wraps the paintings in heavy brown paper, fastens them tight with twine, and delivers them to Annabella at the café. She arrives late to find Annabella alone at a corner table with sunglasses on. When Ruth comes in, Annabella stands, tries to embrace her but is blocked by the canvas.

"For you," Ruth says.

"Thanks, Ruth."

"I like your sunglasses."

Annabella carefully leans the wrapped paintings against the table and looks back to Ruth. Her eyebrows are uncovered and arched slightly up as though she's about to offer pity or ask a favour.

"I guess that's it," Ruth says. "I enjoyed it."

"You thought of me while you made them? I'm looking forward to putting them on my wall. After I open them, I mean. I haven't seen them yet. But I'm looking forward to that."

Ruth puts her hands in her pockets and looks around the café. "I guess I'll see you later."

"Did you want to sit with me?"

"Sorry—"

"Just for a while? It's Saturday so I don't have anything else to do."

"Sorry, Annabella. My husband's coming home today. Didn't I tell you?"

Annabella nods.

"I never see him," Ruth mumbles. "I wait all year for it."

"Okay—" Annabella crosses her arms, swallows.

They stand in silence for a moment before Ruth holds out her hand to be shook. Annabella takes it but, instead of a grip, offers a delicate pinch of the fingertips that lasts, Ruth thinks, longer than it needs to. But she doesn't pull away. She feels acrobatics in her chest reminding her of stage fright but still doesn't pull away.

———◆———

That evening, her husband doesn't come home. Instead he phones from Edmonton to tell her something dire came up and he couldn't make his flight.

"Are you okay?" she asks.

"Yes—and I'm coming. I'll be late though. Midnight. After midnight."

"Should I worry?"

"Never."

———◆———

He arrives through the stultifying rain at two in the morning. From the bedroom, Ruth hears him in the kitchen. Gayle must be able to smell him in her sleep. Man and orange bitters. Gayle crawls from the nook to greet him but hesitates. No hellos, no spinning.

When Ruth comes in, she finds him in a kitchen chair, his hair twice as long as she remembers and a shade lighter. Gayle is standing on another chair.

"It's late," he says to Gayle. "Why don't we talk in the morning?"

Gayle hops from the chair and sulks back to the nook. As always, she goes to the floor and crawls under the curtain instead of opening it. She seems to never want the two rooms to touch.

"How are you, Mr. Husband?" Ruth asks.

He shakes his head and takes his briefcase from the floor.

"It was a joke," she says.

He goes to the bedroom, and she follows him, closes the door.

"What?" she says. "What is it? Shouldn't you be excited?"

"I should."

"Shouldn't you be happy to see me? I've been waiting up. Huh? Shouldn't you—"

"*I am, Ruth.*" A pause. "I am, Ruth."

They sit on the bed. She strokes his thigh as he rubs his nose bridge. Five minutes pass before he explains anything.

"I published the book," he says.

"Oh—*Good.* Good?"

He shrugs.

"It's good news," she says. "Why is it not good? Open your mouth, Al."

"Three months ago," he says.

"And you didn't tell me?"

He sucks in his lips. "I didn't know how it would go. I was rejected—nine times. Even here, the U Vic Press. It was a mistake."

"Whatever," Ruth says. "Every mistake gets you closer to what you want."

He looks at her.

"I didn't say that," she says. "You said that."

Without answering, he removes a letter from his briefcase and gives it to her.

———— ♦ ————

> *Al,*
>
> We've been friends for a long time. I know you are an expert in your field and I'm familiar with your academic publications. I'm not saying the poetry is unpublishable. I'm saying that the poetic climate demands truth right now. It demands answers and someone who pulls no punches.

I get the element of satire in your approach. Why would people take time out of their fatalistic lives to read about birds and trees, right? The world now is in dire straits. Riots in the United States. Violence and wars around the globe. We're caught in a tension between world powers that could lay us all to oblivion at the push of a button. We have murder. We have riots. We have uppers. These are the things the public wants to read about. We need poetry that takes these issues on, not poetry that reinforces what we already think we know. Millions of love poems are written every year.

To put it bluntly: Nobody gives a damn what the sunlight looks like.

I encourage you to try elsewhere.

———— ◆ ————

"A friend," he says. "A good friend."

"It doesn't sound so bad." She gives the letter back.

"He questioned my integrity as a poet and as a man. He didn't really read it. So I sent them elsewhere, a small press in Saskatoon, and they published two of the six parts. They said it was perfect but they had no money and asked me to fund part of it. I did. And I was confident, Ruth. I sent the book to friends, schools, bookstores. And this is what came today—the reason I missed my flight." From his briefcase he removes a small stack of magazines. Literary magazines, mostly from the west. Calgary, Vancouver.

———— ◆ ————

Al Windsor's latest collection of poetry reminds us of the old adage that you can't teach an old dog new tricks—but you can give an old dog a pen and watch him turn it into rubber.

———— ◆ ————

...what rhymes with "sea"? If you ask Windsor, the answer is "lea," "Poesy," "Poesie," "Huckleberry Tree," "sanguine enmity," "thine

atrocity," "angelic horn in reverie," "the C—in cavalry, before the train impedes on we," and, the underdog in this competition for nausea, "sea" itself. Now, shall we move on to page two?

———— • ————

"I did some research into my publisher," he explains when she's done with the magazines. "I learned that they've also put out a bathroom book about railway stations in Saskatchewan and a 'pioneer-inspired' cookbook. That's what I could find, anyway—before I was informed that it's a scam. A week after I was published, the press was charged with fraud."

"I don't know what to say."

"You could admit you married a failure, for starters."

"Get off it."

"Admit it—"

"No—"

"Yes."

It's not how she wanted it to happen, but a warmth rises in her legs and moves to her stomach. She kisses him on the mouth, finds his lower lip and bites. He puts his hand on her shoulders and moves her away.

"Hey," she says. "You're not—being *you*."

"Ruth—I'm a good man—but right now, I can't do this until I get it out of me, this—sick feeling."

She thinks for a moment and goes to the floor, reaches under the bed to find the snowman series. Four failed paintings. He pulls them out. "Here's what I've done. Failure after failure, too. Do you see me moping about it?"

"Ruth—"

"Let's kill," she says. "Kill, kill, kill ... how'd you say it?"

"Kill your children," he whispers.

"Sure."

"But it's late," he says. "How?"

They leave the bedroom and exit the front door, to the lawn where he used to write in a lawn chair. It's still raining. They hold paintings over their heads to stay dry. Under the trees that line the avenue, they stop, and she clutches "Snowman #1," lifts it high and brings it down hard on a tree trunk, breaking the canvas in half. She does it again.

He takes "Snowman #2" and does the same.

She does "Snowman #3."

"Snowman #4," the one that appears to be wearing a mask, she holds up like a matador's flag, and he gives it a firm kick. His foot runs through. She lets go and the painting clings around his thigh. He kicks it off and Ruth laughs.

Before they go back inside, they gather all the broken canvases into a mound and leave them on their sidewalk. The rain makes the colours weep into the asphalt.

————◆————

That night, Ruth screams for the first time in her life. It's sharp and loud, and she immediately stifles it so as not to wake the child or the neighbours.

She doesn't know why it happens, but the orgasm waiting inside her for a quarter of a century finally pries its way out. She shadows the honeyed moans of her husband and his long, staggered thrusts, surrendering her will to become nothing but a ball of energy, a tangled mess, and it's blissful.

When it's over, he rests with one leg and one arm spilling over her, and she folds her hands over her heart, observes the sweat cool and evaporate from her brow. Serene. Lake water rising, cooling the beaches in June.

————◆————

At dawn he leaves to visit Abby the horse. Ruth stays in bed.

The orgasm seems to have realigned the disks in her back. The usual tension is gone. Or, at least, it's shifted into the region of the heart. She presses her hands on her heart and prays that her daughter will not knock. Even thinking about it, the thud on the door, the girlish whine, brings her dread.

Maybe, she thinks, I can phone Annabella. Her voice is the only sound that doesn't seem awful. But for what? What would they talk about? Art? Orgasms?

To prologue her time in bed, she reaches for the magazines on the floor and finds one that her husband hadn't shared—a journal out of Edmonton. In the middle is a blurb about the poetry. It includes a photo of her husband sitting in an office chair with his hand on his cheek, grinning. The blurb was written by a woman, someone named Dr. Hanna Federico:

Professor Allen Windsor's latest collections reads like the letters of an old friend, who is at last setting his pen to paper to share the results of a life spent contemplating romance, nature, and living nobly in a world where it seems so few people are. The tone is close and the language hauntingly nostalgic. The still, sad music of humanity is acutely rendered. The reader senses Windsor's indebtedness to his forbearers, and the elegant restraint with which he approaches the sublimity of daily life. We're proud of you, Professor.

Why didn't he share this one? Ruth wonders. The only positive one, however humble. Unless he's hiding something. Her mind goes to the natural, almost too-obvious conclusion that her husband and this woman are having an affair. They are colleagues, after all.

She drops the magazine, asking herself if she, too, could have an affair. It would be too easy. It would be the obvious thing to do, the remedial thing to do, considering the symptoms.

———— • ————

Ruth is boiling linguine while Gayle reads quietly in her nook. Al returns, rejuvenated by his visit with the horse, leaps up from landing like he used to. Gayle crawls from under the curtain and finds his arms. They spin and laugh.

"Hello!"

"Hello!"

He puts her down.

"Having a nice day, dearest?"

"Yeah," says Gayle.

"Tell me all about it."

He follows her, crawling into the nook, and Ruth listens to her explain what she's reading—something the child found amid the books and papers she is forced to sleep amongst.

Al crawls back from the nook as Ruth dumps sauce over the linguine.

"Thanks, my love," he says, "for dinner."

"You doing better?"

"Better? What do you mean?"

"*Better.*"

He looks at her quizzically.

"Let me remind you how you came home last night and you were—"

"*Oh,*" he interrupts and looks away, "I'd prefer to not talk about it. It's in the past."

They serve themselves and sit at the table, eat the linguine in silence. He occasionally smiles but asks her nothing, complements her on nothing, wonders nothing about the new paintings hanging around the kitchen or the new chair he's sitting on, which she bought six months ago after the old one snapped a leg.

"You have a good one?" she asks.

"Yes," he said. "Maybe you'll find this interesting. I met some lads at the stable today who had a lot to say about something called trekking. You know this word?"

"I don't know."

"Trekking. It's to do with a long journey. Sometimes on foot, sometimes on horse, which is why they were talking about it. They were thinking of doing a trip around the island."

"You want to join them?"

"Not exactly. It's just—how do I say this?—something's been stirring in my mind. Something that I feel I need to do. Like those men. A new start, you could say. A way to clear my head or—"

"You're going on a trip?"

"Maybe," he says, finishing the last of the linguine. "I think it's right. It's been brutal cooped up in the university. There's no respite. None. Stress, offices, the pressures."

"You're leaving?"

He squints at her, observing the look on her face, which she knows is annoyance but he interprets as worry. "Only for a while. After what happened, I need something to bring me back to *myself.*"

"Godspeed," she says, collecting the dishes.

———— ◆ ————

That night a babysitter is called to take Gayle. As soon as she's gone, they are not themselves. They are others. He is a cowboy, shedding dust and musk, and she is something that a cowboy lusts after, which she doesn't have a word for. Not a maiden in distress—that's too old-fashioned—but something helpless all the same. A farmer's daughter, maybe.

She allows herself to scream and rocks dramatically to the rhythm of the bed, following his Gatling thrusts—equally erratic and authoritative. He wants adrenaline.

She rolls over to the edge of the bed, too tired to wipe either of them off like she usually does.

"Oh, Lucile," he calls her. This is her name in their fantasy.

She sighs and soon falls asleep.

———•———

They make less noise when Gayle's in, but they continue the game anyway, every Friday and Saturday for six weeks. The days of talking in the dark, she knows, are gone. The shadow people are dead, dissolved, replaced.

———•———

One morning, he winks at her. It's not something he does, but something *he* does, the cowboy. But the yellow light sneaks through the window, warming her sore body, which she immediately covers with blankets. She's too embarrassed to acknowledge the wink, so he kisses her on the mouth as he fastens his belt and then leaves for the stables.

Gayle's not due back until noon, so she goes to the kitchen and takes the phone.

"Annabella?"

"Ruth?"

She doesn't say anything.

"Are you crying, Ruth?" Annabella asks.

"Yes."

A block of silence. Ruth moves the phone to the other hand. She wants Annabella to read her mind, offer her time, her hand, herself—

"I don't have a lot of time," Annabella says. "I was just on my way out."

"I shouldn't have called."

"It's not that you shouldn't. I just didn't expect it—with your husband and kid. I didn't think you wanted to anymore. Did something happen?"

"Nothing in particular. I just wanted to ask how school is going."

"It's busy."

"Okay—I guess that's all. I'll see you around."

"Take care of yourself, Ruth."

———— ✦ ————

The babysitter brings Gayle home at exactly noon, as planned. Ruth scribbles out a cheque. Gayle walks by her and tries to crawl into her nook, but Ruth catches her elbow.

"Good sleepover, Gayle?"

"Yep."

"Making lots of friends?"

"Just Wendy."

Ruth doesn't recognize the name. "Okay, well, do you want something to eat? I was just slicing up some apples." She wasn't, but now she takes them from the fridge and cuts them into wedges as thin as possible—so thin, sometimes, that they may as well be transparent—and lays them out on a plate.

"You like apples, right?" Ruth asks.

"Yes."

She watches Gayle chew. The slices are so thin, insignificant, that they could nearly melt away on the tongue and retain no trace of the full, complex apple they once were.

What a terrible metaphor I've forced from that apple, Ruth thinks. She imagines a still life of fruit, such as one done by the Dutch and Flemish masters—eternal deliciousness in a black box, preserved in melancholy but preserved nonetheless. Now not even fruit has a stable identity.

"You know your dad's going away for a while?"

Gayle nods.

"Did he tell you?"

"Mhmm. He said he's going away with Abby."

"Right. Next week I think. He'll be gone for a few months. Probably 'til September. It's just us for the rest of the summer."

"He said he's going to come back with a bunch of stories."

"But he's leaving." Ruth turns away. Faces and voices proceed through her mind—Phil Parker, Jean, busy Annabella. "Like everyone, I guess. No one sticks around for your mum."

Gayle takes another apple slice.

"Maybe we should get out of here, too," Ruth says. "I've never left the island before, you know? But I don't like it here anymore."

Gayle doesn't respond. She's seen her mother in this mood before, talking to the wall, and has learned from experience that saying anything can only make things worse.

"But you're not going anywhere, Gayle. I love you."

"Thanks, Mum."

chapter ten
- 1966 -

His goal was Edmonton, but by the end of summer he realizes he hasn't made it nearly that far and decides to end the journey in the nearest sizeable town—Salmon Arm. The hotel receptionist, like those in all the other hotels he stayed at during his quest, looks at him incredulously when he asks for a place to tie up a horse. But they do accommodate him. They can always find a spot in an adjoining yard, or a nearby stable owner willing to house a filly for a night for a made-up fee.

———•———

In the morning, he showers and spends twenty minutes trimming his bundle of beard. Long, smooth whiskers hang to his upper lip, and hair dangles into an upside-down pyramid that just tickles the collar of his checkered shirt. The grey flecks aren't completely unbecoming, he thinks. It's a judicious grey, a hint that he will age gracefully.

Looking equal parts sensible and daring beneath his wide-brimmed hat, he checks out, mounts the horse in the yard, and proceeds with the final fifteen kilometres to Salmon Arm, where he turns heads in shop windows, attracts curious parents and their children, and is eventually stopped by a woman who happens to be a part-time journalist.

"It feels magnificent to finally be here in the Shuswap," he says.

———•———

He stays in town just long enough to see his name and face in print, sends the paper back to Ruth, and finds a company willing to load Abby into a truck and bring her back to the stable on the outskirts of Victoria. Then he cabs to Kelowna and catches the first flight to Edmonton.

Ruth reads:

IT'S A BIRD! IT'S A BEAR! NO,
IT'S ... A POET?

This weekend, Salmon Arm received an unlikely guest. University professor and celebrated poet Allen Windsor has at last completed a province-wide trek on horseback from his home in Victoria to our very own town square, pulling into town last Saturday at sunset like the cowboys of old. Windsor (37) braved the rugged British Columbia landscape to undertake his month-long journey. Along the way, he slept outside and faced storms, wildlife encounters, near starvation, and other dangers in pursuit of his dreams.

"I needed a change of pace," Windsor said.

His route was indirect, as he opted to follow a disused railroad line and took several resting periods in forgotten towns built before Canada was even a nation.

(Insert: Picture of Windsor posing with the captain of the fearless Salmon Arm Rockets)

"What really amazes me about this story," said mayor Belle Forester, "is that he did the whole thing on a whim. He felt the call and he just did it, while the rest of us were enjoying our creature comforts. It's inspirational and ... I hope Al's trip will encourage young people to follow their dreams and see that anything is possible."

When asked if the journey provided inspiration for his poetry, Windsor smiled.

"Do you know John Keats? He was history's most precocious poet, yet his life was cut short by tuberculosis. As a young man, Keats dreamt of adventure, which, in mysterious ways,—complemented his calling

as a poet. During some of his most creative spells, he was constantly on the
move. It allowed his mind to be loosened
from material bonds."

part three

—◆—

black

bird

chapter eleven
- 1979 -

In September, a couple months after arriving in Edmonton, Gayle finds a job that sticks. She isn't sure if her blond hair has anything to do with it or if, as Lewis suggests, the economy has simply improved.

She's a dishwasher in the bar of a hotel, a nineteenth-century, egg-white building by the tracks. It's sleepy every night except Friday and Saturday, when it draws urban cowboys, industry men home for the weekend, gamblers, and students. She stays because she shares in the tips of the bartenders and doesn't need to deal with anyone. It's only temporary, she tells herself.

And washing the dishes is therapeutic. She doesn't even have to worry about doing it well. Her boss tells her so. He explains that alcohol is a disinfectant anyway, and the most important thing is to ensure that the scum is gone, such as dried orange rinds, lipstick, and ketchup stains.

The job gives her time to reflect—the warm water, the grey light, the smoke wafting under the door to the kitchen—

———◆———

Edmonton is a wash of grey. Victoria was turquoise. The farm was gold, burgundy, green, sepia, yellow: the colours that indicate a sound relationship between the ground and the sun, or that Gayle associates with natural rot. The sounds differ, too. Victoria was gulls, the whisper of skin on carpet, and wind, while the farm was a lone chicken, her own breathing, something heavy set atop an old piano, making the strings inside vibrate tunelessly—

chapter twelve
- 1969 -

They leave Victoria in the fall. It takes little time to load their life into boxes. Gayle has nothing, her mother has very little but is attached to some painting supplies and a single kitchen chair that looks different from all the rest. Her father has plenty. Books, mostly. But he isn't concerned with how they're packed.

The boxes are loaded onto trucks, the trucks driven onto a boat, and the boat unloaded onto a train full of tired-looking families, working men, and flower children. As soon as they board, Gayle becomes nauseous and dozes with her head on her father's lap while he reads.

———•———

In her dream—a surreal, meandering dream of sick children—she wants to jump from the window of the train. She doesn't remember going to the window, only that she is perched on the ledge and there is no wind. The darkness is warm and inviting, and she knows instinctively that everything will be okay if she jumps. The darkness can be trusted, like an adult, a teacher or a parent.

It's the right thing to do.

She lands on the back of a giant bird, a black, heavy-feathered creature that blends into the nighttime forest and the jagged silhouettes of the surrounding mountains. The Dream Bird, as she names it, lifts her high in the air and they part from the Earth. With her arms around its neck, she cranes her own to get a better look at the surroundings. The moon shimmers, the sky becomes brighter the closer they come to it. They are going west, back to Victoria.

———•———

She wakes up as the train slows to a halt somewhere in the mountains.

"What's going on?" she asks.

"I don't know, sweet one," her father replies. "Let's watch."

The conductor walks through the car with a headlamp, whispering about how annoying it is for passengers to open their windows when they're explicitly asked not to. "But rebels will be rebels," he insists to anyone listening.

Meanwhile, the passengers whisper to each other, weighing out theories. Electrical issues, logs on the tracks, someone jumped from the window—

The conductor informs them that, no, something has *entered* the train.

"So keep the windows sealed 'til we can figure it out."

Soon employees from the dining car come pacing between the seats with nets, like children searching for butterflies. They peer into the overhead compartments, open and close bathroom doors, kneel to look under seats.

"This is outrageous," says her mother.

Her father leans over to kiss her on the neck.

"We're in public, Al."

Unable to join in the search for the mysterious object, Gayle turns her attention outward, into the darkness, and soon the dream she had on her father's lap returns, hits her so vibrantly that she has a hard time drawing the line between the dream and the moment she woke up.

But now the windows are all sealed, as the conductor with the headlamp wanted, and she realizes with disappointment that it's impossible to jump. There is no Dream Bird. She puts her fingers on the glass.

"Stay put," her father says to both her and her mother. He slides into the aisle and joins the staff in their search.

"Mum," Gayle says after a while.

"What?"

"I had a dream."

"This is a dream, too. A bad one. I'm dying in here. The air is poison now with all the windows closed. And we have moving trucks coming to the station at nine in the morning."

"I flew out of the train," Gayle says.

"What?"

"In my dream."

"You fell out of the train?"

"I *flew*. Where are we, Mum?"

"You're fine." Her mother's knees are shaking. She straightens her sweater, nods to Gayle, and goes off in search of her husband.

Parentless, Gayle too vacates her seat and begins wandering. She has a hard time pulling the lever to open the door between the cars, but no one stops her, concerned as everyone is with finding the alien object that has entered the train. She eventually finds her way to an empty car where the staff have their meals. There a window is still open. It's a larger window than the ones in the rest of the train, and it opens from the bottom.

She goes to it, puts her hand on the sill. The breeze outside is fresh, and she sticks her head outside to breathe it in. The window is slightly too high for her to lift her legs out, so she pulls over a stool. With her bad knee, she has a hard time balancing, but gets her left leg out the window and, for a few minutes, straddles the divide between the inside world and the outside one. The light one and the dark one.

The door slams open and her father bursts in. He clutches a bundled sweater against his chest, his hand stopping whatever's inside from shaking free. In one swift motion, he pulls Gayle in by the elbow and flaps the sweater out the window. The shadowy animal disappears into the nearest trees.

"Gayle, what you *doing*?"

"What was that?"

"A little bird. A little lost, too."

Gayle looks out the window and begins to tremble.

"He's okay though," her father says. "Are you safe?"

She wraps herself around his legs, and he lifts her, supports her in his strong arm, a hand on her back, and carries her to their seats, where her mother is waiting.

When the train starts running again, the conductor comes to thank her father for releasing the bird. "Good thing, too," the conductor says. "People would go crazy if we sat here much longer."

"The bird didn't want to be here either," her father replies.

"No one does," her mother adds.

The train company buys him a bottle of beer for his effort.

Her mother doesn't speak for the rest of the journey but puts her hand on Gayle's forehead and it calms her. Gayle doesn't know why, but she trusts her mother's hand more than the rest of her.

A month after their arrival at the farm near Salmon Arm, Gayle holds her father's hand in the local nursery. In the car on the way over, she thought she was going to be sitting in a pen with other children.

"I'm nine," Gayle reminds him.

"A nursery is a place for plants, too," he tells her when he senses her confusion.

They approach the young clerk. "Young man," her father says, "I'm looking for your crataegus douglasii."

"Umm—"

"Hawthorn, my man. Hawthorn."

Hand in hand, they follow the clerk to the back of the nursery to look at saplings. Along the way, something burns its way into her memories: a row of young sunflowers not yet in bloom. Thin green starfish on stalks, sunken into themselves, using their still-rouged pedals to hide their true colour or stop it from escaping too soon.

"They look shy," she says.

When she speaks, her father listens. He crouches down, sets a knee on the floor, and moves his face close to hers so he can pick up every word.

"It's because they're not getting enough sun in here," he replies and, without another word, loads all seven sunflowers and their clay pots onto a cart and forgets all about the Hawthorn bushes he'd planned to plant along the east face of the flower bed to protect it from the wind.

As they drive back to the farm, he explains that sunflowers are not so named because they look like the sun. "It's because they follow it and learn from it," he says. "They watch it move across the sky and, as they get older, they will look to it as a father and seek to be just like it. Vibrant and true."

———◦•———

Her father is an optimist, her mother a pessimist. When she finds these words in a book later that summer and looks them up in a dictionary, it's easy for her to see examples of them in her own life.

He has strong ears, Gayle thinks, whereas her mother has strong, vulture-like eyes that can see flaws from across the room. Her mother treats the world like something she can smooth out like bed linen—unless, it seems, it's the bed linen itself, which all throughout the house is wrinkled, thin and useless.

"Stand a little taller, Gayle," she often says. Or, "Wipe your spittle." Or, "Finish your damn food."

Her mother doesn't look up, let alone reply, when Gayle softly justifies herself: "My knee always hurts." Or, "I'd rather eat centipedes."

———•———

But her father can read her lips, she knows. Maybe even her mind.

During their time in Victoria, she found her senses particularly attuned to any sound he made. Whenever he arrived home from Edmonton, he would throw open the door. The house would rumble from his weight. He would come to her before removing his jacket, sometimes even before removing his shoes.

Now, whenever he comes home from a ride on the horse, or a trip into Salmon Arm, she can hear him even from the sunflower patch or the woods, beyond the sound of rustling foliage and insects, and go running to him. She forgets her game of pretending to be lost, leaps into his arms.

"Hello!" he says, spinning.

"Hello!"

"Hel-*lo!*"

"*Helllllooo!*"

It lasts several minutes, this round of hellos. It ends only when she is dizzy and asks to be let go. But she holds on for as long as she can, trying to utter one hello for each hour he was away.

———•———

The piano came with the farmhouse, although the former owner must have treated it as mere decoration because it came out of tune. In the first summer of her new life, her father calls in someone to tune it.

The piano man arrives with a tool box full of levers, mallets, mutes, rags, and tuning blocks, and she watches him hammer each string and compare it to the blocks. He wears a sweaty brow and a look of overall intensity. The impression of urgency is increased by the fact that the man wears goggles. She is entranced by the surgical process, the fact that this man can hear things she cannot.

"If a string snaps," he explains, "it could take out an eye."

She holds her breath as each string finds its note. When they're all close, the man starts over again, but this time sets aside the tuning block and presses his ear against the wood, feeling vibrations and listening at the same time, comparing notes to each other in half steps or full steps.

———◆———

Her father is not a virtuoso and knows little more than the basics. But he could listen to a song on the radio and, with care, replicate the melody note by note and experiment with simple chords until he finds the progression. The result isn't always accurate, but he calls it an interpretation and it's good enough for Gayle.

One day, he shows her how to do it herself.

"Major chords are like the sun," he said. "While minor chords are like the moon. Those are the building blocks."

He shows her how, at its simplest, a minor chord is just a major chord with one note dipped in the middle, and how you can add notes to a chord to strengthen it or give it a new accent. You never know which notes are going to fit. You have to try.

"You can put in a note that is one octave above the root—a C chord with an added C—but that's most obvious one. You could also add a seventh. *Here.* It sounds like light humming through a cloud. And a seventh added to a minor chord—like—*this*—is one of the world's most mysterious sounds."

———◆———

All summer she practices when no one is listening but her mother, who never says anything about it and walks in and out of the parlour carrying wet brushes and half-painted landscapes. She treats Gayle's efforts as static, as nothing, until she hits a sour note, upon which her mother flinches as though bitten by a horsefly.

But while her father is out, Gayle learns "All You Need is Love"—her interpretation of it, anyway. The wordless four-chord version. She doesn't like the song. It's just one that plays often on the radio, which gives her a chance to memorize it.

She plays the melody with her right hand and hammers out chords on the left. She even attempts a roll on the low keys, imitating the strings after John Lennon sings the chorus.

———— ◦ ————

"A brilliant performance," he tells her when she shows him. "Did you do it all on your own?"

"Of course."

"For me?"

"Yes."

He claps. "You know how to get right into my heart."

———— ◦ ————

For the rest of the summer, he encourages her to sing. It takes her a while to get used to it, singing and playing at the same time. But the piano faces the wall, which bounces her voice back at her and helps her notice if she's out of tune.

"All children can sing," he explains to her. "Just like all children can dance and paint and build castles in the sky. Not so with adults, unless they're artists—like your mother and I."

———— ◦ ————

In order that she never lose her gift, he hires a music teacher. It turns out to be the same man who tuned the piano. He comes by every week to show Gayle how to read sheet music, something her father doesn't even know how to do.

When her father's out and her mother won't speak to her, Gayle converses with simplified Haydn or Chopin. Music is another language that no one in the world but she and her music teacher understand. It grows more valuable to her as the summer comes to an end and cold wind falls from the mountains at sunset and forces her indoors.

———— ◦ ————

"Music is the purest of arts," her father explains over dinner in August. "It goes directly to the soul and no one can explain why. And if you believe the history books, it's one of the first things our ancestors learned how to do when they stood up from the ground—to grunt, then to sing."

"What, dad?"

"Nowadays, music is the food of love. At least, that's what Shakespeare says." He raises a spoonful of mashed potato in one hand and holds up the empty palm of the other, as though weighing the visible food against the invisible. "I agree with him, sometimes. Do you know that name, Shakespeare?"

"Yep."

She doesn't, really. She assumes Shakespeare is another piano teacher.

———— • ————

The last week of August, a clear day, Gayle stays with the sunflowers as long as she can. She invents a game of turning over the leaves and petals and looking for bees. When she finds one, she follows it through the yard, into the trees, until she knows the whereabouts of all the hives on the property. She tries the game with butterflies, too, but they don't participate the way bees do. They either fly out of sight or else sink into stasis for hours until she becomes bored with them.

She knows he's leaving soon. She's annoyed with him when he comes to find her, but he assuages her irritation by showing interest in her game. She shows him how to play, and late in the afternoon they find, for the first time, a moth. Gayle doesn't know what to do with it.

He gently removes it from the leaf of the sunflower, pinning the wings between his fingers so it won't flutter and injure itself. He goes to his knees and holds it between their faces at an angle that allows the sunlight to run through its wings and surround the frightened creature with a tangerine halo.

"They're under-appreciated," he says.

"They're pretty."

"Just as nice as butterflies, no?"

"Yes."

"But no one thinks of them like butterflies. I think they're lovely, don't you?"

"Yes."

"Would you like to hold it?"

"No." She shakes her head. "I want you to let it go."

"We'll let it go."

He sets the moth on the flat top of a nearby post. He cups his hands around it to protect it from the wind while it recovers from the shock of having been touched by humans.

The day before he leaves, he brings her again to the sunflower patch near sun-down and, with reddish shadows filling the lines of his face, explains that the sunflowers will die soon.

"But part of the miracle of these flowers is that they'll continue to stand. Even throughout the winter, they'll be tough. They turn brown and freeze, but as soon as the sun comes around again next summer, a fresh patch will grow, just a wonderful as the first."

Gayle nods. She understands he talks in metaphors. He's talking about her.

He shows her how it's possible to snip off the flower heads, scoop out the seeds with a spoon, roast them in the oven, and eat them all winter if she wants.

"That way, you'll grow stronger, too. And you'll never forget the flowers. And your mother doesn't like seeds—they get caught in her teeth—so you'll have them all to yourself." They walk back to the house. "But remember to save some for next year so we can plant them again. If we do it each year, the patch will grow bigger and bigger."

She does eat them all winter. She keeps the roasted seeds in a jar in her bedroom and sucks on them while she reads. They keep her feeling strong, like he promised they would. But the sunflowers don't remain looking tough. When a wet snow comes in November, many of them snap.

chapter thirteen
- 1979 -

Lewis works at the convenience store in the morning. Gayle washes dishes in the bar of the Strathcona Hotel in the evening. They rarely see one another and he's asleep by the time she gets home.

As the fall drags on, the rain becomes less frequent and the mornings become more frigid. Edmonton quickly evolves in her mind from being calm, though boring, to being a perpetual murk. The odour of dishwater descends directly from heaven.

———•———

They recline in bed.

"It's funny," Lewis says, "what we're doing."

"What are we doing?" Gayle asks.

"Just the same—washing dishes, stocking shelves, slowly dying in the nine-to-five. I'm not a smart guy, but I know enough to see how fake it really is. People weren't made for this. The disgusting—*sameness*. You know what I mean?"

"Don't be so sour. We have our plan. All this is just temporary."

"Yeah," he says, rubbing his eyes.

"Do you wanna read some poetry again? Remember how we talked about that once a long time ago?"

"You mean a few months ago, when we met?"

"Yeah—I mean, there's a couple used bookstores around here. I used to read all the time when I was a kid. It got me through lots of things."

"Me too," he says. "Maybe something that feels like it comes from far, far away from here. That's my vote. Do you know what I mean?"

"I know exactly what you mean."

"I know."

"Haikus, maybe," she suggests. "What do you think?"

But they have no books now. They have the vent that rattles furiously when the temperature dips toward zero, the neighbourhood dog fights that increase in frequency as the temperature rises above freezing. They have Lewis's coughing fits, which are constant in all weather.

At the start of a Saturday shift, she learns that the previous night there was an exodus of kitchen staff. An older waitress named Arianne, who goes by Ares ("after the god of war," she says), tells Gayle that most of the other dishwashers were participating in a lottery pool. They bought ten tickets every week for several years, planning to eventually split the winnings and move to Tofino.

"'Cause," Ares explains, "if you buy ten tickets, your chance goes from one in a million to ten in a million—but if you do the math, it's actually, uh, one in a hundred thousand. But if you buy it every week, the odds can go to one in a thousand or something. I didn't go in on it 'cause it was just for the guys. And 'cause one in a thousand's still a pretty shitty odd."

"How much did they make?"

"Twenty grand. Someone in Winnipeg won a million."

"So two grand each?"

"But they quit before they thought about how they gotta split it. Two grand ain't enough to live on unless they invest it in something like gold or oil. That's what I'd do. They'll be back in a month, though. I'd bet on that." She chuckles. "But the best part's this—two guys're saying they deserve more 'cause they've always been going to the store to pick up the tickets. So they got more rights, they said."

Gayle shrugs.

"Hun, the shop's a *block* away."

The dishwashers left behind a mountain of unwashed plates, cutlery, and novelty baskets lined with newsprint for serving fries, used to remind the patrons of simpler times.

One of the deserters had also taken a paring knife and carved the word *PRICK* into the wall above the pint glass rack.

———— ◆ ————

Heinz Ketchup hardens into maroon crust and doesn't come off with water alone. For several hours, Gayle attacks it with steel wool.

She invents a game of looking away from the clock for as long as she can and, when she can't stand the anticipation, guesses how much time has passed and compares her guess to the factual clock. She always overestimates, sometimes by as much as forty-five minutes.

She decides by the last plate that the most interesting part of the game is how difficult it is to avoid looking at the clock. Once the job is finished, she craves the time.

———◦———

Her boss is a diminutive man who perpetually rubs his hands, poises hawk-like on a stool by the bar, chews tobacco, scans the room for people who aren't adhering to the bar's "one drink minimum" policy and forces the transgressors to leave.

"You're doing a good job, Ginger," he tells her when the dishes are clean.

"Gayle."

"Who's Ginger then?"

"There's no Ginger here."

"Alright, Gayle, how would you like a raise?" He throws out his hands, gesturing to the empty kitchen. "The boys all took off. I can do three sixty an hour? You gonna stay on?"

She shrugs.

———◦———

The following week, she comes to work to find an automatic dishwasher. It's installed beside the pint rack and the word *PRICK*, the carved letters of which have been filled in brown by spectral kitchen grime. The word is now legible from across the room.

The dishwasher itself is a futuristic machine that blows hot air into the glasses and, when she opens it, erupts with scentless steam that fills her pores. By the end of the night, her hair is curled, the once-shimmering blond a tarnished gold with black roots. Her reflection in the dishwasher door is so downtrodden she laughs.

———◦———

She takes up smoking. Whether it's out of boredom or restlessness, she can't tell. Ares tells her it "takes the edge off."

"The edge off?"

"Of the *grind*, girl."

She doesn't smoke nearly as much as Lewis, just enough to give her a reason to go outside, to observe the alleyway, the occasional fight, bits of litter.

———◆———

Eventually Ares starts distributing joints at the start of each shift.

"Makes the time go by," she says. "Especially if you don't gotta talk to nobody."

"I guess—"

Ares laughs and touches Gayle's elbow. "What are you, a Hutterite?"

Not knowing what a Hutterite is, Gayle laughs and accepts the joint.

———◆———

When she's stoned, unheard music saturates her mind. She doesn't question why. Oblivious to the dropping temperature, oblivious to the dangers of the streets at night, she sings or hums to herself as she walks home.

She hums snatches she remembers learning on the piano as a child—Chopin's "Prelude 20," Sinatra's "Fly Me to the Moon"—or songs she discovered on the radio as an adult. She often doesn't know the name of the song, where it comes from or where it's going. They arrive in fragments. Ten seconds of imagined music. A chorus. Two lines of a verse. A few sidewalk blocks later and the fragment repeats—again—and again.

She is stoned as often as possible.

———◆———

"You don't mind if I wake you up? I wanna hang out but, I mean, you're sick and you should get lots of sleep."

"I don't mind. How's the shift, Gayle?"

"Always the same."

"Sounds about right." Lewis sits up in bed. It's dark, but she can tell he's shirtless by the sweet swish his skin makes against the fabric.

"You know," she says, "the dishwasher's a funny thing—"

"Aren't you the dishwasher?"

"I mean the machine they put in. The fancy new thing. It makes me unnecessary. It could do the job of ten, twenty people."

"Is that so bad? Someday machines are gonna do all the shitty work for us and we'll just lounge around. You know much about computers? I mean those things they have in the university or whatever that can apparently solve any math problem in a couple seconds."

"I don't know much about stuff like that."

They talk this way, about computers, about the death of the service industry, until her eyes grow heavy, the drug wears off.

———— • ————

PRICK appears in several more places around the kitchen and behind the bar, countering Gayle's original suspicion that the deserted dishwashers did it.

In the alley, smoking with Ares, Gayle brings it up.

"It's offensive, ain't it?" Ares asks.

"It's kind of a nice change of scenery. I bought a bonsai tree a couple months ago. It feels a little like that."

"I did it." Ares stabs the night air with smoke.

Next to them is a large grease disposal unit. It's shared by all the kitchens on the block. A sign on the front says not to dispose of cigarettes inside, but everyone does. The unit is even defaced by graffiti of a cartoon man smoking a cigarette and dropping it inside.

"Why'd you do it?" Gayle asks.

"'Cause I'm bored. And 'cause the boss is a prick. You don't mind if I say that word, eh?"

"No."

"You're not a Hutterite or something?" she asks again.

"No."

Ares looks at her watch, shrugs, lights another cigarette. "Okay, well, here's the thing—the guy's a racist. You know how he sits on that stool and looks at people to make sure they're drinking? He's actually just looking for anyone who's not white." She paces, left hand holding up her right elbow, growing agitated. "Look, I've seen all kinds of people come in here and not buy nothing and it's not a problem. When he kicks people out, it's never a white person. I never seen it happen."

Gayle nods.

"You know we're all related, huh? Everyone's part of the same family. That's evolution. It's not right what he's doing, and that's why I'm writing *prick* everywhere, 'cause that prick doesn't deserve nice things."

She throws her second cigarette in the grease disposal unit and they return to work.

———◆———

That night, just after closing time, Gayle takes a knife to the public space of the bar, ensures no one is watching, and quickly carves *PRICK* across the entire face of a twelve-person table. She cleans the residual paint and varnish from the knife with a rag and slips it back into its holder in the kitchen.

———◆———

"You're smoking a lot now, huh?" Lewis asks, sipping a beer.

"Takes the edge off."

"Kinda funny that there's an edge at all, eh?"

"Funny, yeah."

"Everyone says smoking makes you die faster—but you could say the same thing about stocking shelves or washing dishes."

"You ever notice how in old movies, everybody smokes?" she asks.

"What do you mean?"

"I'm just making an observation. I don't know if it means anything." She tries to blow a ring. In the dark, she can't tell if she's successful or not.

The threads of the conversation dissipate and she tries again. "Did you know you can extract the THC and put it in your coffee or tea. 'Green tea' they call it, with quotes around it."

"Who calls it that?"

"I dunno—some woman I work with. Ares. She named herself after a Greek god. She said she wants to open up a 'green café' as soon as the government legalizes the stuff. She has lots of ideas for freeing people from the chains of reality as soon as she's allowed."

"People like that give me the creeps."

"I just like talking to people," she says. "I got invited to a frat party by some boy at the bar."

"You gonna go?"

"Of course I'm not gonna go. I just got invited 'cause I'm blond."

"Guys like that bother me, too."

"When'd you start hating everyone, Lew?"

"I don't hate people, Gayle. Maybe I'm just a little hardened."

"You're talking like an old man." She leans against his shoulder. "You're the sweetest guy I know—Hey, how come you drink beer in the fall? It must be minus ten out and its pretty cold inside, too. Doesn't beer make you colder?"

"It's not that cold out yet. And I heard something on the radio yesterday that drinking cold drinks can make you warmer 'cause it tricks the body into thinking it's cold, so it warms up on its own. It's a natural thing."

"Know what," she says, "I read a play in school one time. *A Streetcar Called Desire* I think it's called. The only thing I remember is that some of the characters have the exact same conversation, about whether beer makes you warm or cold."

"It's a question that's worthy of good literature, I guess."

What she enjoys about her time with Lewis, what she'd always enjoyed, is that he listens. He always responds, regardless of what she says, if she's inebriated, or if she's bothering him. He never interrupts her.

"Hey—you ever wonder how come all the wild rabbits in Edmonton don't get cold?"

"Maybe they're hardened. Like me." He puts his arm around her. "Goddamn world."

"Good to see you still have a sense of humour."

———◆———

The table Gayle engraved with the word *PRICK* is replaced with a cheaper one, the kind used in school cafeterias with fold-out metal legs.

"Did you do it?" Ares asks in the alleyway.

"Yeah."

She gives a thumbs-up. "Good, kiddo. We'll hit him in the wallet. That's where his real nuts are. Hey, do you ever nick stuff?"

"Like what?"

"I dunno—glasses, spoons and forks. *Food* too, of course. And pennies from the tip jar."

"I guess I could."

"Helps to keep costs low, that's all I'm saying."

———— • ————

The next night, Gayle arrives to work with a can of spray paint she found on the edge of a trash can. At the end of her shift, she lingers in the alley until the bar is cleared out, then walks to the front of the building, smokes by a streetlight until there is a break in traffic, and quickly marks the entire front window with a black, stringy letters: *P-R-I-C-K*. She tosses the can in the gutter, pockets her hands, walks home.

———— • ————

"I think about lots of things when I'm working," she says to Lewis in the dark. "I think about my dad a lot, you know. Kinda wondering what he thought about this place. And you, too, Lew. I think about you all the time. Hey, remember when we first got here and we would go out for dinner and movies and stuff. That was fun, right?"

"Yeah—but that was a long time ago."

"It was two months ago at most. I don't remember. When did I get here, Lew?"

He exhales. The smoke lingers in the glow of the cigarette, soft orange hangs in the black—an effect that reminds her of nothing at all.

"How stoned are you, Gayle?"

"A little. Reminds me of high school."

"Me too. Used to dream of a pretty girl to get stoned with."

She laughs. "Yeah—I guess. Kinda funny we found each other."

———— • ————

Over the course of October, she writes *PRICK* fifteen times, never as large as the first two times time, but hitting every table at least once, some chairs, the foosball table, the front of the bar, just below the taps so all the patrons can read it. She tallies her number against Ares, who scored thirty-three *PRICK*s.

"I took a sharpie and wrote the word on the bottom of a bunch of pint glasses," Ares says. "So as soon as somebody's done their beer, they get a prick in the face."

She smirks, tosses her cigarette butt in the grease disposal unit.

———•———

The boss calls them into his office to ask if they know anything about the *PRICK*s that have been appearing all over the premises. He doesn't say the word. He says, "p—" and makes a zipper motion across his lips.

"Probly some coloured person, no?" Ares says sarcastically, looking around the office: the safe, a monochrome photo of the hotel from 1919, a picture of his wife.

"There's a lot of 'em," he replies.

"Crime's up all around the city," Gayle says. "That's what they said on the radio. It's because of the economy."

He shakes his head and spits some tobacco into a cup. There remains some residue in his gums, so he rubs them with his finger, sucks his saliva back, spits again. He continues doing this until the Gayle and Ares assume it's proper to leave.

When they're out of earshot, Ares puts her hand on Gayle's shoulder. "We gotta slow down with the prick stuff. He's gonna see it's us. *Love* what you did with the spray paint, though. Anyway, I got something else up my sleeve." She winks but doesn't say more.

———•———

Gayle is singing when she comes home one night. She wants to wake Lewis and tell him about her boss and the game she's been playing with Ares, but he's already awake. She finds him coughing violently.

"Are you okay, Lew?"

"I'm sorry."

"Sorry for *what*?"

"I don't want to worry you with this stuff. I try to get out all the bad coughing before you get home." He chuckles and chokes on his chuckle, coughs again.

She forces a smile and then drops it because in the dark he can't see it anyway. She sits beside him, puts her hand on his clammy back.

"I heard you singing," he says after a while. "Why'd you hide that from me for so long?"

"I'm not very good."

"You're very, very good—"

"Ah shush."

"Maybe you can be a singer when it all falls through. The world always needs singers."

"Maybe when we get out of here."

———•———

What Ares has up her sleeve turns out to be using pay phones to call the boss's house when he's out and pretending to be his mistress.

"I call once a week," she explains. "And when his wife answers, I ask for him. Sometimes I just make a groan and hang up."

"Is it working?" Gayle asks.

"Yeah," she says, tossing a butt in the grease disposal unit. "I think it's working."

———•———

In the middle of November, Lewis's shop goes under. He gets laid off and is given two weeks' notice.

"What now?" Gayle asks.

"Don't know."

"It'll work out. Look how far we've come already, you know. We have a plan."

"If I was alone, I could haul up"—he shifts to a whisper—"hit the road."

"But?"

"We're together in this—we're in this together. I want it that way. I love you, Gayle."

"Go to an unemployment agency—or an employment agency. What are they called exactly?"

"They're scams. They take most of your money. Besides, I'm coughing a lot, I'm feeling weaker and—it's kind of embarrassing—but the jobs they give out are labour jobs, construction work and garbagemen. I don't think I can lift heavy stuff."

The nicotine sedates them. That night, the temperature drops below minus ten and the snow falls for good. The basement grows cold, too cold for them to sleep.

———— • ————

At three a.m. they touch their feet together. She lends him warmth.

———— • ————

Gayle arrives late for her shift and finds police cars parked outside the hotel. Two officers are standing in front of the building before the word *P-R-I-C-K*, which remains on the window even after several weeks.

"What's happening?" she asks. "I work here."

"Ah," one officer replies, the older one. "There was a robbery."

"Not exactly a robbery," the younger officer clarifies. "Another employee was caught stealing from the safe. There was a fight."

"She was caught red-handed," the first officer adds.

They step aside to speak amongst themselves, return a few minutes later.

"We can't tell you anything else," says the older one.

"You said it was a woman, though?" Gayle asks. "Name's Ares? Or Arianne?"

"Sorry, miss."

"Is she hurt?"

The younger officer clears his throat, stands tall with his hand on his belt, near the butt of his gun. "The woman's in the hospital. Got a broken nose. There's a lot to this case. Apparently they had a relationship of some kind. She admitted to phoning him at home." He steps closer. "Do you by chance have any information that would be valuable to investigators?"

Gayle doesn't answer. She tries to enter the building. It's locked, but the police let her try anyway. Then she goes to the side of the building and looks in another window, a clean one. She sees the office door open, someone in uniform inside, examining what looks like bloodstains on the carpet.

———— • ————

On her way home, she stops at a used bookstore and buys a book of haiku for a dime. She leaves it under Lewis's pillow for him to find when he goes to sleep.

chapter fourteen
- 1972 -

Gayle was used to seeing her father only in the summertime, the sunshine. Only once did he return in the winter for a few days during his holiday break. But he was quiet and irritable the whole time, in one of his "onanistic states," as her mother unhelpfully explained it to her. He wore the same wrinkled sweatshirt the entire time until it began to smell. He ate his meals in bed and split his time between crying and listening to Ruth complain about money—either how it was killing them, or how they didn't have enough of it. Eventually the pressure became too much, and he took a cab back to the airport in the middle of the night.

The following summer, Ruth is six months pregnant. When he comes home, he says "Would you look at *that*," as though unaware of his role in the situation, which even Gayle—who has listened to enough late-night radio to know exactly how procreation works—finds unusual. And with his ear pressed against the expecting belly, he looks just like the piano man pressing his ear against the wood to compare notes. Her parents explain nothing about having a sibling, about what to expect, so Gayle doesn't think much about it.

While her mother stays in bed, her father puts on faded jeans, a straw hat, and a white shirt rolled past the elbows and spends two days digging out a wider bed to plant the sunflowers in. When it's done, Gayle helps him crumble manure, toss the seeds, and soak them with the garden hose.

———•———

The day Ami is born, he drives them all to the hospital. He keeps Gayle entertained in the waiting room with a game. He takes triangular cups from the water cooler, sets them lip-down on the edge of the table, and they attempt to flip them with their fingers so they land with the pointed side up.

While they play, she tells him how sad and lonely she is when he's away, how much she looks forward to him coming home each summer.

"What about your schoolmates?" he asks. "A lovely girl like you must have plenty of kids to play with."

"I don't have friends."

She's twelve now, soon going into sixth grade at an all-grade school. It's true that she has no friends, which she puts down to her limp and the fact that she's older than the other kids in her class. She missed a year when they relocated and had to be held back.

He begins considering solutions to her loneliness but is soon called away by a doctor, and Gayle is brought to the kids' playroom until her mother gives birth.

———◆———

While her mother recovers in the hospital, she and her father have the house to themselves. She learns that he's a far better cook than her mother. Over a bowl of stew and freshly baked bread, he tells her he knows how to fix her loneliness.

"I knew you would," she says.

"Just wait. Let it be a surprise."

———◆———

A few days later, a truck with an animal trailer arrives and drops off three cows, which are taken to the barn. Her father also goes to the store to buy a glossy illustrated book about how to take care of them. But after reading it, he decides it's written by a money-grubbing hack. She agrees with him, being too young to understand the technical language.

So they improvise. They learn by intuition how to milk the animals. It isn't much different than learning to play the piano by ear, she thinks. You experiment with different ways of moving your fingers until you figure it out. The cows are lethargic and, like the piano, they just let it happen.

Her father develops a technique of focusing on the wrist, running the hands down slowly and rhythmically to the teat and applying very little pressure.

———◆———

When her mother comes home with Ami, she seems to Gayle to be stronger and more energetic than ever in all matters except taking care of the baby. Her parents enthusiastically take up the hobby of building storage cabinets and spend most of their time in the shed with old saws and chisels that came with the property. For reasons Gayle can't quite understand, seeing her parents holding sharp objects makes her nervous. She spends her spare time indoors feeding and changing Ami and—once her sister is asleep—feeding the cows and mucking out the stable.

One day, feeling exhausted, Gayle decides she'd prefer not to be home and asks her father to take her somewhere, anywhere, far away.

He takes her to the stables to visit Abby the horse.

The stable yard is full of people cantering and jumping hurdles, training for some kind of competition. Horses weave in and out of each other's paths in synchronized patterns.

They find Abby waiting in the stable. She, like Gayle, waited all year for him to return. She has a large compound to herself and trots to the fence when she sees him.

He takes a handkerchief from his pocket, wipes a line of dried dirt away from Abby's forehead, and kisses it.

"I miss this beast all year," he says. And then to the horse: "Life is a dungeon when you don't have the fresh breeze and open fields for company. In all that noise and decay, I remember you."

"I want to ride her," Gayle says.

"I know." He saddles the horse and they take her to the exercise yard.

"Don't we need other things?" she asks. "The other people have special boots."

"Oh no. Abby's gentle."

He holds Gayle between his knees and she rings her arms around Abby's neck. They ride around the perimeter of the yard for half an hour. Her father speaks not to Gayle, but to the horse. He speaks poetry. "Speaks poetry" is the only way Gayle can describe to herself what he's doing, and soon realizes that he isn't even speaking to the horse so much as to himself. About time, space, the imagination.

Work things, she thinks. Serious things he does in Edmonton.

"Droll—Draughter—Laughter—A lamp that swings—God's conjecture—"

But as they pull back into the stable, something spooks the animal. She bucks hard and both of them fall. Her father lands on his side and smoothly climbs back to his feet, but Gayle lands headfirst onto the hoof-compacted dirt.

He pulls her to her feet, but she falls again.

A crack in time—and suddenly she's in his arms before the doors to the Salmon Arm hospital, and then a nurse is bandaging her head, explaining something about standing as little as possible.

"Until the dizziness subsides, and give her water and this—"

"Okay."

The nurse also suggests crutches to take pressure off her knee. "It appears a little nicked. She's limping."

"No," her father says. "That's hers."

———— ◆ ————

At the farm, her mother holds the baby in the crest of her arm and takes Gayle's shoulder with her free hand, forcing her around to get a better look at the bandage. In the end, Ruth shakes her head, says nothing, and lets go.

Gayle stumbles up to her room and listens through the thin floorboards to her parents fighting. It's the first she's heard them fight, or even raise their voices.

"As far as I see it, you have *one job* as a father. *Not kill your daughter.* You've fucked up the rest, so can you just do that one right?"

"Ruth—"

"*She's not allowed to do high-intensity activities.* Were you not there when she was born? That's exactly what the doctors said when she came out deformed. She's not allowed to do high-intensity activities. Remember, huh?"

Hearing herself called "deformed" makes Gayle cry. Her parents lower their voices, and the discussion morphs into something less spiteful. But when Ami starts crying too, they have to shout again to make themselves heard.

Gayle hears her mother call her father "insane" before immediately taking the word back, apologizing, and replacing it with "useless." She takes this back, too, and finally clarifies that what she means is "unproviding," before asking if this is a word at all.

"You need to sell the horse, Al. How do you justify the fees? We can hardly afford—"

"No."

"We'll lose the fucking house."

"Things like that don't happen to people like us."

"People like us? What, artists? Writers? Writers don't make money, Al. That hasn't been a real career for hundreds of years. You're keeping your job."

"You don't understand how hard it is for me."

"Keep your job or I'll hit you with this pan."

"Ruth—"

"The world is full of goddamn failures. Why don't we try to avoid that?"

"Because we're not the world. We're us. Remember what we've been through? We survived—"

Ami stops crying. There are a few minutes of silence.

"Have hope," her father says. "Dance with me?"

"Will you play 'I Need a Dollar'?"

It's one of her mother's half-jokes. A moment later, her father puts on a Bill Wither record and Gayle hears soft steps back and forth in the parlour.

———◆———

She hears them fight again a few days later. But it isn't a screaming match like before, and she wonders whether it was a fight at all.

Her mother falls to the ground in the upstairs storage room where the new cabinets are, and the thud reverberates through the house. Her father runs up the stairs, and the two of them descend a few minutes later, he with his arm around her shoulders. They look pathetic, lethargic like the cows, moving so slowly that her mother seems to have aged immensely and needs help balancing.

There is a tear on her mother's cheek that neither of them attempt to brush away, although there is only one and, with his ever-present handkerchief, her father easily could. It's as though they want it there, large and poised indiscreetly on her mother's jawbone, gleaning against the backdrop of her mother's abnormally paled face.

Then Gayle notices that her father is carrying a painting under his free arm, the painted side against his body and smearing on his trousers.

"You're okay alone here for a while?" her father asks.

Gayle nods.

"You'll look after your sister?"

———◆———

They don't return until the evening. Her mother's colour is back, the tear gone and so is the painting. He brings her to bed and then goes to the library to smoke a cigar. Gayle follows him in.

"Where'd you go?"

"Just out for a drive."

"You and Mum have a fight?"

"No. Your mother's resting but it's nothing to be worried about. She needs some alone time."

"I get it, Dad—I'm almost thirteen."

"I know you do. You understand a lot for your age."

He kisses her on the forehead and sends her on her way. She doesn't understand.

———◆———

The next morning, her father calls her into the library again. Aside from the light, the scene is the same. He sits on the same armchair, legs crossed. He always sits like that, she thinks. Like a girl. Like her female peers sit on the school steps at lunch. Shoulders pulled together, taking up as little space as possible. Only, instead of ChapStick behind his ear, he has a cigar.

She sits on the sofa across from him. He takes the cigar but doesn't light it, using it rather like a conductor's wand, accenting his words.

"Gayle?"

"Yes?"

"What you saw yesterday—"

"Mhmm?"

"Don't think anything of it."

"I know."

"It's been hard on her recently. Having a baby is—difficult. Do you understand?"

"Yes."

He stands abruptly. "I'm going to let you in on a secret," he says, turning toward a bookshelf labelled *19ᵗʰ CENT.*, cocks his head to scan the spines before taking a slim black volume from between two thick grey ones.

"You know we're not like others," he says as he flips through the book. "You, your mother and me. I know you noticed it."

She nods.

He begins to read: "If you can talk with crowds and keep your virtue—Or walk with Kings—nor lose the common touch—If neither foes nor loving friends can hurt you—If all men count with you, but none too much—"

He pauses, looks at her. She is fixated on the gap left between the two thick grey books, how without the black one between them they lean on each other, a long shadowy triangle cut between their bodies.

"If you can fill the unforgiving minute—" he continues, "With sixty seconds' worth of distance run—Yours is the Earth and everything that's in it. And—"

He closes the book, sets it on the desk and retakes his seat.

"There's more," she says. "It didn't end."

"No," he says, "it didn't. But *you're* the one who must finish it. My flesh and blood. No one else will." He swallows. "No one else will. The world isn't made for us. *We* make the world for us."

He folds his hands on his lap and stares at her. For the first time, she becomes uncomfortable in his presence. It was the words *no one else* that did it. They scared her.

She wants to tell him he's wrong, that there's not "no one," there's *him*. He will help her. She wants to ask him to make sure she's right, that she has him to rely on. But she doesn't—that would dampen the time they have together.

He lights his cigar, signalling that he'd like to be left alone now, so Gayle goes out to the sunflower patch and looks for moths.

———————

By the end of the summer, she's tall enough that he no longer has to lean on his knees and hunch his back to be eye level with her. He only has to lean on his knees. The day before he goes back to Edmonton, he meets her in the barn while she keeps the cows company.

"They're in good hands," he says, eye-to-eye, "but we forgot to name them."

She'd never thought about it. She knows the horse is named Abby, and Abby was smarter and more human than even some humans. That's why she deserves a nice name.

Put on the spot, she says, "How about Ami, Al, and—Shakespeare."

He laughs. "You can't name the cows after your family. That would be confusing."

"Then Haydn, Chopin, and—Shakespeare?"

"Three lovely ladies."

chapter fifteen
- 1972 -

While he's home, Al is enthusiastic to help Ruth with the cabinets. Back in Victoria, they once discussed a common goal of applying themselves tangibly, working with their hands. Now they want something to truly call *theirs*. Not their art, which they pursue separately, but a collaboration.

It takes a while to get used to handling the saws. They spend many afternoons in the hardware storing asking for advice on fitting doors, aligning joints, treating balsam. With every success, however minor, they congratulate each other on how far they've come since their days in the suburbs—now they can not only name the screwdrivers but can discuss the pros and cons of each.

They finish in July. But even despite their honest efforts, the cabinets are nothing special. She sees only when they're done how poor of a job they did sanding. Beneath the lacquer are hundreds of white lines from where they worked the wood against the grain. Most of the cabinets are uneven, and they need to stick small towels under one or more of the legs.

"I'm proud of us," he says.

Ruth places her fingers on the wood, feeling the defects. "Our tall, boxy, wooden kids."

He finds a retractable knife and inside the door of each cabinet carves their initials and the date of completion: *A & R W. 1972.*

"Next summer we'll do the gazebo or finish up the porch," he says.

"Too bad the working season is so short. Otherwise I'd be able to do something right for once."

"Some new gardens, too," he adds. "Edibles, I'm thinking. We'll be self-sufficient before you know it."

———•———

One day, something in Ruth's mind snaps. A synapse misfires. In the upstairs storage room, looking for free space in the cabinets to store a painting, she feels a pang of disgust—for herself, for her work. The incomplete landscape, a woodland scene replete with squirrels and an obscured brown object that may or may not have evolved to become a bear, ends up on the floor, paint-down, and she falls with it.

Her husband runs up the stairs.

"What happened, Ruth? I heard a sound."

"Fuck," she whispers, turning to the fallen canvas. "Fuck me, fuck you, fuck everything." It's a whisper like a scream. It hurts her throat but hardly moves beyond it. Her head is on the floor. "What am I doing?"

"You've made a remarkable forest scene—"

"But why?"

He bends over to rub his thumbs gently between her knuckles. Then he goes to her supply cabinet and finds the retractable knife, turns it back and forth under the sunlight to make sure the blade is fresh and sharp.

He lifts her to her feet and takes the painting under his arm, the painted side against his clothes so she doesn't see it. They're working clothes anyway. They should have some marks. As they leave the room, Ruth spends the last of her energy to slam the door behind them and begins to cry from sudden exhaustion.

They descend the stairs, past Gayle and Ami, to the car, and drive ten kilometres down the road where there's a small turnoff into the woods. They park by the shoulder and proceed into the trees on foot.

There is no traffic on that road, but they go far enough that they couldn't be seen if there was. He leans the painting against the trunk of a tree and gives her the knife.

"Kill?" she asks.

He nods.

She falls to her knees, eye-to-eye with the squirrels and the burgeoning bear, and breathes. Air travels from the pit of her stomach to her nostrils. Breathing meditation. Nothing complicated. When her body calms, she presses the blade into the top of the canvas and slides it to the middle. She jerks it to the far left, then the far right. It falls open and gawks. She stabs, punches it with her spare fist, slashes and tears at random, unconcerned with the possibility of slipping and cutting herself. She doesn't stop until the thing in front of her is no longer recognizable as the woods. It looks like the sail of a long-sunken, long-forgotten ship. The half-bear is dead.

She squeezes the blade between her index finger and thumb. The metal is warm.

———◆———

They return to the woods the next day but not to the same spot. Neither had kept track of where the murdered canvas is. Instead they wander through gentle scenery until they come to a small clearing with a thin creek moving so slow it could be mistaken for stagnant.

He sets up lawn chairs.

She doesn't have the easel, but a blank sixteen by twenty-inch canvas that she can easily position on her knees, and a plywood table to hold her palette, water, and brushes.

They stay all afternoon. She doesn't paint her surroundings, but rather outlines in brown and black the feeling of a murderer redeemed. Like Aṅgulimāla, she thinks, remembering Doctor Phil Parker's lecture on the topic. Aṅgulimāla: the most complex man in history, the serial killer and mutilator who achieved enlightenment after the Buddha told him to simply *stop*. Stop. It was right before his thousandth kill.

After half an hour, her husband rests on a patch of grass by the creek. He lies on his side, not facing her, and falls asleep until she's done what she needs to do. She wakes him by running her fingers through his silver hair.

"Better?" he asks.

They make swift love on the patch of feathery grass. Ruth notices that it's the kind of grass that doesn't receive enough sun and can't grow beyond the length of a finger. It remains in the throes of spring the whole season until it, too, is murdered by winter.

part four

---◆---

alien
corn

chapter sixteen
- 1979 -

"What does the world need of us?" Ruth asks the empty parlour, her husband's ghost. He can't answer, and she can't imagine how he would respond.

Instead, Bill and Elizabeth stare at her from the canvas. Near the highlight on Bill's retina is a miniscule convex blur that could be her, the artist. *L'Artiste*. That's what I would've been called if I was featured in one of those art books, she says to herself, alongside Matisse or Hayez.

She's been there in his retina for months now, since Bill commissioned the painting. Now it's October. He must be wondering when it'll be done, she thinks. In the back of her mind, she's already given up on producing the portrait he wanted—something simple to give to his nieces to remember him by. No, the painting is more *hers* than *his*. It's her closest companion these days.

She smirks to herself.

———◆———

Snow flies in the Shushwap. The yard, the dead sunflowers, the roof of the barn where the cows are dying, and the overgrown vegetable gardens are whitened. Ruth sees her first glimpse of winter, and her first reaction is self-condemnation. I'm too slow, she thinks. I'm wasting my time. Soon the winter will destroy everything. She has no patience to wait for the next season.

Ami is already dressed for the snow in a cotton-filled coat and waterproof pants that whoosh when she walks.

"Are we gonna watch TV today, Mum?"

"Why aren't you outside waiting for the bus? Is it too cold?"

"It's Saturday."

"Is it now?"

"Sammie's mum's gonna pick me up and we're gonna buy a pumpkin."

She digs through her wallet and gives her daughter a few bills. "Come back by dinnertime."

———◆———

This year, like most years, winter comes with a prelude. By noon, the snow has almost all melted, aside from the deposits under parked vehicles and in the shadows of buildings.

Ruth packs her painting pad, brushes, and a selection of hand-mixed paints adapted from Windsor and Newton's Nostalgic Collection. The colours she wants—earthy, cadaver-esque, autumnal, muted as though behind a thin fog—weren't in the catalogue.

She drives to Bill and Elizabeth's farm. It's Sunday. They're at church, so she has time.

Before she finds a subject, she practices ten minutes of strolling around meditation. Trespassing meditation. She walks the perimeter of the house, eyes skirting the parallel lines of the cedar shakes. Then she branches to the pasture and leans against the fence, examining the muscular picturesque black-and-white cows and the alpaca that shares their quarters. The alpaca stands in an opposite corner from the herd, facing north. The outlier, *l'artiste*. Then she turns to view the distant acre of corn. To her the crop is a line, but to a bird, perhaps, it would appear as a rhombus. There's a hill in the middle of the corn—an island with some coppered trees—and a border mown around the perimeter of it, separating the crop from the adjoining woods and allowing one to walk around the corn, even to hide behind it.

She decides to sketch the furrows in the grass that the tractor has left behind, which occasionally break the surface and reveal dirt. The lines undulate toward a distant shed. The waves in the field—they're a pleasing enough shape.

By ten o'clock she feels she's pushing her luck, so she packs up and jogs to the car.

———◆———

She returns several times over the course of October. She goes every Sunday without fail, but also the odd day in between. On those days, she parks her car on the long driveway, behind the trees and hidden from the house, and banks on nobody leaving or entering the property for the next couple hours. She gets the impression that they don't have much company other than herself.

In case they're home, she wears dark clothing and treks through the forest to avoid being spotted. From the treeline she can still get decent angles of the house and the shed. It's difficult to move through the woods with her pencils, pad, and paint box in tow, and by the end of it she's covered in grime and needles. Luckily there are no mosquitoes this time of year.

Being forced to inhabit the woods comes with the advantage of uncovering things such as abandoned wasp hives, bits of litter caught in trees, or the more intrepid autumn flowers.

Her greatest find is an abandoned tree house in the woods east of the house. It's the haunting kind of beautiful. The beauty of things children once loved but no longer do. Many loose boards hang by single nails. The planks are covered in at least two kinds of lichen, which alternate between white-green and yellow.

The tire swing contains an abandoned nest, and a child had long ago carved their name into one of the support beams: *Willy*.

———◆———

She compiles dozens of pages of the house, the vehicles, the shed, the corn, the cows, the alpaca (even if the primary subject is a cow, she ensures the alpaca is included in the background, or on the edge of the field), and Willy's tree house.

This done, she attempts to draft a list of beauties in her head. A list of things that add credence to what she's collected on the page. Things she can point to and say, when someone asks, *this* is what artists are doing. They are finding beauties where no one else can. Things the modern world no longer has a place for, or never did.

To stand in these forgotten parts and extract their beauties: It's like setting a bucket below a waterfall and using it to fill a bathtub.

Bill finds her one morning, poised on a stump beside the yet-to-be-hewn corn.

"Ruth—what are you doing?"

"Hope I didn't wake you."

"Of course you didn't. Lizzy just looked out the bedroom window there and said, 'Hey, Bill, I think there's someone out in the field.' Well I looked for myself and saw you there, and I thought, well, it's not a good idea to be walking around like that in the winter."

"It's hardly winter yet, Bill. I'm just doing some studies."

"I see."

"That's something artists say when they're dicking around."

"Well you better come in and warm up. There's still frost out here and you've got a fall jacket on by the look of it."

"Give me fifteen."

She continues with her labour. But the paints she mixed herself will not settle—perhaps they're old, she thinks, watching oil seeping up through clumps of pigments.

But it's just a study. She aims to lay out a scene in blocks: the house, a childish house of squares and triangles, the trees a flutter. A long, angled boar's-hair brush set on its side and rolled across the pad in an inconsistent line will suffice as a stand-in for the universe of pale morning light moving between stalks of corn, which is the most complex element of this scene and could consume a month if she was so inclined.

——— • ———

"You're gonna freeze to death out there," Elizabeth says as she places a bowl of chowder and a wedge of cheese on the table.

"I'm used to it. Running out of firewood at home. Hey, you have any more newspapers I can burn?"

"Oh, woman."

Ruth tears a piece of cheese and drops it in the chowder, stirs with a spoon. "I'm getting closer to the *feel* I need."

"I really don't think it's so imp—"

"Liz," Bill interrupts. "She's painting our property. She's doing us a favour."

"Of letting us pick the frost from her eyebrows when she's dead?"

Ruth laughs. "I'm good at favours, but not flavours. What's in this, dill?"

"No," says Elizabeth. "No dill."

"I thought I could smell dill. Maybe my senses are going. Anyway, listen, I've been giving a lot of thought to the project. The portrait, I mean. I'll have something for you by December. Once winter's in, I'll have no choice but to paint faster to keep myself warm." She holds her spoon like an epee and pretends to spar with an invisible opponent across the table, dropping melted cheese and chowder on the floor. "Of course, it'll have to dry a bit before I can varnish it."

"That's very nice, Ruth," Elizabeth says.

"I've even had some dreams of putting all these paintings of your farm on display for a while—so the world can see it—see *you*—in a gallery. You know what I mean?"

"I'm familiar with what a gallery is, Ruth."

"People in Victoria fill whole galleries with blotches and triangles and call them 'Marbles' or 'Starfish.' You ever see this collection?"

"Funny."

"It's all a bit funny," Ruth says, shrugging. "But me, I've got honest eyes. I see what's there. That's me, a see-er, a look-er. I see a starfish as a starfish. A field as a field. Life as life. I'm a real looker, wouldn't you agree?"

No one laughs.

Elizabeth walks to the doorway. "Enjoy the chowder, Ruth."

When she's gone, Ruth feels lighter. She smiles at Bill. "Can I call you William?"

"William's fine—Bill's fine."

"Willy?"

"That's fine, too."

"I noticed something interesting out in your woods—a tree house?"

"That's what it was. Still is, I guess, but there's no one playing on that these days. Haven't had kids around here since I was a kid—oh, maybe forty or so—"

"What you have is something special," she cuts him off. "A kind of experiment in paradise. There's *something* here. I can't explain it. It's not new, it's not old, it's sort of timeless. Do you know the Book of Ruth?"

"Ah, the Bible?"

"Do you remember when Ruth lays herself at the sleeping man's feet and they make love with corn sticking to their bodies?"

"Ah—no—I—"

"That's the best way I can explain it because I'm not a poet like my husband. Do you know what I mean?"

"I'm not sure I do, Ruth."

She gazes around the kitchen, the fridge full of magnets and photos of their and other peoples' weddings. "Do you know much about plumbing, Bill?"

"A little, as a homeowner ought to do."

"I don't know spit about it, but I've got a problem with my kitchen sink. I know I keep bothering you with these things, but Bill, I honestly can't afford a professional plumber—and I was hoping you know somebody." She smiles.

He doesn't smile back.

"No money coming in," she explains. "At least not right now. We had a boy working for us for a bit, but I kicked him out for trying to steal my daughter. I paid him off."

"I'm happy to pay you good for the portrait, Ruth. I can give you a bit right now to tide you over."

"That's not what I'm getting at. I just—listen—I don't like talking to people on the phone, so I can't call the plumber. It's strange, right? I can't explain it."

———————◆———————

Before he arrives, she spends a few minutes with the portrait-in-progress.

Elizabeth and Bill side-by-side on the steps of their porch. His face is done better than hers, much better. The lines are more confident, the lips like dips on the edge of a riverbank, the hair feathered like the down of a duck. To represent him, she had to repurpose the things she understood from the natural world to fit the human face.

Now she uses a fat Filbert brush to feel the paint, to smudge, to blend the contours of the cheekbone and pull the shadow away from the invisible sun.

She holds it side by side with Francesco Hayez's portrait of Ruth to compare.

As she does, she notices another distinction between herself and the Biblical Ruth. It has to do with labour—not the quantity, but the quality. Labour is distinct from work, she thinks, because the former carries an inherent hardship, whereas the latter does not necessarily. Labour is livelihood. One labours not for fulfillment or pleasure, but for life. Ruth laboured to make herself at home in an alien environment. She laboured until she met Boaz. Labouring in the sun is not the same as working in the sun, as one can "work in the sun" on a hobby garden, or they build cabinets. But labouring is what Bill does as a farmer: if he stops, he starves.

But an artist, she thinks, if they are genuine, will also starve when the labouring stops.

She hides her portrait when she hears a clunk by the front door. It's Bill dropping his tool box.

"Do you want to wear your hat inside?" she asks as she lets him in.

"It's all the same to me." He leaves it on and proceeds to the kitchen. "Probably just a loose valve. I'm gonna open up your cupboard below the sink there and take a look."

Ruth goes to her knees to be side-by-side with him. He uses the edge of his wrench to tap on the cast iron pipe—why, she doesn't know. Then he reaches deeper, toward a valve against the wall, making his shirt cuffs slide up to his shoulder, revealing a tight, pulsing muscle. Ruth tries to join him in the confined space, to feel his aura in the dark. Using her hands to guide her, she slides into the cupboard until only her legs are outside. He shifts as far away from her as possible and clears his throat.

"I just want to see what's going on," she says, resisting the urge to fall into him and lay her head on his back.

"I can smell something—like rubber. You having electricity problems?"

"I dunno. We did a little wiring back here years ago."

Small footsteps enter the kitchen. Ruth pulls out with hot embarrassment, thinking that if her husband comes home now, this is the worst way to see her.

She turns to see Ami load a pumpkin onto the table. One of the legs breaks, and the table and pumpkin crash to the floor.

Ruth catches the pumpkin and steadies it. "Splendid."

"I got the tools for that in the box, Ruth," Bill says. He stands and brushes his knees.

The guilt fades from Ami's face and is replaced with a shy grin. "Hi."

"Hello there—I didn't know you were home."

"It's Thursday," Ami says, "so kids get off early and the bus driver takes us home super fast 'cause he wants to go home and watch Johnny Carson. That's what he says."

"My name's Bill. What's your name?"

"Ami with an *i*."

He holds out his hand.

"Shake his hand, Ami," Ruth says.

The girl does. "You wanna help me with my Jack the Lantern? Mum's too busy."

"Where'd you get that pumpkin?" Ruth asks. "You didn't steal it, did you?"

"No, Mum. Miss Barker says we get extra points for doing a Jack the Lantern. And you gave me the money, I thought?"

Bill looks to Ruth, as though asking permission to respond to Ami's invitation. Ruth shrugs.

"I can do that," Bill says.

"And it's Jack o' Lantern," Ruth says. "*Oh. Oh.*"

"Oh." Ami rolls the pumpkin out of the kitchen.

It takes Bill ten minutes to fix the leaking faucet because he doesn't have the correct wrench and Ruth has to find an adjustable crescent wrench in the shed. While she searches for it, he fixes the table.

When everything's finished, Ruth follows him to the driveway.

"Thanks, Bill—and listen, I have something I want to tell you—something I was thinking about. It's gonna sound a little crazy, like I'm from another world or something." She laughs nervously, clears her throat.

"Ruth?"

"Sorry—what I was going to say is—"

"Is this about the pumpkin?"

"Ah—no—I wanted to talk about the studies I've been doing of your farm. I had an idea—and for years I've been putting it off, but I think I know how to, I don't know, move forward as an artist. I took a long time. But you've given me—I mean, your place has given me—"

"Don't be worried, Ruth. I'm good with kids. I've looked after kids from church from time to time."

"I'm—" Her mouth hangs open.

"Why don't we talk about this when you come by to carve the pumpkin?"

———— • ————

Bill's table is already covered in newspaper (it's from last week—no headlines about her husband's disappearance), and a metal ladle and a serrated knife are laid out.

"We picked up a couple things at the hardware store," Bill says as he takes the pumpkin and steadies it on the newspaper.

"You didn't have to."

"It'll make things easier—eh, Liz?"

"Don't chuck the guts," she replies. "We can use 'em for soup."

Elizabeth leaves. Ami takes a stool and Ruth moves closer to Bill.

"I've never done this," she whispers.

"I'll show you. I got a couple extra pumpkins so we can all make one." He pulls two more from below the table, smaller but perfectly shaped.

"Your wife isn't into this?" Ruth asks.

"She's the cook of the house. I'm the fun guy."

Bill uses the serrated knife to cut a circle around the stem and hands Ruth the knife to do the same. Then she gives the knife to Ami, who struggles with it. The blade doesn't catch the flesh and it slips, leaving a nick in the table.

"Here," Ruth says. She holds her daughter's hand, which holds the knife, and they force it through together and make a circle.

"Great," Bill says.

Next they toss the guts into a plastic bowl and scrape out the dangling bits.

"Now the fun part," he says. "We get to decide what he looks like. Do we want a *scarrrry* face?" He scowls, and Ami laughs. "Or a *nice* face?"

The face Bill makes is the conventional two triangles and a jagged line. He gives the knife to Ruth, who passes it to Ami, who makes the same face as Bill, except that the jagged line is smiling.

"It's your mummy's turn," Bill says with a wink. "The artist."

Ruth takes the knife handle in a death grip and plunges the blade into the pumpkin, near the top. With messy, imperfect lines, she finds the face of Wile E. Coyote.

"Bravo," says Bill, clapping his hands. He sets lit candles in all three pumpkins, draws the blinds, and turns the lights off. "Ready for all the trick-or-treaters."

"We don't get those," Ruth replies.

"Nah, it must be 'cause you leave your lights off."

"We don't live in town."

"We always get a couple. Their parents drive 'em."

"Well I guess they avoid me."

Elizabeth enters and turns the lights on. "I gotta get dinner going."

"Will you join us?" Bill says, looking at Ruth, then Ami.

Ami looks to her mother.

"I can pick her up at seven," Ruth says.

On Halloween, Bill and Elizabeth agree to take Ami trick or treating with some of her friends. Ruth dresses her daughter as a fairy—a bedsheet thrown over a winter jacket and covered in glitter—and sends her on her way.

The evening news explains how smoke was seen streaming from the baggage compartment of a plane. The flight made an emergency landing in Virginia. There were no casualties, but detectives are drawing lines between this incident and the bomb that was sent to the university in Chicago earlier this year. Ruth mutes the TV and watches the anchor's lips. The face is calm, whispering before a shrunken image of trembling survivors. The cause of the fire was again a homemade bomb. The word TERRORISM appears at the bottom of the screen.

Random, she thinks. All random. Anything could happen at any time. She toys with the theory that the bombs are being sent by no one in particular. That they are simply materializing from the ether, through a tear in the fabric of time.

"What's this, Mum?"

"The news, Ami—again. I don't know why you have to keep asking."

"Sorry." Ami drops a pillowcase of candy on the floor and then brings her hollowed, softening pumpkin through the house, to the back door. Then she carries Ruth's. Then Bill's.

"What are you doing?" Ruth asks.

"Halloween's over, Mum."

"I know—but—"

"Bill said I should give 'em to the cows 'cause it's like candy."

"You sound like Bill, alright."

"Not too much, though. Half a pumpkin a day 'cause they're sick."

Ami leaves them outside by the back door and goes upstairs to change. She comes back in pyjamas and slippers, teeth brushed.

"It's cold in here, Mum."

"Put the sheet back on if you're cold. And don't eat sugar before bed or you'll get in the habit of it."

Ruth turns off the news and tries to leave the parlour, but Ami grabs the edge of her sweater.

"What's this for? You'll stretch it."

"You okay up there, Mum?"

"Up there?"

"Mhmm."

"That's a grown-up question. Did Elizabeth and Bill say that?"

Ami lets go and collects her pillowcase.

———◆———

The next morning, Ami comes to her in tears.

She follows her daughter to the barn, but they don't enter. Ami stands by the door, shaking. Ruth sighs and pushes in.

Lifeless cows in November leave no smell. Filling the barn is the same mix of sour milk and fresh manure that sticks to a person's clothes if they spend too much time in it. But one of them, the cow Gayle called Shakespeare, is dead and lying on its side. One of the survivors is licking the lifeless neck, and the other is scraping its teeth against the pumpkin that Ami dropped when she saw the corpse.

Even dead cows, Ruth observes, produce enough warmth to keep their biggest adversary, the fly, alive and healthy.

"How'd this happen? I just milked them two days ago—she seemed fine."

"Mum—"

"I don't know, Ami."

"Mum."

"What?"

"Gayle'll be sad.... Can we bury it?"

"Bury it?"

"Like the bunny."

"The one you and Gayle stole years ago, buried it by the sunflowers?"

Ruth nudges the dead cow's elbow with her heel—the limb sways easily back and forth. But the rest of it is far too heavy to move.

"What do we do, Bill?" she says into the receiver.

"Well jeez—a farmer's got a couple options here. I've had it happen. I hauled her well away from the house with chains and poured diesel on her, let her burn. It's the safest way if you do it right—doesn't leave nothing but the bones. If it were summer, I'd say you drop her in the woods and let the buzzards get her. But—"

"Ami wants it buried."

"That's right. You don't want her to see all that."

"The ground's not frozen yet."

"I don't have a backhoe. You got any spades, Ruth?"

"Just one."

———◆———

He tows a trailer carrying a tractor. He exits the vehicle and withdraws his own spade from the back seat.

They leave a tarp over the corpse as they excavate around the flower bed. Ruth indicates where to dig so they don't disturb the rabbit bones. The sunflowers are all dead and the soil in the patch is softer than the surrounding earth, so they pull out some of the flowers to allow for more room.

———◆———

The work is slow. It takes them an hour and a half to dig a six-by-six-foot hole one foot deep. But the clay is higher than they thought, and the rainy summer has left it moist. Head-sized clumps stick to their spades.

"It's no good," Bill says.

"We'll try—"

"It'll be sundown by the time get deep enough and we shouldn't let the thing rot in the barn."

"So what then?"

"We make a mound—take some dirt from around and throw it on top so it's covered."

The tractor has a box installed. As Bill drives it to the barn and pushes the lip under the corpse, Ruth uses her spade to chop out the rest of the sunflowers.

Soon Bill drives back and drops the animal into the shallow grave.

One of its eyes falls out when it hits the clay, and it lands with its legs splayed. Ruth pushes the limbs into the hole with the edge of her boot and begins tossing dirt.

———◆———

The sun is nearly set by the time they finish. Scarlet streams in from the west.

The mound is up to Ruth's knees. She walks around the perimeter and uses the back of the spade to pack it down.

"I'll get Ami," she says.

When they return, they see two sticks tied together in a cross and planted in the centre of the mound.

"I had some twine in my pocket," Bill says. "The cross—it's in my nature."

Ami stands between the adults.

"Do you have any words, Bill?" Ruth asks.

"Nothing comes to mind. I've never been to a funeral like this before."

Ami breaks into stifled tears. Ruth holds her hand over her daughter's shoulder and slowly lowers it onto the slippery material of her jacket. The crying stops, but the girl is leaning the other way, drying her eyes on Bill's pocket. He squeezes her other arm gently.

"Okay Ami," Ruth says. "You'd better go now. I left some casserole in the oven for you. It's off but it should still be warm, so use mitts."

Ami trudges back to the house.

"It's almost dark," he says.

"What's going on, Bill?" She turns away, toward the bloody light fading behind a mountain in the west.

"What do you mean?"

"She likes you a lot. It's a little strange, isn't it?"

"We took her out trick-or-treating. That's all. I don't mean to do any harm by that."

"No, no harm. It's good for a girl to have—that. Her and her sister were best friends, you know."

"I heard."

"I get why Gayle would leave me, but I don't get why she'd leave Ami. I sure as hell don't get why my husband would leave his girls. He was the good cop."

"Ami's a brave girl," Bill says.

"She's too young to be brave," Ruth says. "I wish she would break down."

"Ruth—"

"It would ease my mind if she did."

"She's a tough cookie. She takes after you."

Ruth walks a few paces back to the house, crosses her arms, returns to the mound. "No. Not me. Don't even say that."

He moves closer, makes as though he will embrace her but stops.

"Kids just need to get out once in a while," he says. "If you'd be okay with it, Lizzy and I don't mind the company."

"Kids need things, do they?" She wipes her nose on her sleeve.

"You getting chilly?"

"Don't take this the wrong way, but you're not a dad. It's not like you think. You don't *know*."

He coughs. "No, you're right. I don't need to do anything about it."

She looks him in the eye. What a familiar sight, she thinks. She sees her reflection behind the glimmer on his iris, miniscule and submerged in saltwater.

"I'd be happy if you looked after her once in a while," she yields. "She needs it. I'm busy these days with the paintings. Very busy. Besides, I'm hoping to take a trip back to Victoria soon."

"Gonna visit some friends?"

She pauses for a moment. "Yes."

They walk to the driveway and stand by Bill's truck.

"What about the tractor?" she asks.

"It's dark now. I'll come back for it."

———◆———

When he returns the next day to pick up the tractor, she asks him again if he can do anything about the cows, at least the two that remain. He agrees to take care of the problem.

"I can't take 'em in with my herd though, you understand? We know for sure that it ain't milk fever, so it could be contagious, whatever they got."

"How much does it cost—the needle or—the bolt gun—or whatever?"

"It's covered, Ruth. Just keep working on the portrait."

"Bill—"

"Yeah, Ruth?"

She falls to him, hands around his back, finding his shoulder blades. Her right cheek presses to the centre of his chest. He lets her hold him but keeps his arms to his side.

"Why are you so good to us?" she asks.

"It's how I was raised," he responds immediately, as though he'd prepared an answer in advance. "It's the duty of a Christian and a good man."

———— • ————

Where are the cows, Mum?"

"They're gone, Ami."

"Where'd they go? They run away?"

"Yeah—"

"Gayle's gonna be upset."

"I know."

When the snow falls the second time, it stays. The yard, the cow's grave, the roof of the empty barn, and the dead garden disappear beneath it. The thermometer dips a few degrees each day until it valleys at minus fifteen, not counting wind chill. The firewood dwindles to nothing, and Ruth and Ami both wear two sweaters and two pairs of socks indoors.

"Cartoons today, Mum?"

"For a bit."

As Ami walks to the TV, Ruth calls, "Wait—no, it's Monday. Go wait for the bus."

"I have time for one."

"Not if you eat breakfast you don't."

Ami sighs, prepares a piece of dry toast for herself and puts on her coat and boots.

"You going to see Bill and Elizabeth after school?"

"We're gonna go sledding."

"Okay."

The girl leaves.

Ruth has sworn off the news definitively. The growing mystery of American domestic terrorism, the outcome of China's one-child policy, the gay rights rallies in Washington, unrest in Kabul, anticipation around an upcoming Pink Floyd album, the weighed failures and successes of Joe Clark's tax cuts—all are left as loose ends.

Instead she watches *Looney Tunes*.

———◆———

I haven't been sucked in by a memory in a while, she thinks. It worked, then—the TV, the distraction meditation.

Her mind emptied into the cosmos, she goes to the easel by the window and tilts her head at the portrait of Bill and Elizabeth.

Painting alla prima, she did the under layers and the background elements first. As she progressed, she found herself pulling colours from the house, the wood, and the distant corn into the faces of the subjects: into their souls, by proxy, if a painting can be said to emulate the soul.

But the humans—what she was most worried about—are adequate.

The portrait will only need a month or a month and a half to dry before it is varnished and framed.

———◆———

Outside is the grave. Although she's never painted her own yard, the time she spent looking at it while she painted her imagination has left it engrained in her consciousness. The awkward bump in the snow where the sunflowers used to be is subtly upsetting. In the snowy world, the colours she needs for the gallery pieces are no longer present, but it's not a problem. She stored colour swatches, sketches, shapes, and composition ideas in a series of books.

Winter, she thinks—no good for writers, who need to wander; death for photographers, who embrace the world as it is; but ideal for painters, who embrace the world as it isn't, who are rewarded if they are still, if they quit even breathing.

She hears a truck pull into the driveway. The door slams. Soon Ami comes in with a red face.

"You knock the snow off your boots, Ami?"

"Yeah Mum."

Ruth knows she didn't. "Okay—you need dinner?"

"Elizabeth says I can go there for lamb."

"You ever had lamb?"

"No, but they wanna know if you wanna come."

"No, no lamb. I'm a little too sheepish—tell them that. Say your mother's too sheepish."

———◆———

For the rest of November, she is rarely away from the paintings. For the first time in her life, she works methodically. A series of sketches turn into a series of underpaintings, which turn into a series of value profiles.

She condenses Bill's property into a collection on the beauty of forgotten places. A resistance to the modern era: the metal triangle of a distant roof, un-palatable swamp water, paradisiacal silence between leaves, animals being ani-mals, things children loved once, grey, green, black and white. Everything lives in the soul. Even Bill's and Elizabeth's faces, who overlook it all, live in the soul.

Her scoliotic back in agony from countless hours of bending toward the easel, one leg asleep from the way she was sitting, lightheaded from turpentine, Ruth hobbles out of the parlour to the hallway phone.

"Of course I remember you," says the voice on the other line. "Ruth—uh, MacLeod?"

"Windsor."

"Oh yes, you were close with Jackson and Wendel?"

"Sure." She doesn't recognize the names. "I don't know if you heard, but I've moved to the mainland with my family."

"Was that you they had that goodbye party for a couple weeks ago? Aw, sorry Ruth—I was out of town and—"

"It was ten years ago. Listen—I've been working on a large collection—landscapes and more. I was hoping to get it displayed."

"Sounds nice, Ruth—but I'm afraid I can't help. Don't know if you heard, but gallery space is being cut back—"

"I'm a local artist. I know there's a quota for that."

"I thought you said you moved."

"I was born on the island. Lived in Victoria for years. What do you want?"

"You gotta go through the arts council or find a sponsor—"

What the hell is an arts council? she thinks. Back in the day, if you hung around the galleries and the cafés by Yates, looked good, wore black, talked to the right people—that's the way the ecosystem of art developed. She still has one shot—it's a stretch, but—

"Annabella," she says. "A petite girl—well, a woman now, probably forty or so. Did lots of work with blotches, reds and browns mostly."

"Umm."

"And wore sunglasses inside."

"It's not ringing a bell."

"Made paintings called 'Marbles' and 'Starfish' done in the—blotch tradition, as I said."

"Annabella Tavistock per chance? The neo-expressionist?"

Yes," Ruth says, "the neo-expressionist. I left that bit out."

She receives a phone number and calls immediately.

"Is this Annabella Tavistock?"

"Yes?"

"My name's Ruth—Ruth Windsor."

"Okay."

"We were friends once—a long time ago. We used to hang around Yates."

"Ruth. *Oh*—you're the shy one?"

"Yeah."

"Married to the professor?"

"I guess."

The stranger on the phone sounds like she's smiling. They exchange pleasantries for several minutes. The feeling of balled electricity that had been sitting in Ruth's chest—nerves, maybe—fades and is replaced with confidence every time the strangers recalls a detail from their fated encounter years ago. The stranger even remembers Ruth's art. Unusual still lifes, they were. A vase carrying knives instead of flowers, the asshole of a cat, and more.

"So you've decided to live 'off-the-grid,' as they say?"

"That's right," Ruth replies. It's a term Ruth has never heard.

"I'm not surprised at all," Annabella says. "The way you acted back then made me think you really weren't happy in the city at all. I'm glad you've finally found your place."

The conversation continues, and Ruth learns that Annabella has put out several books of blotches, co-authored a book on avant-garde painting techniques, taught at a number of colleges, and now curates a gallery in downtown Victoria specializing in Western Canadian art.

"Still institutionalized," Annabella concludes with a laugh.

"And I'm calling for a reason, actually," Ruth says. "I have an idea—a project. A big one. And I'm looking for help getting it to the public."

"I can't guarantee anything. But we're friends. Tell me."

"I think of it as—a—" she regrets beginning this sentence and stutters trying to find a way to conclude it. "A revival of—no. It's a meditation on paradise—making paradise—under modern constraints, if you will. And an exploration of—forgotten things. Things that don't matter. Now. In sunny '79."

"Hmm?"

"I could go on."

"You have time in December to fly over? How about the Christmas break? Enough material for me to look at? Let me tell you, Ruth, it will be a *treasure* to see you again. It's been forever."

chapter seventeen
- 1979 -

Lewis leaves in the morning for his final shift at the shop before being laid off. It's November, the temperature is falling, and Gayle feels guilty about the warm coat she bought when she came to the city. The coat, like her blond hair, feels like a silly luxury now that they're both unemployed. She decided not to wash dishes anymore, as she suspects the owner tried to kill Ares. Thinking about it all—the vandalism, the bloodstains, the patronizing police officers—makes her want to vomit.

Later Li Yong, the homeowner, descends the stairs and knocks on the door to the basement suite. Gayle dresses quickly and opens it.

"I'm very sorry," he says.

"It's colder than it's been."

"The furnace is kaput. This is a little embarrassing."

"It's fine."

"It's a little finicky. It's happened before. I'm going to take a look. May I?"

She lets him in and follows him to the furnace room. He looks under a panel, examines a few pipes.

"I'm used to the cold," Gayle says. "I didn't have much heat growing up."

"But you're my friends down here—I hate to do this to you—but I can't afford to fix it at the moment. And this is bad timing. If you'd like, you can come upstairs. It's a little warmer there. Hot air goes up."

She's only spoken to him once before, on the day she arrived. Aside from seeing his silhouette in the upstairs window when she returned home from work, that meeting has been the extent of their relationship. She never thought of him as an acquaintance, let alone a friend.

"I wouldn't mind for a bit," she says.

———•———

She sits at Li Yong's kitchen table. He's since put on more layers, the last being an Edmonton Eskimos jersey, and begins boiling water for tea. Newspapers and magazines are scattered about at random. The linoleum is covered in grime. The floor is wet from snow tracked in because no one removes their shoes.

"How is Deadmonton treating you?" he asks.

"It is what it is. I don't plan on staying long, you know."

"With the furnace kaput, I'm not sure you'll want to." He smiles a large, loose smile.

"What happened to it?"

"Who knows? I'm just an accountant."

"And you play football?"

He pours the tea through a pasta colander to remove the leaves and fills two mugs. He sits across from her. "I'm just a fan. Aren't you?"

"I've never seen a game."

"Me neither—can't afford it. I mostly just follow stats."

She picks up another magazine and fans through the pages. "Decorating magazines, too?"

"It's my one guilty pleasure."

She looks around the room, the waste.

"I'm interested in this thing called feng shui," he says. "It's a Chinese tradition, but people only do it in North America as far as I can tell."

"Ah—"

"But I haven't had much time for it. Too busy with work."

"Lewis told me you send it all home. The money, I mean."

"Most, yes. To my father and sister. They depend on it."

She remembers hearing on the radio that, somewhere in the world, there exist people who can tell your fortune by looking at the leaves at the bottom your teacup. It only works in places where they don't filter the leaves. There's a single leaf in her cup, which has somehow made its way through the colander.

"Lewis is gonna lose his job," she says. "And I had to leave mine."

"I'm sorry."

"We probably gotta find someplace else. Someplace cheaper, I guess—until we get new jobs."

"Gayle." He looks her in the eye. "Don't think of it."

———◆———

Gayle and Lewis try sleeping with clothes on.

"I don't know," she says, "but it sounds like he'll let us stay as long as we need—without paying in full."

"I wonder why."

"He's a good guy. Said we could go visit him upstairs whenever we need to. 'Cause hot air goes up, I guess."

"We should. We're in a dungeon, anyway."

She laughs. He looks at her, confused.

"Sorry," she says. "When you said 'dungeon,' it made me think of something risqué."

He laughs too. She loves his laugh and missed it. Innocent and boyish—an impression heightened by the fact that he's now sick, weak, can't lift heavy things.

"I'm happy, you know," she says. "In spite of everything—"

———◆———

Li Yong's brow tightens when Lewis mentions his cough and the pain in his stomach. He moves to the stove and they watch him prepare tea. When it's finished, he removes from the fridge a resealable bag containing a quartered lemon and an ounce of shaved ginger.

"I love these things," he says, referring to the resealable bag. He completes the potion and sets it in front of Lewis. "Tea's an old cure, or whatever. So's ginger. The lemon's for taste. Do you have a hangover?"

Lewis smiles. "Not unless it's permanent. But I've never been a tea guy."

"Try it," Gayle nudges.

He does and, after a few sips, declares he's feeling fine.

"Hey Lee," Gayle says after a while. "I'm not sure why you're doing it, helping us out and all, but thank you. You're kind of—I dunno—a saint, I guess."

"I can tell you exactly why. Because you're friends. In Spanish it's said, 'hay que tener amigos hasta en el Infierno.' Edmonton is a kind of hell."

"You speak Spanish?"

"I used to live in Cuba—was sent there by my school in China. It's a communist thing." He smiles. "So I speak four languages, and a little English."

"You speak French?" she asks. "I speak a little French. Un petit peu."

"Bien sûr. I studied the language of love. I thought it would be easier to find a wife then, too. I learned at the university."

Gayle laughs and takes Lewis's elbow. "The university? Did you know my father? He taught there. His name's the same as mine. Windsor."

"It doesn't sound familiar."

When they all finish their tea, Li Yong looks back to Lewis, who is pale, staring at his empty mug. There are no leaves inside. "Fresh air is important," Li Yong says. "That's not a traditional thing, it's just common sense. It's supposed to be warmer today. Un petit peu. Minus ten."

"I guess we should go for a walk," Gayle says. "Like we used to do, you know, when I got here."

———◆———

She takes him down her favourite streets. They find the university, watch young people strolling with books and ambitions, and discuss the beauty of barren oaks and old brick. They pass the houses with Greek letters on the doors. They head east across 109th and into Strathcona, talking about the lives of strangers who leave their front windows open—people with ceiling fans, people watching television, young people celebrating something and drinking Albertan wheat ale from cans.

"I still try to make up stories about people," she says. "They're like houses themselves, you know, with all kinds of rooms in them for exploring. Fantasies are free, so why not?"

"Better sick than bored, I think."

They pass a house whose living room is illuminated by a novelty green light bulb.

"What about that one?" he says. "Who lives there?"

"I think—an insane man. Or a sad man who believes he's an alien and wants to be green."

"Maybe it was for Halloween and he forgot to take it down."

"Oh yeah—I forgot about that. I never did that one, really. My Mum didn't celebrate anything. She'd probably get along with the green man."

"You know, I used to play a game when I was a boy," Lewis says.

"I couldn't play most games—because of the knee."

"It's simple. I was pretty young, though. I used to go to random houses and ring the doorbell. I was usually with a couple buds, and we had a competition to see who could keep the person talking the longest before they closed the door. Sometimes they'd get really upset, shove us around and stuff like that."

"Funny," says Gayle. "I used to play that with my Mum."

Lewis looks down.

"That was a joke," she says.

"I know."

———•———

Dumpster diving is another game Lewis used to play. Gayle doesn't know it. He tells her it's something he learned in Vancouver after his dad died and he ran away from home. It consists of waiting in the alley outside restaurants, grocery stores, and bakeries, scrounging the trash for edibles or other useful things like clothes or furniture. You could wait at a meat shop, too, but you can never trust what's getting tossed. One bad slice and you'll regret it for days.

"At this time of year," he says, "you gotta know what time the stores bring out the trash and to get to it within an hour. Frozen bread you can thaw out and eat just fine, but fruits and vegetables get ruined by the cold."

This game, Gayle realizes, is also a necessity. They're unemployed and need to eat. So they play it every couple of days.

———•———

Occasionally they wait in alleys with other people like themselves, both young and old. They may or may not have a place to live but can't, or choose not to, spend money on food.

"It's always going on," Lewis tells her. "I mean, every day countless things are thrown away—that's just the way our society is. So the dumpster divers usually *get* each other, they share what they find, they don't judge. It's always like that when people have no money."

It turns out to be true. On good days—like Tuesday and Friday, when the chain grocers do a storewide cull—there's up to a dozen people waiting in the alley. They chat, ask each other where they come from, discuss the weather and the Edmonton Eskimos, share smokes. The youngest and tallest amongst them haul plastic bags from the dumpster and together they sift through them, make piles, divide the spoils democratically.

There's lettuce, ninety percent of which is too slimy to eat, potatoes that have sprouted, tomatoes with white mould. The mould can be removed. The rest of the tomatoes are edible, and Gayle and Lewis put them between two slices of pre-sliced bread or, if they're lucky, old bagels.

They have no toaster, but bread can be thawed by twisting a clothes hanger into a spiral and setting it over the low burn of the gas stove. They twist the hanger in such a way that there is a sizeable handle that can use to flip the bread like a pancake.

———◆———

The best finds are browning bananas that, if rescued in time, stay good for another two to three days at least, and exotic or tropical fruit—cantaloupe, persimmons, guava—which bruise quickly in cold and are thrown away with even the slightest imperfection.

———◆———

"My whole life I've thought about dying," she says one night in the dark.

"Hmm?"

"Or something—"

"What do you mean?"

She takes his arm under the covers. "Since I was young, I felt it's been close. You know, my dad once told me I'd been shocked when I was in the womb—struck by lightning. Sounds crazy, I know. There's a chance I died in there. My dad died, and Mum brought him back to life. That's their story, anyway. It's some freak accident. They never really explained it. But maybe that's why I'm—" She pauses. "I used to read a bunch of psychology books, but I couldn't find the answer in there—so my own theory is that my brain is burned, like my dad's chest is burned, 'cause thinking about dying still gives me a thrill."

Lewis doesn't respond.

"I imagine death as stepping into a dark room with a kind of sweet smell, like someone's lighting incense in there. There's no way of knowing, I guess.

I heard on the radio that people about to have a heart attack can sometimes smell burning toast."

"Are you scared, Gayle?"

"Oh, no."

"'Cause you're scaring me a little bit. I know I'm sick, but I told you already, no one's gonna die. We don't need to even think about that for another fifty years, alright?"

"There's nothing to be scared of. I've been there, I guess." She sing-talks: "I've been everywhere, man."

He swallows, whispers, "Reno, Chicago, Fargo, Minnesota—"

"Toronto," she whispers back. "Umm—Wichita, Ottawa." She can't remember any more. "Since you've entered my life, I've thought about it less—and less—every day. It feels like a childish game now, all this death stuff."

"Don't leave me, Gayle."

———◆———

One evening they walk to the High Level Bridge to smoke with a view. They look at the meagre city skyline on the far side of the river, some government building, offices, old hotels. Neither of them feel inclined to cross the bridge to downtown, the corporate buzz amid the poverty.

"Least we're not living in a ten-storey building," he says, "where you're stuffed into little boxes, given a number. You could go your whole life without ever stepping on grass."

"I've never wanted to live in a place like that."

"I'm glad we have what we have. I'd rather die a beggar than living at the top of one of those high-rises."

"That's the Lewis I know. The fella who drifted into my life one day like magic."

They walk to the middle of the bridge. It's too cold to touch the rail, but she runs her cuff along it, raising it up once in a while, pretending it's a horse jumping hurdles.

The water below is not frozen but will be soon. In the middle of the bridge, the wind is strong. She has an impulse to lift herself over the rail. The feeling reminds her of being a child, being on the train, wanting to jump off and ride the Dream Bird back to her home in Victoria.

She wonders if the air would rip her jacket if she jumped. If the whiplash would make her vomit, give her a nosebleed. Landing on the water may not kill a person. It may just cause a big splash, broken bones, brain damage, crippling. That would be the worst.

Unless it's frozen. She closes her eyes and imagines, instead of falling, gliding through the air, her jacket unzipped and acting as wings, following the turns of the North Saskatchewan, further and further away from the mountains until she comes to a lake.

"Where does this river end?"

"I have no idea," he says. "I guess it's just flat from here until—somewhere. Maybe it goes all the way to the Great Lakes."

——————◆——————

"So the tea's been helping?" Li Yong asks. "In China, sometimes it is said that drinking a cup of tea every day keeps the pharmacist starving."

"I'm willing to try anything," Lewis says.

"How come you don't go to the hospital? All fun aside, tea isn't a miracle. It's just water mostly."

Lewis tips back the last gulp. He shuffles in his chair. "Do you trust me?"

Li Yong and Gayle exchange a look.

"Yeah," Gayle says.

"There's a reason—I've tried to avoid it."

Gayle puts her hand on his. "You don't have to tell me if you don't want to. I mean, if it's—embarrassing, or—"

"No," Lewis says. "Well, maybe a little. I was pretty young, probably eighteen. I was a different kind of guy. Back in Vancouver, things were just like that, the people I was with, the things I did."

"So you're a criminal?" Gayle asks.

"Oh." The syllable sinks. "What?"

"I figured it out—not now but a while ago. I guess because you're a weirdo, you don't go to the hospital, you don't go to the agencies to find work. You don't talk about yourself, really. You don't even sign a proper lease, 'cause you're afraid—"

Lewis stares into his empty mug. "What's a criminal, really? I have a record.

They'd ask for ID—dig something up. I don't know what that would mean. I'd get sent home—put in jail—I don't know."

"You don't have to tell me," Gayle says. "Not if you don't want to."

"Okay."

"Did you kill someone?"

"Jesus, no."

"Then don't tell me," she says. "It's not important."

Li Yong moves to the stove and begins boiling more water. As he does, he whistles through his teeth, something indistinguishable.

On the first day of December, Lewis wakes with a violent cough. Gayle sits him in their kitchen and prepares him a peanut butter and banana sandwich. He eats half and begins to shiver, so she wraps him in blankets and puts him in bed. He closes his eyes for a moment and opens them again wider, as though he didn't expect her there, standing above the bed, arms crossed.

"I was asleep." He's in pain, she can tell, but he smiles.

"This seems familiar."

"What do you mean?"

"Our love at first sight. Remember back when we met? It seems so similar—eerie."

"Keep talking to me, Gayle."

She uses a towel to wipe the sweat off his palms. "After we got to Edmonton, I didn't think it would happen again—but I feel it, the same feeling as before." She can smell him, his illness. "I didn't really believe in that kind of thing—love at first sight. It sounds like something for teenagers or American movies, or those bogus advice columns in the paper. You know those?"

He closes his eyes.

"But those poets and cowboys gotta be writing about something, otherwise why do it? I thought about it when I was washing dishes, how some feelings must be, I don't know, the same for everyone."

He doesn't reply.

"And languages all have their own word for it. Maybe some languages have different words. Like French—they don't really say 'love' the way we do. If they feel strongly about something, they say *aimer*—if they love something really deeply, they say 'adore.' Like j'adore toi. Er, wait—je t'adore. I never really understood when to use which. Lew—Lew? Je t'adore."

He's asleep.

"Do you think Li Yong ever felt love? Maybe he can say it in five languages. That would be good 'cause 'love' in English is used too much, I think. People say they love books, or they love their friends or whatever. But would they give up everything for that stuff? It's like when people say 'make love'—I don't like it. They should just say 'have sex' 'cause making love—if you're really making something—it should be so big that it scrapes the sky, obstructs things, suffocates people, or maybe blows air into them—there should be no world outside of it. It should kill people or save people. Like—"

He's asleep. She puts another blanket on him and closes the door.

———•———

"In Mandarin, it is said, wǒ xǐ huān nǐ or wǒ ài nǐ."

Gayle tries to repeat the words.

Li Yong laughs. "I guess they mean, 'I love you,' and 'I *love* you.' But the second one is not so common. At home, my parents speak some English because they grew up near Hong Kong. Before I left home, they said it to me in English, 'I love you.'"

"Why?"

"Because I think, in a foreign language, things feel beautiful because they are distant. They mean more because they mean less—and because language is language, it is not feelings."

"You've thought a lot about this."

"Yes, because I'm here all alone without a girlfriend."

"What about Spanish?"

"It's the same. Te quiero or te amo—the difference is the *intensity* of the feeling. They are both common in Cuba. I believe that what English does not have is a te quiero. People do not say 'I like you' to their closest friends and family. In English you only say things intensely."

"I guess that's why people learn English, right?"

"No. People learn it because it's the language of colonizers and money. That it's a nice language, too," he adds, "is a lucky accident."

part five

—◦—◆—◦—

apego

chapter eighteen
- 1976 -

For a long time, Gayle believes her family is rich because they live in a big house in the countryside, an image of great wealth she picked up from the novels of Charlotte Brontë and George Eliot. (Both were recommended by her father, but neither could write a book interesting enough to carry her past the first fifty pages.) She also believes this because her father is an educated man with a large vocabulary and her mother is a "woman of leisure," as they say. And because they own a "parlour" with a piano in it, a horse, and room full of antique books.

All the things they do to pass the time, she deduces, are things nineteenth-century writers saw as pursuits of the aristocracy. When she learns the words "proletariat" and "bourgeoisie" in history class, she readily applies the latter to herself and her family.

She never approaches them, but she often tries—and fails—to empathize with the kids who come to class with muddied pants, who are unable to read and have been smoking since the age of eleven. When she tells her classmates she is from Victoria, they gawk at her. She is teased by both the school's poor kids and its rich, who call her "prissy."

———•———

Sixteen now, she decides she deserves independence from her family's—and especially her mother's—ways. She refuses to buy new clothes and seeks to disassociate from the landed European capitalists who, according to the textbook, oppressed the masses, colonized the globe, and caused, by domino effect, at least one world war and the expansion of tyrannical communism on the far side of the Iron Curtain.

———•———

Her mother stops her in the hall one day in autumn and tells her to stand taller.

"And for Christ's sake, Gayle, put on some new clothes. Those are going to fall apart and people don't want to see you naked. In fact, that's illegal."

"I'm not like you, Mum." Gayle looks away. "I'm not gonna be burned like an aristocrat and be spit on for all time."

Her mother looks Gayle up and down a few more times and chuckles. "Look around, silly girl." She brings Gayle to the kitchen, takes a pot of macaroni from the stove mid-boil. She holds it up so Gayle can see the rust on both pot and the stovetop. "When's the last time you were on a holiday?"

Gayle shrugs.

"You know what Ami got for her birthday?"

"Her birthday?"

"Remember what I got for my birthday?"

"No."

"Nothing," says her mother. "You know why? We're in shitloads of debt, Gayle. That's why we got nothing."

"What do you mean?"

"It's not that hard to figure out."

Her mother's speech is dispassionate. She sets the macaroni back on the stove and gazes into it as though it's a crystal ball.

———— • ————

From that day on, Gayle insists they start selling some of the milk from Haydn, Chopin, and Shakespeare. A good quarter of it went to waste, anyway.

They don't make much—most of the milk is sent to Ami's school lunch program, some to a hobby cheese maker—but it's enough to keep Cheerios and Dempster's Whole Grain bread on the shelf and gasoline in the car for a few months.

———— • ————

Soon after, they pay a farmer to come by with a bull and impregnate Chopin, and the male calf—who Gayle names Trotsky—is sold away to be raised for meat. She is disgusted by the whole procedure and swears never to let it happen again.

Her second trip to the hospital (since falling off Abby the horse as a child) was due to an overdose. She can't remember much of the incident, only that she was at a party thrown by her boyfriend at the time—her first and only—Mark Ansell. Everyone decided to go for a joyride through the countryside. Before they got in the car, someone told her to take a pill, and she did, experienced a half hour of intense panic in the back seat, lost consciousness.

She wakes in the hospital under a sheet, her legs propped on a pillow, her body numb, stomach convulsing quietly. There's no pain and the spasms feel like hiccups.

"Gayle?" her mother says.

"Mum—"

"They pumped your stomach, so you're gonna feel some things going on in there."

"Oh."

"And once the morphine wears off, you'll probably be in some pain."

"Okay."

"What do you want me to tell your sister?"

"What?"

"She's asking about you. Want me to tell her the truth or what?"

She feels her stomach (or her lungs, or her heart, or some other organ that she can't name) release something—air, water, fluid of some kind.

"Tell her I got lost in the woods," Gayle says. "Fell down—"

"Can I ask you something?"

"Mhmm."

"What makes you do what you do?"

The sleeves of Gayle's hospital gown are rolled up to her shoulders. Thin horizontal scars, the length of a pinky finger, run across her upper biceps on both arms. Her mother notices them for the first time. She grips Gayle's wrist and slowly runs her fingers down ridges of the left bicep, then the right, as though she is examining the texture of fabric.

"A few months ago," Gayle says.

"I just don't get it."

For the next hour, her mother reads a magazine and waits for her to fall asleep. Gayle wishes she could be alone. With every slippery turn of the page, she feels a cold draft fall on her body and freeze her. The morphine is wearing off.

———◆———

Shortly after her release, she begins to see apparitions. That's what she calls them, anyway, having heard the word in one of her father's many life lessons.

She can't remember which one, or when it happened, only that he said: "apparitions—life is full of them—they tell us something—by 'us,' I mean the real us, not the us we see or others see—"

He saw it coming.

The flittering shadow lives in her periphery and, in a perverse way, makes her happy. It distracts her from the boredom that saturates her life, especially while taking a forced absence from school following the overdose.

The flittering shadow is not malicious. It causes no harm, does nothing aside from brushing the curtain or rattling items on her shelf while she's trying to sleep. It prefers the depth of winter, when things are naturally dark. Occasionally it whistles, but she is open to the possibility that the sound is actually her nose.

It reveals itself clearly to her only once. It happens in February, around Valentine's Day. She comes home miserable after Mark Ansell breaks up with her. Since returning to school, she's been ridiculed daily. One student professes to have seen her remove her clothes, and another claims she was speaking in tongues. Mark Ansell didn't want to be associated with a wreck.

She cries herself to sleep but wakes up an hour later unable to move, as though her limbs have all fallen asleep and she's unable to wake them. Her first suspicion is that she'd been lying funny and somehow severed a cord to her brain. A straw broke the camel's back, already weak from the drugs.

But her eyes are open, she can see the clock on the far wall and for ten minutes considers her new life as a quadriplegic. She would move back to Victoria, she thinks, or at least to Edmonton to stay with her dad.

The shadow appears as a wing through a crack in the door. It waves up and down as though beckoning her to follow it. She tries to open her mouth, but that too is frozen.

Then the shadow speaks. It uses a language other than English, other than any language she recognizes.

"Coming?"

She is able to squirm, but by the time she sits up, the shadow is gone.

———◆———

She rises before dawn, cold from sweat that had yet to dry, and goes to the library. Under the shelf labelled *SCIENCE*, she finds a book of psychological terminology. She looks under the glossary for "Sleep": *Alpha Wave, Apnea, Beta Wave, Circadian Rhythm ... Paralysis.* Page 290.

A disorder usually resulting in reduced or loss of mobility in a state between sleeping and wakefulness and occasionally accompanied by hallucinations. The definition is supplemented by a painting by Henry Fuseli depicting a small demonic figure sitting on the chest of an elaborately dressed woman.

Her fingers tremble in the rotary dial of the phone. It's six in the morning where he is.

"Hmm?"

"Dad?"

"Gayle—that you?"

"I know I'm not supposed to call—I just wanted to because—I had a dream."

"What's going on?"

"It was a bad dream—well, no. It wasn't. It wasn't a dream. I don't know how to explain—it was something else. I was awake but frozen. And I saw a ghost."

"A ghost?"

Her words drip, slop. "Like a giant black bird in my doorway. It was real. It was familiar—like someone I know."

"A black bird—"

"Mhmm."

"It's okay, Gayle."

"I don't want to bother you anymore. I know I'm not supposed to."

"I'm not sleeping," he assures her. "I'm wide awake."

"I'm scared, Dad."

"I'll stay on the line. Talk, talk to me."

She doesn't talk. She listens to him clear his throat and fiddle with a nearby object. She is tempted to ask for a lullaby, a song he used to speak to her when she was a girl because he couldn't sing. She has no doubt he would do it if she asked, but it would be humiliating to request that now, as a teenager.

"I'm scared," she says again. "I've never been scared before—since I was a kid. But I thought it was going to come back someday."

"What's scary about it, Gayle?"

"Umm—"

"I'm listening."

"Because I—don't think anyone can understand. It's like I'm—nuts." She exhales and resumes nonchalantly. "Or something. What should I do?"

"Umm—"

"Dad?"

He doesn't respond. She can hear him shift his position.

"Are you okay, Dad?"

"Don't talk that way," he says abruptly, switching to his instructional voice. "You're fine."

"I'm fine?"

"Yes—I think. Yes. Why don't you talk to your mother?"

"I don't do that, Dad."

"Right."

She looks at the clock, watches the second hand run several laps. There is a noise upstairs—Ami opening her door, creeping out.

"I need to go, Dad."

"Okay Gayle."

"Okay."

"Yes. Be—good."

Ami reaches the bottom of the stairs and sits, eavesdropping.

"Okay Dad, I'm hanging up now. Love you." She talks bravely, for Ami.

"Okay."

"Here I go."

Throughout the winter, Gayle regularly takes Ami into the library to read to her. She pulls books from a shelf labelled *JUVENEILLIA & STICKERS*.

Why, Gayle thinks, does Dad have so many sticker books? And why are some of them filled with stickers?

When she was younger, she remembers, her father read her Christina Rossetti and a poem called "If—," the writer of which she never knew until she found it accidentally in an anthology years later. But Ami prefers normal kid's books like those by Dr. Seuss and the moralistic tales of the Berenstain Bears.

But it was Dr. Seuss alone that could be read again and again to Ami's delight.

They both have a particular fondness for *The Cat in the Hat*, in which two fatherless children are visited by a zany bipedal cat that fills their house with mischievous games and vanishes right before the mother comes back.

"We need a cat," Ami says,

"We have cows."

"But they're not wacky."

"The cat in the story isn't real, Ami."

"I *know*."

"And Mum won't let us get a cat. I asked once."

"We don't have to *tell* Mum."

———◆———

A week later, skipping school and walking through town, she comes across a house with a colony of rabbits living behind a wooden fence. Good enough, she tells herself. And there are many of them—at least eighteen, so the owner won't even notice. She reaches over and takes one, stashes it under her jacket, next to her body.

———◆———

The rabbit doesn't seem to mind its new life. Gayle uses chicken wire to set up a small compound in the corner of the barn. It lives amongst the cows, who don't seem to notice.

The rabbit is Ami's pet. She names it "Cat" and feeds it green beans, sunflower seeds, and hay, the last of which it eats reluctantly.

———◆———

Three weeks later, Ami comes with tears in her eyes and says the rabbit is dead.

Gayle takes it and buries it on the edge of the sunflower patch. The service lasts only ten minutes, neither girl knowing what to say.

While they're standing in silence, their mother approaches from behind and stands between them, looking at the unsettled soil. She waits until the service is over, and they all go back inside together.

Her family doesn't celebrate Christmas. This is never mentioned in their house until one December when Ami is courageous enough to ask her mother why not.

"Because we're not Christians," her mother says.

Later, Ami asks Gayle what that means.

"It means we're atheists, Ami. We don't like God and so we don't put up a tree and buy a bunch of rubbish to put around it, because that's just what God wants. Mum says Christmas and Jesus are a giant Western advertising scam to squeeze the money out of everyone and make them feel guilty. But"—Gayle goes to her knee, her good knee, like her father used to do for her—"I always wanted it, too. I don't think it could be as evil as Mum says. What, are we gonna go to atheist hell?"

"I don't know."

Gayle goes to the store to buy her sister a doll. It's the new kind that just hit the market, according to the staff, and comes in dozens of varieties, outfits, and hair colours. She wraps it in newspaper and leaves it by her sister's door on Christmas Eve.

———◆———

In the morning, she hears her sister shriek.

"She's so pretty, Gayle."

"I got you the one with a puffy jacket so you can take her outside."

She dresses Ami in snow pants and a toque, and they go outside to build tiny snow castles for the doll to live in. The snow isn't wet enough, so they warm up balls in their hand one by one and press them together. It's a slow, laborious process that takes until well in the afternoon.

———◆———

Later in the day, her mother looks up from a painting of a snowscape—all white, unadorned, dashes of grey to indicate ripples in the field. "The hell's that thing?"

"Barbie," Gayle says. She has by this time grown just as attached to the doll as Ami is. "But we call her Cindy because Ami likes the name."

"What's she do?"

"Nothing—she's plastic. She swings her arms and looks pretty."

This makes her mother smile, which in turn makes Gayle smile.

"Her mother ate too much Kraft Dinner," Gayle adds.

Her mother asks to see the doll. She's entertained by the fact that the doll is naked under her skirt, that her hair is frozen to her face, and that she can swing her arms in complete, superhuman circles. "She does yoga," her mother says. "But not very well—all in the arms."

Sensing a playfulness in her mother that she's never seen before, Gayle takes advantage of the moment. She pretends to emulate the doll, swinging her arms in circles while the rest of her remains still.

Ruth, sitting, does the same. Her thin neck and hunched back remain stiff as she raises her arms above her head and puts on a goofy, doll-like smile.

After a few seconds, they break into laughter.

"The young women of our society are in weird, weird hands," her mother says.

The door opens on a long conversation about society's ills—its messages, its unrealistic standards, its tendency toward self-destruction and endless waste. On all these points, Gayle and her mother agree.

"And the doll came with three layers of packaging," Gayle says.

"Good lord."

"I read in a magazine that someone was picking up piles of plastic shit in Africa somewhere. They said it washed up there and came all the way from New York City."

"New York City itself is a pile of plastic shit."

It might be, Gayle thinks, the longest conversation they ever had. As soon as there's a pause, she inserts another cynical remark—about religion, pollution, bad drivers, general rudeness, the price of groceries—and is relieved when her mother bites and begins another rant.

"You should have seen the hell I went through at the post office when I sent in for some more paints—"

"Oh that reminds me," Gayle explains. "In the toy store I had to wait in line for thirty minutes because some idiot was trying to pay for a fifty-dollar thing with pennies and nickels. The cashier asked him if he had anything bigger, and he said, 'I only carry change 'cause it's safer.' He just stood there counting and everyone else was rolling their eyes."

"Like I said," her mother replies, "consumer society's the absolute pits."

Eventually Gayle runs out of ideas and the conversation ends. Her mother takes a deep breath, nods, and turns back to her snowscape.

"Thanks, Mum."

Her father arrives home for the summer in 1977, as he always does.

"Gayle," he says as slowly unties his shoes. Gone are the days of spinning and rounds of hellos.

She doesn't embrace him. Their last phone conversation comes to mind, the fear. "What's new, Dad?"

He pats her on the arm. "Not too much."

"Sorry."

"It's okay, Gayle." It's the voice she heard over the phone—the man without ideas, the man of comfortless Umms. A dark voice, distant and concerned. She sees herself reflected in his eyes—a smudge, a riddle, an issue. "How are you?"

She doesn't answer. He slides by her and into the house.

———◆———

He takes her for a walk in the woods. They drive half an hour north of Salmon Arm to a small dirt lot where hikers can leave their cars while they undertake the "beginner" loop to the midsection of a small mountain. They are the only ones on the trail.

"Tell me, Gayle, what are the joys and sorrows of the year?"

"Nothing, Dad."

"School?"

"I'm not made for education. I got mixed up with a boy, but Mum probably told you that, the hospital and stuff. He was a drooling asshat. I'm not sure why I did it, but it's over."

"An asshat?"

"His head is more of an ass than a head."

"As your father, I'm going to tell you what you already know. Be careful."

Feeling defiant, adult, she responds, "But you're not really—a father—not like other fathers."

He smirks. "I would hope not. I know fathers. They're not a good sort of people, generally. Tyrannical, money-hungry. But don't say you're not made for an education. You're just made from a different cut of cloth. I knew this the moment I saw you."

"What?"

"Humans are born out of a kind of magic—the divine thought, or the imagination—and we trail it behind us like clouds behind a jet. What happens to most of us as we age is that we build a false house around our imagination, which we call a 'real life.' But in it the magic grows hungry and dies. The house remains hollow. But this magic can be retained, and if it's lost, it can be regained. *This* makes for good education. I know. I'm well over forty now, and I haven't lost it."

She believes him but doesn't understand him. That's the way our relationship evolves, she thinks. She moves slowly into his circle of trusted individuals—including her mother and Abby the horse—with whom he talks about things that matter.

"How is the music, Gayle?"

"It's been a long time."

"I see."

They pause by a brook and sit on a flat stone. Another hiker dragged it there to have a quiet resting place along the beginner loop. He crosses his legs and looks around while Gayle clenches and releases her knuckles.

"Dad—something's bothering me."

"I know."

"I know you know."

"But tell me what it is. In your words."

She picks up a handful of gravel and tosses it in the brook. "It's like a *pull*."

"A pull. Yes, a pull. Something that draws you in but moves away."

"Sure."

"Something almost unworldly."

"Very. I never told you about the Dream Bird. I mean, the bird I saw in my dream—when I was a girl—on the train. Like an imaginary friend, I guess."

"No." He pauses. "But I remember. Even then, I understood. Do you believe I understood?"

She thinks back to that moment but, as she expected, it's gone. All that remains is the story she spun over the years as she waited for the right moment to tell him. "I believe you understood. That's why you didn't get mad."

"Don't run away from it, Gayle. The pull. It means you have a gift." He stands, unbuttons the top three buttons of his shirt and pulls it down to reveal an amorphous shape over his heart. "It's always warm. Every day for fifteen years."

"Are you sick?"

"No. This is a memento. The heavens left it in me once, not long before you were born."

"I don't understand."

"Gayle—I never told you, but we died once, you and I. Your mother and I were hit by lightning. But we came back to life." A glow rises in his cheeks. "The universe wants us. It gave me this mark to remind us that we're special. You were still in your mother's belly, but it affected you, too. I know. The three of us are marked."

"What?"

"The world is full of mysteries. You're still pure. Maybe you know better than I do."

"I don't know, Dad."

"We'll find out someday."

———— • ————

From that moment on, he becomes comfortable smoking around her. She watches him puff a cigar in the library. Because she's in his circle now, she assumes, she's allowed to see him at rest. It takes him a long time to finish the cigar and he doesn't seem to enjoy it. But he grins as though there is something delightful in pretending that he does, or he is emulating the image of a cigar-smoking man he once saw on a label or in a movie.

The mature mood, smoke-dimmed, seems right for a question. "Why are you never here?"

"Hmm?"

She doesn't want to upset him, so she speaks slow and chooses her words carefully. "Why don't you come home for Christmas or something—so we can celebrate—normally. Like a family, I mean."

He isn't upset. He takes in the question as he does the smoke. "Because a man needs his solitude. His reflections."

"Oh."

"By which I mean, a man and a sound woman need their solitudes."

"I get it. You're a poet. But I worry sometimes, you know, that one day you're not going to. Come back, I mean."

"What makes you worry?"

"Books are full of people, artists and people like that, who just kinda snap. Mum said the other day during dinner that art is suicide without death. Does that make any sense to you? Because it doesn't really make sense to me—"

"What kinds of books are you talking about, Gayle?"

"I mean biographies. The little biographies at the beginning of books, like Virginia Woolf. Are you like Virginia Woolf? She filled her pockets with rocks and—"

"She was a genius," he cuts her off, "but too given to the mind."

"Mhmm." The diversion from her question, the oddness of the conversation as a whole, makes Gayle think she'd prefer not to be part of her father's circle. She doesn't understand it for one thing but, more importantly, she vaguely suspects there is nothing to understand. His world is a circle of asides. "You must know everything," she says.

"Gayle, no one has time to know everything. One can only look at everything. Do you understand?"

"You're not answering my questions."

———— • ————

He goes, as he always does, as he always will, and there is no ceremonious farewell. It's a grey day in August, the sky the colour of moths.

She graduates high school in 1978 and gives up her lingering acquaintances, drifts away from everyone but Ami. She swears herself into adulthood by forcing off everything that plagued her young life: the pressure to conform, to indulge, to please boys, or chase the darkness through altered states of consciousness. What's left, she doesn't know.

When she's alone in the house one morning, the Dream Bird returns to taunt the absence in her life. It rummages through the parlour, makes the house creak, and she goes down to confront it at last. To see it in the light of day for what it is.

"You again?" she asks from the bottom of the stairs. She cautiously peeks around the corner, sees a blustering shadow retreat beyond the crack in the open door. "I trust you, bird. But I want to know more."

The door closes against the wind.

"Why do you keep leaving me?"

She learns, a month before he's supposed to come home, that her father has disappeared. She finds out by eavesdropping when her mother is on the phone—talking to detectives, or police, or someone official. Her mother doesn't say "disappeared," though. She says "abandoned his post" and answers all the questions posed to her with "Who could say, sir? Who could say?"

"Does this mean he's not coming back?" Gayle asks when her mother hangs up.

"Nope."

"What?"

Her mother laughs—a forced laugh, which she catches with her hand before marching upstairs and slamming a door.

———•———

Two weeks later, the radio says the town of Salmon Arm is bound together in prayer for their missing resident, a once-upon-a-time hero. The newspaper reprints the picture of him posing with the young captain of the Salmon Arm Rockets when he first arrived on Abby the horse.

But in practice, everything is exactly the same. Rain slicks the path to the barn, the cows still need the gentle rhythm of her hands. There is washing and cooking to do. Only now there is no one she can express her thoughts to. Knowing her father won't come home this summer fills her with a sadness like an unresolved melody.

She goes back to the piano, which she hasn't played in years, and tries to revive "All You Need is Love." But the instrument has gone out of tune again, and now they don't have the money to fix it.

On a stormy summer night, she's with Ami in the girl's upstairs bedroom. The radio drones, Ami creaks a rocking chair back and forth. Gayle looks out the window, beyond a scraggly tree, and sees a light flicker between the cracks of the barn. No apparition, no illusion—a human glimmer.

"There's someone in the barn—" she says.

chapter nineteen
- 1979 -

The tire chains on trucks, the disappearance of pedestrians behind their coats and balaclavas until everyone looks criminal, the day-by-day browning and blackening of the snow, the children who pull each other along the sidewalk on magic carpets, clutching ropes, getting injured, bloody noses that run like tar. In Edmonton, she feels like an alien object lodged in flesh. All the city's natural processes work together to force her elsewhere.

The basement windows are frozen shut, covered in thick ice that fills the cracks between it and the casing, but still the draft mouses in like an infestation.

Gayle's routine for December includes sitting on the floor beside the basement refrigerator, which wheezes slight warmth, glancing into the bedroom to see if Lewis is asleep. When she's sure he's out and will be for a few hours, she goes dumpster diving.

———— ✦ ————

During the cold snap, the number of divers dwindles. Occasionally she is the only one. On one of the solitary days, she waits in the alley behind the Safeway on Whyte Avenue and 109th Street, clapping to create jolts of warmth.

A nearby door slams open and a young man jogs out with a bag of culled produce. He sees Gayle, nods politely, leaves the bag by the dumpster for her to rummage through, and runs back in.

She pulls out a box of strawberry eclairs and a mesh sack of mandarin oranges, a variety she's never seen before. The oranges are seasonal. The label is decorated with pictures of Christmas bulbs.

The young man returns wearing a heavy brown coat with the Safeway logo stitched into the front.

"Hi," he says.

Gayle looks at him. He's her age, burly, a soft face. "Sorry."

"Don't worry about it." He pulls from his pocket a pile of loose change and tries to give it to her.

"I don't need it."

"C'mon, take it. I don't want it."

She looks at the change, seventy-five cents at most. "I don't need money—just food."

He goes back inside and returns a moment later with a bag of salted peanuts. "They are not even expired. They're fresh."

She hesitates for a moment and takes the bag.

"Peanuts have lots of protein," he says. "Good for when it's cold."

———•———

When she opens the bedroom door in the afternoon, she notices Lewis's sour smell. He's breathing heavily, cocooned in a motley assortment of clothes and blankets, the sweat locked away. When the door opens, the sudden change in temperature makes the fumes heavy. It's like the way smoke appears thicker, heavier, livelier in cold weather.

Her nostrils revolt. Lewis is rot.

———•———

"How is he?" Li Yong asks, flipping through a decorating magazine.

"He's wrapped up. I thought maybe if it's something in his blood, or below his skin, he'll eventually sweat it out."

"And how are you?"

"I wish I could sleep."

"You should be outside, getting some air."

"I can't last out there."

"In the news, they say it's almost a record low."

Gayle moves to the stove and makes tea with lemon and ginger—she's watched him do it enough—and sits across from him.

"I've been thinking about what we talked about before," he says, closing the magazine. "About language—remember?—and things that can't be expressed in this one."

"I remember."

"There's a word a friend taught me in Cuba. It came to me today."

"Which friend?"

"A friend—well, a lover, really. A fling, as you say in English. Is there a better word? 'Fling' sounds silly."

"I always suspected you were the romantic sort."

They aren't smiling. The sleeper in the basement dampens their mood.

"I never mention this person," Li Yong says. "Even my family doesn't know. It's too close to me."

"I get that."

"But she taught me a word. A special word. It is"—he tilts his head back, searching for the word on the ceiling—"*apego*. It is not a common word, and I never used it again. I have clients who are Spanish speakers. But in accounting, it is not a word that comes up. It is a psychological word, something she wanted me to know before I left for Canada. You could say it was the kind of conversation people have when they know they will never meet again."

"Apego?" she asks. "What's it mean?"

"I wondered this for years, too. In a dictionary—Spanish to English—they call it *attachment*. Sometimes addiction. Or closeness. But it's not any of those things. At least not how I was given this word. It was a gift that keeps on giving, as they say. She was very smart and knew a lot about the brain. It is like when people say, 'wires in the brain.' Do you know this expression? 'I got my wires crossed?'"

Gayle nods.

"When two people have their brains too close together, their wires get tangled. It's not a normal way to be. Maybe some of them get plugged into the wrong person's brain, so all their signals become mixed-up. Replace brain with emotions. Everything you want and feel is connected to what the other person is wanting and feeling, and you know it like it's your own. And maybe it is." He pauses. "It is dangerous to move too far away because you know what happens when you pull wires apart."

"Yeah."

"Apego happens when you pull those wires apart. After that, you can never really be what you were before you got tangled. You are broken, you might say."

She doesn't drink any more. The ginger must have been old. It tastes bitter. "It sounds kind of like an accident. Like people bumping heads or something."

"It is an accident, maybe."

"What did you do?"

"I left her. Because of the visa."

———◆———

One morning, Lewis develops a fever and becomes delusional, lost. She brings him upstairs to sleep on Li Yong's sofa while she goes searching for groceries. It's warmer upstairs, and there Li Yong can watch him.

"You're fine with this?" she asks in the other room so Lewis can't hear.

"Of course," Li Yong says. "I'm the oldest in my family. I took care of my baby sister all the time."

As she rummages, she thinks about Ami. She doesn't know why, but it takes her some time to remember her own phone number, the phone number of the farm. She walks to Whyte Avenue and finds a pay phone in the lobby of the Commercial Hotel.

She's an hour ahead. And it's a weekend, so Ami might still be asleep. If it's Mum, she thinks, I'll just hang up.

The phone rings once, twice. It rings for five minutes. No one.

———◆———

Behind Safeway, she encounters the same young man from the other day. When he sees her, he immediately turns back inside and returns with arms full of cans.

"I thought I'd find you again," he says.

"How come?"

"'Cause there are some regulars back here. I have a surprise. Been stashing this for you." He carries a can of frozen orange juice, two of beef ravioli, two of baked beans.

"You don't need to."

"I do it for everyone."

"Thanks, but I don't need people buying things for me."

"It's stolen," he whispers. "But don't spread that around. Better it goes to you than someone giving their money to the corporation."

"Oh."

"But I don't think that bothers you. You're technically stealing now, any-way. The garbage belongs to Safeway 'til it hits the dump."

As before, she hesitates but takes the cans. She looks behind him into the still-open door to see if anyone's watching.

"Don't worry," he says. "I'm the manager."

"But you're pretty young."

"I am. I'm also a student. Philosophy." As she walks away, he calls after her, "Do you like coffee?"

She turns around. "I'm sorry. You're really generous—but I'm married."

"Jeez, no. I have some bags back here." He goes inside and returns a moment later with two bags of ground Peruvian beans. He tosses them to her underhand.

———◆———

At night she finds Lewis on Li Yong's sofa with a wet rag on his head, a half-empty mug of tea by his side. He's asleep. The book of haiku she bought him is on the table at the head of the sofa.

Li Yong is in the kitchen, dozing with his head on the table. He wakes when Gayle lays a hand on his back.

"You don't have to sit here all night like a watchman, Lee."

"He was making some strange sounds, coughing and gasping. There was blood in the tissue. I wanted to stay in case it happened again, or worse. I'm ready to call an ambulance if he chokes. I'd have to."

She waits for more information. Nothing comes. "He's a smoker, though. That's probably why."

"He should stop that."

"He won't, though. I guess that's why they call it an addiction."

Li Yong works in the morning, so she tells him to go upstairs. Alone, she takes the book of haiku. Two of the pages are dog-eared. Was it Lewis? she thinks. Did he find something peaceful in his fit? Or—

———◆———

A winter morning—
All alone,
Chewing on dry salmon.

—is it arbitrary? A memory fold left in the book by its previous owner, or owners—a beacon to someone, at some point, to encourage them through hardships of winter austerity? The haiku sounds far away. Someplace with salmon jerky, someplace where fish is eaten in the morning.

English also becomes distant, becomes more feeling than language, when it's almost not there.

A winter night, all alone, she eats a package of stolen peanuts, brushes salt on her jeans. Around midnight, she returns to the basement to sleep alone in the dark.

———◆———

For the first time this year, she experiences paralysis. It doesn't come with the confusion it did before. She is better positioned, flat on her back. In the psychology books she'd read, she learned that sleep paralysis can sometimes be brought on by stress. Sometimes by nothing at all. Brain chemicals being brain chemicals. *I got my wires crossed.*

When her eyes open, they are already pointed down, across the room, toward the door. The moonlight is strong enough that she can make out a silhouette. A young person—a girl. Ami? The girl speaks in the voice of a man, but in a language Gayle doesn't know. Then she waves goodbye in a long, exaggerated gesture with both arms, like a sailor saying adieu to their loved ones on the shore.

———◆———

The young manager finds her again, gives her more baked beans and a package of frozen corn.

"By the way," he says, "if you ever find something in the trash with a date on it, don't pay attention to it."

"Hmm?"

"Unless it's obviously rotting. The date means 'best before' not 'expired.' It's a corporate thing. But usually you got another couple months until it's no good to eat."

Lewis stays permanently on Li Yong's sofa. Gayle borrows Lewis's sweaters. She walks to the Strathcona Public Library and signs up for a card so she can look at medical books, thinking if Lewis can't go to the hospital, then maybe she can be his doctor.

She finds a dictionary of symptoms, a thick book containing hundreds of tables with ailments in the left column, symptoms in the middle, and treatments in the right—usually something vague. "Vaccination." "Change in diet." "Sanitation." "None."

———◆———

In the evening, Gayle props him up with pillows and sits on the armrest opposite his head, dictionary in her hands. Li Yong stands in the corner with his arms crossed.

"We need to try, Lew."

"It's alright. I'll be fine."

"That's the biggest lie you ever told me. And you once hid the fact that you murdered someone."

"I told you, I didn't *murder* anyone."

"I'm joking, alright? I'm doing this to save your life again." She brushes hair away from her face and squeezes the book. Her thumbs leave sweat stains on the cover.

"Again?"

"Like when I dragged you from the barn. You woulda died out there, face down in the hay. Don't deny it."

He nods.

"Think of it as a game," she says. "Any coughing?"

"Yes."

"Lee told me there was blood. Is it a sinus infection? Asthma?"

"But the fever."

"That was just the first try. Bronchitis? Chronic bronchitis? It can be caused by smoking, or allergies. You said it comes and goes. Maybe it's allergies."

"It's not allergies. You mean to flowers and stuff? It's winter—"

"Maybe you're allergic to the cold. I heard on the radio that it's possible. It sucks if you live in Canada, but—"

He doesn't respond. She keeps trying.

"Parasites? Some kind of STD? I forgot to ask."

"It's not an STD. We would know if it was."

"Respiratory tract infection." She scratches her cheek. "Do you have a runny nose or a sore throat? Sneezing?"

"No."

"Yeah, and it says it only lasts for a few days. You said you had it for a long time."

"A year or two, maybe."

"Cancer?" she says.

"What about cancer? I haven't been smoking that long—a couple years. Five years."

"Lung cancer: bloody cough, weight loss or appetite loss, feeling weak. If they catch it in time, you can get rid of it. Maybe. It doesn't say. But probably. People get rid of cancer all the time. Sometimes. I don't know."

"If it's cancer, we waited way too long."

"No, we can fix it. It's possible to fix anything if you try hard enough."

"The hell are you going to fix cancer?" He raises his voice. "People have been trying for decades."

"Stop arguing, Lewis."

"I'm not arguing—I'm just saying what's true."

"*Shut up*," she shouts. "I don't care what's true."

Li Yong steps out. Gayle and Lewis lock eyes. She leans over the sofa and kisses his chin.

"Sorry," she says.

"You can leave me, Gayle. I'm okay. You need to do something else. This is too much."

Before she goes, she hides the medical dictionary in a drawer and brings him the radio from the basement.

———————— ◆ ————————

She walks north to the river, to the end of the bridge and back. She follows Saskatchewan Drive to where the road dips to the Walterdale Bridge and cuts down into Strathcona, traces some of the streets she'd walked with Lewis. Late afternoon she stops at a café on 109th Street. She knows the alley behind it well, but she's never been inside.

She orders a coffee and a donut and sits by the window, watches snow fall over the traffic, which moves, stops, drifts slowly like an iceberg. Drivers and passengers caught in their boxes, looking aggravated.

The first donut I've ever eaten, she thinks, that isn't from the trash. The frosting is white, topped with green and red sprinkles in the shape of a Christmas tree. When she's finished, she orders another of the same and leaves it on her plate to remain inconspicuous and not be kicked out.

———————◆———————

The café closes late, and she stays until late.

She listens to music playing in her head, bits and repetitions. First she listens to "Four Strong Winds." And then the new Clash songs she heard on the radio recently, "Lost in the Supermarket," about the shallowness of consumerism, and "London Calling," about the apocalypse.

Three cops at a nearby table discuss the spike in accidents every time there's a snowfall, as though everyone in the city miraculously forgets how to drive, and they joke about wanting to swap lives with their wives.

The donut sits uneaten, and by the third hour the staff begin to give her suspicious looks.

"Need anything else?" a waiter asks.

"Do you have any phones?"

"By the door." He pushes in the chairs vacated by the cops. "We're closing in half an hour, by the way."

She wraps the donut in a napkin, goes to the phone, and uses most of her small change to call Ami, covering the receiver with her spare hand for privacy.

"Hello?"

"Ami?"

"Hi?"

"Don't make too much noise. It's Gayle."

The girl shrieks, as expected.

Gayle shushes her. "I said not to make noise. Is Mum home?"

"She's somewhere—"

"Can she hear you?"

"She's upstairs."

"If she comes down," Gayle says, "just slam the phone and run away. I'm calling you just like I said I would. I'm safe and I miss you. Don't forget."

"I knew you'd be okay, Gayle. I made a picture for you."

"Mail it to me. As soon as possible." She gives Ami her address and tells her to write it on her hand. "But don't show Mum. How's everything over there? Tell me everything you can. How is school?"

"Umm—hmm—I'm having a good time in school, especially with Social, but that's the only one—and gymnastics. It's almost Christmas break and I'm gonna have a real Christmas this year."

"Mum's having Christmas?"

"Nah, she's going away. I'm staying with Bill and Lizzy."

"Who are Bill and Lizzy?"

Gayle hears footsteps in the unseen room across the telephone line, and Ami gasps.

"Gayle?"

Gayle doesn't respond right away. She shifts the receiver from hand to hand, inserts her last nickel. "I can't talk, Mum. I'm running out of change."

"How the hell did you think you could just—"

"To talk to Ami."

"But you're supposed to have run away, huh? Where are you now?"

"Edmonton still."

"With that boy?"

"Yes."

"So your dreams have come true."

Gayle doesn't know if it's a joke. She never knows. "We're taking care of ourselves. Saving up. It was a good decision."

"Magical, Gayle."

"I'm gonna hang up now, Mum."

"*Wait*—"

"What?"

"Did you go looking for your dad?"

"It's a big city, Mum. I'm not a detective."

"Come off it, Gayle." The voice stiffens. "You got everything you wanted. Stop thinking only about yourself for one moment in your life."

Gayle doesn't respond.

"I want *two* things from you, Gayle. In all my life, I've asked nothing. I let you do and be whoever you want. Now I want two things. First, answer some questions, alright?"

"Fine."

Her mother clears her throat. "Are you coming back? Soon, later, whenever?"

"I don't know, Mum."

"That's not really an answer."

"I can't answer you, then."

"I should've expected that."

"What else?" Gayle asks.

"Are you able to forgive?"

"What's *that* mean?"

"Your mother who loves you, who you abandoned, who wants you to say yes. That's what I'm asking for. If you do, we can be friends. And we can try all this again—as friends."

"I forgive you."

"You know what you're forgiving for?"

"Not really, but maybe I'll figure it out."

Gayle hears crying, but it comes in muffled fits away from the receiver. The lights in the café are dimmed, the door jingles as the last few customers step into the winter dark.

"What else, Mum?"

"Do something for me. One thing. Find someone. A friend of your dad's."

"Who?"

"The name's Hanna Federico. They worked together. I think she was a—confidant of his—my replacement. She might be a lover. They go back to the sixties."

"Oh."

"You need the name again?"

"No."

"I don't care who she is or what she's done. But when you find her, ask one thing. Ask if he—my husband, your dad—ask if he believed everything he did had a point. Ask if his labour was worth it all."

Gayle lets the question sink in. Worth it. Worth what all?

"Got it, Gayle?"

"Yeah, Mum."

The café staff catch her attention and point to a clock on the wall. It's five minutes to closing. One barista makes exaggerated movements, miming a mop. The phone dies. The time is up.

She leaves without paying and runs home.

———◆———

"Sorry I've been away so long."

"You can't spend all your time here."

"But I brought you this." She takes the donut from her pocket. The frosting sticks to the napkin and peels away as she tries to unwrap it. "It's a Christmas donut."

Lewis smiles.

"But you don't have an appetite," she says. "I know."

"The tea. It's enough."

"Maybe Lee was right. Tea will heal everything."

He closes his eyes. Gayle sits on the edge of the sofa, thinking about her mother and father—nothing in particular, only their faces, the way they looked on the train from Victoria to the interior, the way they looked in each other's arms in the parlour when things were going well.

———◆———

Li Yong comes down the stairs at dawn in a collared shirt and tie. He goes to the kitchen, walking softly to give them the illusion of privacy.

She does a mental scan of the contents of her cupboard. A single tomato, a carrot muffin with mould. Butter. That's all. When she enters the kitchen, Li Yong seems to know she's hungry. He's never offered food before, but he does now. Some cheese and circular, butter-flavoured crackers.

"You ever get in touch again with the woman, Lee? The one in Cuba?"

"It isn't possible. There are complications sending a letter from Canada. Political complications."

"What about the phone?"

"It's not possible." He straightens a pile of old magazines. "The world's job isn't to bring people together, unfortunately. We need to do that ourselves. I guess if it was necessary, we'd find a way."

"You still love her?"

"Being far apart isn't the same—you know this. With your mother."

"How did you know I—have a mother?"

He smiles.

"I mean," she says. "How did you know we're like that?"

"Lewis told me. He thinks about it a lot. Maybe he feels guilty about it. Told me he wishes you were all still there—on the farm. Salmon Arm, was it?"

"Yeah."

"He told me that showing up was the turning point of his life."

"You're making it up—"

He goes to boil water.

———◆———

She buys a blunt from a drug peddler on Whyte Avenue and brings it home, tears it open and sprinkles the contents into a pan with a cube of butter one week past the best before date.

She lets it simmer on low for forty-five minutes, at which point the butter is luminescent green. Then she transfers the contents to a pot with water and adds tea leaves. She lets this boil for several minutes and then filters the marijuana and tea through a colander and into a mug.

"'*Green* tea,'" she says. "With quotes around it."

"I could smell it."

"It's supposed to have medicinal effects. Even the medical textbook says that."

He looks better today—a glow in his eyes, no coughing.

"Do you have pain?" she asks.

"Yeah—a lot in the stomach, the sides—"

"That's what it's supposed to fix."

He sits up, drinks a third of the mug, smacks his lips, and leans back against the armrest. "Tastes like butter."

"It'll take a bit to kick in."

She tidies the kitchen, washes the dishes to remove the smell. She returns half an hour later to find him still, head back, eyes closed. She slides a pillow behind his head to support his neck.

———•———

The week before Christmas, she notices that the young man at the Safeway hasn't appeared in weeks. Not only that, but the items in the trash are marred—the produce deliberately quashed, cans pierced with a knife, and bottles of bleach opened and poured over everything. The dumpster divers are being poisoned. The empty bleach bottles were left on top as a warning. There is also a handwritten sign posted to the side of the dumpster: *Property of Safeway. Trespassers will be prosecuted.*

———•———

Later in the day, mail arrives. There is something for Li Yong—a package, a box from his family in China. Maybe a Christmas gift, she thinks.

Then there's a letter from Ami. But the writing on the envelope isn't hers, nor their mother's. It's an adult's hand. The return address is also unfamiliar. But it's certainly Ami's letter. It contains a single piece of paper, folded awkwardly to fit the exact dimensions of the envelope. It's a picture of her—she knows only because *GAYLE* is written at the top.

Stick arms, stick legs, wearing pants, black hair—her hair, more hers that what she has now, the faded blond with long, ashy roots. Stick Gayle is standing beside a stick cow.

———•———

Night. She sits at the foot of the couch where Lewis is knocked out.

She thinks now, as she has thought time and time again: What stopped me from jumping from the train as a child? From pushing the razor a little deeper, until I cut the veins straight through? From going feral into the woods around the farmhouse, lying in a clearing, offering my body to the wilderness?

Mum wouldn't have cared, she thinks. Dad wouldn't have noticed. Maybe he'd even encourage it.

When she's in a certain state of mind, these acts seem as simple as flicking off a light switch. It's the hesitation, hovering between *ON* and *OFF—LIVE* and *DIE*—that's hard to deal with. How do you move at all when you have no future?

Nowadays, she proclaims with her quietest of inner voices, there is something large and out-of-sight holding me still, keeping me alive.

chapter twenty
- 1979 -

Gayle finds Hanna Federico's number in the white pages, calls, and is told in few words that it's better to meet in person. The address the woman provides is nearby, so she goes on foot.

The woman comes to the door wearing thick glasses that enlarge her eyes and a beige sweater with Rudolph stitched into the front. Between her fingers is a cigarette holder.

"I'm Al's daughter."

"Oh?"

"You were friends?"

Hanna turns and walks back into the house. "Come in," she says over her shoulder. "Is your name Gayle?"

The house is tidy and small. They proceed through a narrow hallway without decoration, without photos, and enter a small living room lined with bookshelves.

Hanna points to a loveseat. "Sit. Please." She takes a wicker rocking chair, lights her cigarette. When she isn't inhaling, there's a slight crack between her lips, her mouth frozen in expectation. "Are you cold? I could get you slippers or a shawl. I have plenty."

"I'm used to it," Gayle replies. "I wouldn't mind a smoke, though. I left mine at home."

There's a soft pack of cigarettes on the table. They're a luxury style, thinner than usual. Hanna flips open a lighter and holds the flame. Gayle watches it flicker for a moment before she realizes that the woman wants to light it for her—a gesture she's only seen in movies.

"Thanks," she says.

Hanna runs her knuckles down the armrest. "You come in on the Greyhound?"

"I live here."

"How do you like it? It's a peculiar city."

"I don't plan to stay long."

"People come and go. I'm not from here, either. I'm from Calgary. But it's quite similar. So similar that it's hard to compare them. The infrastructure's a little more thought out over there though." She slides an ashtray toward Gayle. "How's your sister, your mother?"

"Fine."

The long cigarette burns at least three times as long as the ones Gayle is used to. "This is a little strange. I—"

She is cut off by a rattling in an adjoining room, clanging metal, followed by a shriek.

"Sorry," says Hanna.

"What's that?"

"My parrot."

"Parrot?"

"A blue-and-gold macaw. Have you met one before?"

"No."

"Oh you're *really* in for a treat. He's very friendly. He just screams when he's bored. I haven't let him out yet today. He's usually not like this. He must know there's company. Would you like to meet him?"

"No."

"Well, if you don't mind, I need to cover him." She leaves the room. There are several more shrieks, followed by the billowing of a blanket and more rattling.

Hanna returns to the rocking chair. "He thinks it's night now."

"Miss Federico—I should tell you why I'm here, I guess."

"Please call me Hanna."

"My mum told me to come. She wants to know some things about dad that, I guess, no one else can know."

"She's a precious woman, I understand."

"Sorry?"

"Your father lives for her."

"Lives, or lived?"

Hanna leans forward. "Are you under the impression that he's dead?"

"I don't know. I'm just gonna ask you what my mum wanted, and then I can go."

"Oh, please stay. Don't be frightened. Is it the macaw? He won't be making any more noise. I promise. Oh *heck*, I should always remember to tell guests there's a macaw in the house. Ornithophobia is more common than you'd think."

"No—I just—this is a little strange for me—to be here with my dad's—mistress?"

Hanna smiles a nicotine-stained smile. "Is that what you think's been going on here?"

"It makes sense."

"Dear Gayle, don't be shy. Your father and I have a very platonic relationship. We were good friends for the years he worked here. He was well-liked at the university, you know. How many years ago did he come in? He came in sixty-two—so plus seven—plus—ah, well. They called him a little Don Quixote."

"If you're not like that," Gayle says, "then why did he never mention you?"

"I couldn't say. But I suppose it's human nature to compartmentalize. It's not a bad quality. Otherwise professionals of anything wouldn't be able to function. Churchill would've brought his drunken artist persona to work and we'd all be speaking German."

Gayle finishes her cigarette. Hanna immediately offers her another.

"What's a little Don Quixote?" Gayle asks. "What's that mean?"

"That's what some people at the university called him. A silly joke."

"I don't get it. I don't know the story."

"Don Quixote—was a victim of culture. He was out-of-joint in time. He read medieval romances and took himself to be a knight, followed a code of chivalry and wandered around Spain trying to help the poor, woo noble ladies, give longwinded speeches about knightly conduct, ethics, war, religion. And so on. An outstanding ideal, but he was a few centuries too late. He got in a lot of fights. Tried to attack a windmill because he thought it was a giant."

"He was nuts."

"*Not. One. Bit,*" Hanna replies, tapping her cigarette holder with each word. "There's a reason we talk about Don Quixote still, and all his two-bit contemporaries have decomposed—just like most people who try to pander to the peers and conditions of their day and nothing more."

"I don't really understand."

"Dear Gayle, why don't you ask me your mother's question. Then I can tell you anything else you want to know."

Gayle takes a moment to remember. "She wants to know if it was worth it. His work, his obsessions—everything he chose instead of his family, I guess— was it worth it?"

"Worth it?"

part six

—◆—

monuments

chapter twenty-one
- 1978 -

An opera by Monteverdi. It's the first time he's played it. He doesn't know the words nor speak Italian but bellows along anyway, sways his large body across the apartment. In his right hand, a glass of vintage port splashes up and stains the carpet.

He sets the glass on the floor by his armchair, sinks his hand between the cushions to fish for a cigar he recalls slipping from his fingers a few nights earlier. He bites off the end, spits it on the floor, and sits. On the end table are his earlier scraps, composed in a leaky red pen. He takes them up again to re-evaluate, strikes out one word, underlines another, sinks a step lower into the trance he seeks.

It's eleven p.m. Every night since he's contracted writer's block, he looks out the window, across the street at the opposite apartment, where's he's found a surrogate muse.

He writes: *Across the avenue is a middle-aged woman who brushes her teeth at 11 p.m. nightly, using her window as a reflective surface—*

Someone pounds the wall of the neighbouring apartment.

"Turn your music *off*, you fucking moron!"

The poet scoffs, moves to the record player, gently lowers the volume knob— the opera recedes but carries on. The pounding comes back, three consecutive thuds before it loses motivation, dissolves into a mutter, a profanity, and then stops.

A victory—the poet smiles. But when he returns to the armchair and reads what he'd written, the smile fades. How to proceed?

His theme is essential—the eternal struggle to appreciate all through the portal of one. One man. One woman—no, not even a whole woman. A woman framed by a square, behind glass, in a blue and green patterned shirt.

For twenty minutes he sits. The woman across the avenue tidies her living room, exits for a moment and returns in pyjamas. As her last act of the night, she gazes through her window. For a moment, focusing on her transparent reflection, she stretches her back and strikes a pose reminiscent of countless standing women in Renaissance art: hands on angled hips, shoulders askew, head tilted, mouth balanced between indifferent and satisfied, lit mostly from the side. Darkness wraps around, emphasizing the textiles and the irregular shadows from cheekbones and brows. Chest centred and inviting. But nothing is aligned. The human form is revealed to be perfect when it claims imperfection.

The poet desires to see her undress. A nude. Not because he's attracted to her, nor because her form reminds him of Ruth—although, aside from lacking a slight hunch, the stranger's shape is remarkably similar—but because it would confirm his belief that the stranger believes she is alone, that what he's witnessing is pure, untampered.

Then she looks beyond herself, into the avenue and, for the third time this month, sees him. He's betrayed by his cigar. Once is an accident, twice a coincidence, but three times is inching toward criminal. To her, he is a nothing more than a voyeur.

She throws her hands up, shouts, and draws the curtain.

When the record plays out, he doesn't reset it, but rather lifts his socked feet to the table, crumples the scrap along with a dozen others and tosses them into a bin that holds the rest of the month's fragments.

From a nearby drawer he withdraws a Mars bar and eats it slowly. He prefers it to melt on its own rather than be forced apart by his jaw. When it's finished, caramel like the end of a miniature snake hangs over his bottom lip, and he closes his eyes.

———— • ————

Fifteen minutes later he is woken by a furious knocking. He answers and is face to face with his landlord whose chin juts forward in frustration.

"Three complaints in one night, Al."

"Three?"

"I got a call from a woman across the street. You know why."

"And?"

"Your neighbour, 'cause you were playing that weird-ass music again."

"*And?*"

"*Me.* I live above you and your goddamn smoke's filling up my place. You know I have allergies."

The poet notices he'd inadvertently taken his empty glass of port with him to answer the door. He lowers it, dangles it between his fingers to distance himself from it and avoid the accusation that he's drunk.

The landlord gestures across his throat. "We agreed on this, Al. Last strike. I don't need freaks in the building. I got enough problems and, you know what, I'm straight-up sick of looking at you."

He slams the door and the poet listens to the dull footsteps find their way back to the floor above. He immediately fills his briefcase with the few things he needs—identification, money, a folder of scraps—and sketches a quick note: *I'm out. Everything here, kill it. Pawn it. I don't care. And give the woman my apologies. I meant nothing.*

He leaves, slips from his warm shame into the scuttling city, follows a bend in the road and emerges onto 109th. He follows it north alongside traffic and soon arrives at a dive bar attached to a pizzeria. He enters, finds the pay phone.

"Hanna?"

"Who's this? It's late."

"It's Al—"

"Oh *Al*—burning the midnight oil?"

He can't resist a single laugh. "I think I'm going to need a place to stay."

"Now?"

"I'm afraid so."

"Explain when you get here. Give me time to straighten things up a bit."

He hangs up, orders a pint of Alberta wheat ale. At the bar is a row of wrinkled men discussing in slurs what they could play on the jukebox to "annoy the kids."

The poet drinks alone at a corner booth beneath a burnt-out light. Aside from the crowd at the bar, the place is filled with students, young people laughing, arguing, playing foosball. One of them he recognizes from his course Introduction to Poetry Analysis. The name he can't remember. A young man, fit and blond and, judging by his all-female company, quite charming. When the young man sees him in the booth alone, he waves and approaches.

"Professor." He stumbles, clearly drunk.

"Good evening."

"This a good time to discuss my term paper?"

"No, it isn't."

The young man smiles. It was a joke. The poet reluctantly lifts his glass in salute.

"Have a nice crawl, Professor."

———◆———

Hanna opens the door.

"Been drinking?" she asks.

"Of course."

"What a coincidence. Me too."

He enters and leads himself to the living room, sits on the loveseat near the macaw's cage and undoes the top two buttons of his shirt. Hanna joins him shortly with two glasses of brandy and finds him gazing into the parrot's eyes.

"So tell me, Al," she says, sitting in the rocking chair. "Why do you need a place to live?"

He breaks eye contact with the parrot, rubs his face. "Things aren't working out at the apartment."

"You seem a bit shaken up."

"For all I know it was a dream. The landlord threatened me and I just walked out. Did everything I could to stop from just—breaking down."

"You left everything behind?"

"I have nothing of value. What day is it, Hanna?"

"Friday." She finishes her brandy in a single tip, coughs once. "Does this bother you at all, Al? Losing your place?"

"Should it?"

She shrugs. "You'll call your apartment later and get things sorted out?"

"Maybe, maybe not."

"Let it be, then." She points to a cabinet next to the bookshelf. "There's some pillows and blankets in there. The bird'll fall asleep as soon as you do. If he bothers you, I can move him."

"No," he replies. "I could use his company."

When Hanna leaves, he goes to the birdcage to test its vocabulary.

"Hello."

"*Ello.*"

"Hungry."

"*Unghee.*"

"Hanna."

"*Nyah.*"

"Honorificabilitudinitatibus."

Silence.

———◆———

The poet runs a hot bath. He soaks until the water is tepid, his hands deeply wrinkled. He pulls the plug but remains in the bath until well after the water has drained.

When he eventually sees himself in the mirror, he is startled and slaps himself in the chest. He expects a dead insect, a spider or a cockroach. He sees the blob above his heart, his mark. A sigh of relief.

"What the hell, Al?" he says to the mirror. "What's going on with you?"

He has no clean clothes, so he wraps his bottom half in a towel.

———◆———

Hanna returns to find the table set for two.

"You're back," says the poet. "I decided to make lunch."

"I didn't expect to find a naked man in my home."

"I have nothing else."

She goes to her storage room to find some clothes her ex-husband left behind. A few sweatshirts, briefs, slacks, socks. Everything one needs.

"Should be about your size," she says.

He slides the briefs on under his towel for privacy, lets the towel fall, squeezes himself into a too-small sweatshirt.

"I'm not as slim as I used to be." He turns to see his reflection in the microwave.

"Don't pity yourself around me. You're a fine man."

They sit down to eat.

"Are you going to call your wife?"

"My wife?"

"To tell her what happened."

"I don't see why I should worry her with that. We have our own lives with our own problems. We deal with them on our own."

"Sounds like the ideal marriage."

———◆———

On Monday, he wakes up in a ball on the loveseat.

"Good morning," says the macaw.

"Good morning," he replies, gets dressed, goes to teach a class.

Weeks flitter by, a routine established. The poet acquires a spare key.
He is forgetful, often leaving the door unlocked, the cupboards open, the
lights on. He enters the house with shoes on. Hanna tapes small paper squares
around the house:

Mid-crime neighbourhood. Lock the door.

Lights off, please.

No writing in my books, please.

Please rinse toothpaste from the sink.

Please don't leave taps running. It wastes water.

Wash dishes, please.

She never reprimands him for not following the rules but every Saturday
opens the newspaper to apartment listings and leaves it on the kitchen table.

———◆———

He holds office sessions twice a week in the afternoon, unlocks the door for
students to come and discuss their term papers. This semester he's teaching
all introductory courses so, he thinks, it's unlikely they will. Yet he's obliged to
spend two hours rolling a paperweight back and forth over a stack of minor
assignments. They are one-page responses to Wordsworth's "She Dwelt among
the Untrodden Ways" worth precisely one percent of the students' term grade.

"She Dwells Among Untrodden Ways" is a poem about impotency, one student writes.

Wordsworth's classic poem is about finding a girl's corpse in the woods, writes
another, *and how scary that was for him.*

The grades, he decides, will be randomly distributed between B and A minus.

Still, the possibility of an intrusion prevents him from concentrating,
and the university's rule against smoking in your office—for which he's been
rebuked several times—prevents him from achieving any sense of clarity he
might need to write.

The paperweight is a heavy glass orb. It reflects a small, wavering man—a beard half-grey, eyes invaded by wrinkles. He cannot resist withdrawing a cigar from his briefcase and opening the window. Outside in the parking lot, a yellow sun shatters upon rows of organized vehicles. Magpies chatter in a maple tree.

"Professor Windsor?"

A student stands in the doorway. A young man, the same from the other day in the bar.

"Is this a good time?" the student asks.

The poet sits on the windowsill, arms crossed. "Close the door. Take a seat."

The young man sits. He appears unbothered by the fact that the poet is smoking.

"I was just reading your assignment," the poet says, "in which you suggest Wordsworth was upset by a dead body in the woods. 'Mopey' is the term you applied to him, I believe."

"I wrote that pretty fast."

"As one does."

"You liked my idea?"

"No." He puffs. "But I can appreciate that you read the poem to the end. Twelve lines is a little much for most people these days. You're receiving an A minus."

"Thanks Professor."

"Now tell me your reason for coming in."

"I was hoping to take the same idea and use it in my term paper. I wanted to know if that's allowed."

"I don't see why not. But. *But*—"

The young man leans forward.

"*But*," the poet repeats, "you need to prove that you *feel* this material."

"Feel it?"

"Feel it. In your heart. Your blood. So what? Wordsworth uncovers a dead body in the woods, you say? So what?"

"So what?"

The poet lowers his voice. "At the bar the other day, you were accompanied by a series of fine young ladies, no?"

The young man raises his eyebrows.

"Any of them very close to you? Any you love, any you trust, any giving you the best sex of your life?"

The young man fidgets. "Maybe."

"I want you to do this. Go down to the valley by the river, find a secluded spot, a place where no one seems to have walked in a while. An untrodden way. Stand there for a moment, fill your nostrils with the greenest air. Then, when you're satisfied, and it's perfectly still, look down and imagine your love's face, cold and dead, staring up at yours from the earth."

"My love?"

"Then," the poet says. "I want you to bend down and look her in the eye. Eyes bright and hopeful and *young*—an infinite number of years ahead for you to delight one another. Lips moist. But, just as you bend to touch her face, an earthworm crawls from her nostrils. It makes its way across her smooth, cream-coloured cheek and dances on the curve of her jaw to mock you."

The young man's mouth hangs open.

"Everything," the poet says. "*Everything* you could imagine loving about her is gone. The world turns ten shades bleaker in an instant. You break down in hideous fits and fall into her cold lap and attempt to rip your own heart out. You sell everything you own and decide you cannot step foot in this city again and retain an iota of who you were. You become an absentee—a zombie."

The young man swallows.

"Okay? Now imagine this. You tell this story to someone, a friend. Someone you know well. And this person replies, 'Sorry, I have no idea who you're talking about.' Perhaps she didn't exist. Maybe she was nothing to begin with. Perhaps the moment she died was the moment you loved her. In a sense, it is *you* who are buried. Life from this point on is irrevocably miserable, unsatisfactory. What do you do?"

"I—I don't know."

"You sit down and write your term paper. You understand?"

The student nods and collects his things. The poet closes the door after him, cries for twenty minutes and resumes his study of the parking lot. He composes in his head.

———— ♦ ————

On the loveseat with his scraps of paper, he tries to remember what he was composing that afternoon. A-A-B-B-C-C. It will not come. He recalls the last word he came to—*Unless*—before he lost his train of thought.

"Unless," he says.

"*Un-eh*," says the macaw.

"Immortality?"

"*Ungree.*"

He removes a bag of peanuts from below the cage, holds up a handful. The macaw pecks twice.

Hanna returns, hangs her coat by the door, enters the living room.

"You're back," she says.

"Of course."

"You're writing?"

"It's all peanuts."

"Oh come on, Al. Your depression's going to affect the parrot. They're very sensitive to human emotions."

He doesn't respond.

"Give me a minute," she says.

She leaves for a while, rummages around the bedroom and returns with a small black typewriter.

"It's '78 whether you like it or not." She sets it on the coffee table. "Happy birthday."

"Is it already?"

"On Wednesday it is. The faculty's been passing a card around. Sorry to spring it on you. How's it feel to be forty-nine?"

"*Appy bird day*," the parrot says.

———— ◆ ————

He assigns his classes group exercises, to read a poem and discuss amongst themselves. Then, one by one, they are to comment on what they found interesting, keeping in mind the broader intellectual context of Romanticism. He doesn't lecture, he doesn't respond, he doesn't even listen. He hasn't prepared anything. The young man from his office drops the course.

———— ◆ ————

Hanna brings him a stack of paper and tells him to practice stream-of-consciousness writing, to write as long as he can without stopping. No contemplations, no doubt or opportunity for depression to break through.

"It's something I tell my students to do," she says, "to beat writer's block. Something will always arise—they have no choice. You become a writer."

"Become a writer?"

"Become a *functioning man*. Is that what you want to hear?"

He frowns.

"A little tough love, Al. It's something I used to do when I had your aspirations."

"Aspirations," he repeats, parrot-like.

"My belief is this. We could spend a year talking about what it *means* to write poetry, like we've done before, or you can write it."

When she's gone, he leans forward on the loveseat and tries to make his fingers comfortable above the keys. He types slowly using only his index fingers but doesn't stop for more than a second or two. When a page is full, he tosses it aside and sets in a new one. He continues until late in the evening, falls asleep in a ball for a couple hours, wakes up and continues. His typing keeps the bird awake and it grows progressively irritable. At two in the morning, it begins to scream.

Hanna comes in wearing a nightgown and flicks on the lights.

"Still at it?"

He finishes his sentence. "It's like digging a hole to Ethiopia."

She calms the bird by rubbing its chin and then sits beside the poet on the loveseat, reads over his shoulder. The page is incomprehensible, ripe with spelling mistakes. "I like the bit about pianos that extend forever in either direction."

"I wrote that?"

"Fourth line—"

He squints. "Tell me, what does that *mean*?"

"Where are your glasses?"

"Left them in the old apartment."

She rubs his shoulders. He doesn't notice. "It's late. I'm going to have a drink."

"Please," he says.

She returns shortly with wine and a bottle of pills. "The pills are to sleep. I take one. You're bigger, so for you, maybe one and a half. Two at *most*." She sits beside him on the loveseat again. "And why don't you call your wife for once? I love you dearly, but I have my limits. She can talk you through this."

"I told you, I can't concern Ruth with this. It's petty. Besides, she's fragile. Bad emotions get into her. I've seen it happen. She absorbs them like an artist."

"Like you?"

"She needs me as a—functioning man, as you would say. I go to her like this—and I'm no longer Al. I'm no use to her. She takes, she doesn't give. I would keep explaining what I mean, but I seem to have lost the words."

"But she does care for you. So you say."

"I learned long ago that our marriage works one way and one way only." He scratches the back of his neck. Silver hairs come free and spin in a draft. "She needs a husband who is pure. A confidant. A mountain. I've tried half my life to be that. If I'm not that, we both fail—and violently."

"Surely she's seen you on a bad day before."

"Hanna," he says, "I have a confession. In all my years, I haven't read a word to my wife. You are the only person with whom I've shared my own lines. Aside from the journals who lampooned me in the sixties, if you remember."

She nods. "She's like your Dulcinea."

"My Dulcinea—"

"From *Don Quixote*."

"I've never read it. These *Don Quixote* references you often make are wasted on me."

"She's the love who's impossible to capture because she exists only as imagination. Or imagination imposed on the real. The transcendent slip—she is a homely peasant girl in fact. I recommend you read it. You *really* should read it. It is essential."

He shrugs, retrieves his briefcase from the floor and opens it on the coffee table. At the back, behind his cigars, documents, money, is a folded sheet of paper. He takes it. It's a pencil drawing of a tree, nothing more. At the bottom is a year, *1962*. He hands it to Hanna.

"Ruth did this," he says, "in her whispery, frail, feminine way. She hasn't changed."

Hanna studies it for a minute. It's nothing remarkable. She sets it aside. "Your eldest daughter. You've often said she's your kin in spirit and body. You're close."

"Gayle's too innocent to understand. Too young. But, I fear"—his voice lowers—"old enough to know a hack when she sees one. She's drifting away from me."

"Keats was young. Would you call Keats if you had a phone through time?"

"I can't call anyone." He scratches his knee furiously. "I've become a mess, Hanna." He looks down at his chest and stomach. "Rather hefty, too, wouldn't you say? I don't have a worthwhile body. Now I don't even have a worthwhile mind. What would these women want with me?"

"Oh *quit* with this self-pity." She whacks him softly on the head. "Is this what your depression is all about? A midlife crisis?"

"I don't like that convention. Men always lose what they had. After the age of thirty, the faculties begin to decay steadily."

"That's simply not true. Plenty of people reach their renaissance later in life."

"Plenty of people are old fish," he says. "When I was a young man, I made a promise to myself. I said I would do what I knew was right. God's plan was poetry. I would be God's. I knew it would be a brutal life, but a life without it would be even more brutal. And by the age of thirty, I thought I was close to knowing God. By the age of forty, I thought I'd been slow, but I still had a few years—"

"Wallace Stevens wrote nearly everything after the age of fifty."

"Tell me what Wallace Stevens has done."

"He's—" She thinks.

"I'm afraid of doing what I've always hated in other men. They bury their nihilism and fear for life behind the gauze of some comfortable *art*. This 'mid-life crisis,' as you call it—it's a pathetic disease."

She throws up her hands. "Pack it in then, Al. Art is nothing but gauze. Go work at Woolco and grow into a raisin."

He shrugs and lights a cigar.

"You don't believe what I just said, do you?" she asks.

"Of course not."

"Then why do you doubt everything?"

"Hanna, I can't be anything but what I am. What alternative do I have? Become a mechanic? A teacher? A salesman? They live as though they're already dead. But once you learn that you can't be an artist and keep your house and bread—that's when you start your life as a lunatic. It's a road that only ends in suicide, sudden or gradual. But now that I'm here, I don't know where to—" He doesn't finish his thought.

"Don't say that word." She shakes her head and whispers, "*Suicide*. It's overused."

He pulls his feet up to the cushion and runs his arms around his legs like a boy trying to make himself smaller. It doesn't make him smaller. "Please don't be angry at me."

"I'm not. Just take a pill, sleep, and set your head straight in the morning." She takes her wine and stands by the doorway. "And for the love of God, Al, good and beautiful things have no age. I learned that years ago." She turns back to him, fighting tears. "Why do you think I take poets into my life, my house? Why get into education? Why live as a patron? Because I believe in it. It's not easy being sensitive—I get it. Most people won't ever know how you feel. But beauty is truth, regardless of how you are right now."

The poet remains awake past midnight, looking at the now well-faded drawing of the tree, the paper withering away from years of abrasion against the inside of his briefcase. Eventually he takes a pill and waits for it to kick in. It doesn't happen right away, so he takes two more.

"Another day," he whispers to the parrot. "I don't know how much longer I—"

"*Donno*," the parrot interrupts.

A peculiar drowsiness comes over him, one accompanied by a light high—a pleasant, ticklish high.

———◆———

He practices steam-of-consciousness writing nightly. When Hanna is home, she joins him in the living room, occasionally looking over his shoulder and reading what he's written but never commenting on it. He knows that it's incomprehensible to her. But she brings him food, does his laundry.

———◆———

One weekend, he walks to Safeway and buys the ingredients for French onion soup gratinée. He can't find everything he needs so replaces Gruyère with cheddar and fresh thyme with rosemary. He drops cloves entirely.

The onions take longer than expected to caramelize. While he waits, he croons to himself. He wishes for Monteverdi, but he left his records in the apartment. His Italian has not improved, but he croons in what sounds to him like Italian, claps at a brisk tempo, and walks room to room.

In the living room, he notices that the parrot is bobbing along to his claps. A receptive audience. He imitates its bobs, thrusting his neck forward awkwardly. "You're a good bird."

"*Parrot*," says the parrot.

"My apologies." He opens the latch and lets the cage door fall open. The parrot soars into the living room and rests on the top of a bookshelf. It unfurls its wings wide and screams. The poet applauds. "Show me what you got."

The parrot dives, completes a full circle of the room, knocks books to the floor. The poet chases it into the kitchen and finds it on the back of a chair, looking at pots and pans scattered around the counter.

"This episode on cooking with Allen Windsor," says the poet to the parrot, "we're making French onion gratin**ée**. I've prepared the onions in advance." He holds up the pan so the bird can see. "The next step is to prepare the broth."

When Hanna arrives, the soup is in the oven, the cheddar bubbling on the surface, the complex scent wafting through the house. "*Where is he?*"

"He's here," the poet says.

Hanna goes to the kitchen, carefully avoiding the bird shit on the hallway floor.

"Good God," she says. Cookware and utensils are sprawled about, the floor scattered with onion skin, water, salt. The refrigerator is open. One of the chairs is on its side and the parrot is under the table. The poet sits before two empty bowls, the typewriter, and a bread knife. There is no bread.

"I made dinner," he says, lighting a candle. "It's the least I can do."

She bends and the parrot leaps to her shoulder. She scratches its belly with one hand and closes the refrigerator with the other.

"You seem better," she says.

"Life is a wide field. Some of its fruits are poisonous."

"Okay." She drops a rag and wipes the floor with her foot.

"That can wait. The soup was ready some time ago."

Reluctantly, she takes her seat. He removes the French onion soup from the oven and sets it on the table. It's an excessive quantity for two people.

As they eat, the parrot flies from her shoulder to his and back. When it grows too restless, it returns to the floor and pecks at crumbs the poet left behind during the act of creation.

"So, the writing went well today," Hanna says after a while.

"Your advice was good."

"The stream-of-consciousness?"

"I've started many ideas from scratch."

"Is the soup a metaphor?"

He shakes his head. "You think I've lost it? It's just to show my gratitude."

"What do you have so far, then?"

He wipes his mouth, picks a sheet of paper from the floor and gives it to her. "It's missing a line. I'm still seeking a rhyme for *truth*."

Hanna reads the poem twice. She responds in her teaching voice, "Your voice, your position—it has shifted slightly. It's more—how you say—*present*. You've come into your own? You've landed on traces of character, and you're playing with perspective. It feels grounded."

"Do you have one?" he asks. "A rhyme for truth?"

"Youth. No—tooth, uncouth, goose. That's a partial rhyme. Noose?"

"Hmm—"

"I'm not a poet, Al. You know this."

"It will come," he says.

"It always does."

Hanna clears the table and begins washing dishes as the poet lights a cigar, turns back to the typewriter and tunnels his mind in search of a rhyme.

It takes Hanna forty-five minutes to clean the kitchen, by which time the sun is nearly set. "Don't worry about doing this regularly. I'm quite a happy cook."

Then she goes to her bag sitting on the counter and pulls out a newspaper, hands it to him. "The student paper," she says. "While you're in a good mood, maybe you'll find this entertaining. Page eight."

The poet takes the paper. It's a cartoon: *A Liberal Arts "Education."*

———— ◆ ————

Panel One: A student sits with a professor in an otherwise empty frame. The professor is obese, wears a pointy hat, shoes with bells, and a scabbard. The student asks: *Professor, can you help me with my term paper on the subject of melodrama?* The professor responds: *Melodrama?*

Panel Two: The professor has drawn his sword and now fills the entire panel. He says: *English literature is the noblest of all fields! It concerns the deepest of human emotions, purest ecstasies, heavenly delights, divine beauty, and the unfathomable mysteries of the soul! And it all begins with research.*

Panel Three: The same as the first. The student asks: *What kind of research?*

Panel Four: In a bar. The characters sit across from one another, between them are two absurdly large glasses of beer. At the next table is a young blond woman. The professor's sword lies on the floor and he's clearly drunk. He is turned around, staring the woman's breasts. He says: *Meloooo there, sexy.*

———•———

The cartoonist's name he recognizes as belonging to the young man from his office.

"I've been slandered," he says, picking up the bread knife.

"What?"

His face turns blotchy red, snot hangs from his moustache. He wipes it away with his sleeve and sets the knife down.

She puts her hand on his back, runs it up and down while he lowers his face to the table.

———•———

He sits in his office, rolling the glass orb back and forth across his desk.

A knock on the door.

"Al," says the dean. She enters and sits in the chair across from him, straightens her shoulders.

"I'm listening," says the poet. He brings his hand to his face to check for tears. There are none. He smiles.

"I suppose you've seen the cartoon in the paper."

"Wit is the candle on a good slice of mind."

"Umm, well, there's work to be done now. I'm not here to talk about the cartoon. It's extraneous. I'm talking about the big-picture concerns that this has brought to light again. Are you prepared to discuss issues of your performance this afternoon in my office?"

"I'd prefer to discuss issues of my performance now, and with the door open, please."

She nods, looks to the door to ensure it's closed. "I'm sure you anticipated this conversation for some time. This is our third meeting in two years. Do you recall when we last met?"

"Yes."

"Okay. Al, since the cartoon was published, and indeed for some weeks prior, several students have contacted us regarding your, for lack of a better word, proficiency as an educator."

"Proficiency—"

"There have been complaints filed regarding your despondency during lectures, frequent absenteeism, seemingly arbitrary assigning of grades, papers simply lost. In other words, not upholding our guarantee to provide students with quality and engaged learning."

He begins rolling the orb again.

"The purpose here is not to place criticism or blame," she says. "I'm here to provide you some options. To help you. Al, listen—you are not being fired. *However*, the board agreed that if a third meeting must occur, you are not to continue with the semester. This third meeting is, at your request, right now."

The orb rolls one and half seconds one way, one and a half seconds back. They both watch it.

"The university covers psychological counselling to tenured staff," she continues. "I've recommended that you complete fifty hours of sessions and, if you are deemed fit to resume teaching, we shall consider this water under the bridge. Do you understand?"

He catches the orb. "Completely."

———•———

"They think I've lost my mind. Lost my mind—"

The parrot says nothing, so he walks from room to room. In the kitchen he takes a plate, weights it in his hands, smashes it. He bends down to pick up the pieces and puts them in the bin.

Hanna comes home and follows him to the living room.

"Sit down, Al. What's gotten into you? I can hear you pacing from outside."

"I've taken down all your notes. All the little guidelines and restrictions. Did you think I was a child? I needed to be reminded of the most basic human functions, things a reasonable person does every single day? I'm surprised you didn't put a note on the sink that says *drink* or a note on the toilet that says *shit*."

Her mouth hangs open for a moment as she looks to the parrot, who is looking out the window.

"Was I so horrible here?" he asks.

"*No*." She spits the word, then clears her throat. "Really."

"Am I out of my mind? Who am I?"

She looks away. "You're scaring me."

"What's happening to me?" he whispers.

"Nothing's happening *to* you—"

"*To* me? But *in* me, you mean?"

"I didn't mean anything. It's just how it came out."

"I need to drink." He goes to the kitchen. "Anything, anything." He pours himself a brandy and returns, breathing rapidly as he sits on the loveseat and pushes his palms into his eyes.

Hanna takes a blanket from the floor and lays it over his shoulders. "It's just stress."

He removes his hands but keeps his eyes closed. He says nothing for a long time. Eventually she kisses him on the forehead.

"Rest," she says. "And in the morning, call your wife."

"You know I'm a miracle."

She waits for more.

"I can only believe the universe has a plan for me yet."

"That's the spirit," she whispers.

———◆———

He takes three pills, stands by the parrot's cage, runs his fingers along the bars.

"How embarrassing this all is."

———◆———

More weeks pass. He does not work or write. He hardly speaks. He disappears for hours at a time as Hanna holds vigil, never sure if she should expect him back. But like a runaway cat, he comes.

"Did you see the therapist today?" she asks.

"I was caught up."

He rises early one day in the summer, feeling light as air. His beard has grown in.

Normally during this time, he would be conducting review for the students' final exams and marking term papers. Instead he finds his life empty. No one to see, no job, no obligations. Except Gayle, who expects him home in two weeks.

"It's been enchanting to meet you," he says to the macaw. "Goodbye."

"*Bye-bye.*"

He boxes the typewriter, opens his briefcase, counts his money.

"It's enough," he informs the bird.

He ties his shoes in the doorway. While he's bending over, he finds a note that had fallen to the floor. *Keep Shoes Hidden. Bird Loves Laces.* He examines his shoes for damage—there is none. There has never been any, and the shoes have been there for months. He writes on the back of the note.

> *The timeless problem for sensitive men is that they risk killing what they love. If they come looking for me (the authorities, the university), tell them the truth. I've disappeared and you know nothing. I am no longer with you, nor worth speaking of. God bless you.*

Briefcase and typewriter box thumping against his legs, he walks to the dive bar. It's closed but the attached pizzeria is already preparing for the lunch rush and they let him in to use the phone. He calls the Honda motorcycle dealership on 96th Street.

"Is she ready to be picked up?" he asks. "Hmm—Yes, yes, the used CB750—I'll be arriving on foot."

chapter twenty-two
- 1979 -

"So I'm not sure what you mean by 'worth it,' dear Gayle," Hanna Federico says. "It implies there's a choice."

"He seems to have no trouble making the choice to abandon stuff—like you, and his job, and his horse, and everything he didn't want anymore."

Hanna lights a cigarette.

"I suppose that's it then," Gayle says.

"Did you learn everything you want to learn?"

"I'm only here for my mum, to ask her question. That's all."

Hanna goes to her bookshelf and takes a slim volume, hands it to Gayle. It's poetry. Her father's poetry. *Cycles Volume 1.* Published in 1965.

"I suppose you've never seen this? There are only twenty copies or so."

Gayle shakes her head.

"Will you stay for dinner?"

"I don't want to think any more about him. Besides, someone's waiting for me. I need to go."

Hanna leads Gayle to the front door.

"But you never told me," Gayle says from the doorway, cold air creeping around her, "where is he? Why is that so hard to answer?"

"Because you never asked." Hanna turns aside to a board hanging by the door containing keys, memos, cards. She takes one down, a postcard from San Francisco.

"A postcard? To you?"

"He's been all around the continent, it would seem."

Gayle leaves without a goodbye, walks home with the book in her inside pocket.

———•———

Lewis is asleep, so she resists clutching his hand to regain some sense of stability and goes to sit alone at Li Yong's kitchen table.

She opens her father's book to the first page. The dedication.

For my wife.

chapter twenty-three
- 1978 -

After leaving Edmonton by motorbike, the poet drives west along Highway Sixteen. First stop, late morning in Spruce Grove, he goes to an Eaton's to buy a tent, cookery, cans of beans.

———◆———

By the afternoon, he's in Jasper National Park, resting by a green lake alongside the highway, joined to a pebbled shore where benches are installed for tourists. He watches young families take their children knee-deep into the glacial run-off, return to their cars, eat French fries and take in the scenery. When they look to him, four months unshaven, they nod. He smiles but speaks to no one.

His fingers long for the vibration of the handlebars. He feels their absence. He decides not to stop in Jasper.

———◆———

He continues until he hits Clearwater and spends the night in a roadside motel.

———◆———

Before the crack of dawn, he heads in the direction of Kamloops, turns right at the sign for Salmon Arm. He passes through town and continues twenty minutes on a minor road. It's a cloudy spring morning. The sun will not crack today, he knows. It will remain dawn until the night comes. But he's early enough that the morning rush—tractors and school buses usually, struggling for dominance of the lane—hasn't started.

He finds a pull-out into the trees and parks his bike to safely examine himself in the left mirror. Black jacket and bandana. Baby-blue veins haunting his right cheek. Frown lines. Hair bristles out below his helmet and meets his beard. It's all whitening at the ends, fading to grey, simmering into black as it comes close to the skin. His hair has started to look like Ruth's older boar's-hair brushes, the ones she's been using the longest.

He pulls the bike behind a blueberry bush and proceeds on foot, helmet under his arm.

Five minutes through the trees and he pulls his black bandana up to his nose, becomes shade and goes to his knees behind a fallen tree. Through a break he can see the house. In the spring dawn light, it looks foreign. He's never seen it at this time of year, the windows reflecting overgrown ochre and sunburnt grass. The sunflowers all adolescent.

The barn door opens and Gayle steps out, carrying two small buckets of milk back to the house. The poet watches her steps, her way of leaving as little space as possible between her feet and the earth, and the endearing limp that says she is her parents' daughter.

He waits another twenty minutes before anything happens. Then Ami springs out for the school bus. When the bus pulls away, the poet turns his attention to the parlour window where a woman in a housecoat stands with hands pocketed and a gaze set across the lawn. She leans back, cracks her spine, struggles to keep the swan-like pose, but soon falls back into her natural position: bent like a branch with a load.

Shortly after, he hears the car start on the far side of the house and pull onto the road in the direction of town. There is no more movement in the house. Hoping the women will be out for a while, the poet approaches through the ankle-deep grass and finds the spare key beneath an empty flowerpot by the back door.

He enters the parlour, removes his note from his pocket.

The house creaks. There are no photos, no decorations, nothing on the walls. Ruth's painting sits on its easel—another nature scene, a meadow and some mountains, unfinished. No shadows yet.

He considers going to the library, but upon crossing the parlour he decides otherwise. There's nothing there, he thinks, but reminders of who he was. The books would hit him like thousands of bullets through time. There is not a single one he does not know the origin of, where he found it, and why he bought it. It's too much right now.

He unfolds his note to Ruth and goes to leave it on her easel.

...for I don't know how long. But for your good, I need to disappear. Until I return, believe I was never here to begin with. God bless you.

"You again?"

He turns. Gayle? he thinks. Is she in the stairwell?

The poet shoves the note in his pocket and makes for the hallway. Gayle reaches the bottom, peeks around the corner to catch the trail of his black jacket just as he pulls the front door behind him. He leaves a crack. He can't resist hearing what she has to say.

"I trust you, bird. But I want to know more."

He closes the door, drops the note in the mailbox and runs for the trees.

———— ◆ ————

That day he passes through Kamloops and breaks south to Abbotsford, bypassing Vancouver on his way to the American border, arrives in Seattle by nightfall.

Upon entering the United States, he slows considerably and peaks at two hundred kilometres a day. He drives in a snake shape down the West Coast, making ventures into the interior, stopping frequently. Some days he drives straight east into the hills, spends the night inland, anonymous amongst trees.

He speaks to few people, aside from wistful waitresses in checkered diners along the interstates where he stops for morning porridge and mid-afternoon pie. In the evenings, he haunts fires surrounded by sawed logs in single-occupant campsites, or motel lobbies with the typewriter on his lap. He fills countless pages, almost all of which he throws away or leaves on lacquered coffee tables to be discovered by the next pilgrim.

He sees the ratio of diamonds to fool's gold as 1:500.

It's December when he arrives in San Francisco. He enters the city but finds it too loud and bright for his taste, decides to leave the ocean and take on the South.

At dusk, exiting east toward to the interstate, he spots a hitchhiker wearing a leather jacket over a black-and-white striped dress, vibrant on a patch of dead grass outside a Baskin-Robbins, her legs covered in road dust. He stops.

"What are you doing?" he asks.

"What's it look like I'm doing? I'm trying to get out of here."

He pulls up his visor, squints into her moon-shaped face. "You look like someone."

"Everybody looks like somebody."

He gestures to the bike. "It's late. Wherever you're going, I'll take you."

She shrugs and follows him.

"Are you a working girl? I've seen plenty."

"Man, I *was*, but I'm going home." She pulls a cigarette from her purse and holds it in her lips, unlit. "That's why I'm standing here."

He starts the bike and she climbs on. "It's late," he says. "Let me take you for dinner and we'll go in the morning."

"Is that what it's gonna take?"

He drives back to San Francisco, finds a candlelit seafood restaurant and orders them both a three-course halibut meal. She picks away at her food, ignores the salad entirely and leaves heavy chunks on the bone. He eats quickly and rapturously, chooses the most decadent of chocolate tarts for dessert and eats them both.

"What's your name?" he asks as chocolate dissolves in her mouth.

"I go by Emma."

"Like Emma Barrett, Sweet Emma?"

"Hmm?"

"I suppose you're too young to know who that is."

He pays the bill and they drive to a nearby motel. There's no shortage of them in the area. The receptionist is used to male guests arriving with younger female company and signs them in without a word.

The room is heavy with something—salted air, he thinks, or sweat. The musk from strangers' bodies has been caked onto the walls and flakes off over time. How many people have stashed their gloomiest memories here?

He lies on the bed and she crawls on top of him. Her fingers make small circles around his nipples and she bites his beard.

"Don't," he says. "You must be tired after the meal. I know I am. Food makes one drowsy."

She continues her way up his beard and to his chin, kisses his bottom lip.

"Why don't you take a shower?" He pushes her gently away.

"Aren't you gonna have me?"

"Have you?"

"Never mind." She slides off the bed and goes to the bathroom. The water runs.

Alone, he removes his typewriter from its box and sets it on his lap, sinks against the headboard.

——————◆——————

She returns later in her underwear, hair still damp, dripping at the back. Her skin is tight in places and loose in others, subtle stretch marks around the edges of her stomach above her hip, and he suspects she's not as young as he originally thought, or that she's recently been pregnant. She sits at the foot of the bed, hands folded neatly on her lap, scratching the carpet with her toes.

"What are you working on there?" she asks after a while.

"My never-ending masterpiece."

"You're strange."

He types slowly with only his index fingers. She lifts her legs to the bed to lie perpendicular on the mattress, her back to him, head propped by her left hand. She looks at her reflection in the dead television and watches the stranger behind her. He looks up briefly from his work to observe her shape.

"What's your masterpiece?" she asks. "You writing a book?"

"I'm a poet," he says, and after a pause, "or so it seems."

"Where're you from?"

"Victoria, Canada."

"You're my first Canadian." She turns around, sits cross-legged by his feet. "This how you do it in Canada? You buy your whores dinner and make 'em watch you work in the bedroom?"

"I don't know. You're my first."

"Are you still gonna drive me out of here?"

"Yes." He stops typing, reaches for his briefcase next to the nightstand and withdraws an envelope containing all his American money, hands it to her. "Keep this."

She flips through it, counts, appears to calculate something in her head, but sets the money aside without taking any. Then she shifts to the head of the bed and retreats under the sheets. He remains on top of the covers and observes the calm ridge the naked stranger makes in the blanket, her shoulders rising and falling with the flow of breath.

"What do you write about?" she says after a while.

"Love."

"Love poetry?"

"It's been my life's pursuit."

"You think it's real then, huh?"

"Love?" he asks.

"Yeah."

"Who could say?"

"That's a man's answer." Her head emerges, hair full of static. "Did you write about me just now, when I was laying on the bed there? 'Cause I saw you lookin'."

He exhales slowly through his nose, removes the page he's working on. "Fragment seven hundred and seven—Emma—A feminine riddle in the motel—"

"Wait," she says. She sits up straight, her elbow against his, looking over at the paper quivering in his fingers. The words are pale grey letters, suggesting the ink ribbon is low "I wanna see 'cause I'm not so good at listening."

"Let's read together," he says. "One line each. Start here, the last stanza."

Her eyes grow wide and she nods. "Of lovers entwinned—"

"Entwined," he corrects her.

"Entwined in fantastical knots—"

"Fanatical," he says.

"With polar-star eyes and hands at their throats."

"At one in their wisdom that loving is merging," he says.

"Of motions soob—lime."

"Sublime," he says.

"—and longings conversing—Hey," she looks up, "it doesn't end."

"I don't write things with an ending."

"Do you have a wife, man?"

"Yes—"

"I thought so. Most of my guys have wives."

"Are you all alone in the world, Emma?"

"All alone in the world? What's that supposed to mean? I got a mum and a sister. They live in Breckenridge, Colorado. That's where you're gonna take me, but I betcha don't know where that is."

"Are you a mother?"

She doesn't answer. He curls onto his side and she to hers, back to back. He reaches to the nightstand and turns off the light.

Darkness.

"Yeah," she says. "He's with my sis and my mum."

———◆———

In the morning, he studies his American road map and estimates that the drive to Breckenridge will take twenty hours. A day and a half.

On the way out of the city, he stops at a department store he doesn't recognize the name of and buys her a helmet. It's slightly too big, but she pads it with newspaper to stop it from moving around.

———◆———

They don't speak until they cross the border to Nevada, pass by Reno, and stop for breakfast at a roadside diner. He buys her a hot dog at her request.

"How long have you been away?" he asks as they sit on a bench outside the diner, below a tree to protect them from the already oppressive desert sun.

She holds the hot dog in one hand, an unlit cigarette in the other. A daub of relish rests on her chin. "'Bout a year. You?"

"I can't remember."

"And where are you goin'?"

"I've yet to decide. Though, I hope, someplace more beautiful than I am."

She doesn't respond.

———◆———

They drive until evening. As they transition from desert to mountains, the temperature drops and the landscape is snowed over. He stops at a roadside shop and buys them both cotton-filled coats.

———◆———

They stop to sleep at a motel a few kilometres shy of Salt Lake City. He requests a single fold-out mattress be laid on the floor at the foot of the bed.

"You don't need to do that," she tells him as they enter the room.

"I respect your privacy."

"It's not like I'm scared, you know, if that's what you think. I been in lots of places with strangers."

She takes a shower as he gazes out the window at an angular hill covered in shrubs, still in the moonlight. Snow descends.

When she returns, she falls asleep almost immediately. The last thing she sees is the poet bordered by a snow-coloured halo.

———◆———

They arrive in Breckenridge at noon. Entering town after nearly two thousand kilometres at highway speed, he feels the buildings and mountains rise up as part of a life-sized diorama. They seem flimsy and false, as though a too-strong wind could break them apart. She directs him through town, along streets of picturesque pine-panelled homes, into another neighbourhood, clearly poorer, where houses are pressed into single-storey duplexes.

"It's here," she says as they reach the end of a cul-de-sac.

She climbs down and looks through the window of a duplex. "I almost can't remember if it's the one on the left or on the right." She takes a few hesitant steps toward the house. "Are you gonna come?"

He shakes his head.

She approaches the front door and rings the doorbell, wraps her arms around her new coat. The door opens on a middle-aged woman smoking a cigarette. Behind her is a young woman carrying a baby.

For a long spell, the poet can't make out what's said. None of the women move their hands, none raise their voices. The one with the baby looks past Emma's shoulder to see him leaning against his bike.

Suddenly they cry, and the middle-aged woman squeezes Emma so forcefully that she's lifted off the ground. The woman with the baby joins the embrace and the child screams.

The poet starts the ignition. When the women hear the sound, they break the hug. Emma beckons him inside.

He carefully manoeuvres the bike around parked vehicles as he exits the cul-de-sac.

Having come so far inland, he decides to carry on into the Midwest. He spends Christmas alone in a highway motel near Kansas City and New Year's Day on the outskirts of Knoxville, Tennessee, from which point he breaks for the coast.

In April, after travelling the rising and falling Atlantic seaboard, he realizes he's almost out of money. Not even enough for a ticket home if he wanted one. He pulls into the nearest sizeable town, which is Rome, Georgia, finds a car wash, meticulously sprays away all trace of his pilgrimage.

That same day, he pawns the bike, puts the cash in an envelope, and sends it to Emma. Briefcase and typewriter thumping against his leg, he walks to a nearby IHOP and shaves in the washroom. He leaves only a moustache, proper and shaped to the arc of his narrow upper lip.

part seven

hunger

chapter twenty-four
- 1979 -

Everything Ruth prepared for the gallery has been loaded into a truck and sent express. Her luggage is packed and waiting by the door. She didn't know what she expected, but it wasn't this, it wasn't fear—fear combined with a great deal of annoyance at the fact that, this being the Christmas season, plane ticket prices have skyrocketed.

———◆———

On the morning of her departure, Ruth brings Ami to Bill and Elizabeth's farm.

"We'll take care of her, Ruth," Bill says.

"You're obliged to say that. I believe it, too."

Elizabeth stands in the doorway behind Bill. "She's a little angel. Don't worry."

"I'm not worried about that," Ruth says. "I'm worried about other things, though—I've never been on an airplane before."

"Never?"

"I took a train once, from Vancouver to here. I didn't like it."

"You're a homebody, Ruth. It's nothing abnormal."

Elizabeth has been more congenial since Ami befriended her. With hands folded politely before her, an oven mitt in one, she even smiles.

"With all the—terrorism," Ruth says. "All those bombs going off in the States. Should I be worried about that?"

"Not in Canada," Elizabeth says and gives her a sympathetic pat on the arm. "You'll do fine at your little show."

"Thanks." Ruth bends to kiss her daughter on the forehead. "See you on the twenty-fourth."

Ami steps toward Bill.

———◆———

Flying, she soon learns, is a surprisingly agreeable mode of travel. A cool wash of sky to her left. The cabin warm and illusory as though for that brief hour it is unconcerned with the cold world entirely.

She stays in a private room in a hostel on Pandora. After calling all potential accommodations in downtown Victoria, it was the cheapest she could find for the two days she plans to be in town. They offer her a discount for travellers over forty even though she isn't. The staff call it an advance Christmas gift.

But the building is loud when she arrives. Although there are no more than a dozen people in the lobby, they are all young, intoxicated and talkative, speaking German, Japanese, French.

Ruth curls on the bed with her clothes still on: paint-splattered jeans and a rustic sweater with fraying cuffs. She cannot sleep against the raging noise and the stifling heat. A previous occupant has turned the furnace to full gallop, and a curled pipe against the wall is too hot to even touch. She doesn't know how to adjust it, so she opens the window, but the smell of marijuana wafts persistently up from the street. Along with music.

It wasn't like this before she left. There is no more Perry Como or free, floating jazz. She doesn't know what music is now. Maybe, she thinks, this is the Pink Floyd the news was sometimes talking about. Cerebral trash, she decides.

She turns on a small TV in the corner and searches for cartoons. She finds *Looney Tunes*—not Coyote and Road Runner, but something regarding the exploits of Daffy Duck—and watches it lying atop of the covers.

———•———

In the morning, she walks to the gallery on Yates. A young man answers the door.

"I'm expected. Ruth Windsor."

"I didn't hear anything—but who knows? A solicitor?"

"What?"

"Sorry, that's lingo in the Community for someone trying to get their works up."

"I'm a friend of Annabella."

"She's coming by later sometime."

"Can't I go in?"

"Sorry, I'm not allowed to let people in. I'm just a volunteer."

Ruth turns to leave, but as she does she runs into Annabella, moving toward her at a brisk pace. She embraces Ruth and presses her red lips to both her cheeks. "A la française," she says. "Welcome home, dear Ruth."

They enter the gallery and turn left into a small studio space that doubles as an office. It's a long room with wooden floors spotted with paint and chemicals, a desk in the corner. The young man follows them in and returns to his work. One of his paintings is of a severed swine's head surrounded by bursts of red and pink. The second, a tiger with its mouth open, which contains another tiger with its mouth open, which contains another, and another, until they're too small to discern. The last painting is of a lion looking at its reflection in a pond of toxic green water.

"So," Annabella says. She wears all black, thin as ever, hair pulled into an elaborate nest, offsetting her sharp, dazzling white chin.

"So."

"So."

"Yep." Ruth doesn't look the woman in the eye. She's thinking of another moment—the time this Annabella wiped a droplet of wine from the side of Ruth's lip. The sensuality of it. The moment never died. Ruth lives in it at all times, like all moments—but the woman, with the years locked in her, seems to have forgotten.

"How is it, Ruth, coming back after so many years? You look glorious." She examines Ruth's dishevelled and uncut hair, her fraying sweater hanging with the light scent of manure.

"Terrible," says Ruth. "The tourists and all. When did the Germans invade?"

"Oh, it's always like this."

"Are we Disneyland now? Don't people have rain and boats in their own country?"

"Oh, Ruth. You bring back so many memories." She laughs a short, well-designed laugh. "I think the international presence does wonders for the Community."

"What's the Community?"

Annabella shifts sideways to observe the progress of the young man's surrealist jungle series. He dries his brush by tapping it furiously on the edge of a metal container. When the commotion is over, Annabella turns back to Ruth. "The Community's a collective of artists around the island who look out for each other, support each other, have showings and other events."

"Like a social club? Like the one we left in the sixties—"

"Not a club. It's a social *movement*—a way of making new paths. Things have changed since the sixties, Ruth."

"You look very much the same."

Annabella smiles. "I've grown to believe that art is everybody's business. Even in its rebellion, because art is always rebellion. It's the rebellion of many."

"I guess."

"It's never really been a solitary affair, has it?"

Ruth points to the young man's work. "Is this the kind of work people do around here? I mean, the abstracts, or kind of abstracts?"

"Sometimes, yes. Come." Annabella leads Ruth through another door to a dehumidified storage space. She opens a deep cabinet and pulls out a work of her own. It's as Ruth remembered. Many blotches and triangles, dozens of layers of texture. Her style is the same. What's changed is her scale. The painting she shows Ruth is a near six-by-six-foot square filled with dark black and blues. The first word that comes to Ruth's mind is *inhospitable*.

"It's called 'Mice,'" Annabella says, smiling.

"Kind of—ironic?"

"Yes, I suppose. I never thought of it that way. I'd like your honest opinion." She lowers her voice. "What do you *think* of this piece, Ruth?"

Ruth opens her mouth, tilts her head and tries to lose herself in "Mice." "I'm not sure. I suppose the word that comes to mind is *free*."

"Free?"

"The feeling of being free. Having a day off, for example. Like on Thanksgiving or another stat holiday."

Annabella looks thoughtfully at her own work.

After a while, Ruth softly adds, "It's beautiful."

"Thank you, Ruth—*Thank you*."

"What does it mean?"

"I wouldn't say it *means* anything. No, there's no such thing as *means* this, *means* that. Not in my work. I'm terribly anti-hermeneutical. I like to think of art as a *conversation*. You would never interrupt someone you're talking to every five seconds and say, *Oh, let me clarify what you mean*. You just listen, take in what they're saying. What do you think?"

"A hundred and ten percent." She clears her throat. "Did my paintings arrive?"

Annabella takes Ruth's elbow. "Of *course*. That is the reason you're here. You want to know what's going to be done for your works." She leads Ruth back to the wooden room. The young painter is gone. The swine's head appears sharper, pronouncedly more in pain, without the painter's body blocking it. Ruth can't tell if she feels relieved or bothered by the absence of the furious, silent painter. The painting alone might be worse.

"Your pieces arrived a few days ago, Ruth. Listen now, I have some exciting news—"

"I'm listening."

"In the new year, we'll be playing host to a transnational tour of artists and art connoisseurs. Our comrades around the globe. The tour goes from here to Toronto, several schools in the States, Spain, France, Japan, Korea, and the United Kingdom. This year's message is"—she holds her hands up, palms facing each other a foot apart as though measuring something—"modernity and tradition."

"Golly," Ruth murmurs.

"The tour starts in Japan, hits Canada by the second week of January."

"Japan, huh?"

"I remembered what you told me on the phone about your work. And I *knew* your pieces would fit perfectly into our exhibit of *Showcasing Canadiana*. A tender look at rural British Columbia. I knew I wanted something by an obscure painter that could showcase our nation's unabashed and—say—complex love of the outdoors, the value we place on hard work, the struggle to find oneself in isolation. Ruth, do you identify as a naïve painter?"

"Naïve?"

"In the naïve tradition. Say, do you take pride in your lack of formal education?"

"Yes," Ruth says flatly, not understanding the question. "A hundred and ten percent."

"A hundred and ten percent? That's a cute expression, Ruth. Is that something people say in Salmon Arm?"

Ruth nods and they exit the room, down an echoing hall, to a set of double wooden doors.

"I know I should have gotten your say in how the works are displayed. But I did my best."

They enter the main gallery. It's a wide hall, dim, with hardwood floors and high ceilings. The only lights are off-white bulbs on metal rods running along the perimeter, illuminating the paintings.

Silently, they walk around it.

The alpaca, the cows.

More of the same.

And more (the alpaca is always included).

Views of the forest, morning light through the branches. The perspective of a trespasser.

Willy's tree house.

The farmhouse.

Rills in the field left behind by the tractor.

The shed with its metal roof.

Moss.

Light breaking through the corn.

Bill and Elizabeth on their porch. His eyes are exhausted but satisfied, lips content with the work he's done. She is glowing, as though her body is filled with fresh mountain air. Their portrait is bigger than the rest of the paintings and more detailed. It appears to watch over everything, through everything, through the gallery walls, across Canada. Ruth painted their eyes to look focused on the distance, an expression borrowed deliberately from Hayez's portrait of the Biblical Ruth.

"I never thought I'd see them in a place like this," Ruth says, feeling a sense of abandonment. A familiar sense. She turns her thoughts inward to pry at the emotion, flip it over like an old stone to see the insects scatter.

"It's always a joy to see your works on display for the first time."

"The first pieces I've finished in years. These two are"—she looks at Bill, who is looking away—"friends of mine."

Annabella doesn't ask about the paintings, what they mean, if they mean anything. "Do you have a pen, Ruth?"

Ruth removes one from the inside pocket of her coat as they move to a small table by the door where Annabella has left a stack of papers.

Ruth signs a document indicating which pieces will be for sale. "You'll tell me the prices later," Annabella says. "I can offer my discretion if you'd like it." There are also documents to sign, allowing the paintings to be photographed and reproduced. "Are you okay with your pieces ending up in magazines, reviews, etcetera?"

"I suppose the paintings say what I can't, even from a magazine. I can't speak to anyone—but the art can, like you said. Like a conversation."

The final document obliges her to retrieve the unsold works within two weeks after the show ends, or else they will be donated or—in lieu of a suitable donor—destroyed.

"Destroyed?"

"It's *never* happened. Artists are pretty protective of their work, as you know."

They exit the gallery. "By the way, Ruth, there's a dinner this evening. It's for the sponsors. It's at a marvellous sushi bar down the block—a sort of chef's table. Where are you staying?"

"In a stifling room on the second floor of a youth hostel, surrounded by addicts and foreigners."

"I see. Well, do consider coming. I should mention, it's *semi*-formal. It's at a sushi bar, after all." She writes the address on the back of her business card. "At seven."

Ruth takes the card, looks down at her fraying sweater. "Okay."

Annabella lingers in the gallery. Before exiting, Ruth looks over her shoulder to see Bill and Elizabeth in the sanitized gallery light and feels an arrow of regret for abandoning them in a world so *inhospitable*. How they will shiver when the eyes of the world are on them—German, French, Japanese? Have they seen anything like them? she thinks.

They've become strangers to her once again, just like the city, like every human on earth, and she feels nostalgic, after a single day, for the soft quarantine of the airplane.

When she's in the doorway, Annabella calls to her: "And please supply me with a short artist statement as soon as possible. A page is fine. Where you work, your inspirations, things like that. It's for the publicity."

———◆———

She finds dinner that evening at a McDonald's a few blocks from the hostel. Realizing she hadn't eaten anything since arriving, she orders a Big Mac and a large order of French fries. She carries the paper bag back to her room, turns on *Looney Tunes* and curls up cautiously on the bed to watch it, a creature of grease, lethargy. This is the way her husband went. But the McDonald's, for all she's heard of it in TV commercials, is even more disappointing than Pink Floyd. It's seven p.m.

She never intended to go to the sushi bar anyway.

When the commercials come, she writes her bio on a napkin.

She includes her name (Ruth Windsor), where she works (Salmon Arm), and her sponsor (ACME), and makes a quick sketch of dynamite.

———◆———

In the morning, she goes to the gallery on Yates, knocks. There is no one there, so she slides her napkins into the mailbox and returns to the hostel, where she is told by the receptionist that she was supposed to have checked out and vacated the room an hour ago.

"Where am I supposed to go? My flight's not 'til six."

"Sorry, ma'am. It's gotta be cleaned for the next guest. Did you have a nice stay in our luxury suite?"

"No."

"Ah?"

Ruth clicks her tongue. "What can I say? Young people make me sick."

The girl shrugs, begins flipping through a binder of check-in and arrival times. "Sorry to hear that, ma'am."

"I couldn't step into the hallway without feeling like I was going to get assaulted and I'm pretty sure I got high off the fumes. I don't understand why you're all—" Ruth leans over the desk. "Can I ask you something?"

"I guess."

"What do people your age—live for?"

She girl looks to the window. Cloudy light illuminates her profile in a way that Ruth interprets as extraordinarily sad. "Just wanna be happy, I guess—like anyone. Does that answer your question?"

"Do you have a mother?"

"Of course."

The hostel lobby is quieter than she's seen it. "What day is it?"

"It's Christmas Eve."

"It's the twenty-fourth already?"

The girl nods.

"Are you spending tomorrow with your mom?"

"Mhmm. She's coming in from Van." The girl looks away from the window and closes the binder. "You seeing your daughter?"

"No." Ruth takes a step back, rolls her cuffs up and down. "Not my eldest. She left me, ran away to Edmonton a few months ago—for love. To be perfectly happy, you know, just like you. It worked out for her. I have two daughters, though. One's only seven."

The girl clears her throat.

"You look like someone I knew once," Ruth says. "Is your mother's name Jean by any chance, a babysitter?"

"No—I'm sorry—and I'm sorry about your daughter, too."

"What do you think I should I do then? I mean, for Christmas."

"You spending it with your little girl?"

"I didn't even get her a gift. We don't celebrate anything, but why the hell not now, eh?"

"Umm." The girl who looks like Jean scratches her chin. "There's a toy store a couple blocks away on Douglas."

———◆———

The store's packed to capacity with parents buying last-minute gifts. Not a single child. Ruth plugs her ears and elbows her way through the crowd.

"Hey!" someone shouts.

"Let me in—I'm sick."

"You can't just *do that*," someone tells her.

She makes her way to the back of the store and finds an employee straightening glossy packaged dolls on a shelf.

"Miss," says Ruth.

"Yes?"

"I need something for my daughter—"

"Join the club," says a nearby man, chuckling.

She seizes the employee's hand. "I left my daughter in Salmon Arm for Christmas."

"What's Salmon Arm?" The woman pulls her hands back, eyes wide, frightened. She looks to the corner where a broad man, a manager and general security presence, watches over the scene. He looks at Ruth's frayed sweater and shrugs.

"*Please*," Ruth repeats.

"What's your daughter like?"

"She had a doll once. A weird plastic girl with eyes like purgatory. B something. You know?"

"Barbie? Sorry ma'am, Barbie's been sold out for weeks. We only have Crissy and Tammy dolls left—see?" She holds up a doll with black hair and a malevolent grin on its non-lips.

Ruth shakes her head. "What else do kids do now?"

"Board games are pretty big, like the Hungry Hungry Hippos."

"What?"

"It's a bunch of hippos eating marbles in a little bowl. Your daughter have friends that she plays with?"

"I think so."

The woman gestures to the back wall.

Ruth moves to the back, finds the small stack of Hungry Hungry Hippos. She recognizes the box from a commercial. It shows four children operating four variously coloured plastic hippos binging on marbles as they roll chaotically around a bright red field. The game consists of pressing the same lever over and over again as vigorously as possible.

Ruth stares into the eyes of the lime-coloured hippo as she waits in the line.

"At'll be forty bucks," says the cashier.

"*Forty?*"

They point to the sticker on the box.

"It's *God's birthday*, though."

"Supply and demand," the cashier says. "That's economics."

"Don't give me those disgusting platitudes. Will you take ten?"

The cashier stands tall, unrelenting.

"Excuse me." A man enters the conversation, the same man who earlier told her to join a club. "It's Christmas. The lady is clearly in dire straits. Can't you offer her a discount?"

"If we offered one customer a discount," the economical cashier replies, "we'd have to offer *all* customers a discount."

The man steps between Ruth and the counter. He provides two twenties for the Hungry Hungry Hippos and gives the box to Ruth. "For the lady."

"You want a receipt?" the cashier asks the stranger, who turns to Ruth and repeats the question.

"I don't know," she says.

"No," the man answers on her behalf.

"Well," the cashier says. "That's something of a Christmas *miracle* right there."

When the surrounding customers see what the man has done for the lady in dire straits, they begin whispering, saying "How wonderful!" and "What a lucky lady." The cashier's miracle comment echoes throughout the store. People begin to clap and half the store erupts in noise, those in the back unaware of what they're clapping for.

Ruth pushes her way out, waits on the sidewalk for the miracle-giver to emerge.

When he comes, Ruth squeezes the game against her sweater. "What do you want?"

"Want?"

"Are you trying something on me?"

He laughs, puts his hand on Ruth's shoulder. She shirks away. "If I want anything, it's only that you say a prayer for me and my family. And I to yours."

Ruth nods.

"And one more thing." He takes from his wallet a small slip of paper and hands it to her, giving her hand a gentle squeeze as he does so. It's an advert from The Church of Jesus Christ of the Latter-day Saints, offering free Christmas dinner to the "less than fortunate," not on Christmas Day, but the day after. *Families Welcome!!!* it says.

When she arrives at the airport, she's told the flight is severely delayed due to heavy snow and ice storms in Kelowna. There's an approximately three-hour wait.

The airport is swarming with people attempting to fly home for Christmas Day. Unable to find a seat in the boarding area where she can be alone, she sets her luggage against the wall near a news and pretzel stand and waits, breathing in the spirit of fried dough.

Soon her vision retreats and she falls into her familiar well—sounds and voices retreat and form a meaningless swirl. She pulls her jacket up over her head, folds her hands atop Hungry Hungry Hippos and closes her eyes.

Eventually she hears someone pull their luggage against the wall a few paces to her left. She lifts her jacket. It's someone in a long orange dress that splays over their legs and across the floor. Their back is perfectly straight, parallel to the wall but not touching it.

She repeats mantras in her head, raising the volume of her inner voice whenever the ambient noise becomes aggressive, when pretzels descend into the oil, when arguments break out between people who want to put their feet on the chairs and people who want to sit.

She expects the person in orange to go but after forty-five minutes she looks out see they're still there. She pulls back her jacket and is surprised to see it's a man—no eyebrows, a shaved head, appearing to be anywhere between eighteen and thirty.

She clears her throat.

The man doesn't notice.

She clears her throat again. "Sir."

He turns and she sees he's smiling. He was smiling before he turned. He may have been smiling the whole time he was sitting there. His lower teeth are concealed by his lips and the upper ones are petite and aligned.

"Make sure nobody takes my spot," she says.

"Sorry?"

"Please make sure no one sits here but me."

"Ah sorry—I'm not good with English."

"I'm *go-ing*," she annunciates, "to the *bath-room*."

"I watch your bags?" He's still smiling, mouth now slightly ajar, wondrous and blameless.

"Yes," she says.

She brings only Hungry Hungry Hippos with her.

When she returns, the man is sitting beside her luggage. The orange robe—she realizes now that it's improper to think of it as a dress—is folded neatly under his knees and no longer poses a tripping hazard.

This time she sits cross-legged on the floor like him. It's been a while since she's sat this way—the spine doesn't want it. She searches for a reflective surface to confirm her deformity, but there is none. Only the face of the smiling man.

"Thanks," she says.

"You are welcome."

She doesn't know why, but she trusts the man. He seems at home here in the well she thought was hers alone. "Where are you from?"

"Thailand." He gestures to his robes and laughs.

"Are you a monk?"

"Monk—yes."

"What are you—doing *here*?"

"I come because there is a Buddhist temple and school—in Victoria—and I learn English. Now home for a holiday."

"That's brave." She looks down at the Hungry Hungry Hippos. "I used to live here. Now I live in Salmon Arm."

"Sal-o-*mon*?" he asks, the last syllable, *mon*, hopping through the air between them and into her mind, clear and delightful as a winter rabbit.

Ruth nods. "I guess you're not allowed to be so close to women, huh? I learned that about Buddhist monks once."

"Women—ah, no, we cannot touch. Is a rule." After a while, he asks, "Are you scared of the airplane?"

She shakes her head no. "I like them."

"You want to hear a joke?" he asks without any clear transition of subject.

"A joke?" She realizes she's crying when she tastes tears. "Yes."

"Knock knock."

"Who's there?"

"*Spell*."

"Spell who?"

"W-H-O," says the monk. "*Who.*"

She begins to sob.

———◦———

They are side-by-side, not speaking, for nearly an hour. In the monk's company, Ruth no longer feels she needs to hide beneath her jacket. She watches the world and, in her head, attempts to guess where people are from and where they're going. The monk, she knows by intuition, is playing the same game in his own head and in his own language. Eventually he leans over and points to Hungry Hungry Hippos still on Ruth's lap.

"A game?"

"For my daughter Ami."

"I never see this before."

"Do you want to try?"

"To play?"

"Yes."

The monk nods.

Ruth opens the box for the first time and places the red plastic bowl on the floor between them. The game, it turns out, is as simple as it looks. Marbles move confusedly in the arena as four hippos look on. The levers make the hippos lunge forward and open their mouths. The players mash the levers and whomever's hippo has eaten the most marbles by the end wins.

They play three rounds of the game until someone reading a newspaper at a nearby bench asks them to stop.

———◦———

Shortly after, an intercom announces that the flight to Tokyo is now boarding, and the monk's ears perk up.

"To Tokyo?" he asks.

"Yes."

He looks around.

"It is my flight—first to Japan and then Bangkok."

Ruth takes note of her surroundings. The gates are all for domestic departures.

"I'll help." She stands and retracts the handle of her luggage.

She doesn't ask anyone for directions, but follows signs through anonymous crowds, the monk a pace or two behind her, as she makes her way to international departures. The flight to Tokyo is not hard to find. They arrive at the announcement well before last call.

The monk pulls his passport and ticket from a pocket in his robe.

Before he leaves, she feels an urge to embrace him but remembers it's against his code.

"Are you coming back to Canada?"

"Yes—in two months."

He bows goodbye, and she bows in return, holding the position for several seconds.

Then he leaves and Ruth sits by the window in international departures to watch his plane accelerate across the tarmac and rise.

———•———

She makes her way back to domestic departures to learn that her flight has been delayed once again. Other passengers curl up on the floor, and she goes to the pay phone by the newsstand to call Bill.

chapter twenty-five
- 1979 -

When the phone rings, Bill goes to the kitchen to answer it.
"A phone call on Christmas Eve?" Elizabeth says, shaking her head.
From the living room, Elizabeth and Ami can't make out what he's
saying over the sound of wind tossing wasp-sized snow pellets against the walls.

A small fire fills the living room with the smell of cedar. There are five
presents below the tree, wrapped in red tinsel paper. Ami lies belly-down on
the rug, eyes shot up the branches of the freshly felled tree whose needles still
hang with mysterious forest dust.

Atop the tree is an angel in a white dress. She is plugged into the wall, and
small bulbs along her hem drop a warm orange light. Several times Ami had
asked to play with her, and several times Elizabeth had said no, that she's a
family heirloom.

"What's her name?" Ami asks. "Is she a doll?"

"She doesn't have a name. And she's not a doll. She's an angel."

"Why's she way up there?"

"Because she's important. My grandma gave her to me, and I wanted to
give her to my own child someday." She sets her knitting aside. "Is it true you've
never had a real Christmas before, Ami?"

"No, it's not true. I had a Christmas with Gayle one time."

"Did you have Christmas snacks?"

"No."

"Well I made gingerbread cookies. Just for you."

"I'm not hungry."

Elizabeth leans forward. "I know what would make you happy. Why don't
you open one present? Just one before your mother comes."

Ami crawls to the tree, finds the biggest present, squeaks her fingers across
the paper.

"Oh no," Elizabeth says. "Not that one. That's for Ruth."

Ami picks up another, slides her fingers into an exposed edge. Before she
can go any further, Bill walks in wearing a jacket and ball cap.

"Ruth's flight's being held up 'cause of the ice."

"I'm not surprised," Elizabeth says.

"And I told her, I said the cabs probably aren't running. It's Christmas Eve, so there's not so many out there anyway. I gotta bring her back in the truck."

"You're going out in this?"

"Can't just leave a woman stranded out there," he says.

Elizabeth rolls her eyes. "Okay Bill, go fetch your girlfriend."

"Ah jeez, Liz. What do you want me to do?"

"We'll just wait here 'til you get back."

Bill moves to the door and laces his boots. Ami drops her present and runs to him. "Can I come?"

Bill ruffles her hair. "You'd better stay here and keep Liz company."

He pushes through the door, enters the storm.

When he's gone, Ami finishes unwrapping her gift, a hand-knitted sweater, bright blue with the red letters stitched to the front: *Ami*.

"Try it on, why donchya?" says Elizabeth.

Ami puts it on reluctantly. It's too big around the shoulders and she needs to roll it up to expose her hands.

"I made it just for *you*," Elizabeth says. "The one and only *Ami*."

"Thanks." She returns to the floor and watches the angel until she drifts to sleep.

Elizabeth takes a pillow from the sofa and slides it under Ami's head. Then she takes her favourite Bible from its spot atop the hearth and reads Luke's account of the angels coming to the shepherds to announce the birth of Christ. When she concentrates, the corners of her lips dip and she mouths the words quietly to herself.

———◆———

Ruth's second time on the plane is not as agreeable as the first. There is no colourful wash of sky, and the other passengers complain about the delay and the fact that Christmas is ruined.

When the plane lands, Ruth jumps for her bag in the overhead and pushes through bodies blocking the aisle. She finds Bill waiting for her in arrivals and runs her free arm around him, the other occupied by Hungry Hungry Hippos. Instinctually, he follows the motions as though she were his wife. He lays a firm hand on her back and pulls her close but quickly stops himself.

"Thanks for coming," says Ruth. "You saved me."

"My truck's just out those doors. It's gonna be a rough ride but she can handle it."

She lets go. "It feels like I've been away for a long time."

The truck is still warm from the drive over.

"It's really been coming down," he says. "I'm surprised the planes are still goin.'"

"They needed to de-ice the tarmac. That's why it took so long. How is Ami?"

"She's doing good, Ruth. Just like we thought she would."

"What's she doing now?"

"She's just waiting at home with Liz. We're gonna open presents tonight if they're still up."

Ruth holds up Hungry Hungry Hippos. "I got her this. Has she been asking about me?"

"Well—"

"I've never left her alone before," she says.

"We've all been worried about you with the storm and all. How'd things go over there in Victoria?"

"I left everything behind."

"The flight good at least?"

"Yeah—no terrorism on Christmas."

The dark along the highway obscures everything. Snow sticks even to the road signs. Buildings and names all hidden, it looks to Ruth like it could be anywhere. A land where there are only two—truck headlights illuminating a new world.

———————

The fire starts at ten p.m. in the kitchen. It's caused by faulty wiring installed by inexperienced homeowners and begins as a soft smoulder behind the empty refrigerator. It soon melts the insulation around the surrounding nest of wires belonging to the stove, the percolator, and a small lamp. Within half an hour, it catches countertops and eats away the drawers. A sudden conflagration when it reaches the stash of tablecloths and rags below the sink. It skirts the walls, jumps to the dangling curtain by the table, then the table itself.

By eleven p.m., it's a tall, bright column. The smoke alarm screams in the hall but there is no one to hear it. The flame travels along the faded wallpaper, licks away stains left by dripping pipes, carves a rough circle in the ceiling below the upstairs storage room. Cabinets of unfinished paintings groan against the thinning floor joists. At eleven-thirty, one cabinet breaks through and lands in the hall, the doors burst at the hinges. Canvases scatter across the floor.

Shortly after, a box containing oil paints and a two-litre tin of turpentine falls to the kitchen. Under intense heat, the turpentine explodes.

Several more electrical fires start on the second floor. In an abandoned bedroom, a carpet and a twin-sized bed are taken. The other bedrooms are taken shortly after, and the fire stretches to the upstairs loft.

At midnight, the fire hits the stairs, the hall, and enters the parlour. It eats the table, the easel, the sofa, melts the screen of the television. It breaks through a wall and enters the library. Thousands of books ignite in less than ten minutes, an enormous ball of flame bursts through the library door, and the fire doubles in size.

———•———

Four and a half kilometres to the west, a neighbour smells smoke. Drunk on his annual Christmas rum, he isn't sure if his senses are deceiving him and decides to call the non-emergency line. There is no answer. He returns to his family in the other room with a shrug.

When there's no longer any doubt that something is burning, the family worries it might be the forest and pressures the man to call the authorities.

"On Christmas though?" he says, staggering. "Ah well, fires don't celebrate."

He chuckles and calls the emergency line.

"I'm not sure," he says into the receiver. "Could be, ya know, a bonfire. It's Christmas Eve so maybe someone's out having a good time. Think I caught a whiff a s'mores in there, too."

The operator remains firm, asks him if he knows which direction the smoke is coming from.

"You askin' me to go out there right now and see which way the wind is blowin'?"

The operator replies that it isn't necessary, that someone has been dispatched.

"I know you weren't hopin' for a big emergency on Christmas and all. But the family's right, could be a forest fire. You know fires don't celebrate, eh?"

The man pours himself another rum. Over the sound of the wind, he hears sirens singing. The pitch shifts higher and lower, higher and lower as trucks speed along the byroad.

———————•———————

Elizabeth is sleeping on the couch, Bible on her lap, when she hears boots banging off snow on the porch.

Bill comes in first, Ruth behind him in a coat too thin for this weather, looking mischievous like a child with her hands behind her back, holding something.

Elizabeth looks to a clock above the hearth. "You were gone a couple hours."

"Can't move any faster," Bill says.

Bill steps aside and Elizabeth goes to Ruth. "Merry Christmas."

"You too," Ruth replies.

Elizabeth stands in her way for a moment, blocking her entrance into the living room, and then nods, smiles, steps aside.

Ruth sees her daughter curled up by the fire in an electric blue sweater, labelled *Ami*. She puts the board game under the tree and kneels by her daughter's side, rests a hand on her shoulder. The light from the kitschy angel fills Ami's eyes.

"Mum?"

Ruth leans forward to kiss her on the forehead. The girl lets it happen. "Did you have a good time?"

"Mhmm."

"You'll tell me all about it?"

"Okay, Mum."

"I even got you a little gift. But maybe it should wait 'til morning."

Bill moves. "I was thinking in the truck, Ruth. It's a mess out there, so why don't you two spend the night? Liz and I can take the spare room where Ami's been sleeping. Or I can take the sofa. You ladies can take the master bedroom.

Then in the morning, we'll have good old-fashioned Christmas breakfast like my mum used to make for me. Could open gifts, too." He looks to Elizabeth, who folds her arms and looks away. "I suppose you've got a toothbrush and all you need in your bag?"

Ruth helps Ami stand. "Sounds fun, huh? You and I are having a real sleepover."

"I'm tired, Mum."

Elizabeth sighs, quickly installs new sheets in the master bedroom and leads Ami and Ruth inside.

"It's cold at night," she says from the doorway.

"Say goodnight, Ami," Ruth whispers.

"Goodnight," Ami repeats.

Elizabeth leaves them in the darkness and Ami shifts to the far-left side of the bed. Ruth occupies the middle and takes her daughter's hand. It's dry and delicate, bones that may be the hollow bones of a bird. She leads the delicate hand to her own chest and lays it over her heart.

"What's that, Mum?"

"I just wanted my heart to feel your hand."

Ami says nothing.

"Did your sister call again?"

"She doesn't know Bill's phone number."

"Makes sense." Ruth pulls Ami closer, lays her hand on the back of the girl's head, feels her invisible hair and jaw. She cradles her daughter's head against her chest like a newborn.

"I'm never going anywhere again," Ruth says. "I'm sorry, Ami."

"How come, Mum?"

Seven years of pacing the farmhouse arise in Ruth's soul like fog from a valley. "You'll realize someday," she says. "And when you do, remember that I'm sorry now."

"Okay."

Ami falls asleep with her hair flowing over her mother, tendrils journeying to Ruth's neck.

———— • ————

At the crack of dawn, a woman on her way to town sees a mess of beams and metal where she could have sworn there was a farmhouse. The driveway is snowed over and there's a car buried up to the headlights.

She pulls over and turns on her flashers, trudges to the foundation of the missing house and looks around. The east-facing wall is still mostly intact, but thoroughly blackened, the windows impenetrable. There's a toilet, a sink, and a tub, all seemingly unscathed but filled with snow. And she can see into the basement—a washing machine, a chest of drawers. They too are unharmed. Everything else is cinders, and a cold wind pushes black dust across the property, dirtying the fields for a mile around.

She stopped out of mere curiosity, but when she sees the disaster up close, she realizes it's her duty to confirm whether there are any human remains. She circles the debris and, finding no one, returns to her car and proceeds to town.

She tells the staff at a gas station what she's seen, who repeat the information to their friends and families, and rumours spread.

——————◦——————

In the morning, Ruth and Ami descend the stairs and find Bill curled on the living-room couch. The angel is still on and the fire is still going. He's must have stayed up all night feeding it, Ruth thinks, to keep us warm.

"Merry Christmas," he says, yawning.

He goes to the kitchen to mix batter for pancakes. Ruth takes Ami to the tree and finds the board game.

"I'm sorry I didn't wrap it, Ami—I didn't know where to find that stuff."

Ami examines the box.

"Do you know it?" Ruth asks.

Ami opens the game on the floor and they play a few rounds, Ami growing more competitive with each one. Ruth pretends to be an expert, hammering the lever with vigour until there are only half a dozen marbles left, and letting Ami take them and win by a narrow margin.

"You've done this before, Ami."

"No Mum, I swear."

They laugh.

Eventually Elizabeth descends the stairs, washed and dressed. "Was wondering what all that noise was."

In a diner in Salmon Arm, a group drinks coffee by the counter and gossips.

"Could be an exploded boiler," someone says. "The house was *old*. Was there even when my granddad was a boy."

"Could be arson," someone replies. "With what the world's coming to these days, a bomb going off in the States every week it seems. Wouldn't surprise me."

"My money's on something Satanic," says another, smirking.

"Could've been done to collect property tax," says yet another. "I read in the news a while back that someone in Prince George pulled a stunt like that. Spending a good twenty years in prison."

"Murder," says a voice further down the counter.

"Suicide," says a voice in a nearby booth.

"Murder-suicide," replies the first voice. "'At's why the car's still parked out front. They never left."

"But there's no remains," says someone at the counter.

When someone points out that the house was owned by the "manic professor" who once rode his horse all the way here from Victoria and his bitter wife who used to scoff at people at the church rummage sale, the crowd agrees that the wilder theories seem possible.

"But the professor was a good man," says the cook, entering from the kitchen with a plate of fried eggs. "Came in here time to time. Was good to talk to. Loved his family, too. Had two daughters, if I remember correct."

At the mention of children, an offshoot of the crowd decides to drive over and search for more clues as to the whereabouts of the owners.

———◆———

Over pancakes, Ruth asks what they've all done since she left.

"We made a little snowman, didn't we?" Bill asks.

"Mhmm," says Ami. "But there was so much snow he got lost."

"And we watched some movies, right? What movies did we watch?"

"We watched Frosty the Snowman and—umm—"

"Rudolph," Bill says.

"Did you watch any *Looney Tunes*?" Ruth asks. "I love *Looney Tunes*."

"No," Ami says, "'cause Bill doesn't have that number."

Elizabeth reaches for a jar of apricot jam in the middle of the table. "You get your artsy stuff all wrapped up, Ruth?"

"She said she didn't wanna talk about that," Bill interjects.

"But that's why she left."

"It's fine," Ruth says. "You're both in a gallery now. Gonna be admired by Japanese and German tourists pretty soon."

"We'll be famous then, eh?" Bill says. "Look at that, Liz. Ruth's gonna make us famous."

"I thought we were going to get that painting," Elizabeth says.

Ruth lays her fork on the plate with a clink. "When the show's over, I'll have it sent back."

"So what are you going to do now, Ruth? Now that you're done with us?"

"Liz," Bill says firmly.

"Done with *painting* us, I mean," Elizabeth says, raising her voice.

"I don't know," says Ruth. "I haven't thought about it."

They open presents after breakfast. Bill and Elizabeth give Ami some new mittens, and Ruth a lacquered picture frame from the church rummage sale.

"And," Bill says, "I'm gonna give you some firewood. The needle's dropped the past couple days and I remembered you're running out."

"You don't need to."

"It's already chopped and stacked up in the shed—just gotta load it into the box."

He goes out to load enough wood to tie Ruth and Ami over until their next visit. He returns twenty minutes later.

"I guess it's time," he says.

He leads Ruth and Ami to the truck and they all sit on the front bench. "The road still looks a little rough so make sure you got your seat belts done up."

———◆———

They see it from a distance, but neither Bill nor Ruth process it until they're idling out front.

A small group is standing on the lawn of now well-trampled snow. A man approaches the car and sees Ruth. It's the cook from the diner, who recognizes her from the photos her husband used to carry in his wallet.

"Stay in the car," Bill tells her.

He goes to the crowd. They tell him everything they know, which is that a fire burned overnight, but because of the circumstances no one could report it until it was too late. The first fire truck got stuck in the snow. No one was able to locate either of the owners, nor even the eldest daughter, who they assume is an adult now.

When Ruth looks up, she sees Bill keeling over. Two strangers have their hands on his back. Beyond the crowd, where the house used to be, she sees the empty barn, the yard stretching to the treeline. In the middle is the cow's grave and the cross Bill planted on top. An indistinct black bird circles above it, caws, and descends behind the mound.

Bill returns to the car, puts the keys in the ignition and, saying nothing, drives back to where they came from.

———◆———

The next day, dull echoes accompany Bill as he walks through the drafty nave of the Anglican church. The priest is in the office, hunched over a desk and scanning the church's year-end financial reports: donations in one column, fundraising in another, expenditures in the last.

"Hi, Bill. I heard someone coming."

Bill removes his cap. "You probably heard what happened, Father."

The priest nods, gestures for Bill to sit. He does, balls his cap above his lap. Tears drip into it.

"*Why*, Father?"

"You are a friend of that family?"

Bill nods.

The priest shifts his notes aside and waits for Bill to look up.

"Bad things happen to good people," Bill says. "I seen it before. It could happen at any time."

"No one is harmed. That's a miracle."

"The girl was staying with us. If they'd been home, though—I don't want to think about what would've happened. It's the devil's work, I have to believe. But what'd they do to deserve it? This only a test like what happened to—Job?"

"God sees your confusion, son. And he understands. As long as we take refuge in God, we will have gladness forever. You've heard it before—but God works in mysterious ways."

"What should I do?"

"To begin with, thank God for bringing us into his design. And secondly, pray and be patient. The church is here to help you through it."

"It's not about *me*. Ruth and the girl—they're not Christians. They don't know God or think about Him. They're strangers to Salmon Arm and don't know the truth like you and me know."

The priest leans back, thinks.

"I never had kids," Bill says. "God made me like that. But the girl's been a kind of daughter—"

On the wall is a clock with a grey cross screwed into the front of it. The cross indicates twelve, three, six, nine. There is no one on the cross. Where there would be a spear, there is instead a thin minute hand. Each tick appears to move the needle nowhere, but through increments of imperceptible movement, it advances.

chapter twenty-six
- 1979 -

On Christmas morning, a ferocious storm hits Edmonton, and the radio issues extreme weather warnings. It advises people to call elderly relatives. The streets are devoid of vehicles. The city is smothered in white.

Gayle stays in with her father's book but reads only so far as the dedication: *For my wife*. She has a memory of her parents dancing in the kitchen in the evening when they lived in Victoria, young and smiling. Ruth hardly older than Gayle now. She doesn't know where the memory comes from, if it's real or imagined, but she holds onto it, tries to fill in the part of her father's hair, the slope of his shoulders, the colour of her mother's socks.

For my wife. The rest of the book is worthless to her, esoteric and obtuse. If anyone might get it, it's Al and Ruth Windsor. And she believes they do. That's enough.

———•———

After her meeting with Hanna Federico, she spends all her time with Lewis in Li Yong's living room. The mystery of her father's disappearance, though not solved, no longer has the tragic finale she thought it would, and she sets it aside. Sitting by Lewis's feet, the current of her heart is aimed only toward the man she loves and who reflects her love back to her even from his sick bed.

Lewis shivers himself awake, sees her flipping through the pages, not reading but fanning.

"Merry Christmas, Gayle."

She reaches over and sets her hand on his cheek. "Merry Christmas, Lew."

"In my dream, I got you a present."

"What was it?"

"I don't remember."

She brushes aside his bangs, which have grown long and creep into his eyes. "That's the best present I've ever had—a dream. I don't need anything else. Was Dream Gayle happy?"

"She was beaming."

Shortly after, Li Yong emerges from the stairway carrying a box wrapped in newspaper. "You're awake," he says. He hands the box to Lewis. "Maybe I should have gone about this another way, so forgive me"— he looks away—"because I know this is not the merriest occasion."

Lewis tears away the newspaper to reveal cardboard covered in Chinese characters. He tears the tape away, drops his hand into the packing peanuts, removes a small brown bottle with a label he can't read.

"That's what came for you in the mail the other day," Gayle says.

"Yes," says Li Yong. "I called my sister and explained the situation. She sent this."

"What is it?" Lewis asks.

"I have been thinking about you and your symptoms. I listened when you two were here with the book, remember? Then I thought of my sister. When she was little, she had something very similar, with the coughing, the blood and the fever. And please forgive me for staring, but you never said if you had … irritation. I've seen you scratching"—he shifts to a whisper—"*down there*. Perhaps you were trying to avoid embarrassment by not mentioning it."

Lewis shows no signs of embarrassment now. He unscrews the cap and sniffs the contents. "Smells like absinthe."

"I'm sorry to ask this in front of Gayle," Li Yong says. "But Lewis, did you see anything in your stool—dots, lines?"

Lewis shrugs. "I didn't think about it. Thought I was falling apart on the inside."

"This thing you two do, this digging through the trash for food—did you do this in Vancouver?"

"Yeah," he says. "For a while."

Li Yong nods. "This is my suspicion. I don't know what it's called in English, but in China we call it huíchóng."

"What is it, Lee?" Gayle asks.

"It's a kind of—worm. It lives in the body." He points to his stomach. "Sometimes in the lungs, I believe. I'm not a doctor. I only know from experience."

"A worm?" Lewis asks.

"Many worms, most likely," Li Yong replies. "If you'd eaten food that was thrown away, then possibly you took in the eggs. I'm not sure. I just put two and two together, as you say."

"Many worms," Lewis repeats despondently.

"Whatever, Lew," Gayle says. "Is it deadly?"

"Could be," says Li Yong. "Lewis should take that medicine. A tablespoon every day for a few days, maybe two weeks—until it's better and before it's worse. My sister was cured after a few days, but Lewis will take more because it's been in him much longer. So inside that bottle is concentrated wormwood oil mixed with other things—herbs. It's a medicine."

Gayle looks to Lewis. "Why not, Lew?"

"We put it in tea," Li Yong says. "It's better than drinking it straight."

"That's it?" Lewis hands the bottle back to Li Yong. "I drink it a few times and I live?"

Li Yong goes to the kitchen to boil water. "Merry Christmas."

———◆———

The wormwood tea is palatable with large amounts of honey stirred in. Lewis drinks it lukewarm, and quickly, before gagging and rinsing his mouth.

"How do you feel?" Gayle asks.

"The same—"

"Wait," Li Yong says. "It'll take some time."

———◆———

An hour later, Lewis throws off his blankets and hobbles to the bathroom.

"*What* Lew?" Gayle asks, following him.

"*Pain.*"

"What do you mean pain?"

She hears him vomit violently, followed by dry, choking sobs. She rushes to Li Yong. "Did we give him too much?"

Li Yong shakes his head. "I don't know. He's reacting badly. It's possible—the bottle says it's possible." He reads the label. "Nausea, dizziness, and, yes, yes, vomiting."

"What is this, poison?"

"Yes."

Lewis's reaction worsens in the days to come. He acquires a wide catalogue of symptoms. Frequent diarrhea, spells of dizziness, headaches, uncontrollable jittering. He cannot sleep for more than an hour at a time.

Gayle drops her head one night and cries. "I'm useless."

"It means it's working," Lewis says. He sits up but immediately grows too dizzy and spits up in a pail Gayle set by the sofa.

"Have you—umm—seen any?"

"What?"

"Lines and dots."

He nods with a glint of a smile and closes his eyes.

———◆———

Gayle doesn't leave his side until New Year's Eve, when the weather suddenly improves, the weather warning is lifted, and the city creaks back to life. Li Yong tells her to go for a walk. She does and takes the opportunity to call her mother and tell her about her meeting with Hanna Federico.

She returns to the pay phone in the Commercial Hotel. Unlike before, there is no ring. The line is dead. Instead she buys an envelope and a single stamp from the receptionist and writes a letter on hotel stationery:

> I tried calling but the line is dead. I assume you didn't pay the
> bill. I met with Hanna Federico. Dad's not really gone. He's
> just in America. Don't know when he'll be back. What else
> to say? I'm worried he lost his mind. Was it worth it? I guess
> if everything works out, then what he did was not the worst
> thing in the world. But I'm done thinking about him and I
> hope you are, too.

Writing, she finds, is easier than speaking. In her mind, the mother she's writing to is not just Ruth. It's the mother of her imagination (in mismatched blue and black socks, she finally decides). She is her father's dedication, the "wife" in *For my wife*.

She signs off: *Your friend, Gayle.*

———— ◆ ————

Lewis's symptoms plateau. He tells her to leave the radio off, that the noise makes things worse.

"It's kind of dull," he says. "I can't remember what it's like to not be dizzy."

"Are you hungry?"

"Not even a little."

It occurs to Gayle that he hasn't eaten in days, and she's had almost nothing. She hasn't been scavenging, and the cans of soup and beans have run out. She tells this to Li Yong and he offers to cook them a meal to celebrate the holiday. He leaves and returns an hour later with potatoes, greens, and a block of firm tofu.

"What's this for?" Gayle asks as he sets the watery brick on the table.

"It's the best I can offer. I'll bake it."

"Tofu?"

"I'm a vegetarian."

"I didn't know that."

They spend the day together preparing food: two kinds of potatoes, a salad with cranberries in it, and fragrant sauce for the tofu to bake in.

———— ◆ ————

In the evening, while Lewis is trying to sleep, Gayle and Li Yong eat together, speaking in whispers.

"I can't believe it's almost 1980," he says. "Only three hours left of the decade."

"If someone told me three years ago that I'd be here in Edmonton, eating tofu, sitting with you—that I'd find the love my life and almost lose him—I wouldn't believe it."

"Why not?"

"Didn't even think I'd be alive."

"I don't see what you mean."

"I have a hard time seeing past my nose," she says, "let alone, you know, everything else. Nineteen-eighty still feels like a void to me. What do you think?"

"Show me your left hand."

Gayle stretches her arm across the table, palm up. Li Yong rolls up the sleeve of his jersey and takes it, squints.

"Like I thought," he says. "Your life line is off the map."

"My life line?"

"And your love line—it *just* touches your life line—It happens when you are—let's see—nineteen to twenty-two. Otherwise the lines are parallel."

"A deformity," she suggests. "Like the knee."

"No, no. It only means your love moves through life with you. And you have grooves in your life line here and here and here." He taps his finger three times, seemingly at random. "It means big life events at the age of twenty-five, thirty-one, and—hmm—about sixty-six—and another at one-hundred-and-eleven, more or less."

"Maybe that's when I move to Mars?" He lets go of her palm. "How 'bout you? What's your palm say?"

He shrugs. "I read it once a long time ago. I can't remember. Something about money, fame, women, rock 'n' roll, being an accountant. Things of that nature."

———•———

A few minutes before midnight, they hear someone setting off fireworks.

"Downtown?" Gayle asks.

"No—it sounds close."

They put on jackets and walk half a block to an intersection where the roads stretch in straight lines in all cardinal directions. A few blocks to the north, someone is lighting fireworks one by one.

A green burst in the sky followed by a sizzle. Fifteen seconds later, another.

"It's pretty," Li Yong says. "He's a bit early though."

They watch until the renegade fireworks are finished. A moment of silence, and the stranger continues with hissing Roman candles. Soon another person a few houses away does the same. A minute later, another comes a few blocks closer to them. Another from the east. The artificial lights are the only ones. The clouded sky blocks out even the moon. With each passing minute, more people contribute, until Gayle and Li Yong are surrounded in all directions by green, blue, and white. Some explode, some merely pop, some dissolve, some are defective and make no sound at all. Gayle turns in a slow circle, watching splashes of colours and hazy brown tails blending into the sky.

At midnight there are, by her count, twenty houses celebrating the new decade by tossing ephemeral lights into an absolutely dark universe.

———————◆———————

The first morning of the year, Gayle pulls her hair into a ponytail with an elastic band, takes a pair of orange-handled scissors from the kitchen, and cuts off what remains of her as a blond. The rest of her hair, black, sits as a lopsided bowl across her ears and neck.

Lewis sits up when he sees her. "You look older."

"I don't know why I did it in the first place. No more pretending. Hey, you don't seem dizzy."

"I slept like a baby last night."

"No nausea, diarrhea, no shaking?"

"Not really."

She kisses him on the forehead. "Happy New Year, Lew."

"I almost forgot."

"I hope the worms weren't the ones doing the thinking for you."

———————◆———————

A week and a half later, Lewis announces that he no longer sees worms and eggs in his shit. He stands, wobbles slightly, but can walk without feeling lightheaded.

"Guess we killed 'em all," he says.

"It could be," says Li Yong. "It's been some time."

"Those bastards," Gayle says.

Lewis walks to the window and gazes at the street. "I'd like to see the sun." He puts on his jacket and goes out. Gayle follows and they stand on the sidewalk. The sun hides behind a veil of clouds, scattering cool gold across the sky. Lewis puts his hands in his pockets.

"*Here* they are," he says. "This whole time, I haven't had a single dart." He lights one and they share it. "I don't know how to thank him."

"Me neither." She looks at his face. The colour is returning, taking on the gold of the sky. His beard obscures his sweet, thin lips, but his eyes are boyish and dark.

"He may have saved me," he says. "Saved my life. This is the second time someone's done that—"

"Don't try your luck again. Lee's not gonna be wherever we're going."

"Where are we going?"

She lets out a short, airy laugh. "We're going?"

"You said so."

"I just assumed. No reason to be here, is there? I know it isn't spring yet, but—"

"No." The cigarette is finished, but the conversation isn't. He lights another. "But we have a little stashed away. A *little*. My emergency fund. Some of what your mom gave me when I left."

"We'll go east," she says. "As far as possible."

"Far, far. Mountains, water, forests—I don't care. I don't wanna be in Edmonton anymore."

"The coast?"

"Halifax?"

"How?"

"Hmm—"

"By thumb?" she asks. "It's still cold."

"Or—the train."

"There's a train all the way there?"

"I think so."

"I haven't been on a train since I was a girl."

"I've never been."

"It must take days. We'll get to see everything swept away—"

"Yeah."

"And what do we do when we get there?"

"I don't know," he says. "But it can't be any worse than this."

"So what's stopping us?"

"I thought—what about your father? He's—"

She shakes her head. "Forget about it."

"Forget about it?"

"It's okay."

———◆———

"I don't like goodbyes," Li Yong says a few days later.

Their bags are packed in the basement. They intend to leave with no more or less than what they arrived with, aside from one hand-drawn picture of Gayle, a book of haiku, her father's poetry, and the bottle of wormwood oil.

"I've never said one before," Lewis says.

They embrace, pat one another on the back.

"Did you remember the wormwood?" Li Yong asks. "In case it comes back."

"I got it." He turns around, toward the screen door where their cab is waiting.

"I'll never forget our conversations," Gayle says. "Or everything you did for us."

"It's nothing," Li Yong says.

"I'll write to you. Don't change your address."

He shakes his head. "I'm never leaving this place."

The screen door clicks shut, and Li Yong returns to the kitchen. Still a mess. He sits to read a newspaper, not realizing until halfway through that it's three days old.

chapter twenty-seven
- 1980 -

The cab drives through Sunday morning traffic. Gayle and Lewis exit outside the downtown train station.

Yellow lights illuminate the faces inside: expectant, bored.

The woman at the ticket desk asks them if they're going west or east. When they say east, she informs them that the Toronto-bound train is delayed due to electrical problems on the line from Jasper. They wait on a bench, backpacks between their legs, and she lays her head on his shoulder.

"I forgot how tired I am," she says.

"Sleep. I'll stay awake."

She closes her eyes. He rests his chin atop her head, eavesdrops on a nearby conversation between two British tourists waiting for the westbound train.

"The Rocky Mountains," one says with astonishment, "are *just over there*."

———————◆———————

The priest of the Anglican Church in Salmon Arm stands before the unusually small congregation, whispers to himself whether it was everyone's New Year's resolution to finally turn their backs on God. He is briefly distracted by someone in the front pew nervously tapping their foot. It's Bill, alone. He and his wife usually sit somewhere near the back.

After a reading from the Book of Common Prayer, the priest says that, before they begin, there is an announcement from a member of the congregation. He nods to Bill and steps aside.

Bill clears his throat and ascends the three shallow steps to the pulpit. He stands beside it, removes a folded piece of paper from his pocket. The congregation leans forward.

"Hello—my name's Bill.... I think you all know who I am. I've been part of this church since I was a boy and never missed a day unless I was sick.... I don't say much unless I really got something to say, and today I'm standing here because there's no one else who can....

"As many of you know, there has been a tragedy in our community involving a woman and her young daughter whose house burned to the ground on the very birthday of our Lord.... Since then, these two have had no place to go because there is no husband or relatives to take them in and show them mercy.... The little girl is so hurt that she stopped speaking all together.... She cannot go to school.... She's a very sad little girl.... And from the bottom of my heart I, fear for her future....

"We don't understand the ways of the Lord, but I have no doubt we know what he wants us to do.... Although they are not part of our community, we owe Ruth and Ami Windsor our Christian hospitality.... As Paul has said:"— Bill raises his voice—"'Don't forget to show hospitality to strangers, for by doing this some have delighted the angels without knowing it.'"

On his way to his seat, he whispers to the priest, "Thank you, Father, for helping me write my speech."

The priest retakes the pulpit and announces that, all participants willing, the Salmon Arm rummage sale will for the next several months donate twenty percent of its profits to helping Ami and Ruth Windsor get back on their feet.

"And anyone with skills in carpentry, plumbing, and so on," the priest concludes, "can talk to Bill."

When they at last board the train, they find it surprisingly empty. Not even half the seats are occupied.

They move slowly out of Edmonton and emerge into fields of seemingly endless white, grey, smoky blue, occasionally brushed by deciduous woods.

The further they move away from the city, the more the landscape carries notes of ochre and red. Thousands of kilometres of prairie lie ahead.

Hanna Federico wakes up later than usual. The conversation with the poet's daughter has left her melancholic. Guilty, too. Was it I, she thinks, who let him disintegrate on my watch? With no one to discuss this with, her thoughts just pool.

Meanwhile, the condemnations of colleagues' flutter to her head like bugs to a light bulb. A madman, a wack-job, they continue to call him. Sometimes a mere narcissist.

"Bullies," she says to the macaw.

"*Bullocks.*"

This mess has had repercussions on others. There's a daughter the poet claimed to love but abandoned. What about his other daughter? What about his wife? Hell, what about his job, his house, his debt? Mixed emotions surface in Hanna's daily freewriting exercises, which she undertakes to understand her feelings with no barriers. She seeks a way to carry on with her own life as though the poet, as she knew him, had never existed—just as he requested in his farewell letter. Al is over. Now he's a just ghost who sends kitschy postcards.

But forgetting him is impossible, considering all the scraps of paper he left around her home. The ones that fell from the typewriter and he chose not to pick up. She finds a new one every day.

"Fragment forty-four," she reads. "Upon looking a Chevy straight in the face and emerging the victor—"

———◆———

The train crosses the border to Saskatchewan. There are fewer trees. The landscape breaks into frozen lakes. An attendant walks from car to car, smiling at those who haven't fallen asleep against the sedative rumble of the tracks, and welcoming everyone to the "Western Red Lily Province."

Gayle pulls her forehead from the window, where it had been lightly adhered for the last hour. "I guess we'll be in Saskatoon soon."

"Looks like it."

"I don't know anything about Saskatoon. In my head it's just a big old nothing."

"Seems about right."

———◆———

"I been talking to some friends about this, Bill," says Elizabeth on the way home from church.

He keeps his eyes on the road. "Hmm?"

"Ruth and Ami and their—*condition.* This kind of *unsocial* behaviour."

"Unsocial behaviour?" he asks sharply, shakes his head. "These friends you're talking about—they just a bunch of vets?"

"Jeez, Bill. What happened to them's a big tragedy. It's horrible for anyone.

But their response is not normal. The girl's become a mute, and Ruth on the other hand's not bothered one bit. I'm saying it 'cause it could be something *inside*. You know the father was a strange, strange man, too. That's the word around town."

Bill pulls over and shuts off the engine. "*Cut it out, Liz. Cut it right out.*"

Her mouth hangs open.

"They're God's children," he says. "I've opened up my heart and I think you ought to do the same." Bill starts the truck again. "Ruth's holding up good considering everything that happened to her the past years."

"I don't think you'd do it for anybody, Bill."

Bill doesn't respond.

Elizabeth looks out the window, murmurs, "That woman's special to you—I see it. I know you better than anybody."

———— • ————

The train crosses into Manitoba, waits for twenty minutes in Winnipeg and continues past Elma, Ophir, Winnitoba, the Ontario border, Malachi, Ottermere, Minaki, Redditt, Farlane, Canyon, Richan, Sioux Lookout, Armstrong, Ferland, Auden, Nakina, Longlac, Caramat, Hillsport, Hornepayne, Elsas—

———— • ————

In Victoria, the gallery on Yates Street opens its doors for the exhibition *Showcasing Canadiana*. The works of one Ruth Windsor of Salmon Arm are on display for students and connoisseurs from Japan, Kore, England, Spain, France, Germany, South Africa, the United States, Chile, and Eastern Canada.

The crowd hangs raincoats by the door and is led through the hallway to the gallery.

"We decided," announces Annabella Tavistock, "to take an unconventional approach to this year's theme, focusing not on the artists living in urban spaces, or career artists within the academy, but rather on the naïve artists who live isolated lives in our province's rugged interior, meshing fine arts with the rigours of daily life."

The connoisseurs flood around the sign that is illuminated by a small white light. It contains the artist's bio and an explanation of the works. Annabella didn't print the bio Ruth provided on a napkin—the dynamite—but wrote her own, emphasizing that Ruth is the wife of a vanished poet and ran away from the city to rebel against modern society. A kind of female Thoreau.

The connoisseurs proceed through corn, trees, cows, an alpaca, and a rustic farming couple, discussing amongst themselves the deliberately inconsistent brush strokes and how they ingeniously reflect the rigours of life.

As the crowd moves on, a middle-aged German man approaches Annabella.

"Please," he says, "if you could be so kind, tell me a little more about the woman who produced these works. I am enthralled by the sense of desperation I see in them, the struggle to *communicate* with the world as it—hmm—responds only with brutal silence. Such *Sehnsucht*. Have you met her?"

"We've been friends for years. I assure you, she is every bit the character you just described. No mind for others, nor touch, nor society. She works for herself."

The man nods.

She continues: "And as Dostoyevsky might as well have said: If there is no audience, then anything is permissible. She came to the city dressed as a scarecrow, her hair down to her waist, and she provided her biographical information on a McDonald's napkin."

"How fascinating. How curious."

———◆———

The train passes through Foleyet, Gogama, Westree, Ruel, Felix, Laforest, Capreol, Parry Sound, and Washago, and approaches Toronto Union Station after a long churn through the parks and suburbs orbiting the city. As the train slows, an attendant informs passengers that those continuing their journey to Montreal can catch the morning train at six a.m.

Gayle lifts her face from a sweater, folded over itself three times, which she'd been using as a pillow, and says in a voice that has become hoarse from not speaking, "We made it somewhere."

"Toronto."

"I know this one."

"Let's go out for a smoke and walk around."

They exit the station into a snow-covered square lined with buildings of pinkish glass.

They walk until they grow cold, duck into underground malls to keep warm. When they return, they prepare to spend the night in the station.

———— • ————

Ruth sits with Ami in the master bedroom of Bill and Elizabeth's farmhouse, where they've been staying since Christmas. Ami's despondency, her selective muteness, leaves Ruth no choice but to spend every waking minute with her, to touch her, to rub her knees and her back, lay endless kisses on her forehead, offer games and television. Once in a while she breaks through, the girl responds, but it's rare.

"Do you want to play, watch a movie? Do you want to read?"

The girl nods, whispers, "The Cat With the Hat—"

Ruth's breath accelerates. "*Who's the cat with the hat?*"

"Dr. Seuss book."

"In the library?"

"Gayle knows it."

The name of the other daughter creates fissures in Ruth's chest, now more than ever. Gayle was supposed to call back after talking with that Hanna Federico woman. She never did. Or maybe she did, but the phone is ashes. Gayle could reach her sister, though. She always has. But now there's no way to reach her—no number, no address.

"Ami," she says. "You sent something to Gayle in the mail. You talked to her on the phone."

Ami says nothing.

"Do you remember the address? Anything else about where Gayle lives?"

Ami shakes her head.

"Do you remember anything?"

"No numbers."

"Seventy-eight—umm—Avenue. And—"

———— • ————

Lewis finds another traveller waiting for the train to Montreal and asks him to wake them up when it's coming. He and Gayle lay sweaters on a narrow bench and curl up on it. She on top of him, hands under his head, knees alternating, the protrusion of her hip slotted perfectly into the dip below his stomach. An awkward human puzzle falls asleep surrounded by station commotion.

———— • ————

The German connoisseur puts in a bid for the entire collection with the intention of relocating it to his own international art exhibition in Hamburg.

Annabella calls Ruth to tell her the news, but the number is no longer in service.

———— • ————

At six a.m. the train to Montreal arrives at platform three. They peel apart their bodies.

———— • ————

After sitting for two hours at the kitchen table, Li Yong signs off his letter to Cuba: De quien te adora. He sets it atop the arbitrary stack of magazines, folds his head in his arms.

This, the pain of living alone, he doesn't discuss with his family. The letter to Cuba he'd just completed is the only time he's seen this recurring thought expressed in print: el dolor de ser invisible.

With the young lovers gone, he's free to break down multiple times a day—a sudden release of what's infested him for months. It's good for a while, like the amputation of a gangrened limb that keeps growing back in the same place.

As he cries, he laughs at the cold planet on which he chose to spend the rest of his life alone. When the clock hits seven, he tightens his tie and puts on his jacket.

The cold makes him forget himself.

On the way to the bus stop, he drops off the letter, not expecting a reply.

———— • ————

The train stops thirty kilometres outside Belleville to let a series of westbound cargo trains pass. The track runs between two snowed-over fields. Many of the passengers take the opportunity to stand outside for fresh air, look around, smoke. Gayle and Lewis go, too. They stand on the edge of the tracks, snow up to their ankles. They light up and watch a white sun glow behind a cloud.

"I like you in this light," she says.

He smiles.

"You look so young and clean and delicate."

"You're younger than I am." He laughs.

"But you're like an angel descending on a cloud of smoke."

"Cut it out."

———◆———

The poet lives near the arts college in Rome, Georgia, renting a mouldy room in the basement of a student apartment. He's been living there for a month, the madman in the cellar, embracing his poverty, waiting for his trickling funds to align with his destiny.

The students are useful to the poet because they donate loose paper and staples.

This is the end, he thinks. The students have given him the supplies needed to collate the manuscript. Exactly one thousand fragments. Poems to grace one thousand shades of life and love—just like the particles that constitute the sky, he often thinks. The sky is love, each poem a particle. It means nothing in the end, but perhaps the most a single human can do when faced with infinity is make their soul as inflated as possible.

He carries the pages to a small communal lobby on the first floor where the arts students sometimes linger. One is there, a girl in a beret who came from Houston to study painting. She's his favourite, with her small chin, knotted and sand-coloured hair, fingers always daubed with paint. Here in Rome, the eternal city, she is a creature out of place and time, as though she stands with one foot in the deep past.

Whenever he wrote in the lobby, she'd observe him, sketch his figure and his face and later submit his likeness for grades in her Introduction to Perspective class.

The last three fragments are for her.

"You really finished it?" she asks.

"Nothing is ever finished. But I'm done."

She flips through the manuscript, dropping her daubed finger on random pages. The last hundred pages get progressively lighter as the typewriter ran out of ink. The very last one, which bears her name, is hardly legible.

"It's as thick as a dictionary," she says. "What's the title? I would *love* to call my mom and tell her you've finally finished it. I told her about you on the phone a couple times."

"I haven't thought of a title. Seemed like the most trivial of concerns, considering."

He retrieves the typewriter, installs himself at the table in the lobby. In letters light as smoke against a cloud, he writes *Dictionary of Beauty*. On another page, fainter still: *For my wife*.

"Now what?" the girl asks.

———◆———

The train stops in Montreal. They have two hours until they board the *Ocean* train to Moncton. Gare Centrale is filled with people speaking French and English. Gayle lingers on the platform, listening to the chatter of strangers filling the chilly station air.

"It's so pretty," she says.

"What is?"

"French. It's so pretty it makes me want to cry."

"C'mon, let's find something to eat."

"Something French," she insists. "Oh, let's get croissants—maybe at that bar over there. And café au lait. I wanna try to order in French."

———◆———

Participants of the Salmon Arm rummage sale are more than willing to donate proceeds to the woman who lost her home. There's not a whisper of protest. A few individuals recall that the woman in question, a Ruth Something, used to operate a booth next to the man selling handmade clay pots. They recall that she would set her paintings at an exorbitant price—but the paintings that were always a bit *off*. Something to do with the shadows.

The man selling pots glances to his right, where the lonely painter used to sit.

"She saw the world a little differently," he says to a friend. "She would watch everyone walking by talking about her art. She pretended like she didn't care one bit about what they thought, but she clearly cared about it very much. Gosh, she was rude. But I could tell she liked the rummage sale. Otherwise, why'd she come? I though her whole schtick was pretty funny, honestly."

———•———

Gayle and Lewis wait in the dining car of the *Ocean*, watching mist try to cling to the countryside, eventually catching sight of the Atlantic Coast. They cross the border into New Brunswick—Campbellton, Charlo, Jacquet River, Petit Rocher, Bathurst, Miramichi, Rogersville.

———•———

The post office clerk looks at the stack of paper, neatly arranged, ghostly grey type on the first page.

"A dictionary?"

"Of beauty," the poet replies. "Send it fast."

The clerk nods. "Canada?"

"Edmonton, Alberta. Hanna Federico. F-E-D-E-R—"

———•———

They transfer at Moncton to the *Atlantic*. The last leg of the journey takes place on an empty train through a tunnel of blue skies.

———•———

"I found the cat with the hat," Ruth tells Ami as they prepare for bed. "I know where he is. He's in Edmonton—"

Ami moves to the bed, crawls under the covers.

"We're going to go see him."

———•———

The train arrives in Halifax. Mist falls from the sky. Not knowing what else to do, they lock up their bags in the station, walk through a small park, continue down Barrington Street. The snow here is heavy and wet, and soon it starts to rain.

They buy an umbrella from a corner shop.

"It's kind of warm here," she says.

———•———

Hanna Federico hears a knock and answers the door.

"A package?"

"Sign here."

She takes it inside. It's a box posted from the States—no return address. It's heavy. The contents shuffle around as she walks with it. She cuts through the tape with a spare key.

Dictionary of Beauty. Nothing more. No note, no explanation, no instructions to tell her what to do with it, but she knows. Oh, she thinks, the wondrous logistics of publishing a one-thousand-page book.

"You crazy bastard."

She divides the papers into five more manageable piles on her coffee table, takes the first one, and sits in her rocking chair. "Here we go."

"*Ungree*," replies the macaw.

She flips past the title page to the predictable dedication, then to the first poem, "Fragment one. Written in the hospital bed, 1960."

———•———

Li Yong hears a clatter in his mailbox. He puts on pants in case the neighbours are shovelling.

A glossy card. A picturesque photo of the Halifax harbour in the summertime.

> *Hi Lee. Lewis and I made it to Halifax and the first thing I wanted to do is send you this postcard. It's a nice city, smaller than I thought and very calm. And there's a lot of music here. Even in the snow, people play fiddle on the street. It makes me want to sing. Haligonians (that what you call them) are fine. It's easier to talk to people than it was in Edmonton.*

*After only a couple hours, we found a bar with a notice board
and both landed jobs on the docks. Haven't started yet, but I
guess we'll be working sorting tools and stuff. And we found a
place to stay. There's a little trailer park outside of Dartmouth
(that's across the basin from Halifax). I'll put the address at
the bottom. Write when you get a chance. Yours, Gayle.*
    p.s. Lewis is healthy as can be.

He attaches the card to the fridge with a magnet.

———•———

Few photographs of Gayle ever existed. The ones that did were taken when Gayle was a child and were destroyed in the fire. Instead, Ruth draws Gayle's face in pencil, relying only on her memories, the library of her soul.

Ruth and Ami arrive in the heart of Edmonton and park on 78th Avenue. Ami couldn't remember the exact address, so they begin by knocking on the door of every house on the street south of a schoolyard, Gayle's sketched face in hand.

Of the houses that answer, responses range from annoyance to gushy pity. But only two of them say anything she wants to hear. The first says the face belongs to the girl who used to pick through the trash behind a Safeway—except that her hair was blond.

"When?" Ruth asks. "Where is she now?"

"I'm sorry," the man says. "I haven't seen her in a while. I don't work there anymore. And a lot of the people who do that come and go. Transients, you know."

The second clue comes from someone who insists that the face belongs to a girl who used to wash dishes at the Strathcona Hotel.

"Had some problems with drugs, from what I could tell."

———•———

Ruth and Ami spend the night in a motel and try again the next day, this time with the north side of the school. Around noon, they approach a bedraggled house with a single dying pine out front and duct tape on the windows.

They knock once with no response. The second time, they hear lethargic footsteps. A man in a green football jersey opens the door.

"Does this girl look familiar to you?"

The man looks carefully at the drawing, then straight into Ruth's eyes. "It's Gayle."

Ruth seizes the man's sleeve. "Where is she?"

He swallows. "Are you Ruth? Are you her mother?"

"*Yes.*"

"And you," he says, looking down. "Ami with an i?"

Ami nods.

"Gayle used to live here. Please come in. And excuse the mess. I live alone."

Ruth and Ami step into the disastrous living room.

"Would you like something to drink?"

"Listen," says Ruth. "Just tell me where Gayle is because you're making me nervous."

"Gayle is in Halifax." He runs to the kitchen and returns with the postcard.

Ruth looks at the artificially sunny harbour. "Halifax?"

"She took the train."

"With that strange boy."

Li Yong nods.

Ruth copies Gayle's address to the bottom of her portrait. "What else could I have expected?"

She opens the door and stands on the porch, looking out at the street.

"Ruth," Li Yong says.

"Yes?"

"Your daughter—she's a good person. In spite of everything. For her age, she understands a lot."

Ruth nods, feels a ghostly shimmer in her skin, a magnetism binding her and her daughter and this stranger in the green jersey together in eternity.

"Let's go home, Mum," Ami says.

part eight

———◆———

completely
unlike
anything

chapter twenty-eight
- 1980 -

That poet emerges from the basement of the student apartment and makes his way to a candlelit Italian restaurant on Broad Street. He requests a window table and space between himself and the well-dressed couples with whom he silently shares his aperitif.

Not having much of an appetite, he skips the antipasto and moves directly to chicken risotto, followed by salmon, and at last a spring salad. He eats with measured bites, occasionally leaning back in his chair as though finished, which repeatedly alerts the attention of the waiters until he assures them he's only trying to savour his meal. He opts out of dessert, satisfied with a simple espresso.

He has no change for a tip.

———•———

He returns to the basement after sundown and lights three candles, one by the side of the bed and two across the room. They are scentless, the smoke smelling only of smoke. He undresses completely and slips into his bed, which consists of a twin-sized mattress, two thin sheets, and an abrasive wool blanket.

With his back against the headrest and his shoulders, chest and blob exposed, he feels a chill. He lays his fingers on his forehead. A fever, he thinks. His left knee shakes so he holds it with his left hand, squeezes it until, like a frightened animal, it stops.

He sits this way for half an hour.

The single window is closed, but moonlight bleeds from the bottom of the curtain, and the occasional noise—anonymous footsteps, cats, laughing students—joins him in his shrine.

At eleven p.m. he runs his tongue slowly around the inside of his mouth, clears his throat, and withdraws his pills from the nightstand. He begins swallowing two at a time, easing them down with tap water. But after the first sixteen, he slows down. Now he takes one, cradles it in his tongue until he can feel the almost imperceptible weight of it, lets it slide to the summit of his throat and fall. The pills have no taste. A few minutes later, another. And another.

Finishing all fifty-one takes him almost twenty minutes, at which point he feels full as though he'd eaten a second meal.

He puts his hands behind his head, opens his mouth wide to let the smoke-scented air sink deep into his stomach.

chapter twenty-nine
- 1980 -

When March comes, the ice melts, the winds settle. Life begins to travel upward from the earth, making everything it touches a little lighter—the sky, their bodies.

————•————

The trailer is small. Two rooms: the bathroom and everything else. A fold-out bed, a fold-up table, an attached kitchen with a mini-fridge and a hot plate. Beyond the window, a cluster of birch trees and the sea.

Gayle sits cross-legged on the bed with a used Harmony guitar, the cheapest she could find in a pawnshop downtown. It's painted sunburst orange with black birds stencilled across the pickguard.

She's working on a song. Two verses and the first chorus are fine, but she has a hard time with the chords. She remembers the way her father used to do it with the piano when she was a girl. The most important thing, she remembers, is that chord progressions are not random. There's a reason why they follow each other the way they do. The distance between chords is significant, and how they're shaped can make a difference: how many times a note is repeated, whether the root is on top or not. Chords are complex units, like paragraphs in a book, and each one needs to resonate both with the ones around it and with the song as a whole. A chord might take you by surprise, but that doesn't mean it's bad. It means the musicians wanted you to be surprised. In the end, it's all a kind math, but she prefers to not think of it that way. She plays with them until they fit.

The hardest part is to work with the minors, the sevenths, the minor sevenths, the sixths, and so on. The diminisheds and augmenteds sound odd no matter how she strums them.

She plays it again and again, sometimes loud, sometimes quiet. Sometimes she pretends she's Joni Mitchell, sometimes she's Bob Dylan.

When she's done, the door opens.

"Hey Lew," she says. "How long've you been standing there?"

"I didn't want to pop in when you were concentrating. You do a better Bob Dylan than Bob Dylan."

"*Wyelll, I'm glayd you thiynk so,*" Gayle says as Bob Dylan. "*I thyink I'll talk like thees from nyow on.*"

Lewis laughs and pulls from his bag a bottle of Quebecois red. "Just thought we'd celebrate."

"Celebrate what?"

"Nothing—everything."

"Sounds good."

———— • ————

Side-by-side on the bed, wearing sweaters, drinking directly from the bottle, they listen to the radio: a program featuring Celtic-inspired music performed by locals, sometimes Acadian music in French, during which Gayle tries to pick out words she knows.

"I was thinking we'd stay here 'til May," Gayle says. "When the weather's good enough to sleep outside every night if we want to."

"That's exactly what I was thinking. We could save up a little more and pick up the gear we might need. You know, camping gear, cooking gear. We'd be self-reliant."

"And enough for the boat if we want. To England."

"But first we could drive the car down to Maine and then to New York City and watch some shows and walk in the parks, you know. We would deserve it by then. I can't remember the last time I've seen a show. A movie, I mean. I've never seen a *show* show."

"Would I have enough space in the car for the guitar?"

"Definitely," he says. "I bet you'd knock the socks off people wherever we go."

"But I've only been playing a few months—"

"Sure, but what's that place on Spring Garden that keeps bringing you back?"

"I'm playing there tomorrow. You're gonna come?"

He always comes. "Are you gonna play 'Black Jack Davy'? I love that one. Reminds me of us."

She nods.

"I'm amazed at you," he says.

"I'm amazed at *us*."

"What about the rest of the weekend," she says. "What should we do?"

"Let's go for a drive around, see how much is budding."

———◦———

Gayle receives occasional letters from Ami. Never from Ruth directly, but her mother's words always find their way in: …*mum wants me to ask when you will come for a visit.*

She replies:

Tell her I'll try for next Christmas. But here's a late Christmas gift for last year. Three for you and three for her. And please send me another picture that you drew—I look at the other one every single day. Love, love, love, Gayle. In the envelope she inserts six seashells of assorted colours that she'd found on the beach last weekend. She wraps them carefully in cotton and writes the word "Fragile" on the envelope.

The address she's writing to has changed. It's not the family farmhouse, but judging by the numbers, it's nearby. Not in town, though. She can't place where it is exactly, and nowhere in Ami's letters has there been an explanation. Perhaps, Gayle thinks, Mum's finally come to her senses and moved into a reasonably sized place.

In April, she receives a letter from Li Yong. She opens it while Lewis is out:

> *I should have written you sooner, but I didn't know how to*
> *go about it. I've contemplated this for a long time, and I've*
> *decided that, knowing you, you'd prefer to know. My deepest*
> *condolences. If you have the time, I wouldn't mind a phone*
> *call. Your friend, Li Yong.*

Attached to the letter is a short article clipped from the *Edmonton Journal* several months earlier:

> Police have solved the mystery of the dis-
> appearance of Allen Windsor (50), who was
> reported missing last year by his col-
> leagues at the University of Alberta after
> refusing to undergo a mental health evalu-
> ation. Windsor's body was recently discov-
> ered in the basement of a student apart-
> ment in Rome, GA, United States. He had
> no identification on his person and his
> name was not attached to the rental, which
> stalled local police in their efforts to
> confirm his identity.

Gayle folds up the article and paces across the trailer—three steps one way, three steps back. She finds her hands shaking but is surprised by the absence of tears. Lewis pulls up in the car.

"I need the keys for a bit," she tells him as he gets out.

"Gayle? You're hyperventilating."

"I'm going to the store for a minute."

"Should I come with you?"

"No, no."

———◆———

She decides that all coasts are similar. Saltwater is saltwater. It crashes. Even if it has a different tide or hides different fish, it resurrects the same memories. They move at the speed of light, and the distance of the whole country collapses under them.

She removes her shoes and leaves them on the rocks, one of them standing and the other one lying on its side. She runs her hand into her pocket and feels the newspaper clipping. From her other pocket, she takes her lighter and a pack of cigarettes. She lights the clipping and lets it fall, lets the paper dissipate along with his name and the monument to himself he'd built inside her. Then she lights a cigarette and leaves the pack and the lighter inside her shoes.

The smoke is finished by the time she reaches the water. She drops the butt and begins taking small strides toward the horizon where the sun is setting, as though its gravity were enough to pull her in. Her clothes become heavy with water. The stones underfoot are large, sometimes jagged. She takes each step carefully, tensing her muscles so she doesn't lose her balance in the current.

Up to her chest, her body pushed and pulled by the weight of it, she begins to feel how large it is, with too many glints of light to be counted, a face with infinite teeth: the Atlantic in the springtime.

She leans back, lets the water lift her legs until she is floating on her back, cradled.

chapter thirty
- 1980 -

The new house, funded by the Anglican Church and a variety of secular donors from the city of Salmon Arm, becomes a sensation in the community newspaper, which publishes biweekly progress reports congratulating the town on its overwhelming generosity. Bill recruited several volunteers from the region—carpenters, draftsmen, and electricians amongst them—who agree to spend weekends and the odd evening on the project.

It's a slow process. Cleaning the debris from the old house took over a month, and construction couldn't start in earnest until the weather improved.

During the planning stages, before the scaffolding is brought to site, Bill receives a phone call and gives it to Ruth. It's one of the head volunteers, asking what she has in mind. How many bedrooms, if she wants a living room or a pantry.

"And perhaps a painting room as I understand this is your trade?"

"Yes," she says, overwhelmed. "I mean—I have two daughters—and—we don't want much. Really not much. Nothing. Well something, but very little of it."

"Hmm." The scraping of a pencil. "That's all, ma'am. Bless you, and we'll be in touch."

———•———

In the evening, after Ami drifts off to sleep in the master bedroom, Ruth descends the stairs, hoping to find Bill lying up in the living room, wanting his face, wanting to be alone with him and sop up some of his soul, overflowing, refreshing as water.

But he's with Elizabeth. She can hear them whispering for privacy. Elizabeth is crying and she can only make out bits of the conversation.

"...the week ... but nothing for *me*. Your *wife* ... soulmate, Bill."

"I'm sorry Liz," Bill whispers. Ruth feels guilty for listening but knows that whatever they're talking about involves her. "It's not that ... a long time, like you said ... Jesus ... and I don't want it like that."

"I'm so sorry I couldn't ..."

"...*Jesus's* ... a child ..."

"...It's gotta be ..."

"...supposed to *be like this!*" Elizabeth shouts.

Bill begins to cry, too. Ruth ascends the stairs, which creak more on the way up than on the way down.

———•———

Well into the night, Ruth listens to the sound of doors opening and closing, boxes and other objects shuffling around, footsteps up and down the stairs. But no human voices.

———•———

In the morning she finds Bill alone in the living room drinking a coffee. It's still chilly enough for a small fire, and he stares into the crackling twigs, one foot stretched toward it for warmth. His Bible is on the shelf across the room. Ruth knows which one is his—the faux leather-bound New King James Version, the one that replaces "thou" with "you." He didn't need it.

"Bill," she says.

"Morning, Ruth."

She pulls a wooden chair next to his, sits on it sideways, facing his profile.

"Liz left a couple hours ago," he says flatly.

"I heard."

"It's got nothing to do with you, Ruth. I want you to know that. You been a great help here with the animals, the cleaning and everything else you been doing." A pause. "It was coming for a long time."

Ruth puts a hand on his shoulder, firm but not too firm, the way he'd seen her do for Ami when they stood before the cow's grave. "You're the best kind of man."

Bill struggles to smile.

"Gone to stay with her sister in Kamloops," he adds. "She's taken care of over there. You got nothing to worry about over that."

———•———

The days go on with a new routine, which is, Ruth notices, hardly different than the old routine. Bill moves into the room vacated by Elizabeth and no longer needs to sleep on the sofa. Ami returns to school full-time, her mood seemingly restored by the contact, however contrived, with her older sister, especially since those seashells came in the mail. The food around the house becomes significantly worse as Ruth takes up cooking. Otherwise, she continues to look after the cows and the alpaca, takes long walks around the property, just looking.

———— • ————

Bill doesn't mention Elizabeth again until the documents arrive in the mail filing for divorce. He sheds a few tears. Ruth runs her arms around him to console him. He quickly recovers, drops the papers in a drawer, returns to the fields. It's planting season.

———— • ————

Since returning home from Victoria on Christmas Day, Ruth has paid no mind to her paintings. What's the portrait of Bill and Elizabeth worth now? It's spring before she calls Annabella Tavistock to apologize for leaving her works behind.

"I suppose they were trashed," Ruth says. "Shame. I could see one or two of the cow paintings looking nice on the shelf at Salvation Army."

"*Ruth.*" Annabella is incensed. "What in the hell happened to *you*?"

"It's been strange here."

"I believe you, Ruth. A hundred and ten percent, as you would say. But *no*, you're works were not trashed. I wish you had called sooner because they're sitting in my office and taking up a fair bit of space."

"You kept them?" Ruth asks. "I got the impression you thought me a good old-fashioned simpleton."

Annabella laughs. "Your works have been sold. All of them. They're destined to be part of the collection of the Helmut Albrecht." Annabella tells her everything she knows about the prestigious art collector and dealer of Hamburg and his plans of showcasing Ruth's work alongside a number of other naïve North American artists. "He's a Canadaphile, tried and true. I just need to you to sign a few things before I can ship them."

Ruth doesn't respond right away. She feels nothing, having already pronounced the works dead, property of no one. "Why Germany?"

"Who knows? It's about the Canadian exotic. You should see the sensation *Anne of Green Gables* has caused over in Japan. Whatever the reason, your work struck a note. You must have a new number. Do you accept long-distance calls? I'm going to pass it along. And I'll give you his number too. It's long. You have a pen?"

———◆———

Soon documents arrive from Annabella, something about allowing the paintings to be shipped overseas and displayed in Germany. Something about insurance, which Ruth doesn't have. She signs them and sends them back, and then calls the number of Helmut Albrecht.

"Wer da? Es ist *nach Mitternacht*."

"Umm."

"English?"

"It's Ruth Windsor."

"Ruth Windsor? Ah—how delightful. *Excuse* my manners. I'm not used to receiving calls at this hour. I was just up in the kitchen fetching a glass of milk."

"I can't speak long. It's international."

"I will comply." The man quickly explains that he'd already paid in full, and she should be expecting a cheque via Annabella in the near future. "Is there anything else I can do for you Ruth? How would you feel about a visit to fair Hamburg?"

"I'm not planning on going anywhere further than the shop."

"I understand."

"But—is that it? The paintings—they're finished."

"Finished?"

"The work is over. They've found their shrine—far, far away, for strangers' eyes."

"I wanted to speak to you about this at length, but as you're pressed for time, I'll just say it. I'm interested in seeing more. I see here the work of someone just getting started. I can't say what it is about your art tells me this, but—"

"Please," Ruth interrupts, "can we continue this by letter? I'm more myself on paper."

—•—

When the cheque arrives from Annabella—more than Ruth ever expected—she cashes it and goes into town to buy a camera and film. Her husband took photos of her and Gayle when they lived in Victoria—all destroyed now—but she's never taken a picture in her life.

She teaches herself how the camera works. Fiddling with settings, playing with lights, learning by trial and error what an aperture does. She quickly fills up a roll of film and starts on another. Something about it is nice, but she doesn't know what. Maybe, she thinks, it's because there are no results so there's no pressure. She can't see a single shot until it's processed and doesn't want to. She only wants to walk around and collect, content that somewhere, on some invisible slip of acetate, the world is being remembered for what it is.

At four-thirty, the school bus stops on the road and Ami hops off, walks slowly up the long driveway, chin up, looking around at the trees, unaware of her mother sitting on the porch.

It's a great distance, great enough that it could be anyone's daughter she's watching. She takes a series of photos of the girl moving closer and closer, the small human framed by the hall of trees, growing steadily until she's up close and says, "What's that, Mum?"

"A camera. You've seen one before?"

"Of *course*, Mum. I'm not a doofus."

Ruth laughs.

"What is it for?" Ami asks.

"For you," she says, thinking and recalling almost nothing of Gayle's lost childhood, "so we don't miss anything."

—•—

When the film is developed, she finds most of it blurry and overexposed. Ami is a spectral figure, and angel with a long trail, as though she's being pulled away by an invisible vacuum at the top of the road. Ruth doesn't mind. She takes the photos, puts them in an envelope, and labels it *May 10—1980*.

—•—

She lost her paints in the fire but takes up drawing again to make another portrait of Bill, alone this time. She remembers that the reason he wanted a portrait done in the first place was so that he had something to give to his nieces to remember him by.

She buys charcoals and an easel, and in the evening brings Bill out back and tells him where to stand. In the background is the fledgling corn and the pen where the alpaca is standing in the opposite corner from the other animals.

"I know your face so well, I could do it with my eyes closed," she tells him. But the hair has grown longer since she worked on the last portrait. And he has dust on his neck, stubble stretching from his nose to his Adam's apple. She'd been so insistent on doing the sketch now that he hasn't had time to wash off the day's grime. On second thought, she decides, he looks much older than he did. But this, exactly this, is how she wants him.

"I'm awfully dogged," he says.

"Let me capture the feeling. Then you can take a rest. Your nieces will be proud to see you after a day's work."

As she shapes up the blocks of shadows around his brow, she tells him about the camera, about her plan to take more photographs of Ami.

"It's a good idea, Ruth."

When the sketch is done, he goes inside, finds Ruth's camera on the kitchen table, and comes back out to find her in the same spot. The easel is folded, the sketching pad under her arm, and she's looking out over the field of corn. She turns around when she hears his footsteps, and before she can say anything, the camera clicks.

chapter thirty-one
- 1300 BCE -

Used to sleeping on the ground, he'd been peacefully unconscious before the door creaked open and bits of grain whispered to life across the threshing floor. He sits up. Moonlight leaks through the cracks, lays a row of silver tails across the floor. He can see tiny footprints in the dust, all deeper on the toes than the heel.

The tracks imply hesitancy, but he cannot tell where they lead. A few steps into the barn, a few steps to the left. A few more toward him. Then nothing. They seem to disappear—to have floated up into the corn.

"Who are you?" he asks.

It takes a few minutes for his eyes to adjust to the light, and when they do, he jolts in surprise. How could he not have seen? Not an arm's length away, tightened into a ball next to a shallow pile of threshing, directly next to his feet—a body. In the darkness it blends in with the husks of corn. Despite the breeze rustling the adjoining field, he can hear a shallow, concentrated breathing, the kind of breath that is aware of itself, trying to not make too much noise.

It's a woman.

He leans over and places his fingers on her wool hem, gives it a gentle tug.

"I'm Ruth," the woman responds. "Please spread your cloak over me. I am very cold and mine is thin."

"Ruth? I don't understand why you are acting this way."

Ruth sits up, pulls the hood away from her face to reveal her eyes, which are wet from sobbing.

"Wipe away your tears, dear Ruth."

"I'm crying because, under the circumstances, I don't know what else to do. Dearest Boaz, I am here to ask for your hand in marriage."

She removes his shoes, slides them from his heel and sets them behind her so they won't interfere. Then she leans forward, brushes bits of corn from his chest, kisses him on the mouth.

"I have never seen you like I see you now," he says.

"In the dark?"

He nods. "And what happens when we wake?"

"When we wake? Do we ever wake?"

"Surely we must."

"Why?"

"Because this is a common mortal feeling. It is foolish to believe it's eternal. It's not any more lasting than a field of corn."

"Are we nothing more than corn?" she asks. "Are we not simply Boaz and Ruth, as never any Boaz and Ruth have been before?"

They are naked now. He runs his eyes over her, the hair pulled straight back from her brow, the egg shape of her chin, the crescent shadows below her breasts. She runs her eyes over him, too, and places her hands on his hips.

"Each field may be as brilliant as the last," she says, "but they are not the same. They look the same to the human eye, but they are made up of thousands upon thousands of stalks. They are infinitely complex, brushing one another in the wind. Each touch is completely unlike anything that existed before or will ever exist again. Only to an ignorant person—or a false god—do all souls move and touch each other in the same way."

———◆———

Lying naked below their blanket of coats, they are warm. Sweat and fluids evaporate and combine their bodily scent with that of the corn. At the crack of dawn, Ruth is the first to wake. She rubs life into her eyes, dresses quickly and ensures Boaz is wrapped up safely, protected from drafts and spiders.

Feet in sandals, she leaves the barn to a green lawn sodden with dew and proceeds to the fields to get an early start on her day's labour.

chapter thirty-two
- 1980 -

The walk from the water back to the car is not enough to dry her off, but she is warm because there is still some sun and the wind blows from the south. In the parking lot by the beach is a van where fishermen are stowing away their gear. They stare but don't ask her why her clothes and hair are dripping. She ignores them and rings herself out as carefully as she can without removing her clothes.

As she drives back to Lewis, she watches Nova Scotia's countryside in the spring. She feels a small shoot growing in her, pumping sadness all through her body, heating her up and weighing her down. This sadness, thick and circulating, reaches all her joints and limbs and then cools.

Spring colours grace the roadside and far-off hills. She longs to touch the colours, to rub a sun-warmed infant leaf between her fingers or place it on her chin or her lips or her wrists where the body is more sensitive, or stand up to her knees in the deep-green grass on the edge of a town where earlier that day, perhaps, a small wild animal had done the same.

As she drives, madly in love with the colours, she is pulled through time. A new pair of eyes appears, and she looks around. A panorama of eighty years. The colours of Nova Scotia become just one amongst many things that will have pressed into her by the time she dies. She sees in translucent, watery reflections a lover who dies too young, a man who works at an airport, a brown eye with a streak of gold, Ami's eighteenth birthday, a bicycle moving through flowers, a friend who writes a novel that comes to nothing, five hours in a restaurant famed for its chocolates, all the adjectives in French she needs to describe music, Li Yong and his thousands of letters, falling asleep in a moving car in winter, a certain kind of bird that she only ever hears but never sees—

———•———

"Are you okay Gayle?" Lewis asks, jogging out of the trailer. "You're all wet."

"I walked out into the ocean."

"Huh?" His eyes are wide open.

"Then I turned around and came home."

"Someday you'll tell me what you mean by that?"

She runs her arms around him, links her hands behind his back.

"And I saw the letter on the table—from Lee. What's going on?"

"Nothing," she says and lets him go. "We'd better start packing for our trip, huh?"

chapter thirty-three
- 2011 -

Gayle is sitting by the water when her cell phone rings.

"Hi Mum."

"Hi Gayle—I'm returning your call—"

"Oh—It's nothing. I just wanted to know—Mum?—Mum, you there?"

"Ah—Son of a bitch—I can never figure out this thing. I'm trying to get it so I see you and hear you at the same time. Ami *said* I could do it when she gave it to me—Feels like I haven't seen you in years."

"I'll explain it to you some other time, Mum. Anyway—I was just calling to check in and see how your flight was. You're in Victoria now?"

"I'm staying in a little hotel outside the city. My meeting with Albrecht is tomorrow but not 'til three. Hey, while I have you—something strange happened recently—I thought you'd find it interesting."

"What's that, Mum?"

"I got an email from someone. A woman from the States—Colorado I think it was. It was the strangest thing—It was a long message, and she was asking me if I was the wife of Allen Windsor and went on to tell me this wacko story. Apparently she knew your father when he was down there and—she didn't give me all the details—but she said he rescued her from a prostitution ring in San Francisco, took her on his motorbike thousands of kilometres back to her mother—Her *mother!*—She said something like, 'The whole time I thought he was a guardian angel'—It's really a crazy story. Didn't know your dad was into whores, but I'm not surprised. I guess I have to believe it all—The woman knew who *I* was, which was eerie."

"How did she know?"

"That's what I thought, so I went to Ami's house and asked her to Google his name—Apparently someone published a book of his after he died, did you know that?

"I knew that, Mum."

"How?"

"'Cause I have it on my shelf. It came out a while ago. I thought you knew. There's a big internet community around it, too. Like, forums and stuff. You should check it out. He's a real hero for people, I guess—I wouldn't be surprised if your name was on some website somewhere and that's how the woman found you."

"Sounds a bit culty to me—"

"Probably, Mum."

"Mhmm."

"Anything else?"

"Hmm—How's—Umm—How's Lewis?"

"Good—I guess—We're on holiday soon."

"Good for him. Good for you."

"Still warming up to him, huh? After all these years?"

"No, Gayle—*No*. I love him because—well, because you love him."

"I'll tell him that, Mum."

"You'll be coming for a visit soon, then?"

"Maybe, Mum. Maybe not. I'll let you know."

"Well is there anything you can tell me, Gayle?"

"Not really—I'm just looking at the ocean now."

"Me too."

"Okay—"

"Okay. I guess that's it, then."

"Guess so."

"Talk to you later?"

"Sure, Mum."

"Okay then."

"Okay then—I'm hanging up now."

"Okay."

"Here I go—"

end

acknowledgements

I would be nowhere without community, and neither would this book. I would like to acknowledge all of those who encouraged me to lead a creative life and, in doing so, prepared my heart for the beauties and terrors of this world. In being around, you have made it all more bearable.

Thank you to Ken Lee, René Schumacher, Jordana Hon, Lina "Maligna," Eric Yaremko, Jordan Pike, Brandon Mackenzie, Corinne Riedel, Christine Stewart, C.J. Bogle, Kyler Chittick, Todd Anstett, Josh Bookhalter, Matthew Pünyi, Damian Hockley, Josh Carson, and so many others who have offered their support and kindness over the years.

Thank you to Paul, Yolanda, and Darrell Holowack for decades of patience and love.

Thank you to the Writers' Guild of Alberta and Margaret Macpherson, without whose mentorship I would have been lost.

Thank you to the staff at NeWest Press and my editor Thea Bowering for their constructive criticism and faith in my work.

Finally, thank you to the anonymous strangers in the streets and cafés who reached me with their laughter and sorrow. Maybe you are among them, dear reader. My sincerest wish is that this book provides you some consolation and entertainment.

Kevin Holowack is a writer from Edmonton who has his M.A. in English from the University of Alberta. He has lived in various places across Canada and Europe. His work has been published in *Glass Buffalo* and *Lemon Hound*. Kevin's debut novel, *Light on a Part of the Field*, is a Nunatak First Fiction Series book.